Retreat From New York

Also by Robert J Shade

The Forbes Road Series

Forbes Road

Conestoga Winter

The Camp Follower Affair

Lord Dunmore's Folley

The Rebellion Road Series

Pursuit Through Chaos

Flight From Bonniecrest Manor

Freedom At Gwynn's Island

Fetching Captain Henry

Retreat From New York

A Rebellion Road Novel

Robert J Shade

Sunshine Hill Press

Sunshine Hill Press LLC
2937 Novum Road
Reva, VA 22735

ISBN 979-8-9946582-0-8

Artwork with specific permission
Front cover: *Bitter Winter at Jockey Hollow*
By Pamela Patrick White

Major Characters

Historical

George Washington	Lieutenant General commanding Continental Army
William Howe	Commanding General of British Army in America
Richard Howe	Admiral commanding Royal Navy North America
Charles Lord Cornwallis	Lieutenant General in British Army
Charles Lee	Major General in Continental Army
Hugh Mercer	Brigadier General in Continental Army
John Glover	Colonel of Marblehead Regiment of sailors/fishermen
Thomas Stirling	Colonel Commandant of 42nd Foot (Black Watch)
Alexander Hamilton	Captain of New York Artillery Company
Elizabeth Loring	'Friend' of William Howe
Banastre Tarleton	Cornet in British 16th Light Dragoons

Fictional

Wend Eckert	Captain of Frederick County Light Foot Company
Peggy McCartie Eckert	Wend's wife
Simon Donegal	Company Sergeant of Frederick County Light Foot,

Joshua Baird	Scout for Frederick County Militia, Wend's mentor
Reese Newkirk	First Lieutenant of Frederick County Light Foot
Shay O'beirne	Second Lieutenant of Frederick County Light Foot.
Edward Childers	Ensign of Frederic County Light Foot
Geoffrey Fairfield	Lieutenant commanding 1st Troop of Palmetto Light Horse
'Quinn'	Senior sergeant of Fairfield's troop
Barrett Penfold Northcutt	Colonel Commandant of the King's Loyal Virginia Legion
Clive Harfeld	Loyalist lawyer living in Morristown, New Jersey
Mary Fraser	Matron of the Hospital, 42nd Foot (Black Watch)
Charles McDonald	Major in 42nd Foot (Black Watch), Mary Fraser's protector
Alexander Tresh	Colonel, Swiss volunteer on Washington's staff
Catherine Tresh	Wife of Colonel Tresh
Harold and Elise Moulders	Couple in domestic service to the Tresh family
Ernst Ludwig Wolff	Captain commanding 4th Hesse-Cassel Jaeger Company
Colleen Alison McGraw	Proprietress of the Red Vixen Sutler Company
Edna Farley	Colleen's forewoman
Charlie Farley	Edna's son, scout for Red Vixen Sutler Company
Andrew Horner	Gunsmith providing services to Continental Army
Emily Crider	Member of Red Vixen Sutler Company, Horner's lover

Contents

Part I

A Futile Campaign

Chapter One

Philadelphia

The merchant ship *Lady Felicity*, the sails on her three masts barely feeling the light wind, moved slowly, almost imperceptibly, through the water. An impenetrable fog enveloped the vessel, blocking out sight of the surrounding sea except for a precious few feet on either side of the hull. Wend Eckert, Captain of the Frederick County Light Foot, whose company was embarked on the ship, stood by the quarterdeck rail, not far from where the helmsman struggled to keep the vessel on course. Eckert was a man of medium height, with a wiry figure and a high cheekboned, stone face topped by dark brown hair. He wore a blue uniform with red facings, which denoted him an officer of the Virginia line.

Eckert stared into the fog off the side of the ship, then looked forward to see that the end of the ship's bowsprit was barely visible. He glanced skyward and was surprised to see bright stars in the night sky in clear view.

Foley, the master, walked over to where Eckert stood, and seeing him look upward, commented, "Yes, this damned fog is thick, but it's low-lying—a blanket spread over the sea, if you will. It's caused by the difference in temperature between the air and the water: warm air hitting the cold water. You get it many mornings in these Summer months."

Wend nodded his understanding. "Yes, we see stuff like this on Shenandoah mornings often enough, particularly in valleys and hollows."

The two men stood silently for a minute staring into the gloom, then Foley said, "Despite this lack of visibility, it's sure enough we've passed through the capes and entered Delaware Bay."

Puzzled, Eckert asked, "Sir, with due respect, how can you tell in this blindness?"

"I can feel it in my feet. It's the way the ship moves. Don't you sense how the roll of the ship has quickened over the last hour?"

Wend concentrated, then nodded. "Yes, now that you mention it, the movement of the deck has changed. I hadn't noticed."

"Aye, well at sea the feeling in the bottom of your feet on the deck is as important as seein' with your eyes. We've left the long swells of the Atlantic behind and are into the choppy waves of the Bay."

Another period of silence ensued, the two men staring into the mists. Presently Wend said, "I make it nearly two hours since we've heard any cannon fire."

Foley stared astern and concern flowed over his face. "Yes, I think things have been decided between the *Firefly* and whatever British ship that was. And I don't have much hope for *Firefly*. I had a good look at that Britain and she was a two masted schooner, purpose built for naval service—undoubtedly more heavily armed and sturdily constructed than a little coastal sloop converted for war by simply adding a few two pounders."

Eckert replied, "When Governor Henry told me that my company was going from Yorktown to Philadelphia by sea, I expressed my worry about British ships intercepting us. He assured me that the blockade had been weakened because they were using most of their vessels to help move Howe's army from Halifax to New York. He was very proud that he had founded a navy for Virginia and that one of its ships would be protecting us." Wend shook his head. "When I saw the *Firefly*, I lost all confidence in his assurance."

Foley's facial expression changed to amusement. "Now my dear captain, it wouldn't be the first time a politician overstated matters." Then he was silent and looked around the ship. "Right now, our greatest protection is this weather. If that Britisher has defeated *Firefly*, they'll have the devil's own time catching up to us in this light wind or finding us in the fog. Keep your fingers crossed that it persists."

Wend looked along the deck of the *Lady Felicity*. "You have cannon. Would we not be able to do something to defend ourselves?"

Foley laughed aloud. "Those are little four-pounders. They serve to give pause to rogues like those Barbary corsairs when we're in the Mediterranean and native pirates who come out in small boats from islands in the Caribbean. I have only one or two good gunners, and my men and their six guns could in no way stand up to trained navy crews." Then he turned and waved his hand along the ship's deck. "And, in any case, there's no way we could work the guns, not with the parts of your wagons stowed all over the deck and those eight horses in their improvised stalls." He took a deep breath, then waved out toward the fog. "That British schooner out there would have at least eight guns, a couple of them probably six- or nine-pounders. And it might even be armed with carronades."

Wend turned to look at Foley. "Carronades? I've never heard the term."

"It's a devilish new kind of cannon, just devised a few years ago: very short in length, but with a great bore to fire heavy shot. They are only good for close range, but the damn things are so powerful and can be reloaded so swiftly, a small ship like that schooner could get close and chop us up posthaste." He shook his head. "Word is the British are starting to equip small ships with them."

Wend shrugged. "Well, God willing that Britisher won't find us in this fog."

Foley nodded and echoed, "God willing." Then he walked over to the helm and stood beside the man at the wheel.

Wend continued in his place by the rail, and nearly an hour later, he became aware of the sky above the fog becoming illuminated with the soft light of morning twilight. The stars had faded and the sky was beginning to have color. No sooner had he realized that then there was a call from the lookout on the main top.

"Deck there! Deck there! A mast! I've got the mast of a vessel off to starboard! On the starboard quarter and close aboard!"

Wend looked up to see the man shielding his eyes with one hand, the other grasping a rigging line for support and staring off to the right side of the ship. Foley dashed over to the rail and peered out into the fog. Then he called up to the lookout, "You say one mast only?"

"Aye, looks like some kind of sloop."

Wend looked at Foley. "A sloop? Could it actually be the *Firefly*?"

"We can only hope. It'll be a damned miracle if she beat off the Britisher or somehow got away from her."

The master had no sooner spoken when Wend saw a ship, ghost-like, materialize through the mist, perhaps seventy-five yards off the side of the *Lady Felicity*. It was indeed a sloop, but after a few seconds, Wend realized it was not their consort.

It looked different—larger and it had a long poop deck. Wend turned to the master. "That's not *Firefly*."

"You're bloody right. It's a damned sight bigger and more heavily armed."

Just then a voice from the stranger called out, "Ahoy, the ship! Heave to! We're going to board you."

Foley went over to the compass binnacle and took up a speaking trumpet from its rack. He called out to the sloop, "Who are you?"

The voice came back, "Continental sloop *Providence*. Now heave to forthwith!"

Foley swore, then called, "There's no need to heave to! We're moving so slowly your boat can make us easily!"

The response came, "All right, we'll parallel you. We're lowering a boat now!"

Foley turned and growled to his first mate, "Tanner, get a ladder over the side."

Meanwhile, there was a flurry of activity on the deck of the *Providence* as a boat was hoisted up and then over the far side of the sloop. After about ten minutes, the boat, manned by several oarsmen with a blue-coated officer in the sternsheets, appeared from around the stern of the Continental vessel and pulled for the *Lady Felicity*. Shortly, the boat came alongside, the rowers tossed oars, and the officer grabbed hold of the rope ladder and ascended to the ship's deck.

The mate met the Continental officer and spoke a few words with him. Wend saw that the officer was in his thirties with a handsome face and dark hair. He was of medium height with broad shoulders, muscular build, and a complexion darkened by the sun and wind of the sea. As he watched, Tanner led the officer aft to where Foley awaited.

As the two approached, Tanner motioned toward the master and announced to the officer, "This is Captain Foley."

Foley immediately demanded, "Sir, pray tell, what is your name, and why have you boarded us?"

The naval officer stared at merchant master for a moment, then glanced over at Eckert, before saying, "Jones, sir. John Paul Jones, lieutenant commanding the Continental sloop *Providence*." He motioned toward Wend. "And who is this, if I may ask?"

Foley answered, "That is Captain Eckert of Virginia. We are transporting his company to Philadelphia." He pointed along the deck of the ship. "That's why we've got these damned horses and wagons on deck. His men are down below."

Wend touched his hat to Jones and said, "We're on our way to join Washington in New York, and I am carrying dispatches from our Governor, Patrick Henry, to Congress and to General Washington."

Jones nodded, then said, "Ah, yes, I quite understand." Then he smiled at Wend and said, "As it happens, in '74 and early '75, before hostilities broke out, I spent some time in Virginia. I found it quite pleasant and considered residing there." He shrugged. "But then this conflict arose and I left to offer my services to the Congress."

Wend said politely, "Well, perhaps after the war you will find your way back."

Jones made a tight grin, simply nodded, and then looked back to Foley. "It happens we are also on our way to Philadelphia. I'm escorting a convoy of colliers from the northern colonies. But last night, shortly before midnight, we heard numerous broadsides bespeaking a sea battle. When I saw your masts above the fog I approached and boarded to see if you could shed any light on that incident."

Foley answered, "Indeed we can, sir. That fight was between our escort, the sloop *Firefly* of the Virginia Navy, and a British schooner of war." He shrugged. "We have no idea of the outcome."

Eckert added, "The *Firefly* is smaller than your ship, Mr. Jones. We are not optimistic of her survival. The fighting was out of our sight and the gunnery subsided hours ago."

Foley added, "And since this fog closed in, you are the only ship we have sighted."

Jones turned toward *Felicity's* stern and stared over the taffrail into the fog, lost in thought. Then he glanced upward at the rapidly brightening sky. Turning back to Foley and Eckert, he said, "Right, gentlemen. This wind, though light, is fair for you to proceed up the bay." He waved out into the mists. "And the same is true for my convoy. I shall fall astern of both you and the colliers, as a rearguard if you will, ready to amuse that British schooner or any other Royal Navy ship which might find us, although I think that highly unlikely."

Foley shrugged. "That is our intent in any case. We shall trim our sails to make best use of the breeze, which I believe will increase as the day progresses."

"Quite, sir!" Jones extended his hand to Foley. "Thank you for your information. Then he turned to Wend. "Mr. Eckert, you said you were going to join our forces defending New York. Well, sir I can say this: You shall have a busy time of it. In mid-June, before sailing on this voyage, I received word that large numbers of Howe's army have been landing on Staten Island, amounting to many thousands. And less than a week ago I encountered a massive British convoy. The largest number of ships I have ever seen together. Scores of them. Mostly transports, Mr. Eckert, escorted by a squadron of frigates, twenty-gun ships, and brig sloops. There could not have been less than ten thousand soldiers being carried. From their course, the destination could have been nowhere else but New York City. Sir, the British mean business and you shall have your work cut out for you."

"I have never thought different, Mr. Jones."

"Good, sir, then you shall not be disappointed." He shook hands with Wend and said to both men, "Perhaps we shall meet again in Philadelphia. That would be my pleasure. And now, gentlemen, I will return to my ship."

Foley said, "Let me accompany you to the ladder."

Wend watched as Jones descended to his boat, which then cast off and set course back to the *Providence.*

The master came back to the quarterdeck and, waving toward the sloop, said, "Well, I believe we can put paid to our fears of being overcome by the Royal Navy. Now we can concentrate on getting through the Bay and up the river to Philadelphia—and I can assure you ascending the Delaware river is a quite challenging matter in itself." He looked up at the sails and continued, "Pray the wind holds in a favorable direction."

Wend Eckert stood on the waterfront quay in Philadelphia, looking up at the *Lady Felicity,* which, after two days of lying at anchor in the stream, had finally been warped alongside. The sailors were rigging the ship's yardarms with block and tackle to enable them to be used to lift off the company's horses, disassembled wagon parts, and barrels of provisions and gunpowder. Standing next to Wend was his first lieutenant, Reese Newkirk, a man in his late twenties, slightly taller and more heavily built than his captain, with dark hair and a continually intense expression on his face. Reese had recently lost both his wife and first child in childbirth, the melancholy of the event lingering in his demeanor.

Wend looked over at Newkirk and said, "I'm going to see the Virginia delegation at Congress and deliver these dispatches from Governor Henry. He motioned to the leather case in his left hand, then continued, "Send young Childers out to find the military authority here in Philadelphia and have it advise us of a place where we can bivouac until we're ready to travel. It would be most advantageous if the site were on the north side of the city, making it easier to depart for New York when the time comes." Wend pointed up to the deck of the ship. "Get Horner to work on assembling those wagons as soon as all the parts are offloaded and look closely at the horses to see how they have fared during the voyage."

"Aye, sir. I'll get it all arranged. And I suggest we send out Billy Wood and Melinda to locate a source of fresh meat and produce. We can sure use it after all the time on the ship."

Wend nodded. "Yes, good idea! We could all stand some decent meals after that wretched food." He looked around the harbor, at the mass of shipping alongside the wharf and in the river. Among them were the *Providence* and her convoy lying at anchor in the stream. Then he said, "I should only be gone a couple of hours," and headed off into the city.

Wend had a rudimentary knowledge of Philadelphia, having traveled there from Lancaster with his father two times to pick up shipments of parts for firelocks which had come in from Germany and England. Suddenly he felt a knot in his stomach, as the memories of the days with his family in their home just west of Lancaster flooded back into his consciousness. And that spurred the indelible images of the terrible day in 1758 when Mingo warriors had massacred all of them along Forbes Road. He alone had survived, left lying in the road severely wounded and unconscious. Then he recalled when he watched with tear-filled eyes as men of the 77th Highlanders carefully placed the bodies of his parents, sister, and younger brother into a common grave alongside the road. Without thinking, he put his right hand up to the back of his head and felt the scar where a Mingo, thinking him dead, had taken a circular part of his scalp. Then he took a deep breath and, literally shaking his head to dispel the memories, picked up the pace of his steps through the city.

He had been informed that the congress was meeting in the Pennsylvania Statehouse, and he knew where that was, so he walked briskly, soon turning onto Chestnut Street. Immediately the red brick building with its bell tower came into sight. Shortly thereafter he entered through the door at the center of the building into a wide hallway. Numerous groups of well-attired men were conversing in animated fashion. Looking around, he saw a clerk sitting at a desk, talking with two men. Wend made his way through the crowd and stood waiting until the two finished their business and then approached the desk. Clearing his throat, he gave his name and said, "I'm looking for the Virginia delegation; I have official letters from the governor."

The clerk, who appeared to be in his early thirties and was prematurely balding, looked up at Wend with appraising eyes, then after hesitating a few seconds, shrugged and said, "Well, you won't find them here today. There's no general session scheduled. I would say your best bet is to go to the Graff House. That's Jefferson's lodging and they often gather there for meetings."

Wend said, "I'll do that. Can you give me the address?"

"Indeed, it's not far from here. It's at the corner of Market and Seventh Street." He picked up a quill and wrote out a small note, then handed it to Wend. "Here are directions. It's a brick house." He laughed. "In fact, a brick house *owned* by a bricklayer. That's Graff's trade."

Wend thanked the clerk and quickly left the statehouse. Ten minutes later he was standing in front of the Graff House. It was a tall, rather narrow structure of red bricks, and eyeing it critically as a craftsman, Wend had to admit it was well designed and skillfully built. After a moment of hesitation, he stepped up to the front door and pounded with the knocker.

A young African servant answered the door, saying in a heavy accent, "Yes, suh. Are you here to see Mr. Jefferson?"

Wend responded by giving his name and saying, "I'm looking for anyone from the Virginia delegation. I've got dispatches from Governor Henry."

The servant gave him a once over, sweeping his eyes up and down, then opened the door wide. "Now you come in, suh. It happens all the gentlemen are here, discussing matters. If you'll wait, I'll tell Mr. Jefferson."

With that he turned and walked down the hall, tapped on a door and went in, shutting it behind himself. In just a few moments, the door opened and a tall, slender, long-legged man came out, followed by the servant.

The man looked Wend over, then walked up to him and proffered his hand. "Good day, Captain Eckert. I'm Thomas Jefferson. Welcome to Philadelphia, sir." He paused and motioned to the leather pouch under Wend's left arm. "I understand you have some correspondence for us."

"Yes, there are several letters from the governor." He reached out to pass the pouch to Jefferson.

Jefferson didn't take the pouch; instead, he put his hand to his mouth, thought a minute, then said, "You hold onto the pouch and join us. We'll look them over, and while we're doing so, you can answer any questions." He smiled. "And you can bring us up to date on news from Williamsburg." He motioned Wend to follow, and headed back toward the room.

There were six men in the room, seated around a large table. Papers were before each man, and others spread out on the table surface. Jefferson said, "Gentlemen, this is Captain Eckert, just up from Williamsburg with dispatches for us."

Wend said, "Good morning, gentlemen."

Jefferson waved toward the table and made introductions. "Captain, you have caught the entire delegation together. We're preparing Virginia's position on matters to be discussed in tomorrow's session of Congress." He went around the room. "This is George Wythe, Benjamin Harrison, Francis Lightfoot Lee, Thomas Nelson there at the bottom of the table, and on the other side is Richard Henry Lee—yes, Eckert, we have two Lees here—and finally Carter Braxton.

Each man nodded in turn. Then Wend handed the dispatch case to Jefferson, who in turn handed it to Braxton. "Carter, will you be so kind as to take a preliminary look at these so that we may query Eckert on any questions which may arise?"

Then Nelson spoke up and asked, "Captain, we're glad to see that Virginia is finally sending troops to Washington's army at New York. He'll need every man he can get, and we are all somewhat embarrassed that Virginia is not well represented, all because of this Dunmore business." Then he thought a moment and asked, "Have you and your company been long on the road?"

Wend smiled. "Actually, sir, we've not been on the road at all. We came by ship—we embarked at Yorktown and sailed around to here. Governor Henry, like you gentlemen, was anxious that Virginia be represented as rapidly as possible in Washington's army."

Richard Lee spoke up. "We've heard that the Royal Governor Lord Dunmore and his forces have finally been ejected from Virginia—is that accurate?"

"Indeed it is, sir. He was driven away from his stronghold on Gwynn's Island by forces under General Andrew Lewis. We believe he and his people sailed for

New York to join Howe." He looked around the room. "Several Virginia regiments of foot, now freed by Dunmore's departure, are preparing to march to join Washington."

Braxton looked up from the dispatches. He glanced around at his compatriots and then at Wend. "I've just finished the cover letter from Henry. He says you and your company played a major role in the defeat of Dunmore. He's quite complimentary of you and your men." He looked back to the others at the table. "Henry says they defeated an entire regiment of Dunmore's men in a battle near Mobjack Bay and then led the assault on Gwynn's Island."

All the men looked up at Wend. He felt himself flush slightly and hurried to say, "Well, sir, the regiment we defeated was Northcutt's King's Loyal Virginia Legion, and it was a regiment in name only. Its total strength was only slightly greater than my company of one hundred men, and we caught them raiding a number of farms, broken up into details, which we were able to defeat individually, leaving only a nucleus of men on the shore of the Chesapeake. We were able to destroy that last detachment before they could take to their boats."

Richard Lee spoke up. "Did you get that damned scoundrel Northcutt? He was Dunmore's chief advisor before the war." He looked around the room with a smirk on his face. "Everyone in Williamsburg called him the Governor's Brain."

Several of the other men grinned and nodded, and Jefferson said with an impish smile on his face, "I'd say that was quite accurate: both scoundrel and brain. He certainly was a schemer."

There was laughter around the table.

Wend continued, "Mr. Lee, in response to your question, Northcutt was not with his regiment that day. It was led by a major named Welford, and he was killed." He shrugged. "As far as I know, Northcutt sailed to New York with Dunmore."

Richard Lee nodded his understanding and exclaimed, "Damn shame!"

Then Braxton held up several pieces of paper and said to Francis Lee, "Sir, these three dispatches deal with military matters, and I commend them to you since you are a member of the army committee. The others are of civil matters, and I will review them to decide to whom they should be sent."

Francis Lee took the proffered papers and looked down at them for a moment. Then he said, "Mr. Eckert, it occurs to me that you could be of great assistance to me and to the army committee."

"How so, sir?"

"Recently, a Swiss professional officer arrived by ship and has offered us his services as an advisor to the army. His name is Colonel Alexander Tresh. If his references are to be believed, he has considerable wartime experience with different armies of Europe." Lee looked around at the others. "For your information, Eckert, we are planning to encourage senior officers from Europe to join us. Heaven knows, although Washington is a good man with experience fighting on the frontier, the committee feels that the organization and tactical ability of the army would benefit from an infusion of formal military experience from the continent."

Jefferson interjected, "Yes, we're sending a diplomatic delegation to France, and one of their missions will be to recruit professional soldiers. In fact, the first of that delegation, Mr. Silas Deane of Connecticut, has already taken ship."

Lee said, "Quite right, Thomas." Then he turned back to Wend. "Now, sir, Tresh is completely unfamiliar with our country. So, Captain, you could be useful to us by escorting him up to New York and *delivering* him, as you might say, to Washington. We'll prepare a letter of introduction for Tresh, but we're worried about making sure he gets there expeditiously and safely."

Wend nodded. "It will be my honor to assist you, sir. However, this Colonel Tresh needs to be ready to travel soon, for I intend to waste no time in departing. I just need to assemble my wagons and obtain fresh provisions, and then we shall march. I expect to leave tomorrow or the next day at the latest."

Lee said enthusiastically, "Capital, my dear Captain! The good colonel is staying at the City Tavern. I'll write you a quick note of introduction, and you can go right over and make arrangements with him. I'm sure he will be eager to ride with you." Lee took out a blank page and began scribbling with a quill.

The other men went back to their papers, and Wend felt like the odd man out. Presently, Lee finished the note and handed it to Wend. Jefferson rose from his chair. "Let me see you out, Captain Eckert." He ushered Wend into the hall and escorted him to the front door. "Take care with our Colonel Tresh. It is to be hoped that he will correspond with fellow officers in Europe about his treatment here in America, and perhaps others of his experience and prestige will be encouraged to volunteer."

"I shall endeavor to show him the utmost hospitality."

Jefferson smiled and opened the door. "Excellent, sir. Are you familiar with the location of the City Tavern?"

"No sir, I don't recall it from when I was last here. That was as a lad in 1758. I thought to get directions along the way."

"Yes, well, you wouldn't have seen it back then, for it was just constructed four years ago. It is actually quite near to the State House; for that reason it is favored by many from Congress and those who have business with Congress. It has become quite prosperous and has some of the best food and lodging in the city." Then he gave Wend directions to the tavern and added, "Now, sir, I am confident that you and your men will represent Virginia well in Washington's army, and I wish you Godspeed."

Wend said, "I hope we will live up to your expectations, Mr. Jefferson." And with that, he departed for the tavern.

City Tavern was an imposing building: red brick and sporting three stories plus a basement. The entrance was at the top of a set of stone steps. Wend climbed them, went through the door, and found himself in a hallway with an opening on the right leading to a large common room. It was full of patrons sitting at tables and standing before the counter. The buzz of talk and laughter permeated the room, while a cloud of tobacco smoke hung over the assemblage.

Wend went to the counter and waved to the barkeep. The man, dressed in well-pressed and clean clothing, with a spotless apron, came over and asked, "Can I get you a libation, Captain?"

"Later, perhaps. Right now I'm looking for a Swiss military officer who is staying here."

"Oh, the foreigner." He motioned upward. "His rooms are on the second floor. Numbers two and four, across from the ballroom door."

Wend walked back out into the hall and up the wide staircase to the second floor. On one side of the hall were doors to guest rooms, and on the other was a set of double doors, which stood open. He looked in to see a well-decorated ballroom with tables around the edges. Two maids were at work, laying cloths on the tables, obviously at the beginning stage of setting the room for some event.

Wend came to a door with a brass numeral '2' tacked to it. He knocked, and the door swung open almost immediately. Inside stood a tall man with blue eyes, blond hair arranged in a queue and a thin mustache. Wend estimated he was in his late thirties. He was dressed in a white shirt and white breeches, the stock of the shirt open. Instead of boots, he had on a pair of slippers.

Upon seeing Wend, the man's face changed to a surprised expression, and he seemed baffled for a long moment.

Wend took the opportunity to ask, "Are you Colonel Alexander Tresh?"

The man nodded, "At your service, sir."

Wend continued, "Sir, I am Captain Wendelmar Eckert of the Frederick County Light Foot Company, from Virginia." He handed Lee's note to Tresh. "This will explain why I am here."

As he opened the letter, Tresh said, "Captain, I apologize for looking so at odds. I was actually expecting a serving maid bringing our midday meal, so I was surprised at your appearance at the door." Then he looked down at the open letter, his lips moving silently as he read the contents.

He looked back up at Wend. "Ah, Captain. I am quite glad to see you. We shall be most pleased to accompany you to New York. I have been frustrated having to wait here when events are moving rapidly with the army."

Wend was puzzled. "Sir, you said 'we.' Do you have others in your retinue?"

Tresh smiled but didn't respond directly to Wend. Instead, he turned to an open door which led to an adjoining room. "Catherine, my dear, please come out here. We have a visitor."

Wend was stunned to see a strikingly beautiful woman emerge from the other room. She was tallish, with a thin, high cheekboned face framed by raven hair. She wore pale green gown that exposed a bit of her cleavage and flattered her elegant figure. Her hair was put up with nary a stray hair evident. Wend was instantly reminded of his wife, Peggy.

"Captain, this is my wife, Mrs. Catherine Tresh. My dear, this is Captain Eckert of Virginia, and he is going to escort us to New York to meet General Washington."

Wend made a slight bow. "It's my pleasure to meet you, Mrs. Tresh. Excuse me if I'm a bit surprised, for Mr. Lee did not inform me of your presence."

She smiled broadly. "We have not long been married, and I had no intention of remaining in Europe so soon after our nuptials. I'm determined to share my husband's life, wherever it may lead."

"Very commendable, Mrs. Tresh, but following the army can be a hard life. However, we have a number of women in our company, and they will be glad to help you while we travel."

"Oh, I do have my own maid. She will be with us."

Wend looked over at the colonel. "That makes three in your retinue. Is that all? Do you have a manservant?"

Tresh nodded. "Yes, a former soldier who has been with me for years, Captain. He is the husband of Catherine's maid, so there will be four of us." He stopped for a moment in thought. "But, I fear we do have considerable baggage. It will require a wagon or cart to carry it. I should like to purchase one, along with a team, for if Catherine is to follow the army, we'll need adequate transport with us." He thought a second, then said, "And we shall need two saddle horses. My wife and I will ride; the servants will travel in the vehicle." He looked over at his wife. "Catherine is an accomplished horsewoman."

Wend felt a touch of irritation, fearing that the time needed for Tresh to find a wagon and horses would inevitably delay their departure from the city. But he mentally sighed—there was nothing for it. He said, "I shall send some men to assist you in locating a suitable conveyance and animals. My former apprentice, Andrew Horner, is traveling with us to become an armorer with the army. He's a good man with wagons and has a fine eye for horses. And I'll send my second lieutenant, Mr. O'beirne, along also. He has some familiarity with Philadelphia and may be able to expedite locating a dealer for both."

Tresh looked at Wend with raised eyebrow. "Your apprentice? You were a tradesman before you accepted a commission?"

"That's right, Colonel. I was a gunsmith living near Winchester, Virginia. And I wish I were back there now. However, for some reason, the local committee of safety thought I would make a good captain and essentially pressed me into the army."

"Well, things seem quite different here in America. If you don't mind my asking, have you ever been in action before?"

"I don't mind your question, Colonel. As a matter of fact, I've seen war—on the frontier of course—not the type of war you are used to. In my youth, in 1763, I served as a scout in Pontiac's War. I was with Colonel Bouquet of the Royal Americans during the campaign to relieve Fort Pitt."

"Bouquet, you say? Henry Bouquet?"

"Yes, I fought with him at Bushy Run, the critical battle of the campaign." Wend motioned toward Tresh. "He was Swiss, like yourself."

"Ah, yes. I know of Bouquet by reputation and have studied his tactics. He had an impressive career, being the only foreign officer raised to the rank of brigadier by King George himself." He shrugged. "A pity that he succumbed to fever at such an early age."

"Indeed, sir. I consider it an honor to have served with him."

"As it turns out, I know several officers who served with Bouquet. Most particularly Thomas Stirling, who is now the commandant of the British 42nd Highlanders. Did you make his acquaintance?"

Wend smiled broadly. "As it happens, I served as his scout on a diplomatic mission to the Ohio Country in late 1763. Bouquet had dispatched Captain Stirling and his company to present an ultimatum to tribal leaders to come to negotiations or face an advance by a strong force in the forthcoming year. We were together for nearly two months." Wend thought a second, then asked, "How did you come to know him?"

"Stirling and I had companies in the same regiment in the service of the Dutch. When war with the French in America was on the horizon, Thomas went back to Scotland and raised a company, which earned him his commission in the 42nd." He shrugged. "There were numerous British and Scottish officers serving in Europe before the Seven Years War erupted and necessitated the expansion of the English army."

Wend raised his eyebrows. "I was not aware of that bit of Stirling's past. Thank you for educating me."

Tresh looked sharply at Wend. "Is that time as a scout your only previous experience?"

Catherine spoke up. "Alex, you are being very nosy. It is quite impolite."

He stopped and raised a hand. "Captain Eckert, my apologies. Forgive me if I seem overly inquisitive about your past. I am trying to ascertain what the experience is of American officers in the Continental Army."

Wend shrugged. "No offense taken, sir. As for my further active service, I was a lieutenant in the campaign against the Shawnee, Mingo, and Delaware under Governor Dunmore in 1774. There was considerable fighting. And then my company and I saw action last month in the battles which drove Dunmore and his men out of Virginia."

Tresh cocked his head. "So your company has actually been blooded." It was more of a statement than a question."

"Indeed, sir. My lads performed well in action against Dunmore's King's Loyal Virginia Legion."

"Well, when we have more time, you must tell me about it."

At that moment, the maid arrived, carrying a covered tray. Wend said, "Sir, I will take my leave now, so that you and Mrs. Tresh may take your meal. But my men will be here very shortly to assist you with the purchase of the wagon and horses."

Tresh nodded. "That will be most satisfactory, Captain."

Wend made a bow to Catherine and said, "My pleasure to have met you, ma'am. I look forward to your company on our journey northward."

And with that he took his leave.

—⁓—

After leaving the Treshes' rooms, Wend descended the stairs and entered the common room. He had decided to have a drink and think about how having the two Europeans along on the march northward would affect his plans. He went up to the counter and ordered whiskey. As he stood there waiting, he realized one thing was sure: He could not expect to get the company out of Philadelphia the next day. It was already mid-day. Procuring the wagon and horses and getting the Treshes ready to travel would extend their departure at least until the day afterward. He wondered how young Ensign Childers was doing finding a place for the company to camp.

The barman brought his whiskey, and Wend had just taken his first sip when someone tapped him on the shoulder. He looked around to see a young tavern maid, tray in hand, at his side.

"Sir, the gentleman at the corner table has invited you to join him." She motioned to a table at the far end of the room. Surprised, since he had no acquaintances in the city, Wend looked to where she indicated and saw that Jones, the *Providence's* captain, was sitting there. He had pipe in hand and a tall drink on the table. The naval officer, seeing Wend looking at him, waved and then pointed to a chair at his table.

Wend picked up his glass and made his way through the crowded room to Jones' table.

"Sir, will you join me? I hate drinking alone, particularly when I'm celebrating."

Wend smiled and sat down. "What, perchance, are you celebrating, sir?"

"Well, my promotion to the rank of captain, for one thing."

"In that case, you have my congratulations."

"Yes, I visited the naval committee today and they gave me the good news. It is in recognition of a cruise I made with *Providence* this Spring along the northern part of the coast. We took many prizes and gave the British considerable indigestion." He took a long pull on the pipe. "My only regret about it is an encounter I had with a British dispatch schooner. It was just south of Halifax and her name was *Raven*."

"Why the regret, if I may ask?"

"I had to decline combat with her." He gritted his teeth. "Not because she was larger and more heavily armed than *Providence,* which she was indeed. Not because I didn't think I could take her."

Wend's brows furrowed. "I don't understand. If what you said is true, why did you decline combat?"

"I had only a skeleton crew onboard. Most of my men and officers had been detached as prize crews to take captured vessels into port. I didn't have enough men to properly serve the guns or rapidly handle the sails." He sighed deeply. "I vow if I did, our little *Providence* could have made short work of the Britisher, or at least have given her a fight they would have long remembered."

"Surely now you will command a more powerful ship."

Jones laughed. "That's the other reason why I am celebrating. I've been told that I will shortly get orders to command the *Alfred,* a three-masted ship with twenty 9-pounders."

"Well, congratulations again."

"Actually, I'm quite familiar with *Alfred*—I put her in commission as First Lieutenant and served many months onboard." He took another pull on the pipe. "But I hope this is actually an interim command. *Alfred* is a good ship for one converted from a merchant, but the weight of all the guns added to her has affected her sailing qualities and made her damnably slow." He raised a finger. "However, I have hope for something better in short order." He leaned toward Wend and spoke in a soft tone. "Confidentially, several members of the naval committee are trying to line me up to get command of a brand new ship being built in Maine—a fast, 18-gun ship-rigged sloop of war." He smiled. "A swift ship suits me well, for it will enable me to engage when I meet a suitable foe and escape from heavier ships. With our small navy, I hold speed to be essential, for we can never take on the Royal Navy's heavy ships."

Wend put his hand to his chin. "Well, what you say is interesting. I admit that I have never paid much attention to matters of the sea."

Jones gave Wend a knowing smile. "No, I dare say not, but I propose that you are about to get an illuminating lesson in naval power."

"Sir, what are you implying?"

"I'm not *implying* anything; I'm *predicting*. I'm speaking about the forthcoming battle at New York City. I believe the presence of the British fleet will make it indefensible."

"You mean they will be able to move their ships around the harbor and bombard our forces?"

"Yes, but that's only part of it. More importantly, they will be able to use the fleet's small ships and boats to transport their troops rapidly to unexpected places. Washington will never have enough troops and artillery to cover every potential landing place. They'll be able to outflank him, perhaps divide and trap parts of his army to defeat them individually. He will find it hard, if not impossible, to respond. And the same waters which will help the British will limit Washington's own mobility. New York City is really a collection of several towns and villages separated by rivers and bays. He'll have to spread his troops out into isolated positions, and they will find it impracticable to support each other." Jones cocked his head and said, "What say you to that?"

Wend thought a moment. Then he said tentatively, "Washington must have taken into account all that you have just said. If what you say is accurate, why is he preparing to defend the city? Why doesn't he withdraw to fight in another place more advantageous to him?"

"Because, my dear Eckert, he has been told by Congress that he *must* make every effort to hold the city." He raised a finger. "Here's the truth of it: Defending the city was the New York delegation's price for agreeing to the Declaration of Independence. It had to be unanimous—all the colonies—and New York has a strong loyalist faction. The only way the New Yorkers would sign on with independence was if the other colonies would agree to the all-out defense of the city." He smiled and shrugged. "A clear case of politics dictating military action and frankly not to the advantage of our cause."

Wend thought about all that for a moment, then said noncommittally, "Well, we shall shortly see if your assessment is correct."

"Indeed, sir." Jones took some of his drink, as did Wend, and there was silence at the table for a few seconds. Then the naval officer said, "What is the news from Virginia? As I said onboard your ship, I spent some time there, looking at land. I thought perhaps to go into the plantation business."

Wend raised an eyebrow. Then he said a bit playfully, "A sailor interested in a farm? That is not what one would expect."

Jones laughed. "You would be quite wrong, Eckert. Many sailors long for nothing more than to settle down on their own land." He grinned mischievously. "There is an old saying: When a sailor is ready to leave the sea, he should get an oar and carry it over his shoulder as he walks inland. When he gets far enough from the coast that someone asks him, 'What is that funny thing he's carrying?' he knows that's the place to settle."

Wend smiled and responded, "An amusing thought, sir." Then he paused a moment, reflecting on what Jones might find interesting. "Well, in news of Virginia, Lord Dunmore has finally been driven from the state. Virginia forces defeated him at a place called Gwynn's Island. He and his followers sailed for New York to join with Howe."

Jones nodded. "I know of Gwynn's Island. It's near the town of Gloucester."

"Indeed, sir." Then Wend continued, "Also, a constitution for Virginia has been approved by the legislature. It was ratified just after word of the Declaration of Independence was received in the state. And Patrick Henry has become the first governor."

A thoughtful look came over Jones' face. "Ah, yes. I know of Henry, although I never met him. He was from near where I was looking for land in Hanover County, out to the northwest of the town of Richmond. I dealt with several men who owned property in the area, particularly Nathaniel Dandridge, who was an acquaintance of Henry's."

"Well, then you know that the Dandridge family is one of the most influential in the state."

"Yes, I'm quite aware of that. Dandridge had a large plantation with an elegant mansion. I quite liked the countryside in that area. I would have been most satisfied to settle there." He stared into the distance for a long moment as if deep in reflection. Then, with the faraway gaze still in his eyes, he continued, "Dandridge had a stunning young daughter, named Dorothea. She was a raven-haired beauty and quite popular among the young men of the gentry in that locale. I wonder what has become of her."

Wend thought for a long moment, deliberating on what to say. He was well aware that Jones had attempted to court Dorothea, only to be rebuffed by her father. Finally, he said, "Actually, I can enlighten you on that matter."

Jones slowly turned to look at Wend. "Are you familiar with the Dandridges?"

"Not the family, but I have met Dorothea—briefly, as it happened—during a ball celebrating independence at the governor's palace in Williamsburg, just earlier this month." He looked directly at Jones. "She's as lovely as you say and has the most genteel manners. She'll make a fine governor's lady."

"What did you say?" A shocked expression came over Jones' face. "Governor's lady?"

"Yes, she has just become betrothed to Patrick Henry. He lost his first wife in '74."

Wend watched Jones as shock momentarily appeared on his face. Then he regained control and again looked into the distance. In a moment, the naval officer said, almost under his breath, "Well, it seems that Nathaniel Dandridge got exactly what he wanted for his daughter in marriage."

Wend nodded and said in a matter-of-fact tone, "Yes, everyone is saying that it is an ideal match. It helps ensure the Dandridge family's influence in government, and it propels Henry, who has worked his way up from a hardscrabble background, to a place in the gentry. Both sides achieve their ends." Wend shrugged. "Given the beauty and intelligence of Miss Dandridge, I would say our governor is a lucky man."

Now having recovered his composure, Jones smiled and said, "Indeed he is." Then he took another sip of his drink and asked, "And what other news of Virginia do you have?"

Wend told him all he knew of things in Williamsburg and the state in general and how its regiments were preparing to march to join the Continental forces.

In a few minutes, Wend had exhausted his supply of information and emptied his glass. He said, "Sir, this has been quite pleasant and interesting, but I must rejoin my company. Much must be done today in preparation for our march northward." He picked up his hat and added, "I wish you much fortune in your new command."

Jones touched his forehead with two fingers of his right hand—the sailor's salute—and replied, "And to you, sir, in the arduous campaign which lies ahead of you."

Shay O'beirne, second lieutenant of the Frederick County Light Foot Company, climbed the front steps of the City Tavern. He was tall, lean, black Irishman with a narrow face, piercing eyes, and a ready smile. An observer would have had trouble deciding whether he was on the upper side of thirty or the lower side of forty. Beside him was Andrew Horner, Wend's former apprentice who was now traveling with the company to serve the army as a journeyman gunsmith. He was a young man of medium height, thin build, with dark brown hair, just beyond his twentieth birthday.

When the two entered the hall, the Irishman turned to Horner. "Why don't you wait here while I introduce myself to Tresh? Then I'll bring him down, and we can be off to the horse trader's place."

"I'll be happy to do that, but don't be long. I'll be at the counter."

Shay grinned. "That's the first place I would have looked for you in any case." He motioned toward the common room. "And tell the barman Shay O'beirne will be there presently."

"You've been here before? He'll know you?"

"I was here often in my brief stay in Philadelphia, and that was only a few weeks ago before I was off on my way south to Carolina, where I would be now if I hadn't fallen in with Eckert in Winchester and joined up with the lot of you."

O'beirne quickly mounted the stairs to the second floor and in a few moments was knocking on the door with a brass numeral "2" on it. Almost instantly it was opened, and a man of about forty stood before him.

"Colonel Tresh? Sir, I'm Lieutenant Shay O'beirne of the Frederick County Light Foot. Captain Eckert sent me."

"Ah, yes. Please come in, Lieutenant."

O'beirne stepped into the room and said, "Captain Eckert asked that I and Gunsmith Andrew Horner, who is down in the common room, assist you in procuring horses and an appropriate conveyance."

"Indeed. I'm glad for your help." Tresh turned and motioned into the room. "And let me introduce you to my wife, Catherine." O'beirne had seen the woman on the settee out of the corner of his eye and now turned to her, bowing as he did so. As he straightened out and looked at her directly for the first time, his face turned to an expression of shock, but he was able to control it in an instant and return to a normal countenance. "A pleasure, Ma'am."

Catherine smiled broadly. "The pleasure is mine, Lieutenant."

Tresh, oblivious to O'beirne's reaction on seeing his wife, said, "Catherine, will you entertain Mr. O'beirne while I fetch Moulders?" He turned to O'beirne. "Moulders is my manservant, and he will drive whatever conveyance we purchase."

Catherine nodded and said, "I'd love to, Alex. I should get to know the lieutenant, since we shall be traveling companions for some time."

Tresh responded, "Just so, my dear." Then he said to O'beirne, "Excuse me, sir, I shall not be long." And with that he walked out and shut the door behind him.

There was a momentary silence as Shay and Catherine stared at each other. Then he said, "Well, Aiethne, it seems you found a way out of that brothel in Paris."

"Please, Shay, it was a *Woman's Social Association*." A look of anger passed over her face. "And don't ever call me *Aiethne* again. It's now *Catherine*. Catherine Tresh. Aiethne is merely a dim memory."

"Well, now, my darling lady, whatever name you use, we both know you are an Irish lass who ran out on her husband. Does the honorable Colonel Alexander Tresh know about your past and membership in the association?"

"My husband was a beast. Leaving him was the best thing I ever did. And as far as Alex, where do you think we met?"

Shay grinned broadly. "So you turned a client into a husband? And he's comfortable with your past?"

"Quite comfortable. And I feel great gratitude to him for taking me out of that place. In any case, I'm not the first courtesan who moved on to a respectable situation."

"Oh, I'm quite aware of that. My congratulations on your success." A smile came over his face. "Are you in love with Tresh?"

"Love? What's that? Merely a young girl's fantasy! I was disabused of the idea of love long ago. What *is* important is that Alex is quite enamored of me and has the fortune to support me more comfortably than I ever expected to live." She shrugged. "And in truth, I do feel considerable affection for him."

A thought struck Shay. "Did you ever bother to get a divorce from your Irish husband?"

"Given the way I left? Don't be silly, Shay. And in any case, bigamy is probably the least damning of my sins in the eyes of the Lord. But let's get on to the important matter. You are not going to betray me, are you? You're not going to tell your fellow officers about my past? I beseech you!"

"Now, now, er, *Catherine.* Why should I do that? Especially after the many happy, intimate hours we spent together? Pleasure for me, profit for you."

"That's a crass way to put it, Shay. And you know I always thought of you as special."

"Yes, as indeed you should." He grinned broadly. "I invested a small fortune in you." He shrugged. "But have no worries; I vow, for old time's sake, I'll shield your past. Your secrets are safe with me."

Catherine sighed. "My past is one of the reasons we came to America. Alex thought it would be less likely that we would run into men I had entertained. We plan to stay here when the war is over, whatever the outcome. Our dream is to buy land for a plantation and assume the life of the gentry."

"Well, that's a long time in the future. This war will see a lot of twists and turns, and we both may have picked the wrong side."

Catherine cocked her head. "Which leads me to ask a question, Shay. Last time I saw you, you were a captain serving with one of those small German principalities. How do you happen to be here, and serving as a junior lieutenant at that?"

"I had a small disagreement with my regimental commandant, and given the general outbreak of peace in Europe, other situations were hard to find. So I thought to cross the ocean and throw in with these colonial rebels. Then I was here in Philadelphia negotiating with a Pennsylvania official about a place in one of their regiments when an *unfortunate* problem arose regarding the daughter of a prominent family in the city."

Catherine smirked. "Knowing you, I'm not in the least surprised."

He grinned again and shrugged. "Needless to say, it became convenient to depart promptly and head for South Carolina, where I heard they needed officers to fill out their state regiments."

She pointed to his uniform. "But you are in a company of Virginians."

"Well, I arrived in a place called Winchester rather short of funds and it happened they were looking for a lieutenant."

"Ah, yes. Now I see. Necessity became virtue."

"Ah, now Catherine, we know how that can happen."

They both laughed loudly.

At that moment, Tresh re-entered, accompanied by Moulders. The colonel said, "Well, you two certainly seem to be getting on well."

Catherine gave her husband a pleasant smile and said, "Lieutenant O'beirne is quite charming and even more amusing."

"Ah, yes, I understand." Tresh motioned toward his manservant. "Moulders, this is Lieutenant O'beirne of the Frederick County Light Foot."

Moulders snapped to attention and simply said, "Sir!"

Tresh said, "Moulders is an old soldier. He has campaigned with me for many years."

Shay nodded to him and said, "Well, shall we soldiers be about our business?"

Tresh responded, "Indeed, let us be off." He turned to Catherine. "My dear, I'm sure you can entertain yourself while we are gone, and I assure you we will be as swift as possible."

"Oh, by all means. And make sure you procure a spirited horse for me."

"Dear. I well know your tastes." He turned, opened the door, and departed, followed by the other two.

Chapter Two

The Jersey Incursion

In the morning twilight, the four officers of the Frederick County Light Foot sat on camp chairs around the fire in front of Eckert's tent. All had coffee cups in hand, and the cook of the officer's mess, Melinda, a light-skinned, formerly enslaved African, was collecting their breakfast plates from where they had set them on the ground. The company was bivouacked in a large field to the north of Philadelphia just off the main road which they would take for their march to New York.

Reese Newkirk looked up at the sky. He swallowed some coffee, then said, "It will be dawn soon. We could be packed up and on the march within the hour if we didn't have to wait on that colonel and his entourage. And given the heat we're likely to encounter later in the day, that would be a good thing."

Wend raised his eyebrows. "I told him to arrive as close after dawn as possible. He will understand our anxiousness to start the day's march."

Newkirk took another sip of coffee, then responded, "I'm not worried about the colonel, but I wonder if he can impart the same sense of urgency to his woman. Shay tells me they're recently married." He shrugged. "Undoubtedly she's not accustomed to life in a military camp or on the march."

O'beirne spoke up. "Now, my dear Reese, I spent a wee bit of time with Mrs. Tresh the day we went to find them that cart and their horses. She seemed quite keen to learn the ways of the camp. It's not surprised I'll be if they arrive in goodly time."

Wend drained his cup. "We have to take Tresh at his word, even if in the end they do arrive late." He looked over at his first lieutenant. "Reese, go ahead and get the word to Sergeant Donegal to make preparations to break camp. When Tresh gets here, I want to be ready to march. If anyone's going to hold things up, I don't want it to be us."

The officers rose and went to make their preparations. Wend entered the tent to pack his kit. Meanwhile, Billy Wood and Melinda began packing up the chairs and other camp equipment. As he worked, Wend could hear the voices of the soldiers and camp women and children as they stowed equipment, doused fires, and struck their own tents. Down at the picket line, a horse whinnied, presumably as someone began putting on harness. He stepped out of the tent to see Billy Wood standing by. Melinda was about to carry her cooking things to a wagon. Wend nodded to the African man, "Go ahead and get my kit, then strike the tent, Billy." Billy, his parents, and sisters had been the house servants for the Eckert family at their farm, Eckert Ridge. Seven years earlier, Wend had bought the entire family at an estate sale. He had then had James Wood, Frederick County's representative in Burgesses, negotiate their manumission. In gratitude the family had taken Wood's surname. When the company had been formed, Billy had asked to join and thus had become a private and Wend's personal servant. The lad had performed superbly during the campaign against Lord Dunmore and, in response, had recently been promoted to corporal.

Wend had no sooner spoken to Billy than he saw Andrew Horner bringing his horse, Sonny, saddled and bridled, toward him. The muscular, long-legged hunter's black coat gleamed in the morning light, and he pranced as the young man led him through the camp.

Horner smiled as he approached where Wend stood. "He's anxious to get going, Mr. Eckert, tired of standing around on that ship's deck all those days."

"Well, Andrew, he'll settle down after a few miles on the road."

Horner handed him the reins and went to tend to his own team and wagon. Wend checked out the horse, then tied him to a nearby tree. He returned to the tent and got his holstered pistols and saddlebags and laced them to the saddle.

He had no sooner done so than Billy called out, "Mr. Eckert, someone's comin' along the road toward us—two people on horses and a cart followin' behind."

Wend looked down the road. In the twilight, he could make out two riders—a man and a woman—and a cart pulled by a powerful Conestoga horse. He recognized Tresh, dressed in a dark blue uniform coat, white breeches, leather riding boots, and a black cocked hat. Catherine rode sidesaddle on a high-stepping bay horse. She wore a two-piece, dark blue riding habit consisting of jacket and skirt, with a white stock showing around her neck. It was topped off with a flat straw hat sporting a plume. Moulders drove the cart with Elise riding in the seat beside him. The whole entourage was coming at the trot.

Newkirk joined Wend. "Well, I stand corrected. They've arrived in good time, women and all."

Wend nodded. "Indeed, Reese. I rather suspected they would." Then he had a thought. "Find Donegal and have him get the men into formation with firelocks and full marching kit. Form in company front by half companies. We'll give Colonel Tresh the honor of inspecting the company. I expect it's his first view of American light foot in the field, Make sure we give him a good impression."

"Right, sir. I'll see to it." And with that, Newkirk was off, shouting for Donegal.

Wend walked over to the side of the road to greet Tresh and his people. It wasn't long until they arrived and pulled up.

Wend touched his hat in salute to Tresh, then doffed it momentarily to Catherine. "Good day, Colonel and Mrs. Tresh. Welcome to our camp."

"Our pleasure, Captain." Tresh slipped to the ground and went to help his wife down.

Wend said, "Colonel, before we march, I've arranged for you to inspect the company."

Tresh smiled broadly. "That would be my honor, sir."

Wend motioned toward the campfire where his tent had stood. "Mrs. Tresh, there's still a camp chair available for you to take your leisure while we inspect the company."

Catherine grinned. "That would be very nice."

"And," responded Wend, "I believe we still have some coffee, if that would be to your pleasure."

Catherine pursed her lips and hesitated momentarily, then asked, "Might there be something a little stronger available? Something to fortify me for the long ride? We left the inn in rather a hurry."

"Well, we do have whiskey."

She put her hand to her chin and raised her eyebrows. "American whiskey? Now that sounds interesting. I should like to try that."

Wend motioned to Melinda, who was standing nearby. "Melinda, please fetch Mrs. Tresh some of our whiskey." He turned to the colonel. "Perhaps you would enjoy some also while we wait for the company to assemble?"

"Indeed, sir. I tasted some local whiskey in the inn and found it quite appealing."

Melinda hurried off to get a jug from the officers' wagon. Catherine stared after the girl for a moment, then said, "That girl is very light-skinned for an African, and her face seems to have Caucasian features."

Wend said, "She was enslaved on a plantation in Tidewater Virginia. Now, there's no delicate way to say this, Catherine, but the master had his way with her mother, and she was the issue of the affair." Wend sighed. "It is a fact of life that such things occur on plantations throughout the Southern colonies."

Catherine nodded. "No need to feel embarrassed, Captain. I quite understand."

"Yes, well, Melinda was motivated to escape the plantation because the master's oldest son began taking an interest in her, and—how shall I say this—she had no desire to cooperate. She joined the forces of Lord Dunmore, the royal governor, but after a while, she became disillusioned by how the Africans were treated in his camp and found a way to stay behind when he evacuated his forces from Gwynn's Island in the Chesapeake. She joined us when we occupied the island and stayed voluntarily as the cook for the officers' mess." Wend smiled. "I should say, she's very good at it, because she worked in the cookhouse at the plantation and served meals to the family in the mansion."

Melinda returned carrying a jug of whiskey and poured both Catherine and the colonel a measure. They sipped the libation and Tresh looked over at Wend. "Well, as I said, I had some whiskey at the City Tavern, but this is far superior. If I may ask, where did you get it?"

"Actually, Colonel, it was distilled on my farm. The company sergeant, Simon Donegal, and I are partners in the production of the whiskey. I grow the grains and Donegal runs the distillery. It's based on a recipe he learned while working in a distillery in Scotland, modified for the grains we grow here."

Tresh looked down at his cup, then over at Wend. "So your senior sergeant is your partner in trade? Is that not unusual?" He raised an eyebrow. "I mean, a soldier of the ranks in a business arrangement with an officer? Are there no disciplinary complications?"

There was a moment of silence, with both of the Treshes staring at Wend with puzzlement in their eyes. Wend grinned and explained, "You have to understand, although this company was raised to be a regular unit of the Continental Army, it is a product of the colonial militia system. One year a man may be a corporal or sergeant, but the next a lieutenant or even a captain. It will depend on what men, with what experience, are recruited for a specific service. Donegal spent seven years in the 77th Highlanders during the late war with the French and their tribal allies and rose to be a corporal. He was sergeant major of a militia battalion in Virginia's war with the Shawnee in 1774." Wend looked from Tresh to Catherine and then said, "In fact, I asked Donegal to be my first lieutenant when I was given the commission to recruit the company, but he turned me down, saying he would be more effective as the company's senior sergeant."

Catherine looked after Melinda, who was carrying the jug back to the wagon. Then she scanned the bivouac area with her eyes and turned back to Wend. "I see other women with the company. How many do you have?"

"Catherine, we have six, besides Melinda—all wives of soldiers," he smiled, "and four children of various ages."

Suddenly Catherine's eyes opened wide in surprise. "There's a pregnant woman. My God, she's near due. And she's very, very young." She looked surprised. "This life must be very hard on her."

Tresh interrupted. "Yes, my dear, hard on the woman, but not unusual. You are new to military camps, but you will see that the families become adapted to the rigors of this life."

Wend said, "That young mother-to-be is Patricia Carver. She's only fifteen." He smiled, "And she was pregnant before Jedediah found it in his best interest to marry her, if you take my meaning."

Catherine laughed. "I quite understand."

Wend continued, "Martha Flanagan is the leader of the camp women. She is the wife of one of our sergeants. She's quite experienced, for she and her husband marched with the Virginia Regiment during the late war with the French and then served in the militia against the Shawnee in '74. I am sure she will do what she can to ensure your comfort during your time with us."

Catherine smiled at Wend over her cup. "I should be very grateful."

At that moment, Newkirk approached, the officers of the company with him.

Wend motioned to the group. "Colonel, I should like to introduce my officers to you and Mrs. Tresh."

Tresh nodded. "That will be our pleasure. Of course, we have already met Lieutenant O'beirne."

Shay spoke up. "My pleasure to see you again, Colonel," then he touched his hat and continued, "And of course you also, Mrs. Tresh."

Catherine grinned broadly. "Yes, Mr. O'beirne and I had a lovely conversation at the inn yesterday."

Wend nodded and motioned his hand toward the other two. "This is our First Lieutenant, Reese Newkirk, and our most junior officer, Ensign Edward Childers."

Both officers acknowledged Tresh and touched their hats to Catherine.

Tresh swept his hand to include Newkirk and Childers. He said, "Well, I'm aware that Mr. O'beirne has been a professional officer in Europe. May I be so bold as to inquire what military background you two gentlemen possess?"

Wend answered for them. "Mr. Newkirk is an accomplished surveyor, but he also served some active time in the militia. During Dunmore's campaign against the tribes in the Ohio Country, he saw considerable action as a lieutenant leading a half-company." Then Wend grinned and indicated Edward with his hand. "Mr. Childers is new to the military service. He was just appointed Ensign before we formed the company, but I am well aware that he had considerable action in the taverns of Williamsburg while a student at the College of William and Mary."

Childers' face broke into a sheepish smile. "I would plead guilty to that accusation."

Tresh laughed. "I am quite familiar with that kind of action."

Wend raised a finger and added, "I am a bit remiss about Mr. Childers' background. We had a brisk skirmish with some of Dunmore's troops on the shores of the Chesapeake, and Edward acquitted himself quite well leading a detachment of men, including closing with the enemy using the bayonet."

Tresh nodded and smiled at the young ensign. "Good fellow! Sir, you may be proud of your first action."

Wend agreed. "Indeed he can, sir."

Then Newkirk spoke up. "As we came over, Donegal informed me the company is mustered and ready for the colonel."

Wend looked over and saw the company standing in formation. "Well, Colonel, shall we go take a look at the Frederick County Light Foot?"

"By all means."

As they walked, Wend gave Tresh a background briefing. "Our strength is one hundred men, the full authorization for a company. Half the men are armed with rifles, the other half with muskets—namely the British King's Arm short land pattern."

Tresh stopped and turned to stare at Wend. After a moment he said, "Now that is unusual, sir. The British and most other nations arm their light companies with muskets, while of course the German principalities are known for their Jaeger companies, which carry rifles. I confess I don't understand the reasoning behind mixing the two weapons within the company."

"Donegal and I worked out the idea, based on our experience when marching with Bouquet. He formed a scouting squad of four men, which by chance had two men who were Highlanders armed with muskets and the other two were scouts with long rifles. On several occasions, the men with the muskets, because they could load faster, protected the two of us who had rifles, which of course take much longer to reload."

"I see, but how does that figure into your tactical use of the company?"

"We imagine that the company can be used in three ways: in line formation by half companies, if it comes to that in battle; but obviously our most important use is in skirmishing. As I'm sure you know, the standard method is to have the men fight in pairs, one ready to fire while the other loads."

"Yes, yes, Eckert, I understand. But what is this third way you speak of?"

"We have established in the company ten of what we call field squads, or sections if you prefer, made up normally of ten men each. Eight of the squads contain four riflemen and six men with muskets. The remainder of the riflemen form two squads with rifles only."

Tresh squinted at Wend as if trying to understand the reasoning.

Wend continued. "The idea, sir, is that during skirmish warfare, in each squad the riflemen will act as marksmen for important targets, while the musket men will cover and protect them with rapid fire. With six men using muskets, there will always be at least two ready to fire, forcing the enemy skirmishers in our front to take cover." Wend held up a finger. "And there is one other tactical benefit: In case we encounter a line battalion of superior force advancing rapidly, I believe we can space out our squads, with gaps between each, and by combining the high firepower of the muskets with the precision shooting of the rifles, slow or check the enemy's advance temporarily while our own main force properly deploys to meet the enemy."

Tresh stood still, hand to his chin, considering Wend's words. Finally he responded, "It is an *intriguing* idea." He cocked his head and smiled at Eckert. "But one which will have to be proven in the face of the enemy."

Wend nodded. "Indeed, sir. We have practiced the system and I look forward to doing just that in action against the British." He then motioned toward the company. "Well, the men are waiting. Shall we proceed?"

"By all means!"

As they approached the formation, Tresh turned to Wend and said, "Captain, I see that you, all of your men and officers, are dressed in a linen frock. I have heard of such a thing on the American borderlands known as the *hunting shirt*. Is that what I am seeing?"

"Indeed, sir. The shirts were all made to the same pattern for the company by the women of Frederick County. There wasn't time to make all the men proper uniforms, and in any case the hunting shirt is much more appropriate for our function as scouts and skirmishers. Most of our men have worn them before when hunting or serving as militia. The officers have official Virginia line uniforms, but we wear the shirt in the field." Wend smiled. "In fact, the British call light foot and rifle companies who wear it 'the shirtmen.'"

Tresh nodded his understanding. "Well, I would say that they do give your men the look of uniformity. While in Philadelphia, I was advised that many regiments of Washington's army have no uniform at all." Then he continued, "I see all your men also wear black hats with the rear brim turned up." He motioned toward Donegal, who stood in front of the company, waiting to receive them, and said, "Except for your sergeant there, who is wearing the bonnet of a Highland regiment."

Wend laughed. "Donegal said he wore it through seven years of campaigning in the 77th Highlanders and it brought him luck, so he's determined to wear it through this war. And I assure you, no one in the company would try to dissuade him."

The colonel looked over Donegal. "Yes, he seems a hard man."

"He is that, and the best soldier I've ever known, save one named Kirkwood, who was his comrade in the 77th. But that man is home in Scotland."

They approached Donegal, standing in front of the formation. When they were a few steps away, the sergeant turned and saluted. Then he said to Eckert, "Company all present and correct, sir!"

Wend returned the salute and introduced Donegal to Tresh. Then the sergeant led the way to the ranks of the half-company armed with muskets, where Sergeant Flanagan took over and guided the way along the line.

Tresh commented, "Ah, yes. As you said, Captain, the King's Arm. If I may ask, where did you obtain these?"

Wend responded, "They were made in my shop. Before the war, I had a contract from the colonial government to refurbish and cut down long land pattern muskets from the armory in Williamsburg into the short pattern. So we had the experience and practice manufacturing the parts we could and arranging for fabrication by other craftsmen of those we couldn't make ourselves. And of course, we had considerable experience at carving stocks for the long rifles we made as a matter of routine, so it was not difficult to move on to manufacture of muskets."

The colonel raised an eyebrow. "Quite impressive." He thought a moment, then said, "I assume you had to shut down your shop to take this commission for service with the army."

"No, colonel. I have a very competent journeyman who assisted me, and he and my apprentices are carrying on the work in my absence. And my good wife Elizabeth, or Peggy as she is called, maintains the records of the business and pays the bills." He smiled. "She does the same for our whiskey business."

Tresh smiled and remarked, "Very convenient." He looked at Donegal. "I presume you have a similar arrangement for running the distillery."

"Aye, I have a man who helped me with the distilling. And he is runnin' it now, watched over by the wife of a friend, a certain Mrs. Baird."

"Ah, I see. So you are not married, Sergeant?"

Wend quickly interjected. "Sergeant Donegal's wife, a lovely young woman, was killed last year during a loyalist raid on our farm."

A puzzled look came over Tresh's face. "A raid? On a *family* home? Does it happen often?"

"No, colonel. Lord Dunmore, the royal governor, sent the loyalists specifically to stop the manufactory of muskets and to punish me for not taking a commission in his royalist forces. He felt I owed him loyalty because of the money I had made for years refurbishing the colony's muskets and serving as a lieutenant on his staff during the war with the Shawnee in the Ohio Country."

Tresh stared at Wend for a long moment, considering, then said, "Ah, yes, I understand." He turned to Donegal and said in a sympathetic tone, "My condolences on the loss of your wife, Sergeant."

Donegal simply nodded.

Wend spoke up briskly. "Shall we move on to the rifle half-company?"

They walked over to the ranks of the riflemen, where Sergeant Tom Wilder saluted, and Wend introduced him.

As they walked to the front rank, Tresh said, "I've heard of these American long rifles which hunters use, and I'm very interested in examining one."

"Well," responded Wend, "there's no better time to do so than now." He saw that the first man in the rank was Corporal Joseph Schreiber. "Schreiber, hand me your rifle."

The corporal did so, and Wend passed it to Tresh. The colonel examined it with the eyes of a professional. Presently he said, "Well, I have seen many Jaeger rifles in Europe, but this is quite different. The lock is not as heavily built, and of course there is the longer length of the barrel. But what surprises me most is the bore of the barrel—much smaller than I have seen on any rifle. And naturally, the weight of the ball would be considerably less than the Jaeger model."

Wend responded, "Well, the long rifle was born from the Jäger, which German gunsmiths brought to this country. But the long rifle was developed to meet the needs of hunters in the backcountry who could carry limited amounts of powder and lead on long trips. The longer barrel makes more efficient use of powder, and the smaller bore means less lead for the balls. The longer barrel also makes for greater accuracy, which British officers have learned to their dismay."

Tresh's brow furrowed. "You mean you Americans specifically target the officers?"

Donegal laughed and spoke up. "Aye, they're the first target of our riflemen. And my lads are wagering among themselves on who will get the most."

The colonel stiffened, then said in a serious tone to Donegal, "You speak of it almost like taking game in the forest."

Donegal didn't answer, just staring quietly at the Swiss officer.

Wend said, "Colonel, some aspects of war in America are considerably different than on the Continent."

Tresh didn't respond. Instead, he looked down at the rifle in his hands, then spoke to Schreiber. "I'm told American riflemen carry their own personal firelocks. If I may inquire, how did you obtain this?"

"Sir, I bought it at the sale of an estate. The first owner bought it from the gunmaker himself. Lucky for me, it was sparsely used, so it was almost like new."

Tresh nodded. "And is this rifle typical of what all the men have?"

Wend waved his hand along the length of the rifle. "They are generally similar, but different localities have their own style, and each gunsmith has his preferences in matters like size of bore and the pattern of the carvings on the stock." Wend thought a moment. "Many rifles made in the southern colonies have little or no carving, but their reliability and accuracy is as good as any."

Tresh turned to Schreiber. "And do you know who made this firelock? And where it was made?"

Schreiber looked at Wend conspiratorially. "You had best ask the captain that question, sir."

Tresh looked at Wend with puzzlement in his eyes. "Ask Captain Eckert?" Then understanding passed over his face, and he smiled. "Am I to take it that you were the gunsmith?"

"Indeed, sir. I made it shortly after we moved to Winchester from Pennsylvania. That is what we call the Lancaster County Pattern."

Tresh smiled. "Well, Captain, you have my compliments. It is indeed an elegant piece of craftsmanship." With that, he handed the rifle back to Schreiber.

Wend motioned to Wilder. "Let's move on, Sergeant."

When they finished, Newkirk was waiting for them. "Captain, everything is loaded into the wagons. Fires are out. We're ready to march, sir."

Wend nodded. "All right, Reese. Let's not delay any longer. Get the company on the road and lead off."

In short order, the company was on the march. Wend and the Treshes mounted and took the lead, with the company marching behind in column of threes. After the soldiers walked the camp women and children, followed by the company's two farm wagons, Horner's tool wagon, and the Treshes' cart carrying the two servants. Bringing up the rear were two hired Conestoga wagons, carrying provisions which had been arranged in Philadelphia.

As they began their march, the sun rose above the horizon, dispelling the pre-dawn gloom and promising a bright day for their journey.

—∞—

Mary Fraser, Matron of the regimental hospital of the 42nd Highlanders, dressed in her traveling gown, her hair tucked into a bonnet, stood on the deck of the fifty-gun ship *HMS Prefect* near the entry port in the starboard bulwark. As she looked out on New York Harbor, she could see the massive fleet of warships and merchant ships which lay at anchor around the great ship of the line. Everywhere she looked were vessels of every rig and size. There were warships ranging from small schooners and cutters up to frigates and ships of the line even larger than *Prefect*. But most of the ships were merchants: three-masted transports, two-masted brigs and brigantines, even single-masted coasting sloops. All were carrying men or supplies for the army's use.

Mary was quite familiar with the harbor and the surrounding land, for she had spent considerable time in New York during the French War as a child growing up first in the 77th Highlanders and then the 42nd. Now, looking to the west, she could see the flat expanse of Staten Island. To the northeast, she could see the tip of the island of Manhattan and beyond that, the wide Hudson River. Looking more to her right, she could see the mouth of the East River and the western end of Long Island. She was pleased to make out familiar landmarks.

In a few moments, Mary looked aft to the quarterdeck and could see that the 42nd's senior officers, Colonel Thomas Stirling and Major Charles McDonald, stood talking with *Prefect's* Captain Denholm and Commodore Royston, commander of the squadron which had escorted the convoy of transports carrying both the 42nd and 71st from England to Halifax and now down to New York. Near them stood Surgeon Potts, head of the regimental hospital, and Lieutenant Lachlan Campbell, the adjutant.

Then her thoughts were interrupted by the sound of a youthful voice. "Miss Fraser! Miss Fraser!"

She looked around to see young Midshipman Henry Blandford, aged twelve, standing a few feet away, and with him were all the other midshipmen of the ship.

Henry was speaking again. "Miss Fraser, we've come to say goodbye and to thank you for all you've done for us since you came aboard in April." The other six boys, ranging in age from Blandford up to seventeen, nodded. Sandy Richards, the eldest, said, "Indeed, Ma'am, we wanted to thank you for teaching us French and telling us those stories about the French War and the fights with Red Indians on the frontier. It was all so exciting."

The others nodded and touched their hats to her and expressed thanks in their own words. Then Henry spoke up again. "Ma'am, we've got something for you—a token to remember us by." He looked over at Midshipman Hawley. "Give it to her, Archie."

Young Hawley grinned shyly and handed her a piece of parchment rolled up into a scroll. Mary took it and spread it out. She was surprised to see a drawing: It was a picture of the seven boys, all sitting on deck, looking up at Mary standing with book in hand, as she had many times, teaching them their French. And at the bottom, each boy had signed the picture.

Blandford said, "Archie drew it up. It took him all last week." He smiled. "It took longer because we had to hide what he was doing from you. Every time you came into the gunroom to go to your stateroom, he had to stop and hide it."

Archie grinned. "Sometimes I took it up on deck and worked on top of one of the capstans."

Mary felt tears coming to her eyes. "Well, you did a wonderful job, Archie. Everyone's likeness is perfect. And I vow, this is the first time I've seen a drawing of myself."

"Well, Ma'am, I wanted to get it right. But I don't think it makes you look as pretty as you are in real life. And of course, it's only an ink drawing, so I couldn't show your beautiful auburn hair."

Mary squinted to prevent the tears from escaping her eyes and running down her face. Then she said softly, "Gentlemen, I shall remember our time together fondly, and I shall keep this wonderful drawing with me always. I thank you so much."

Just then Surgeon Potts called over, "Miss Fraser, they're ready for us to take to the boat. The chair is ready for you."

Mary nodded to Potts, then returned her glance to the boys. "Once again, I vow it has been my pleasure knowing all of you. Perhaps we shall meet again."

Then, with tears blurring her vision, she turned and walked over to where her chair dangled from a line that had been fairled through a block at the ship's main yardarm.

Beside it stood Harley Farrell, the *Prefect's* fourth lieutenant. "Mary, I'll help you into the chair."

She gave him her hand, and he seated her, then secured the safety strap over her lap.

"Mary, I can say on behalf of all the wardroom officers, it's been a pleasure having you aboard. We so enjoyed the times you dined with us. We shall miss you and recollect your time with the ship fondly."

"And I feel the same, Harley. Please express that on my behalf to all the other lieutenants."

Farrell smiled broadly. "Indeed I shall. Best fortune to you, Mary Fraser." And with that he signaled to the bos'n in charge, and Mary was lifted into the air high above the deck. Below, she watched sailors heaving on lines which rotated the spar around until she dangled over the side and could look down at the boat moored alongside the *Prefect's* hull, moving gently in the small waves of the harbor. She could also see Midshipman Blandford, who would be the boat officer, scurrying down the ladder to the boat. When he had arrived, he waved to Farrell and called out, "We're ready, sir. Lower away!"

Farrell called out to the bos'n, "Stanley, lower the chair, and mind you make it smooth!"

Mary began to descend, and she reflected it was indeed a smooth ride, affected only by the gentle rolling of *Prefect*. As she approached the boat, Blandford called out to a seaman, "Catch that tail line and hold it steady!"

The seaman grabbed the line hanging from the bottom of the chair and pulled it in as the chair reached the boat, keeping her from swinging out over the water. Blandford grabbed the chair, released the strap, and helped Mary down into the boat. Then he signaled to the ship, and the chair rose rapidly.

"Miss Fraser, let me get you to your seat. You and Mr. Campbell will be forward."

Mary looked up and could see Lachlan climbing down the ladder. Soon he reached the boat and carefully stepped aboard. He joined her in the seat ahead of the oarsmen. They sat facing toward the stern, so that their backs would face any spray which came over the bow. Mary knew that according to naval etiquette, officers boarded a boat in reverse order of seniority. So now Surgeon Potts was descending, and Major McDonald stood ready to follow him. Colonel Stirling, commandant of the battalion, would be the last to descend and would be given the most comfortable seat near the stern of the boat, right in front of the steersman's position.

Soon the two senior officers had descended and taken their places in the sternsheets. Blandford ordered the boat to push off and the rowers to give way with their oars.

As the boat made its way toward their destination—Staten Island—Campbell leaned over and said, "Our camp is near the center of the island. It's just west of a town called in Dutch, "New Dorp." He smiled, "Or, *New Town* in English."

Mary smiled. "Oh, yes. I know it from our days here in early 1763. The old 77th was billeted on the island for a while after we got back from the West Indies. Many men—and women—were regaining their strength after having the fever."

The lieutenant thought a second and said, "Yes, I sometimes forget how long you have been with the army, even though you are so young." Then he continued, "The Colonel's Company is already ashore, to lay out the camp. They'll have both the headquarters and hospital tents ready for us when we arrive. The rest of the regiment will come ashore tomorrow morning."

Mary nodded. The Number One Company, or the Colonel's, besides being a regular line company, was the home of the staff officers and other support elements. The hospital was generally encamped close to the colonel's company. Her good friend, Ian McGregor, who had been her suitor long ago at Fort Pitt, was now senior sergeant of the company.

Lachlan was speaking again. "Colonel Stirling is keen to get the bivouac set up and move on to training the men for war here in the colonies. Drilling in a two-rank, wide-interval formation instead of three ranks. And he's especially eager to start training for skirmish order and fighting in the bush. He knows, from his days in the French War and that Pontiac Insurrection in '63, that we'll be using it often against the rebels."

Mary smiled. "There's no better officer to lead the regiment here in the colonies."

They sat silent for a few moments, watching as the oarsmen relentlessly pulled them toward the shoreline of Staten Island. Mary could see Stirling and McDonald engaged in earnest conversation. She surmised they were making plans for the regiment's daily routine and training. Then she felt Campbell put his hand on her arm.

She looked over and saw that he had leaned close to her. He spoke softly. "Mary, you know that as adjutant I spend my time close to the colonel and those that visit him in the course of a day. That means I sometimes overhear things which are not meant for my ears. And it's my business to keep those things to myself."

"Of course. That goes with being the adjutant."

"But I've just heard something that concerns you, and I feel I must share it with you."

Mary turned to look closely at the lieutenant. "What might that be, Lachlan?"

"We received dispatches from headquarters just two days ago. Among them was a listing of the regiments due to arrive in forthcoming convoys."

"I don't understand. How does that affect me?"

"I heard Stirling and McDonald talking about the regiments and their officers who were arriving. One of them is the 16th Light Dragoons. McDonald was actually reading off the list to Stirling, and when he read off the name of the 16th, the colonel said sharply, "Damn, Charles! Haldane's nephew is in that regiment!" Lachlan paused a moment, looking at Mary, then he continued, and McDonald responded, "My God, that could mean danger for Mary."

Mary felt a knot in her stomach.

Lachlan said, "When I heard your name, I made it my business to listen closely to their conversation." He looked at her and sighed. "Mary, now I know the whole story: that when you were the governess at Bonniecrest Manor, your master, a man called Gerald Haldane, attempted to force himself upon you and that you dispatched him with a dagger into his back, and that you are wanted in Scotland for murder. And that General Murray and Stirling and McDonald have shielded you by allowing you to rejoin the regiment as the matron so that you could escape here to the colonies." He hesitated. "I know that you can never go back home." He paused for a long moment. "But I vow I will never tell anyone else, and if I can help you in any way, you can count on me."

Mary felt a knot form in her stomach. Dougal Haldane, Gerald's younger brother, and Nevin Haldane, his nephew, had been at Bonniecrest Manor when his attack on her had occurred. After she had fled, they had pursued her relentlessly through Scotland, until she had finally managed to escape with the assistance of old friends from the army and had been given sanctuary by General Murray, the proprietary colonel of the 42nd. Both men were in the army—Dougal was a captain in the 1st Foot, the Royal Scots, and Nevin was a cornet in the 16th Light Dragoons. She had hoped neither regiment would be sent to America, or at least not close to where she was posted. She had managed to suppress worries about the pursuit by the two Haldanes, but now she knew she must again fear discovery.

"Mary, did you hear me?" Lachlan was looking at her with concern in his eyes.

"Oh, yes, Lachlan." She smiled at him. "I'm most grateful that you have told me and are so understanding of my situation."

"I shall keep my eyes and ears alert for any more information on the 16th and will keep you advised of what I find out, so that you may be warned of any prospect of encountering young Haldane."

Mary touched the lieutenant's arm and said, "That will give me much comfort, Lachlan."

Lieutenant Colonel Barrett Penfold Northcutt, commandant of the King's Loyal Virginia Legion, approached the Rose and Crown Tavern, near the center of Staten Island's village of New Dorp. The tavern had been taken over by the British Army as General Howe's headquarters. Given its modest size, numerous tents had been erected around it to accommodate the staff officers. Northcutt, after picking his way through the tents, entered the tavern through the main entrance and found himself in a hall which separated the two sides of the building. An officer was sitting at a small desk in the hall, and he recognized Captain William Gardiner, Howe's secretary. He had met the captain at Halifax two months before, when he had been acting as a courier for Lord Dunmore, the Royal Governor of Virginia.

Gardiner looked up. "Ah, yes, Colonel Northcutt. We've been expecting you for your meeting with the adjutant general." He rose from the table. "Let me check with Colonel Paterson to see if he's ready for you."

Gardiner went into a room which opened off the left side of the hall and was back in a few seconds. Standing beside the open door, he said, "Colonel says go right in."

Northcutt walked past the captain and entered the room. It was small and looked as if it might have been a storeroom or large pantry. James Paterson sat at a desk with his back to the wall, which had built-in shelves running up the whole length of it. Stacks of notebooks and files were on the shelves.

Paterson looked up from his work on the desk. "Ah, Northcutt! Glad to see you again."

"And I you, sir."

"I think you are aware that Lord Dunmore is headed back to England."

"Indeed, sir. I just left him. He and his household are in the process of moving his baggage to the *Foxhound* from that worn-out old East Indiaman he's been using as his flagship."

"Yes, *Foxhound's* going back with dispatches. We thought the frigate would be the most comfortable and rapid vessel for him." Paterson bit his lip and raised an eyebrow. "Although confidentially, Northcutt, I imagine Dunmore is not particularly keen for a fast crossing. We have word that Lord Germain is not happy with that proclamation he made last November freeing slaves who agreed to fight for the crown. He may have some sharp words for him regarding the matter. It clearly violated Crown policy."

Northcutt felt the need to defend his former governor. "I was with him when he made that decision. There seemed no other way to obtain the manpower necessary to defend the King's rights in Virginia."

Paterson looked down at the paperwork on his table, saying nothing for an interval. Finally, he looked up and said, "Perhaps there is some merit to what you say. However that may be, we're here to discuss *your* future in the King's service." He cleared his throat. "Dunmore says you were quite valuable to him in your position as a senior advisor." He shrugged. "And confidentially, General Howe was quite impressed with that briefing you gave us back in Halifax on the status of the war in Virginia." He shrugged, "As were I and the other officers present."

"I'm grateful for your kind sentiments, Colonel."

"Now, sir, to present business. Lord Dunmore made it known to us that you had spent considerable time here in New York and New Jersey prior to your service with him."

"That's correct. I lived in New York City when Dunmore arrived to become Governor of the Colony of New York in 1771. I was dealing in land." He smiled. "I own considerable acreage in both colonies. I met Lord Dunmore at the card table and then assisted him with some of his land purchases throughout this region. Then he asked me to accompany him as an aide when he was appointed Governor of Virginia."

Paterson nodded. "Yes, I'm aware of that. The point is, Howe believes that your experience could make you quite useful to the King's cause. I'm sure you are familiar with many people in this area of the colonies."

"Of course, sir. I spent the better part of a decade here before Dunmore arrived."

"Just so, Northcutt. Let me cut to the chase: We are certain that there are many people loyal to the King here in the colonies. We think you could be highly effective in helping recruit and organize them to the cause of preserving his authority. To be precise, we intend to form Loyalist military formations as auxiliaries to our regular forces. And in furtherance of that, the general desires that you take a position on the army's staff to perform the function of doing just that."

Northcutt felt a surge of excitement. "It would be my pleasure to accept such a duty."

Paterson held up a finger. "Let me add one thing before you fully agree. We would also hope that you could establish," he paused, and his face wrinkled up as he considered his words, "We would also want you to organize a web of, how shall I say this? A web of watchers to help us keep informed of the movements of the rebel army."

There was a momentary silence as Northcutt considered Paterson's words. Then he said, "So, in addition to organizing Loyalist military units, you want me to be a spymaster."

The adjutant general raised his hands in supplication. "A web of spies is absolutely necessary to the success of our endeavor. We must know what the insurrectionists are up to. And you seem to have the qualifications for recruiting and managing such a resource." He gave Northcutt a direct look. "Now, there might be some personal danger associated with the effort. Are you willing to accept the job on that basis?"

Northcutt didn't have to think. "Of course. I'll do whatever I can to serve. After all, my interests in a considerable amount of land are directly related to the King's retention of the colonies."

"Excellent, Northcutt. Now, even though your regiment was reduced to a remnant at that battle on the shores of the Chesapeake, we're going to keep The King's Loyal Virginia Legion on the books so that you can maintain your rank." Paterson smiled. "I trust that pleases you."

"Naturally, and express my thanks to the General. However, I would ask that you suffer me two bequests."

"Bequests? Please advise me what you mean."

"The strength of my regiment now consists of one cavalry troop, of about forty men. I ask that you keep them together, whatever occurs. They could be useful in the duties you have assigned to me. Moreover, I should think that an organized, equipped, and well-mounted troop of light horse would be of great use to the army."

Paterson raised his eyebrows. "You transported your horses with you by ship?"

"Indeed we did. Excellent, well-bred Virginia hunters."

"In that case, I see no difficulty with your request. Indeed, we have a shortage of cavalry of any kind. We're expecting the 16th Light Dragoons in the next convoy, but that will be but one regiment, and they may arrive short of horses after weeks at sea. It's damn hard to keep the animals alive for that long on shipboard." He waved a hand. "Now, you said you had two requests."

"Yes. The second request is that Captain George Markwood, who is the one officer that survived the Chesapeake skirmish, be assigned to the staff as my assistant."

Paterson shrugged. "Consider it done."

"Thank you—may I call you James?"

"Certainly, Barrett."

"Well, James, if I'm to get on with recruiting people for the King's service, I must be able to get off this island periodically. And I would like to make my first trip soon. Can some arrangement be made so that Markwood and I, along with our horses, can get onto the mainland?"

Paterson smiled broadly, the biggest grin that Northcutt had ever seen him make. "Funny that you should ask. Quite confidentially, we are organizing a little expedition to cross over into Jersey soon. It will include some barges to carry horses. You could go along with it."

"Well then, James, both I and Markwood will be ready."

—ɱ—

Lieutenant Geoffrey Fairfield, commander of South Carolina's 1st Troop of the Palmetto Light Horse, dressed in his uniform of gray coat with green facings, white breeches, and highly polished riding boots, escorted Mrs. Colleen Alison McGraw into a private dining room on the second floor of the Britannic Crown Inn, located in lower Manhattan. Fairfield was a tall, wiry, strikingly handsome man with blond hair, blue eyes, and a youthful face such that most people, and particularly women, took him to be in his mid-twenties. He didn't disclose the fact that he was in fact thirty-two unless there was some particular advantage to be gained by projecting maturity. Colleen McGraw was a willowy, auburn-haired, high cheek-boned lady of thirty-three, who also could pass for a younger age, particularly when she had taken care with her facial makeup, which she decidedly had done this evening.

As they entered, Mrs. McGraw looked out the large window which graced the room and exclaimed, "Why, Geoffrey, what a beautiful view of the harbor! And the sun will soon be setting. We shall have a charming sight as it sinks into the western horizon."

"Yes, Colleen, the view is beautiful. Unfortunately, it's marred by that fleet of British ships anchored off Staten Island. It would be perfect if they were to disappear."

"Well, despite that, I love it, so please seat me at the table so I can look out the window."

"My pleasure, Colleen." He pulled out the chair and assisted her to settle in. Then he took his seat next to her. "Our serving man should be here momentarily."

"Geoffrey, I do so enjoy these dinners. You find such charming places for us to have supper."

"It is my pleasure, dear Colleen."

Mrs. McGraw nodded and stared out the window at the harbor. Fairfield looked at the woman he thought of as one of the most intriguing females he had met in the colonies. Colleen was a widow, having lost her much older husband, a tavern keeper, to pneumonia several years earlier. She had taken over management of the tavern, located in Fredericktown, Maryland, and had enhanced profits greatly by adding a bevy of personally selected prostitutes, which had essentially converted the tavern into the best brothel in the town and county. With the beginning of the insurrection, striving for even greater profits, she had sold the tavern and organized a combination traveling store and brothel, catering to the officers and soldiers of the army. She named it the *Red Vixen Sutler Company* after herself, and it operated out of a collection of wagons, including four great Conestogas which carried the store's inventory. There were also numerous tents, several of which the girls used for privacy in providing services to the troops. Since arriving in New York, her company had been encamped in a pasture on the outskirts of Manhattan, and it had become a mecca for men of the regiments stationed nearby. Fairfield thought to himself, *Given all the money she's making, Colleen should be treating me to a meal.*

The door opened and a server entered the room. He nodded to the couple. "My name is James, and it's my pleasure to attend to you this evening." He looked from Fairfield to Mrs. McGraw and then asked, "Shall we start with a libation? Some wine for the lady?"

Colleen grinned broadly. "A drink would be wonderful, but I'll wait for wine until the meal. Do you have any rum? If not, whiskey would do."

The waiter raised an eyebrow, but said, "We still have a limited amount of rum. The blockade, you know."

Geoffrey nodded. "The rum will do nicely."

"Indeed, sir. I'll go to the barman and bring some up. Then we'll discuss your meal, if that's satisfactory."

Fairfield nodded. "Yes, quite."

The waiter went out the door, and immediately Fairfield rose to his feet. "I forgot something I wanted to discuss with the waiter about our meal. I'll be right back."

Colleen looked up at him coyly. "Why, Jeffrey, are you planning some sort of surprise?"

"You'll just have to wait, my dear."

He caught up with the waiter just as he was starting down the stairs to the common room on the first floor. "Excuse me. I reserved a room here for tonight. Are you aware of that?"

James smiled knowingly. "Ah, yes sir. The proprietor told me about that. In fact, it's room three, right down the hall. The door is unlocked, and the key is on the night table."

Fairfield smiled broadly. "Thank you."

The waiter turned and went on down the steps. Geoffrey smiled to himself. He had been pursuing Colleen for weeks and had invested a small fortune in entertaining her on occasions like this evening, and he felt that she had become increasingly receptive to his advances. So he had decided that tonight, after a cozy supper and generous amount of libation, he would tactfully invite her to spend the night in his company. He was no novice at enticing women to his bed and was excited by the challenge of possessing Colleen McGraw.

With that on his mind, he re-entered the dining room, where Colleen was staring out the window at the sunset.

She turned and smiled at him. "I've been sitting here trying to guess what kind of surprise you were planning. A special meal? A musician to entertain us while we sup?"

"Now, my dear, it wouldn't be a surprise if I told you. You'll just have to be patient."

The waiter came back and ran through the bill of fare with them. Both selected roasted beef as their main course, with potatoes and vegetables. Fairfield chose a red wine recommended by the server.

After an interval, James brought their food and wine. After laying out their table, the waiter withdrew. Geoffrey raised his glass. "Well, my lady, to us—a fine supper and a lovely evening."

Colleen joined him in the toast, saying, "I could not agree more."

As they were just finishing their first sip, there was a knock on the door and James re-entered. "Sir, there's someone here to see you, and he says it's urgent."

He had no sooner spoken when a soldier, dressed in the same uniform as Fairfield, pushed past the server. "Lieutenant Fairfield, I must speak to you!"

Geoffrey looked at the soldier, irritation spreading over his face. "Trumpeter Bloom, what the devil are you doing here? What is the meaning of this?"

"Sir, Colonel Grayson on Washington's staff sent me. The British are up to something in New Jersey. A man from a town down there came in to warn us. They've come ashore from Staten Island."

"The deuce you say! Are they in Jersey? We thought they'd make their first move to Long Island."

"It's true, sir. And the general wants you to get down there and find out what's happening."

Fairfield stared into the distance for a long moment, then shifted his gaze to Colleen. He smiled and said, "Tell Grayson I'll be there posthaste as soon as I finish my supper and escort Mrs. McGraw back to her camp."

"Sir, I was ordered to bring you back with me. Grayson says Washington himself wants to speak with you. In any case, you are to get across the harbor tonight to join the troop in their camp so that you can ride at first light. I've got a horse for you to come with me."

Fairfield felt anger and frustration flash through his body. He took a deep breath and looked at Colleen. "My dear, I regret leaving you, but it seems I have no choice. The hired driver and his carriage will take you home."

Colleen sighed. "Geoffrey, I'm so sorry this happened. But good luck on your mission."

"Thank you, my dear. I shall see you again in a few days, and we shall finish our evening."

"I shall look forward to it with great anticipation, Geoffrey."

With that, he was out the door with Bloom trailing behind.

James asked, "Shall I have the driver bring the carriage around to the entrance, Mrs. McGraw?"

Colleen frowned. "You shall most decidedly *not.* I'm going to finish my meal."

The waiter nodded. "Yes, ma'am. I understand." Then he approached the table and made to pick up Fairfield's plate. "Here, ma'am, I'll take the lieutenant's food back to the kitchen."

Colleen raised a finger. "Has Lieutenant Fairfield made arrangements to pay for everything?"

"Indeed, madam. He has an account with us. He told the proprietor he would settle everything."

A look of pleasure came over Colleen's face. "Yes, take it back. But," and she smiled up at him, "pack it up, if you please, so that I may take it with me when I leave. I'll not see it wasted."

The waiter hesitated for a moment, then said, "Yes, ma'am. I'll see to it." And with that, he picked up the plate and left the room.

Colleen drained her wine glass, then refreshed it from the bottle, and with a broad smile on her face, lifted her fork and attacked her roast beef. After the first bite, she looked up and out the window to see that the last sliver of the sun was about to disappear below the horizon. She thought, *All in all, the evening had turned out most satisfactorily.*

Chapter Three

First Encounter

Washington's Headquarters was located at the corner of Varick and Vandam Streets, less than a half mile from where Fairfield had been dining. *Richmond Hill,* owned by Abraham Mortier, was a substantial, white, two story building with porches in the front on both levels. It was sited on a large plot of land for a residence in the city and a number of tents had been pitched on the grounds around it to shelter members of the staff who could not be accommodated in the house.

Fairfield and Bloom dismounted and gave the reins of his horse to the trumpeter, then bounded up the steps onto the porch, past a couple of sentries and entered the building through double doors into the center hall. His nostrils instantly told him that Washington and his official family were at supper. He felt a pang of hunger, thinking of the savory beef he had left sitting on the table at The Britannic Majesty. The dining room was off to the left and he could hear the banter of men at the table. An aide normally manned a receptionist desk in the hall, but nobody was present at the moment. Geoffrey stood there, hesitating about what to do other than cool his heels until the diners emerged. Then a server came into the hall from the rear of the house, balancing a covered serving tray on one hand. He started for the door to the dining room and reached for the knob. Fairfield held up his hand. "Lad, I'm here on urgent business. Could you tell Colonel Grayson that Lieutenant Fairfield is here? He summoned me."

The server looked him over, not impressed by the presence of a lieutenant, then said with no enthusiasm, "I'll mention it to the colonel." As he opened the door Fairfield caught a brief glimpse of diners seated around a table with Washington at the head. Then the door closed behind the steward and he was once again alone in the hall.

But he didn't have to wait long: Just a few moments passed until the door swung open and Grayson came out. Fairfield was surprised to see Washington right behind him.

Grayson said, "Sorry to pull you from your evening distractions, Fairfield." He smiled knowingly. "Particularly with the enticing Mrs. McGraw. However, the matter is most urgent."

"Yes, Colonel, so I was informed. What are the particulars?"

"An informer from New Jersey came in just a couple of hours ago. He says the British have sent a force across the narrow channel between Staten Island and Jersey, toward the southern end of the island. It's quite a surprise—we've been expecting them to land on Long Island. We don't know their strength, we don't know their intent. Is it a raid? Is it a reconnaissance? Or most gravely, have they got a different idea for a campaign than we have supposed, and this is the beginning of a major movement? We need you to get down there and find out what the devil is going on."

"Right, sir. I'll lead a patrol to get a feel for the size of their activity."

"No, Fairfield. Not some *patrol.* We want you to take your *entire* troop so that, if necessary, you will have the strength for a proper probe. And you are to ride at first light tomorrow. I've arranged for a boat to get you across the harbor from Fort George to your bivouac tonight so that you can make preparations."

Washington, who had been standing by silently, now cleared his throat and spoke up. "Lieutenant Fairfield, we must find out, as early as possible, what precisely is going on down there in Jersey. You must get *definitive* information. This is not a scout where you simply locate the enemy's position. We need you to press matters until you have certitude as to what they are about and particularly their strength on the ground." He hesitated a moment, gathering his thoughts. "If that takes going into action to break through the enemy's pickets, you must do so even if it means taking significant casualties." He paused again, his eyes drilling into Fairfield's own. "I presume you understand how serious I consider this matter?"

Fairfield felt a knot forming in his stomach. "You have made yourself quite clear, sir."

"Then we shall delay you no longer. It is urgent that I get accurate word from you as soon as possible. Good evening, sir, and may God speed your mission and bring you success."

Washington turned and returned to the dining room, followed by Grayson.

Fairfield took a deep breath, then turned and left the house. Bloom brought up the horses. "What's toward, sir?"

"We ride to the boat landing down by old Fort George. We're crossing to the troop's camp immediately. And Trumpeter, I can tell you, we're going to have a very long day tomorrow."

—※—

"Coachman, that's my tent. Pull up right here." The driver obligingly reined in the team and quickly jumped down from his seat to help Colleen to the ground. She thanked the driver and walked through the darkness to her tent, which had a large canvas fly erected before it. Colleen was glad to see that Charlie, the son of her company manager, Edna Farley, had just put some wood onto the fire that burned in front of the fly and was busy stoking it up with a poker. Under the fly were two comfortable chairs and a table. She put the box which had the leftover food from supper, down on the table.

Charlie stood up and said, "Evening, Mrs. McGraw. Hope you had a nice supper."

"Excellent, Charlie. And please be a good lad and ask Edna to join me."

Colleen looked around her establishment's camp. It was noisy with considerable business in progress. The bar tent was open, and a number of soldiers were enjoying ale and whiskey. A large pavilion was just beyond her headquarters tent, and she knew a group of officers from a Connecticut regiment were partying with her girls. She could hear raucous male and female laughter within the tent.

She pulled off her hat and entered the tent, dropping it on the cot. Colleen went over to a humidor which sat on a small table. Her pipe, with a long, curved stem, lay beside it, and she quickly packed the pipe with tobacco and went back outside. She used a taper to light the pipe from the fire and then, with a sigh of contentment, sat down in one of the chairs and took a long pull on the pipe, savoring the taste of the tobacco. Then she exhaled, amused by watching the stream of smoke until it disappeared into the night.

She heard footsteps approaching, and momentarily Edna appeared from around the side of the tent. The stout, fiftyish lady with graying hair stood, hand on hip, by the fire. "Now, Colleen, did you have some sort of falling out with that lieutenant?"

Colleen looked up, puzzlement on her face. "Falling out? What makes you think that, Edna?"

"Why, Charlie said you came back *alone* in the carriage. Lieutenant Fairfield always brings you back himself."

Colleen laughed. "No fight. Actually, General Washington saved me tonight."

"Saved you? General Washington? And why did you need saving?"

"Geoffrey was going to attempt to bed me after supper."

"For God's sake, it's obvious that has been his purpose from the time months ago when you first met him that night in the camp outside York."

"Yes, well, I suspected from our arrival at the inn this evening that he planned for this to be the night. He had everything set up to be very elegant. It was obvious I was going to have to make a decision by the time the evening was over." She grinned at Edna. "But just as he was getting ready to become very serious about it, a messenger arrived with orders for him to report to headquarters immediately. The British are up to something."

"So you had to come back alone."

"Indeed. But not before I finished the meal and had the waiter pack up Fairfield's food, which had arrived just before he left." She pointed to the packet on the table then leaned back in her chair. "But it was what happened just as I was leaving that gave me certitude about his intentions. The server said, "There's some wine in the bedroom Mr. Fairfield reserved. Would you like that also?" Colleen laughed. "That's when I was assured of what he had planned." She shrugged. "So of course I said *yes* and insisted on going with the server to the room. It was impressive! Geoffrey had it all set up for a tryst: the wine bottle with two glasses, a bouquet of flowers in a lovely vase, the bed covers turned down."

Edna gave Colleen a knowing look. "If you keep seeing him, sooner or later you are going to have to give him what he wants."

"When we first met, back at that camp near York, after he found out about the girls, he very delicately asked if my services could also be bought." Colleen raised her finger. "And I told him everyone has a price, but mine was very dear. So he knows the conditions."

"But Colleen, he's been entertaining you at the best establishments in town for weeks now. He has put a lot of money into you. He is undoubtedly of the mind that he's met your price, in *kind* if not in hard *coin*."

"Well, I tell you this: I'll not break it off whatever happens. He's been far too useful to us. Since his troop works directly for Washington, he knows what's going on all the time, and that's been greatly beneficial. And more importantly, we'll need his information once the campaign actually begins. It could save us from disaster, if it comes to that." She put her hand to her chin. "I'll find a way to keep him interested." She sighed deeply and shrugged. "If it comes to that point, I will give him his way." She shrugged. "God knows I've slept with far less attractive men when it served my purpose."

"That sheriff in Fredericktown comes to mind."

"We both know that was simply good business." She laughed. "As did the sheriff." Colleen motioned toward the pavilion. "It sounds like that party is going well. Are those officers spending a lot of money?"

"I'm glad you brought that up. They are indeed, but there's a problem. One of the officers took Sally to bed but only paid her half what was agreed. He told her she wasn't worth it." She grinned. "Sally told me that despite her best efforts, he couldn't get it up, probably because of all the drink he's had."

"What!!!" A fierce look came over Colleen's face. "Damn it! Nobody cheats my girls or me!" Without saying more, she sprang from the chair and went into the tent, returning momentarily with a pistol in her hand. "Let's go! I'll settle this immediately!" She set off toward the big tent at a brisk, determined pace, with Edna close on her heels.

Colleen arrived at the pavilion and pushed aside the flap at the entrance. In the bright candlelight, she saw twenty or more officers mingling with all seven of her girls. Some of the men had shed their coats and were in shirtsleeves. Molly had one of their tricorn hats perched on her head. Edith was actually wearing a regimental coat. It was indeed a jolly affair, with many of the men well into their cups. Colleen didn't hesitate: She cocked the pistol and immediately fired it into the ground in front of her. The loud bang echoed throughout the tent, and everyone immediately ceased their celebration and snapped around to look in dead silence at her and the smoking firelock.

Colleen called out, "Who is the senior officer? I will speak to him immediately!"

A stout officer who she estimated was about thirty-five came forward. "I'm Major Prentiss. I say, what has you so upset, my dear Mrs. McGraw?"

"I'm not upset; I'm damned mad! One of your officers paid Sally Croft only half of what he agreed, just because he couldn't get aroused." She glared at the major. "Undoubtedly, he couldn't get it up because he had too much to drink before he went with her." She leaned forward until she was almost in Prentiss' face. "Or maybe he just doesn't have what it takes to start with. Major, I assure you I've seen it both ways more times than I can count." She waved her hand around the tent. "This party's over right here and now unless Sally gets her money!"

A look of distress came over the major's face. "Now, my dear lady . . ."

Colleen continued in a loud voice. "Don't 'Dear Lady' me! If she doesn't get paid immediately, this bloody regiment is banned forever from the Red Vixen. Forever! You'll not buy another thing here! No liquor, no girls, no provisions for the officer's mess. Do you understand me?"

There were murmurs of distress all around the room. Then one of the officers called out, "*Paulson,* that was you that took that little blond to a tent. I saw it! For God's sake, pay up!"

Prentiss turned and looked at a young lieutenant. "Frank, were you with that girl?"

The lieutenant bit his lip, and a sheepish look spread across his face.

The major stood up to his full height. "Lieutenant Paulson, you will immediately pay the woman what was agreed. Immediately, do you hear?!"

The youngster came forward, head hung down, and walked over to where Sally stood. He reached into his pocket and counted out some coins, then handed them to her.

Colleen asked, "Sally, is that the proper amount?"

"Yes, ma'am, that makes it right."

Colleen put her most cordial smile on her face and turned to the major. "Now you gentlemen may continue with your revelry. And I hope you find great enjoyment and pleasure and partake of everything we offer."

With that, she turned and left the pavilion, and soon the sounds of laughing voices returned, although a little more subdued than before.

Colleen returned to her tent, picked up her pipe, which had by now gone out. She lit it again and sat down in the comfortable chair. She puffed away, staring into the fire and reflecting on her real problem: how to deal with the relentless advances of Lieutenant Geoffrey Fairfield.

—☙—

Under the midday sun, the First Troop of the Palmetto Light Horse, Lieutenant Geoffrey Fairfield at its head, trotted down the coast road from New York in a column of twos. Just behind him rode Sergeant Quinn and Cornet Henry Middleton, a lad just out of his teens. The other sergeant of the troop, Freddie McCrae, rode at the rear of the column.

Presently, Fairfield held up his hand to halt the troop. He pointed along the road to a grove of pines several hundred yards distant. A man dressed in the uniform of the troop stood on the road, waving toward them.

Quinn said, "Yeah, I see it. Corporal Conner's advance guard."

Fairfield said, "Quinn, come with me. Middleton, hold the troop here."

The two men rode forward, reining in their horses where Conner stood.

The corporal pointed eastward. "We've got a Redcoat picket in sight. Light Bobs by the cut of their uniforms. They got short coats and caps with bills."

Fairfield nodded. "What else have you seen?"

"There's another picket we sighted just a few hundred yards south. I figure there be a line of them. And there's smoke from a lot of fires toward the coast, in the direction of Shoreham Ordinary. Looks like their main camp."

Fairfield replied, "All right, Corporal, have someone signal the troop to come up. Meanwhile, let's go take a look, and you can show Quinn and me what's out there."

Conner nodded and led the way through the grove to where one of his men knelt behind some underbrush, scanning the landscape beyond. He pointed. "There's the picket's position."

Fairfield saw wisps of smoke from a small fire across a large field, near another stand of trees, but at first could not make out any men. Then he saw some movement, and a soldier with musket in hand emerged and stood looking over the countryside. He showed no sign that he was aware of their presence.

Quinn raised his arm, indicating beyond the picket. "Look—way to the east toward the coast. There's the smoke of a large bivouac. Many fires. Could be a battalion in strength." He thought a second. "I'd say it's right at Shoreham."

Conner nodded. "Yeah, Sergeant, that's what I figure. But I got more information." He pulled a rolled up piece of paper out from underneath his jacket. "We found this nailed to a tree alongside the road." He handed it to Fairfield.

The lieutenant quickly read it. "Why, they're basically on a forage mission. They want to pay farmers to bring them fresh meat and vegetables!"

"That appears to be the case, sir."

As they talked, Middleton and McCrae came up.

Fairfield briefed them on the situation, then told Middleton and Conner to go back and have the troop dismount and ease their horses' girths. He said, "The sergeants and I will discuss what we'll do next."

After the others had left, Fairfield grinned at the sergeants. "Well, Washington told me to do whatever it took to find out about the intentions and strength of the British. He said we might have to press through the pickets to get that information." He shook his head and held up the handbill. "But this answers the question. The British have put ashore a small force simply to get provisions." He shrugged and grinned. "We've found out what we need to know, as far as I'm concerned."

Quinn took off his helmet, fully exposing the ugly saber scar on the left side of his face that ran from his chin to the ear with the bottom half missing. He winked at McCrae, then said to Fairfield, "That's not quite all, Fairfield. We don't know the full strength of the British, which you told us Washington wanted to know, and we don't know their complete intentions. Maybe they're ashore in limited force now but are making preparations to expand their holdings. That's what the general wanted to know and that handbill doesn't answer those questions." He turned and looked back toward the British position. "We've got to penetrate their picket lines to find out the answers."

McCrae nodded. "Quinn's got it right, Fairfield. We got to take a little trot down through there to find out what we can. Quinn and I done it before during the French war when we was together in the old 11th Dragoons."

Fairfield bit his lip. "Damn your words! We stand a good chance of taking casualties: Men being shot out of the saddle or unhorsed in some other way."

Quinn scowled at Geoffrey. "We been here for two months. We done a lot of scouting but the lads ain't been near a fight yet. Time they get blooded."

McCrae shot a crooked grin at Fairfield. "That includes their lieutenant who ain't never faced the enemy or led a charge."

Fairfield reddened and retorted, "I've taken plenty of fire from sheriff's men and others back when we were highwaymen on the roads of Virginia. I've had balls whistle past my face, just like you, so keep your scorn to yourself."

Quinn laughed and said, "Not to mention being shot at by angry husbands after you bedded their wives. And between sheriffs and husbands, all the action you've seen was with you runnin' or riding away fast as you could. You ain't never rode into troops firin' right at your face."

Geoffrey stifled his rage. He turned to Quinn. "So what are you proposing? A mad charge down through the pickets to see what's going on around Shoreham? That's crazy!"

Quinn looked up to the heavens and took a deep breath. "No, Fairfield, there's a way to do it that's much safer and has a better chance of success."

"So tell me what you propose."

Quinn exchanged another knowing look with McCrae, then turned and waved his hand around the terrain below them, taking in the picket and the smoke beyond it. "We spend the rest of the day scoutin' out their picket line hereabouts. Then, 'bout the time they settle down to their evening meal, we move on them." He grinned at Geoffrey and began to explain: "Now here's how we do it."

Sergeant Quinn stood before the troop, in the gathering dusk, all eyes on him. "Now listen sharp, you bastards. We're going on a little evenin' ride 'round that British camp down there." He waved his hand toward the Redcoat positions. "We're goin' to start off on foot, in single file, leading the horses. Mr. Fairfield and I have scouted out a way down through the fields and woods where we will be behind trees out of sight of that picket to the east until about a hundred yards from it. Keep your damned mouths shut and keep your horses quiet. Then when

I signal with my hand, we're goin' to mount very quietly, rush past the picket station at the gallop and head for Shoreham Ordinary. Once we're riding, keep a wide interval between men. Make it harder for the British to hit someone." He raised his finger. "No shootin' as we go past the picket, even when they fire. Hunch down over your horse's mane to make less of a target. Save your pistol loads for when we are down around the main camp. We're sure as hell going to need them then, for by that time they'll have some idea what's going on and may be ready for us. That's when we'll need to use the firelocks to make them keep their heads down. Wait for the order to fire—we'll need to do it all at once as we swing past the bivouac." He looked around. "Now, you all got that?"

Twenty-four heads nodded.

"Once we ride past their camp, we'll turn south for a while, then swing back eastward to the road. We may encounter another picket on the way out."

Quinn looked over at Fairfield and in feigned deference asked, "You got anything to add, sir?"

Geoffrey thought a moment, then said, "Cornet Middleton, you will bring up the rear and help anyone who may be wounded and having trouble staying on their horse."

Young Middleton nodded. "Right, sir."

McCrae, who had been standing quietly by Quinn, looked up at the sky. "If we're going to have enough light, we need to go now."

Everyone looked at Quinn, but Quinn eyed Fairfield, who immediately took the cue. "Indeed, it's time to go. Sergeant Quinn will lead the column, and mind what we said about maintaining silence!"

Quinn took the reins of his horse and left the grove of trees in which the troop had been sheltering. He headed toward another grove some distance away which screened them from the picket station. Geoffrey followed immediately behind, and one by one the men fell into a long single file.

Supper was underway in a small private dining room at Shoreham Ordinary. Major John Maitland, commandant of the British Second Light Foot Battalion, presided over the table of several officers. Maitland was in command of the force which had landed two days previously. Also at the table was Major Percival Howard of the quartermaster department, who was supervising the purchasing of produce from the local farmers. In addition to the foot battalion, a detachment of marines gathered from various warships was part of his force, and Captain Forsyth, officer in charge of the marines, was seated at the table. Also present were Maitland's second in command, Captain Colly, and the battalion adjutant, Lieutenant Wright.

The final members of the party were Barrett Northcutt and George Markwood. They had been rowed ashore in mid-afternoon, and their horses had been landed via a barge towed by a Royal Navy boat. Maitland had invited them to sup with his officers.

Conversation, which had been sprightly through the meal, momentarily lagged. Maitland looked over at Howard, the quartermaster, and asked, "Well, Percy, how are things going as far as the provisions?"

Howard smiled. "Actually, quite well. We've only been ashore two full days, and we're already starting to get produce from local farmers. We've had four wagons come in, and numerous other locals have approached us to see what we want and how much we are willing to pay." He shrugged. "The lure of hard coin has a most beneficial effect."

Forsyth, the Marine, nodded. "I should think so. I expect trade will get heavier as more farmers learn we're here."

Howard smiled. "Indubitably, sir. I expect a busy day tomorrow."

Maitland looked over at Northcutt, who was sitting at his right hand. "Well, Colonel, that should facilitate your departure on the morrow. The busier we are, the less likely any rebels who may be watching will notice you riding out."

Barrett shrugged. "We'll be leaving at dawn tomorrow. In any case, I don't expect trouble. From my memory, the traffic along this road is busy and quite varied. We'll merge in with the stream of travelers. No one should pay much attention to a couple of gentlemen heading northward."

Maitland looked thoughtful. "Ah, yes. I understand you spent some time up here before moving on to Virginia."

"Indeed, sir. The best part of ten years. And I have many acquaintances in both Jersey and New York. In any case, we intend to head for northwestern Jersey posthaste, an area where I don't expect many questions about a couple of travelers or their business."

The adjutant, Wright, patted his mouth with his napkin. "Still, sir, I don't envy you the job of moving through the rebel countryside out of uniform. It could be trouble for you if someone asks questions."

"Well, Mr. Wright, I don't expect problems. As I mentioned, I'm quite familiar with the area and have some significant land holdings throughout the region, which will give me a believable reason for traveling—inspecting my properties. And truth be told, I'm quite confident that a large portion of the populace are sympathetic to the crown. On the whole, I'm satisfied there's not much to worry about."

As he spoke, a young serving girl came in to begin clearing their dishes, and Maitland suggested a round of after-supper libations. Everyone readily agreed. A server had just delivered the drinks when a young ensign hurriedly entered the room.

"Major Maitland, sir!"

"And you are?"

"Ensign Wiltshire, of Captain Tolliver's company, sir."

"And what, may I ask, is the source of all your excitement?"

"Sir, beg to report, we heard shots fired. They seem to be coming from the direction of Number One Picket, sir. First one up to the northwest, close to the coast road!"

"Anything else seen or heard?"

"No, sir. Not yet. But the captain has ordered the company to stand to just in case, and the other companies are doing the same!"

Maitland took a pull on his drink. "Very reasonable precaution. I certainly approve. Thank you, Mr. Wiltshire. You may return to your company."

The ensign saluted and departed. Maitland looked around the table. "Gentlemen, I'm not sure what is toward, but I suggest you take your posts." He looked at Colly. "Make sure the battalion is ready to receive any eventuality." He looked at Forsyth. "And the same for our colleagues of the Marines. I shall remain here, at least for the moment."

The officers, save Northcutt and Markwood, rose and headed for the encampment.

Northcutt thought for a moment. "My dear Major Maitland, while we're waiting for developments, might I suggest we all share a bit of tobacco to accompany our libations?" He reached into a pocket of his coat and produced three cigars. "These were made by the good ladies of Norfolk, of excellent Virginia tobacco, which I consider the most tasteful in the colonies."

Maitland smiled. "Delighted, Barrett. I've heard of the Virginia leaf, but never had the opportunity to try it. This seems as good a moment as any."

Markwood rose and took a taper from the mantel of the fireplace and lit it from the fire. Then he helped Maitland and Northcutt ignite their cigars, followed by his own. He had just finished when he cocked his head and put a hand to his ear. "Sir, I believe I hear the sound of horse hooves! Moving at the gallop!" Cigar in hand, he hurried to the window and peered out. "Gentlemen, you may want to see this!"

They all gathered around the window, which afforded a panoramic view of the encampment and the fields and tree stands that formed the landscape to the west of the ordinary.

Markwood pointed to the northwest. "There—coming out from behind that grove of trees!"

Maitland exclaimed, "Well I'll be damned! A troop of light horse!" He thought a moment, then said, "Damned if I've ever seen organized rebel cavalry before. They certainly had none at the siege of Boston!"

Northcutt said, "Interesting—gray coats and white breeches. Not a common combination for the colonial army."

"Quite right," replied Maitland. "And look how they ride—spread out in a wide group, not massed to make a good target."

The troop was closer now, and suddenly came the sound of firing.

Maitland pointed with his cigar to the troop. "Good move—pistol fire to distract our men." He took a pull on his cigar. "Not much chance they'll hit anything, galloping like that, but I dare say whoever is leading knows their business, keeping our lads' heads down as they ride by."

Suddenly a ragged volley of musket fire erupted from the battalion. Maitland shook his head. "Not likely our men will take down any of them the way they're spread out."

Northcutt commented, "In any case, they've swept right past the battalion now."

Maitland took another puff. "Yes, they'll loop back to where they started now.

They've seen what they wanted. They know our strength, which I take was their intent from the beginning—a nicely executed probe." He shrugged. "I would not have anticipated the Colonials to have that skill." Reflecting a moment, he continued, "We didn't expect them to have much effective cavalry. Right now, we're short of cavalry ourselves. Only Burch's 17th Light Dragoons are here, and they're short of horses. Harcourt's 16th is on the way. They're expected to arrive any time now." He looked at Northcutt. "I should hope, in your recruiting effort, Colonel, you might organize a few mounted units."

Barrett looked down at his cigar, took a sip of his drink, and replied, "Well, Maitland, that has always been part of my plan. In fact, I already have a troop of light horse that I brought with me from Virginia. Good horsemen mounted on Virginia hunters. I expect to make them the start of a Loyalist cavalry regiment."

"Excellent, sir."

At that moment the young adjutant came in and said rather breathlessly, "Sir, we exchanged a volley with them. Captain Colly says we're standing ready should they return."

"Very good, Mr. Wright. But in all truth, they'll not be back. You may tell Colly to stand down and send the men back to their suppers. And pass that on to the Marines."

"Sir?"

"Indeed, Mr. Wright. There will be no further action here tonight."

A look of disappointment spread over the youthful lieutenant. "Yes, sir. I'll get the word out." With that he hurried off.

Maitland looked down at his cigar. "You know, Barrett, you damn well were right about this Virginia cigar. It's quite fine. Let's sit down and have a drink, and perhaps have another cigar, if you would be so kind."

"My dear sir, that would be my greatest pleasure."

Lieutenant Shay O'beirne swallowed a sip of his coffee and remarked, "This is going to be a damned hot day." It was a general statement for the benefit of the other five people gathered around the fire in front of Eckert's tent, which included all the officers of the Frederick County Light Foot Company and their traveling companions, Colonel and Mrs. Tresh. All were engaged in finishing their breakfast in the predawn twilight. Billy Wood stood nearby with a coffee pot, and Melinda was busy at the tailgate of a wagon, which served as an improvised side board for the mess. Nearby was the main camp of the company, with the men and women also finishing their morning meal around the squad fires.

Wend Eckert responded, "Well, Shay, I don't doubt you are correct. But if my map is accurate, this will be our final day on the march. If we push it, and I intend to do so, we will encamp across the harbor from Manhattan by dusk tonight. We'll just have to bear the July heat. And tomorrow we will see about being ferried over to the city." He looked over at the colonel. "With luck, sir, we'll deliver you to army headquarters by tomorrow evening or early the next day, and you will be able to establish Mrs. Tresh in more elegant quarters than a tent and camp cot."

Catherine smiled at Wend. "Now, Captain Eckert, I'll not let you imply that I haven't been comfortable or enjoyed my time with your company." She held up her cup. "In fact, I'm even getting used to drinking this coffee instead of tea."

Tresh smiled at his wife. "Yes, my dear, I daresay you've done well in your first few days of marching with troops. But I think you will be ready for the comforts of an inn by the time we arrive in the city."

Catherine grinned. "Well, I'll not deny a soft mattress and a warm bath do have some appeal."

Wend was about to speak again when the sound of horse hooves pounding at a gallop was heard by all.

Reese Newkirk said, "Now, why would someone be pushing his horse along the road at such a pace so early in the morning?"

O'beirne put his coffee down, rose from his seat, and took a few steps toward the road. In a few seconds, a horse and rider appeared. Wend saw a man dressed in farmer's clothing, holding a fowling piece across the pommel of his saddle. The rider pulled up and stared at the camp for a few moments. Then he slid down from the saddle and led his horse by the reins toward the fire. Shay called out, "I'll see what the fellow wants."

All eyes turned toward the horseman as Shay went to meet him. They exchanged a few words, then both came toward the mess.

A serious look was on O'beirne's face. "Captain, this man is named Jebediah Hays. He's from the local militia. He says there are British soldiers just a couple of miles away. They crossed over the narrow channel from Staten Island two days ago."

Howard touched his cap to Eckert. "Yes, sir, Cap'n. That's the truth of it. My cap'n sent me here to let you know. He figured Continental soldiers should be aware of this matter."

Wend was puzzled. "How did you know we were here?"

"A traveler riding on the road passed by where we was assembling and told us about your camp." He shrugged. "So we thought you ought to be told 'bout what's happening."

Wend thought for a moment. "Well, what have you seen them doing?"

"That's it, Cap'n. We ain't seen nothing but pickets. Cap'n Halliday figures they be shieldin' whatever the main business of the Redcoats is. He figured you could bring your company up to see what's toward. And then we could go back to our places. We got to take care of our farms and trades."

Wend stared at the militiaman for a few seconds. While he was doing so, young Ensign Childers said, "Are we going to march to join the militia? To defend them from the Redcoats?"

Wend shot Childers a hard look. "No, Edward, we're not going to go rushing to fight the British. Our orders are to join the main army."

Childers looked crestfallen.

Wend continued, "However, I *would* be remiss if I didn't try to find out something about what they're up to." He looked at Howard. "You say the British haven't done anything but stay in one place? The pickets haven't been moving or advancing?"

"Yep, that's it. The captain's right puzzled about it, same as you, sir."

Wend said, "All right, here's what we're going to do: Childers, go find Donegal; tell him to get Sonny and a horse for himself and join me." He looked at Newkirk. "Reese, you stay here with the company. Donegal and I will do a short scout. I would be derelict if I didn't get some information on the British to pass on to army headquarters when we arrive in New York."

Newkirk nodded. "Makes sense to me, sir. But we're going to lose a lot of time. Likely it's going to delay us a day in getting to New York."

Wend gritted his teeth. "I don't like it, but it can't be avoided."

In a few minutes, Donegal appeared leading Sonny and another horse with one hand, musket in the other. Wend explained the plan to the sergeant, then he turned to the militiaman. "Hays, take us to your captain."

The three of them rode off along the road, going northward for a mile or so. Then Hays turned off onto a trail which led eastward, toward the coast. They now had a rising sun before them—Wend pulled his hat brim down to shield his eyes. After about a mile, they came to a well-traveled wagon track, and the militiaman turned northward. They climbed a rise and found a knot of armed men sitting along the road at the crest.

Hays pulled up and slipped to the ground. One of the sitting men rose to his feet.

"I found them Continentals, Halliday." He waved back toward Wend and Donegal. "This be their captain. Eckert's his name."

Wend dismounted and walked over to where the militia captain stood. "I'm Captain Wend Eckert, of the Frederick County Light Foot Company. Who am I talking to?"

"Ronald Halliday." He swept his hand around to take in the sitting men. "This is my company of the county militia."

"Howard tells me you're watching some British who landed from Staten Island."

Halliday nodded. "Yeah, there's a picket just to the east. Come on, I'll show you."

He led Wend and Donegal past the tree line at the edge of the road and through some pine scrub. Presently they came to a place where two men, hidden in the bush, were stationed where the hill began to drop down toward a plain covered with scrub pines.

The captain pointed directly eastward. "Look, you can see the picket." Wend covered his eyes to shield them from the glare and could see several men, one standing by a tree, the others seated around a fire.

Halliday said, "They are making themselves comfortable, like they plan to be there for a while."

Wend raised the small brass telescope he had brought from the saddle bag of his horse. He adjusted it and examined the men in red uniforms. He scanned the countryside beyond the picket and was rewarded by numerous pillars of smoke well to the northeast, obviously coming from the fires of a troop encampment. He remarked, "I see the smoke of picket posts stretching northward. Their main body is a couple of hundred yards beyond the picket line." Then he said to Donegal, "Simon, I don't recognize the uniforms. You know more about that than I. Here, take the glass and see what you think."

Donegal examined the men of the picket for a couple of minutes. Then he lowered the glass and handed it back to Wend. "Na I'll say this: It appears to me they are Royal Marines, not army."

Wend nodded. "All right, that would make sense if they've made a landing from the water." He paused a moment, then continued, "I wonder what this is all about. They are obviously settled in as if planning to remain in that position."

Halliday reached into a pocket of his jacket and pulled out a rolled-up piece of parchment. "Here, look at this handbill. We found it posted on a tree after Hays rode off to find you. It seems to explain what this is all about."

Wend read the handbill. After finishing, he nodded. "You're right: This explains a lot, if true, and there's no reason not to believe it." He looked at Donegal. "It says they want to buy fresh provisions. They've set up a trading station in a village named Shoreham Ordinary for local farmers to bring in meat, flour, grain, and vegetables." He looked back at Halliday. "Where is this village?"

"Just east, near the coast." Then he pointed northward. "There's a wagon track up that way which leads into it. We checked, and there's another picket up there at the junction where the track into Shoreham joins this road." Then he pointed northward. "Probably more pickets up that way, but we ain't scouted that out."

Wend shrugged. "It looks pretty obvious. The British haven't anything on their ships but salt meat and other dry goods which won't perish on a voyage. Now that they are ashore on Staten Island, they are opening a supply post to obtain fresh provisions, probably for both the army and the ships." He thought a moment. "Do you think the local farmers will cooperate?"

"I'm damned sure some will. There are a lot of loyalists around here and others who will want the hard money which the British are offering. It will just be business."

"Yes, I imagine so."

"Captain," responded Halliday, "There's something else you ought to know. Last night, just before dusk, we heard some firing coming from up to the North."

He shrugged. "It weren't much, like just one quick exchange. Ain't got any idea what it was all about."

"You didn't send anyone up to investigate?"

Halliday hesitated a moment, then made the faintest of smiles and shrugged. "I ain't about to get my lads mixed up with British army or marines, not unless they start movin' on our homes. I just figure we're here to watch and let the proper authorities know what we see and hear." He motioned toward Wend. "Which I just did."

Wend considered for a moment. "Well, there's nothing to be done. It's possible the British will try to occupy more land beyond the post they've set up, but between my company and yours, we don't have sufficient men to dislodge them." He shot a hard look at Halliday. "Even if you were inclined to join in." He paused to let his words take effect. "In any case, my duty is to join Washington's army, not start a battle."

The militia captain nodded. "All right, let's get back to the road and my men. We'll just keep a watch on the Redcoats to make sure they don't make any big moves."

When they arrived at the road where Halliday's men were posted, Wend turned to the captain. "I'm going to rejoin my company and continue our march. When we reach Manhattan, I will report on this development to headquarters."

Halliday was about to respond when there was the sound of several horses approaching at the trot along the road from the north. Everyone turned to look and soon sighted a group of four mounted men riding toward them. The militia captain said, "Why, that's some of those Carolina dragoons that patrol down here once and a while. We've seen them often enough."

The dragoon patrol rode to the militia position and reined in their mounts. Wend saw that they wore gray coats with green facings, white breeches, and black helmets. Their leader was a corporal, and Wend was surprised to see the man staring down at him from his horse, a startled look on his face.

After a long moment, the corporal lifted his gaze from Wend and, looking around, said, "I'm Corporal Conner from the Palmetto Light Horse. We've been sent by Washington to investigate and watch the British position ashore here in Jersey."

Halliday introduced himself, then said, "This here is Captain Eckert, commanding some Virginia soldiers their way to join the army in New York." He waved in the direction of the picket. "There's a picket line of Redcoats along here and an encampment beyond that just close to Shoreham."

The corporal nodded. "We're well aware of that. I'm scouting to find out how far south the line extends."

Halliday handed the handbill to the cavalryman. "This seems to explain their purpose. They're looking for provisions."

The corporal nodded. "Yes, we've got the same handbill."

Halliday said, "There's something else. We heard some firing last evening, up to the north of here. I don't have no idea what that was about."

Conner laughed. "That was us. We rode through the picket line and right up to the British camp. We exchanged a round of fire with them. Then we rode back out. Our lieutenant, Mr. Fairfield, wanted to find out the strength of the British." He grinned widely. "We surprised the hell out of them, and didn't have any casualties, 'ceptin' a couple of men who got grazed by balls, and one man who had his helmet knocked off by a ball. Pissed him off at losing it, but didn't hurt him none."

Halliday thought a minute. "So are you Carolina lads going to be watching the British?"

"That's right. We'll be leaving a detachment here to keep an eye on them. I'll be rejoining the troop once we find out the extent of the picket line."

Halliday pointed toward the Marine picket post. "That's the last one to the south. We checked it out." He hesitated a second, then waved at his men. "We been here since yesterday. If you lads are going to be watching, is there any need for us to stay around?"

The corporal shrugged. "Captain, far as I'm concerned, you can go on back home."

The militiamen, who had been lounging along the track, enthusiastically rose to their feet. Halliday said, "Someone go get the lads who are down watching the British, then we'll be out of here."

The corporal looked at Wend. "What is your intention, sir?"

Wend waved in the general direction of his company. "I'm going back to join my men. Then we'll be marching to join the army in New York."

"Right, sir." The corporal saluted, then said to his men, "All right, let's head back to the troop." And with that, they pulled their horses around and trotted back up the road.

Wend motioned to Donegal. "Let's get going. We've used up too much of the day already." Then he turned to the militia captain. "Good day, sir."

As they rode back toward the company encampment, Wend turned to Donegal. "Simon, did you notice anything familiar about that cavalry corporal?"

Donegal's face wrinkled up. "No. Why should I be thinkin' someone from Carolina would be familiar?"

"He shouldn't. But I swear that when he first arrived, he looked at me as if he knew me. There shouldn't be any way that could be true, but that's the impression I got."

"You must look like someone from down there he's seen before. Na there ain't no way he's ever met you."

Wend nodded. "You're right, of course." He looked up at the sun. "Come on, let's hurry and get back to the company posthaste. We got to make as many miles as we can today."

—ꝏ—

The morning after the raid on Shoreham Ordinary, Geoffrey Fairfield and his two sergeants sat on blankets around a fire beside the coast road. The rest of the troop were at their own fires. All three men were smoking—the two sergeants with pipes and Fairfield with a cigar.

McCrae took his pipe from his lips and said, "Bloom says the two men with flesh wounds are fine. He's got dressings on them and they're good to ride and to perform all their duties." He waved his hand. "Bloom likes doing the medical work. Says he wants to become a doctor when the war is over."

Fairfield grinned. "I've seen worse who already call themselves physicians. He's got good hands dealing with wounds."

At that moment, Quinn took the pipe out of his mouth and looked southward down the coast road. He called out, "There's Conner and his patrol coming back."

The four horsemen dismounted and led their horses to the picket line. Conner came to the fire to make his report.

Fairfield asked, "Did you find out how far their picket line extends?"

"Indeed, sir. Met up with a group of militia. They been watching the British for a couple of days. The last picket is manned by Royal Marines, down to the south." He waved his hands. "The militia were anxious to go home and I said that would be fine."

Fairfield nodded. "That's good. They'd just complicate things."

Quinn said, "All right Conner, get yourself something to eat. Most of the troop will be riding north to our regular bivouac soon."

But Conner didn't leave. Instead, a nervous smile came over his face and he said, "But meetin' with the militia ain't all that happened on that patrol. It turns out we got a problem."

Quinn took the pipe out of his mouth. "Problem? What are you talking about?"

"Yeah, well, when I met that captain of the militia company, there was another captain with him. A captain of a company of foot from Virginia going to join Washington's army. The militia found out about them and asked for help."

Quinn shrugged. "So there was a Continental captain there. Why is that a problem?"

"I'll tell you why: That captain was that gunsmith *Eckert*. Eckert of Winchester."

Fairfield stiffened and sat upright. Quinn exhaled the smoke from his mouth and scowled. McCrae was more vocal: "Damn!"

"You're *sure*," asked Fairfield, "that it was Eckert?"

"Yeah, I'm *damned* sure. I was with Quinn when we robbed him and his wife on the Berryville Road east of Winchester back in '74. And you well know I was there the night we came across him with those men down by the Shenandoah—the night you let him shoot that merchant trader—Grenough was his name." Connor looked around at the other three. "And now he's in command of a company called the Frederick County Light Foot. Can't be anyone else but Eckert."

Quinn, a bit of concern in his voice, queried, "Did he recognize you?"

Conner shook his head. "Ain't no way. I was wearing a hood the night we robbed him on Berryville Road, and I wasn't near him that night on the Shenandoah. Anyhow, he was too concerned with Grenough and you to be lookin' at me or any other of the men."

McCrae said, "Whether he recognized Conner ain't the point, at least right now. The point is Eckert will recognize the three of us."

Fairfield held up a hand to silence McCrae. Then he said, "All right, Conner, that was good work. You've alerted us. Now go get something to eat while we discuss what it all means."

Conner nodded and walked back to one of the squad fires.

When he was out of earshot, McCrae spoke up. "That tears it! Eckert will spill the beans on us when he finds out we're with the army. We need to take our leave. Gather up the other five lads of the crew who worked with us on the road in Virginia and Maryland and get out while there's time. We can find a good territory and live off the wealth of travelers. It was a good life before, and it can be again."

Quinn took his pipe out of his mouth, looked down at it for a moment, then said to Fairfield, "I told you we damn well should have let that man Grenough kill Eckert that night at the Shenandoah ferry. Or we should have killed him after he shot Grenough. Either way, we wouldn't have this problem now. Now or ever." He pointed the stem of his pipe at Fairfield. "But you had the hots for his wife, that raven-haired Ulster woman. So you let him go as a gesture to her. Your stupid idea of chivalry or something."

Rage swept over Fairfield's face. "Damn it! That's enough, Quinn!"

There was a long moment of silence with Geoffrey glaring at both sergeants. Finally, he took a deep breath, controlled himself, and started to talk in a quiet and serious tone.

"Now listen, both of you: we've never had it so good as here in the army. We work directly for headquarters. Washington needs us because we're the only fully equipped and well-horsed cavalry troop in the army. The only other cavalry they've got is some ill-disciplined and ill-equipped militia troops. And think about it: No one in this army lives and eats better than we do, thanks to the discrete foraging we're able to do." He smiled. "After all, we're *quite expert* at that."

McCrae said, "It won't matter if Eckert tells them who we are and what we've done. Washington is a bloody gentleman and he ain't going to take well to highwaymen working for him."

"Look, Freddie," replied Fairfield, holding up his finger. "First, I don't think Eckert's going to do that. After all, he owes his life to me." He raised a second finger. "And given his sense of fairness and honesty, he's likely to respect that."

Quinn scowled. "Maybe he will, and maybe he won't. You can't count on his good graces."

McCrae shook his head. "Why the hell are you so determined to stick with the army, Fairfield? It could cost you your life if Eckert talks to someone on Washington's staff."

Quinn leaned back, a knowing smile on his face. "I'll tell you why Fairfield is so determined to stick it out with the army. He's thinkin' about that young, rich, good-lookin' widow of the Charleston gentry who got him his commission and authority from the governor to raise this troop. That's why." He raised his eyebrows. "He's thinkin' about goin' back to that low country and marryin' her. It's what he's always wanted, a comfortable situation as a gentleman. That's why he's spent years learning all those fine manners and how to speak with a cultured style in front of the gentry. He figures that the street urchin from London is someday going to end up as the master of the widow's plantation, sittin' on the portico of that big house overlooking the Ashley River, drinkin' cool juleps in the hot afternoons. Yeah, that's what's keepin' him with the army." He turned and stared at Geoffrey. "Tell me it ain't so, Fairfield."

There was a momentary silence. Fairfield looked from one sergeant to the other. He managed to control the anger welling up inside and think of words which would change the direction of the argument. After moments of silence, he said, "And what's wrong with that plan? Money, good food and drink, a lovely woman to bed, and soon enough, children running around. Games of chance in the evening with other gentlemen from plantations along the Ashley. Not to mention a substantial town house in Charleston."

Quinn made a face. "Yeah, that's good for you. But what about us? We ain't makin' any money in the army. You go back to Carolina and high livin' off the widow's gold and we got nothin' to do but go back to the old work on the road."

Fairfield took a puff on his cigar, then exhaled the smoke in a smooth stream. "What makes you think I'll forget about my companions of the road and the army? Have faith that I'll share my fortune with old comrades. Any large establishment like a plantation needs many functionaries—overseers of the Africans, managers to sell and move the rice crop, and clerks to procure supplies and other goods." He smiled conspiratorially. "I'll not forget either of you. We can be fixed for life without worrying about sheriffs and magistrates. We can all die comfortably in bed from old age with a woman crying over us instead of gasping out our life with a pistol ball lodged in our chest or stomach from the firelock of an outraged traveler or some minion of the law. Or dare I mention the threat of the gallows?" He shrugged. "Think about that."

His words had their effect. The two men sat staring at him, obviously thinking about what he had said. Fairfield raised his eyebrows and spoke again. "There's something else. You two are old soldiers. The fact is, you like this life and the adventure that comes with it. I watched you riding on that raid yesterday, excitement in your eyes as we galloped by that British camp. Me, I was scared nearly out of my mind, expecting to get hit by a ball at any moment."

After he finished, the two others sat silent, looking at him for a time. Then McCrae asked, "You really serious about takin' care of us if we go back to Carolina? You ain't just spinnin' a story to keep us with you?"

Fairfield raised his hand as if taking an oath. "You have my word. When I marry the widow and take over River Oaks Plantation, you will be with me."

Quinn had a fierce look in his eye. "You damn well better be right about dealing with Eckert and then keep your word about Carolina. If it don't work out, you won't have to worry about some sheriff's pistol or the noose. I'll do the job myself."

Geoffrey smiled broadly, feeling a sense of relief. "Well, then it's all set." He took a deep breath and continued, "Now let's leave Mr. Middleton and Conner here with a detachment to watch the Redcoats, and we'll take the rest of the troop back to bivouac. And then I'll go tell Washington all about what the British are up to."

Chapter Four

The Gathering Time

Geoffrey Fairfield tied his horse to the hitching rail in front of Richmond Hill, climbed the front steps, and entered the hall. He identified himself to the staff captain sitting at the desk and said, "Please let Colonel Grayson know I'm here. I have urgent information he's waiting for."

The captain was unimpressed. He raised an eyebrow, then said in an officious tone, "The colonel is with a high-ranking officer now. I'll let him know of your presence when they've finished." He casually motioned toward the front porch. "In the meantime, you can wait out there."

Fairfield wasn't having it. "Look, Captain, I've just come back from Jersey, where there is an outpost of British who have been there for the last four days. General Washington *personally* sent me down there with my troop of light horse to find out what was going on. I suggest you promptly enter Grayson's office and whisper in his ear that I'm here. Or slip him a note. Let me be clear, this is of the *highest* urgency."

The receptionist stared at Fairfield for a long moment, skepticism in his eyes, obviously irritated at being told what to do. Finally, he rose and said, "All right, I'll notify him. But you better be right." He walked down the hall, tapped on a closed door, and slipped into the room.

Almost immediately a lieutenant colonel Fairfield didn't recognize came out of the room, followed by the staff captain, who had a rather surprised look on his face. He motioned to Fairfield. "Please go in, sir."

Fairfield couldn't resist shooting the officious captain a victorious smile as he walked past.

Grayson was at his desk when Geoffrey entered. Without preliminaries, he demanded, "All right, Fairfield, what did you find out?"

Instead of answering, Geoffrey reached into his coat, retrieved a copy of the British handbill, and handed it to Grayson. "This is what it's all about, sir. Fresh provisions."

The colonel scanned the paper. "Is this all? How did you confirm that?"

"We pushed through their pickets, rode right by their camp, right to the village of Shoreham Ordinary and got a good view of the waterfront. They had a few boats and some barges moored there. No sign of bringing in more troops than the light foot battalion, perhaps 400 men, that they've landed along with a few marines and sailors." He laid a rolled-up piece of paper on the desk. "I've written a report which adds a little more detail."

Grayson stared at Fairfield for a moment, a thoughtful look on his face. Then he said, "Come with me. We'll take this right to Washington." Then he walked over to a connecting door in the wall which separated his office from Washington's, knocked and then opened it. "Sir, Fairfield is back from Jersey. You'll want to hear what he has to say."

Washington answered, "Come right in."

Grayson waved Geoffrey to follow and went through the door. When he entered, Geoffrey saw Washington had risen from his desk and was standing by a window which looked out on the grounds. He turned and asked, "Well, Lieutenant, what have you found out?"

"Sir, the British position is just an outpost established for the purpose of procuring fresh provisions." He went on to explain the situation in somewhat more detail than he had to Grayson, particularly describing how they had raced past the pickets and then the main camp and had observed the waterfront.

Washington asked, "You say only a light battalion and a few Marines? And you saw no evidence of them adding troops to their presence on the ground?"

"No, sir. I got a glance of the beach where they had their boats, just beyond the village. Nothing there looked like preparations to reinforce the battalion." He shrugged. "They may stay there, but I don't believe they are any threat to us." He thought a second. "Of course, a brigade would be able to easily dislodge them if that was considered desirable."

Washington crossed his arms and stared out the window into the distance. Then he shook his head and said, "It's not worth the effort of moving a large contingent of troops across the harbor and into Jersey, just to bring them back when the operation is complete."

Grayson nodded and replied, "I strongly agree. We need to keep our forces massed for the British main push on this side."

"Yes," said the general, "and particularly since we can't be sure of when or where they plan to land to begin their actual operations."

Fairfield felt emboldened to speak. "Sir, I left a contingent of my troop—ten men including Ensign Middleton, a corporal, and eight troopers—to keep watch on the British. We'll know immediately if anything further develops."

Washington nodded. "Good. That's precisely what is needed." A thoughtful look spread over his face. "Now, what were your casualties making your probe? How many men did you lose?"

"We were fortunate, sir. We surprised them and moved swiftly. No one killed, only two men slightly wounded and able to continue their duties."

A small smile came over Washington's face. "Excellent, Mr. Fairfield." He clasped his hands behind his back. "You have conducted a most effective reconnaissance."

"Thank you, sir."

"No, Lieutenant, it is I who must thank *you*. You and the state of South Carolina. Let me say, your troop has provided us with essential services since your arrival just a few weeks ago. Your patrols have kept us informed about the arrival of the British expedition and the status of their progressive occupation of Staten Island. You have been my eyes." He looked quickly over at Grayson, then back to Geoffrey. "Sir, please prepare a dispatch to inform Governor Rutledge of the troop's good work and to thank him for sending us a unit that, while small, has proven so valuable to our cause. Tell him we wish we had more of the regiment with us."

Grayson said, "I'll draft it immediately, General."

Fairfield felt a thrill of exultation rush through his body. He hurried to formulate an appropriate answer. "I am *most* grateful for your kind words, General. Rest assured we will continue our endeavors to provide the information you need for your decisions regarding the army's movements."

Washington raised his hand. "Indeed, sir, we are quite confident you will."

Taking that as his dismissal, Geoffrey came to attention, saluted, made an about-face, and exited the office.

Walking out onto the porch, Geoffrey could hardly restrain a feeling of exuberance. A letter to Governor Rutledge commending the troop and himself would undoubtedly be passed on to the Governor's wife's second cousin, Susan Middleton Guerard Beresford, widow of Colin Beresford and now the mistress of River Oaks Plantation. And that would be another step closer for him to return to her arms—and bed—from honorable service in the army. He would definitely mention it to Ensign Thomas Middleton, a nephew of Susan's, who would likely also communicate the news to her. He thought about Quinn's description of him sitting on the portico of the manor house, looking over the rice ponds to the Ashley River. He smiled and thought, *That vision was now a long step closer to reality.*

He was standing there, full of happy thoughts, when he heard the sound of drums beating a marching cadence, coming up Varick Street from the direction of the harbor. In a few moments, a column of troops came into view. They were dressed in linen hunting shirts, brown breeches, and black hats with the rear of the brim turned up and pinned to the crown. Having seen the amateurish drilling of many units of the army, Fairfield was quite impressed by the precision of this company. They were in precise step, their firelocks all at the same slope, shoulders squared, their accouterments all carried in the same place and manner. Then he looked at their commander, who was mounted on a magnificent, long legged black hunter. The animal was prancing with irrepressible energy. Geoffrey moved his gaze to the rider, and a shock ran through his body, erasing the pleasurable thoughts which he had just been contemplating and replacing them with a gut-wrenching sense of dread.

Eckert!

Fairfield suddenly realized that in seconds the gunsmith would be close enough to see and recognize him standing on the porch. He scrambled down the steps, grabbed the reins of his horse, and led him away from the house to where rows of tents for staff officers were pitched. He quickly gained shelter behind one where he could not be seen from the road. Then he looked around and saw a path to lead the horse to the next street under cover. He headed that way with the horse trailing behind, ignoring the stares of several officers and servants who wondered why the devil he was taking this way on his exit from the headquarters.

—∞—

Washington was busy with papers on his desk when Grayson entered. "General, there's a new company of light foot which has just reported."

Washington responded, without looking up, "Was that the fife and drums I heard approaching? They were playing a tune I swear I've heard before, long ago. Can't place quite where it was." Then he looked up at his adjutant general. "Did you say it was just a single company? Not part of a regiment?"

"That's correct, sir."

"Well, Grayson, any addition to our force is welcome. Assign them to a regiment from their own state."

"With respect, sir, that might be impossible. You might want to give these troops a little more attention. In fact, they're drawn up in front of headquarters."

Washington looked up, mild exasperation on his face. "William, what are you trying to tell me?"

Grayson grinned. "This company is from *Virginia*. From Frederick County."

A broad smile spread across the commanding general's face. "Well, Patrick is finally making good on his promise to send us troops."

"Indeed, sir. And as a matter of fact, the captain gave me a pouch of dispatches from Henry. I read this one, which is the introduction. You might want to take a look at it." He handed a single sheet of paper to Washington.

The general quickly read the missive. He looked up. "Very interesting. He says he'll be sending several battalions to us now that Dunmore has been driven out. And he makes the point that this company is his very best."

"Yes, they rushed it up to us by ship to Philadelphia and then a rapid march from there." He paused. "Oh, yes, and there's something else: Congress sent us a European volunteer along with the Virginians—a colonel named Tresh. He's Swiss and served professionally with several armies. It is suggested you accept him as an aide."

Washington nodded. "Yes, I shall be glad to meet with him. I've had correspondence from Congress that they are sending a delegation to France to recruit professional officers." He shrugged. "We will welcome this Colonel Tresh and see what use we can make of him." He bit his lip, and a thoughtful look came over his face. "Who is the captain of this company? I've spent a lot of time in Frederick County and Winchester. I may know him, or at least his family."

"The name is Eckert—a German fellow. First name is Wendelmar."

Washington's face wrinkled up in reflection. "Eckert? I can't recall any man or family of that name from my time there as a surveyor or during the French War with my regiment."

"I should doubt you would have met him. He's a gunsmith."

"A gunsmith?"

"Yes, a mechanic. However, I will say that he is quite well spoken, and I got a look at his company out the window. They're actually well-uniformed in hunting shirts, brown breeches, and black hats, and it seems there are fully one hundred of them."

Washington's eyebrows went up. "A company recruited to full strength? That is rare." He thought a moment, then got up from his desk, picked up his hat, and said, "Perhaps I *should* look them over." He shot a smile at Grayson. "Not the least to see some faces from the Valley."

Grayson led the way out to the porch and motioned toward the formation of men standing silently in the street before the headquarters. The company was in two ranks by half companies, their arms grounded, officers in their places with Eckert out front. He said, "I told Eckert to stand by, that you might want to look them over." He looked over at Washington. "Sir, they do make a good appearance."

"They do indeed, William. Go tell the captain that I shall conduct an inspection of the company."

Grayson nodded, then formally strode down to where Eckert stood before the company, drawn up in two ranks, their firelocks grounded. "Captain Eckert, prepare your company for inspection by the commanding general."

Eckert saluted and ordered the men to slope their firelocks. In good order, they brought their weapons to the shoulder.

Eckert turned and drew his sword, then ordered the company to present arms. Washington returned the salute, and Wend reported, "Frederick County Light Foot Company, all present and correct."

Washington accepted the report, then asked, "What is your strength, Captain?"

"Sir, four officers and one hundred men, one civilian contract gunsmith, ten women and children accompanying."

"Very good, Captain. I shall inspect your company. Please lead."

"Aye, sir."

Washington walked through the ranks silently, taking in each man but saying nothing. He acknowledged the officers with a nod. Then they came to Donegal. The general stopped and stared for a moment. "Captain, your men are commendably uniformed, but why is this man wearing the bonnet of a Highland regiment?"

Wend responded, "Company Sergeant Donegal has my permission to wear the bonnet. He was a corporal in the 77th Highlanders, sir, Montgomerie's regiment, throughout its service here in America. He was with them in Carolina against the Cherokee and on the campaign with Forbes in '58. He marched with Bouquet in the relief of Fort Pitt in '63. His wearing of the bonnet commemorates that service, and I feel it shows his experience to the men of the company."

"Ah, yes, Captain. I take your point. In fact, I quite remember the 77th. In 1758, they were encamped beside my own Virginia Regiment at Fort Bedford during the march to take Duquesne." Then he spoke directly to Donegal. "Sergeant, which company were you in?"

"Na, sir, my captain was Robertson. James Robertson, sir."

Washington thought a moment, then said, "Ah, yes, I remember him quite well." Washington looked over Donegal for a few seconds, then said, "Well, Sergeant, we are quite pleased to have such a long-serving veteran in the army."

When they arrived at the musket-carrying half-company, Washington stopped and gave Flannagan a direct look. "Sergeant, you look familiar. Have we met?"

"Can't say we've met, sir, but it's sure you have seen me. I was a corporal in Captain Mercer's company in the old Virginia Regiment during the French War. In the days we were manning the outposts along the line in the Valley, sir, you came by our fort often enough. And then I was still with the regiment on the Forbes march in '58, sir, when we took Fort Duquesne."

Washington smiled. "Now I remember, sergeant. Mercer had a fine company, and it's good to see an old compatriot from the regiment."

They moved on and finished the inspection without further comment from the general. When he finished, he turned to Wend and said, "Captain, you have a commendable-looking body of men, and they seem well-disciplined."

"Thank you, sir. Most of the men have previously served in the militia, and at least half marched on Dunmore's campaign against the Shawnee in '74."

Washington simply nodded. "Well, Captain, hold your company here. Presently one of the aides will come and take you to a site for bivouac, and in due course we will determine your assignment within the army."

Wend said, "Yes, sir," and saluted. Washington turned and strode back up the walk to headquarters, accompanied by Grayson.

As they walked, the adjutant general said, "Sir, Colonel Tresh is waiting to meet you."

"Good. Bring him into my office. I'd like to meet and have a discussion with him."

"He's brought his wife with him."

Washington sighed. "That's a complication." He thought briefly. "Grayson, I'll briefly meet with them both. While we're talking, get one of the junior aides to help them find accommodations. Then schedule a meeting between myself and Tresh in a day or two after he's had time to get her settled."

Grayson nodded. "I thought you might make that decision." He leaned over and said quietly as they walked, "By the way, Mrs. Tresh is quite attractive and considerably younger than the colonel."

Washington simply nodded. They entered the headquarters, and the general entered his office. Grayson ushered the couple from his own office, where they had been waiting, to Washington's, where the general had remained standing. He made introductions, then excused himself to find an officer to help the couple arrange accommodations.

After about a half hour, Grayson, accompanied by one Captain Hanley, tapped on Washington's door. All three were seated. He introduced Hanley, and Washington rose.

"Well, Colonel, it has been a pleasure meeting you and Mrs. Tresh. Grayson here will arrange for a longer meeting, a serious discussion of how you can assist us in our quest, once you have settled in quarters."

Hanley said, "Yes, I have some familiarity with the city and know of some lodgings which you might find to your liking." He looked from Tresh to his wife. "Shall we go?"

After making their final goodbyes, he led the couple out of the office. Grayson closed the door. "Well, sir, what do you think of the colonel?"

"I think we can make use of him. I was impressed with his service in Europe." He looked over at Grayson. "William, what was your impression of Mrs. Tresh?"

"A stunning woman, with that lovely face, fair complexion, raven hair, willowy figure. Seems to be quite cultured." He looked at Washington. "Why do you ask, sir?"

"William, she is all that you say. However, it was her eyes which drew my attention. She was smiling the entire time we talked, but that smile did not extend to her eyes. Her eyes said something much more serious. It was a look of *calculation.* I confess, once I noticed, it was a bit disconcerting."

"Well, sir, whatever is behind those eyes, it's more Tresh's concern, not ours."

Washington shrugged. "Naturally, you are quite correct. In any case, I shall be interested to have a serious discussion with Tresh as soon as you can arrange it."

"Indeed, General. I'll have him meet with you at the earliest time that is convenient." Then Grayson recalled something else. "What shall we do with the Frederick County company?"

Washington raised a finger. "Ah, yes. I was thinking about that. Since we have no Virginia regiment to assign them to, let's keep them under our direct command, at least until Virginia troops arrive in numbers. We'll consider them part of our reserve, ready to move in case the British attack somewhere besides where we expect."

"As you wish, General."

Barrett Northcutt pulled his horse up at the top of the small rise some miles west of Morristown. He was dressed in the riding attire of a gentleman of some means, including a broad-brimmed beaver hat, a brown shell jacket, tan breeches, and riding boots. Markwood stopped his own horse alongside. He wore the rough clothing of a servant and held the lead reins of a packhorse which carried their baggage. Before them in the distance was a large farm surrounded by fields and pastures.

The colonel turned to Markwood. "That's Harfeld's plantation. It's a rather substantial place."

The captain responded, "I should say so. The house is impressive, not to mention the stables and other outbuildings. Have you been here often?"

"Twice, George, both of them for shooting parties." Smiling, he continued, "And the card table in the evening. Harfeld is a deft gambler. Of course, it helps to have the money to back it up."

"Is he married?"

"Yes, to a lovely lady named Adele, but they are childless, at least the last time I saw him, which was in 1772 just before I went to Virginia with Dunmore." He looked over at his companion. "Let's ride on in."

In a few minutes, they had trotted up the drive and reined in their horses in front of the large, two-story house with a wide porch at the front. An African stable boy came running and took their horses.

Northcutt led the way up the steps and across the porch. He used the brass knocker on the door to announce their presence. In a minute, a Black butler opened the door.

"Can I help you, sir?"

Barrett nodded. "Indeed. Please tell Mr. Harfeld that Barrett Northcutt is here. I'm an old friend; he'll recognize the name."

"Please wait here, sir. I'll announce you."

There was but a short wait and the butler returned, followed by Harfeld himself. The plantation master was a man of above average height, thin body, and very dark brown hair. He was dressed in a well-tailored suit.

He smiled when he saw Northcutt. "My dear Barrett! So good to see you. Deuced if I don't believe it's been four years if it's been a day!"

"Yes, indeed, it's that long." He motioned toward his companion. "This is my friend, George Markwood from Virginia. He owns a plantation on the James River, south of a town called Richmond."

Harfeld looked over the captain with a raised eyebrow, clearly noting the lower-class clothing. A look of puzzlement came over his face, but politely he said nothing except to greet Markwood.

Northcutt hurried to resume the conversation. "Clive, we stopped at your place in town, but they told us you had departed for a few days out here. So we took the liberty of coming to the plantation."

Harfeld smiled. "Well, of course, you are welcome." He glanced at a clock on a small table. "It's approaching the supper hour. You will, of course, stay for the meal?"

"That would be our great pleasure, Clive." He smiled. "And it will also be a pleasure to see your lovely Adele again."

A cloud came over Harfeld's face. He sighed and said, "Barrett, sadly, my wife has gone on to a better place. She became sick last year, which progressed to lung fever. She succumbed in November, to my great distress."

Northcutt reached out and put his hand on Harfeld's arm. "My friend, I'm so sorry for your loss. Besides being a woman of beauty, she was endowed with marvelous grace and wit. It must be lonely for you here."

Harfeld made a tight smile. "One carries on, Barrett. I have submerged myself in work at my law practice and the management of this estate." Then he hurriedly said, "Please, let us adjourn to my study. You've had a long ride, and I suspect you would welcome a bracing libation."

"Your suspicion is quite accurate, sir!"

They followed Harfeld down the hall, past the parlor, and into a cozy room with a desk, comfortable chairs, and a fireplace. Windows on either side of the fireplace offered a broad view of fields and forest. Harfeld went to a cabinet and took out three glasses and a decanter. He turned to his guests and said, "I happen to still—despite the blockade—have some rum. Would that be to your pleasure?"

Both men nodded and took the proffered drinks.

Harfeld motioned to several leather chairs, and they all took seats. After a sip of his rum, he said, "Well, Barrett, excuse my curiosity, but what brings you here?"

Northcutt had a story ready. "Well, since I've been in Virginia since '72, I thought I might take a look at my land holdings hereabouts. They're fairly extensive, as you are aware."

Harfeld raised an eyebrow but simply said, "Indeed they are. I remember when you bought the acreage."

They chatted for the better part of a half hour until the butler tapped on the door and announced that the evening meal was ready.

The jovial conversation continued at the table. With the conclusion of sweets after the meal, Harfeld had brandy served. A pause in conversation took place as the three sampled the libation, and Northcutt took the moment to offer cigars, which the host readily accepted.

After they had all lit up, Harfeld exhaled his smoke, then turned to Northcutt. Looking over his cigar, he said, "Well, now, Barrett, you've had my rum, my supper, and my brandy." He smiled wryly. "Would you now do me the honor of telling me the *real* reason you are here? And don't repeat that blather about looking over your land. You bought that purely as speculation: it's virtually all in woodland, and there's no bloody need to inspect it."

Northcutt laughed. "Same old Clive Harfeld. I didn't much think that would fool you." He paused, looked over at Markwood, then back to his host. "Let me be frank and direct, sir. When I was here in the past, I was well aware that you were quite firm in your support of the King's party. Has anything changed in the ensuing period? Have the events of Boston and Bunker Hill, and the actions of this Continental Congress changed your view and led you to become a sympathizer of the so-called Patriot cause?"

A gleam appeared in Harfeld's eyes. "So I was right! From the moment you arrived, I suspected that you had come on British business. I'm aware that the Virginia governor—Lord Dunmore—has recently been expelled from the colony. And you were his advisor. Those recent events explain your return to these environs. So, logically, you have come to ask something from me or for me to do something for the British. Am I not correct?"

"Quite correct, my dear Clive. I am presently the colonel of a loyalist Virginia regiment and serving on General Howe's staff." He waved toward Markwood. "And this gentleman is a captain and my assistant." Northcutt waved toward Harfeld with his cigar. "But you still haven't answered my question: Are you still of the King's party?"

"For God's sake, Barrett! I fought for the King in the French War back in the fifties and sixties. I was at Ticonderoga and many other fights, large and small. Do you think I would change my colors now?"

"I was hoping you would say that, my dear Clive. The fact is, I'm here on behalf of Howe to ask you to take up active service for the King amidst this insurrection."

Harfeld's face brightened. "I consider it an honor to be asked. What is it that you desire—for me to raise a company of troops? I know many men who would come to the colors, and it would be my honor to serve as their captain."

Northcutt and Markwood exchanged glances, then Northcutt said, "My dear Clive, I know you would be quite effective in raising and training a company or even a regiment." He paused and leaned toward Harfeld. "However, what I would ask of you is something even more important, more critical to the suppression of this insurrection."

Puzzlement spread over the lawyer's face. "More important than raising troops? You have me stumped."

"From our days together, I recognize that you have a talent for organization and daring action found in few others."

Harfeld cocked his head, pondering Northcutt's words. "And?"

"The most important thing that Howe needs now is *information*: information on the rebel army, it strength, movements, and the support they are receiving throughout the countryside. In short, he must have a web of watchers who can provide news of the enemy to our army. And such a web must have someone to recruit it, organize it, and lead it in operation."

Clive stiffened in his chair. "So, in short, you are asking me to organize a ring of spies?"

"My dear Harfeld, that's *precisely* what I'm asking."

Clive Harfeld rose from his chair and paced back and forth in the space between the table and the sideboard. As he walked, he puffed on the cigar, frequently exhaling the smoke.

Northcutt added, "Clive, you are the perfect person for the job. You have rental properties in various places here and in New York, and you are a lawyer. Both provide reasons for you to travel widely, which would be essential for managing a net of watchers."

Harfeld paused his pacing and took the cigar out of his mouth. "There would be some expenses associated with such an endeavor. I don't mind spending some of my money, but I would expect some reimbursement. There will be travel expenses, and some of the spies would want payment for their services and loyalty."

"A very good point, Clive, and I have assurances from Howe's adjutant general that such funds would be made available."

Harfeld smiled and nodded. Then he resumed pacing.

Northcutt cleared his throat. "Clive, there's something else for you to think about."

The lawyer stopped, took the cigar out of his mouth, turned, and looked at Barrett. "And what would that be?"

"Just this, Clive: When this insurrection has been suppressed, it is certain that the ringleaders in each colony will be punished. Their lives, and certainly their property, will be forfeit."

"What are you implying?"

"It means, my friend, that the King will most certainly reward those who have stood steadfast and loyal, and most particularly those who have actively assisted in the suppression of the insurrection—rewards of both honor and material." He looked at Harfeld. "Let me be clear: There will be considerable rebel property to be distributed to deserving loyalists."

Harfeld smiled. "An important consideration, Barrett."

Markwood spoke up. "We should need to caution you, sir, that of course such a role would put you in danger of discovery and retribution by the rebels—retribution which would indubitably be mortal."

The lawyer stopped and looked at Markwood, "Sir, naturally I am aware of that. I told you that I have fought on the battlefield for the crown." He shrugged. "What, pray tell, is the difference, in the end, of dying by musket fire on the field of action or from musket balls delivered by a firing squad in an execution?" He smiled. "The result is the same, and a soldier of the king should not shy from either."

Northcutt looked up from his seat at the table. "A noble sentiment, Clive. Does that mean you are ready to accept the duty?"

Hatfield stopped his pacing, turned, and looked directly at Northcutt. "Yes, Barrett, I accept the charge. I believe I am the man for this service and, by God, I'll carry it out with all my heart. Tell Howe he will soon have a functioning ring of spies in Jersey and parts of New York." He turned to the sideboard and picked up the brandy decanter. "Gentlemen, I suggest we adjourn to my study. We have much to discuss." He thought a second, "We shall need some time to work out details of this scheme. Will you stay the night?"

Barrett looked over at Markwood and winked, then turned back to his host and laughed. "Clive, we thought you'd never ask."

—∞—

Adjutant General Grayson had suggested to Washington that Tresh accompany him on his daily ride through the army camps in lieu of an office interview, and the general had readily agreed. Washington and the Swiss colonel, mounted on their horses and escorted by cavalry of the general's life guards, had left the headquarters in mid-morning and rode northeasterly through the bustling streets of Manhattan, headed for the open fields where much of the army lay encamped. Tresh was impressed with Washington's sleek, long-legged gray hunter, which was nearly two hands taller than his own bay mare. The size of the horse meant that Washington's head was even further above Tresh's than it would normally have been due to his tall stature.

The party soon arrived at a rural area of farms with green pastures and fields. Tresh saw that many of the open areas were the site of sprawling military camps.

Tresh said, "General, I'm impressed with the number of troops I see. May I ask how many are in your army?"

"You may, sir." Washington waved his arm to take in the surrounding camps. "This area holds the main part of the army." He pointed to the south. "But a significant body has been transported to Long Island. That is where we expect the first thrust of the British when they are ready to begin their campaign. To directly answer your question, our strength is nineteen thousand men, but perhaps a third of those are militia, and I cannot be sure of their reliability in a hot action." He looked at the colonel. "We estimate that Howe has at least 25,000 at present, but clearly they are still in the process of building up their force. More ships arrive every day."

"I saw their fleet when we crossed the harbor from the New Jersey side. It was impressive—I've never seen so many vessels."

Washington nodded. "We, of course, cannot be certain, but there are indications that they eventually may have 30,000 men at their disposal."

Tresh looked over at the general. "Before I left France, I had it on very good authority that the British have arranged for a large number of troops from the German principalities to join their expeditionary force here. The talk was of perhaps 10,000 men. I've worked with German regiments. They are first-rate, well-disciplined soldiers."

"I would not argue with you. We have been advised that they are coming. In fact, I am of the opinion that the reason Howe has not already started his campaign is because he is awaiting the arrival of at least some of the Germans to bolster his force."

They rode on in silence for a few moments. Tresh commented, "I see that few of your regiments are uniformed. It appears that the uniformity presented by the Frederick County Light Foot is the exception rather than the rule."

Washington sighed. "Regrettably, you are quite correct. It is the responsibility of each state to raise and equip their regiments, and in most cases, funds for both uniforms, weapons, and equipment are inadequate. I have regiments without a single proper musket in the ranks." Washington thought a moment, then pulled up his horse, turned to face the Swiss colonel, and changed the subject. "My dear sir, there is something about which I would ask your opinion. When the Frederick County Light Foot arrived, Eckert presented us with a case of dispatches from Patrick Henry, the governor of Virginia. Among the correspondence was a personal letter to me from Henry which introduced Captain Eckert. He was very complimentary about the man, calling him both intelligent and an excellent tactician. He described a battle in which Eckert's company annihilated the better part of one of Dunmore's regiments which was raiding plantations along the Chesapeake shore. Then his company participated in the assault which drove Dunmore's forces from his island bastion. He finished by saying that the Frederick County company was the best in Virginia's force and recommended Eckert for positions of great responsibility." Washington paused to collect his thoughts. "Now, I will tell you that I have known Henry for some time; he is exceedingly proficient in the law, political maneuvering, and oratory. But I confide that I find his credentials as a military commentator suspect. Now, sir, here's the point: You accompanied the Virginia company from Philadelphia. So I would ask what your time with Eckert has shown you about his military ability? What is your opinion of his company's discipline and organization?"

"I must admit, General, that I was surprised to find it very efficient. The men are well drilled, camp routine and sanitation were very much to military standards, and they were well equipped with proper weapons and accouterments."

"Indeed, that was also my impression from the brief inspection that I made. I am glad to have a fellow officer of experience concur in that assessment."

Tresh thought a minute. "However, I must admit that I was quite startled to find the captain of the company was a man who appeared, at first impression, to be a simple tradesman. In Europe, it is customary for a man of means and at least middling status in society to raise a company, then receive a captaincy in an appropriate regiment."

A tight smile spread over Washington's face. "I should tell you, Colonel, that right after the war started, when we were besieging Boston, I asked for, and Congress directed, the formation of ten rifle companies from the middle colonies. The first one to get there was also from Frederick County. It was led by a man named Daniel Morgan, who I knew from my days when my regimental headquarters were in Winchester during the late French War. Morgan makes his living as a wagoner. He is also the best rifle marksman that I know. He proved during the French War and Dunmore's campaign against the Ohio tribes that he is a superb woodsman and fighter against the Indian tribes." Washington paused for effect. "You will get used to the idea that our officers come from all classes and levels of education."

"Clearly, I have much to learn about you Americans." Tresh shrugged. "But regarding Eckert, he is clearly educated beyond the level of most mechanics. Interestingly, the man at first seems rather emotionless—indeed, he has what is called a stone face." He held up a finger. "But it soon became clear that there is a lot going on behind that countenance of his. You see it in the eyes. And his conversation is quite intelligent, bespeaking some classical study. At one point he quoted Shakespeare during a talk we were having beside the campfire one evening."

Washington raised an eyebrow, but said nothing.

Tresh continued. "I had a long conversation with one of Eckert's lieutenants—an Irishman and professional soldier with considerable experience on the continent named O'beirne. He told me about Eckert's military background. It seems he marched as a volunteer scout with Bouquet in the relief of Fort Pitt in 1763 and fought at Bushy Run. Ten years later he was a lieutenant in a battalion which fought in Dunmore's War against the Shawnee, and led troops during several skirmishes with Indians. In fact, Lord Dunmore made him an aide on his military staff during the latter part of that campaign. O'beirne took part in the fight on the Chesapeake shores, which occurred just a few weeks ago, where the company destroyed Dunmore's regiment. He was quite adamant that Eckert knows his business. He literally destroyed the regiment by a coordinated attack on both flanks while holding the center. The Loyalists were broken and destroyed in detail as they tried to escape."

Washington nodded. "I thank you for that frank analysis. We are holding Eckert's company in reserve until we determine its best employment. You have assisted me in my eventual decision."

There was a silence as they rode on. Then Tresh noticed a group of large and small wagons parked by the road, with tents arranged around them. An exceptionally large pavilion-style tent was at the center of the camp. His eyes fell upon a wooden sign planted by the road. It read, "Red Vixen Sutler Company." Then he noticed several men and women moving around doing chores, and a group of young girls sitting by a fire, one of whom was doing some sewing. A slim-waisted, auburn-haired woman was standing in front of the girls, and suddenly all of them broke into laughter at something she said. Tresh motioned toward the camp. "Ah, a group of camp followers. They are always with an army, here as in Europe."

Washington responded, "True enough, sir. That is Mrs. McGraw's establishment." And then the general broke into the broadest smile Tresh had ever seen him make. "Mrs. McGraw follows the army with a stock of everything a soldier would want, if he has the money for a purchase."

Tresh stared at the girls then turned back to Washington. "Everything, General?"

"Precisely, Tresh. And that auburn-haired lady is Mrs. McGraw herself, who is a widow."

"She is quite handsome. I find it surprising she remains a widow."

"Yes, she is indeed. I have some knowledge of her because the younger aides of my staff find her quite intriguing and often speak of her and her female associates when we are at the table." He paused and smiled again. "However, I am led to understand from Colonel Grayson that a lieutenant who commands a troop of light horse from South Carolina is Mrs. McGraw's frequent escort and seems to have earned, to some degree, her favor."

Tresh looked at Mrs. McGraw again and remarked, "Ah, yes, a fortunate man."

They rode on in silence for a few moments, and then Washington spoke in a businesslike manner. "Colonel, I am glad you have joined us. As you will have discerned during the course of this ride, we need all the professional counsel about military matters that we can obtain. Many of my soldiers have extensive experience fighting native tribes in the bush on the frontier and, to a certain extent, the French during the late war. But I am well aware that we must learn to fight the

British in the open field, using European drill and tactics. With your knowledge and experience, my hope is that you can help us achieve that competence. So it is my pleasure to offer you the position of aide-de-camp on my staff, to advise us on how to proceed toward that goal."

Tresh felt a surge of delight. "That would be my great honor, General."

Washington turned and extended his hand. Tresh had to rise in his stirrups to take hold, and they shook hands. The general smiled and said, "Welcome to my military family, Colonel."

—∞—

Barrett Northcutt entered the office of Howe's Adjutant General, Colonel James Paterson. The colonel looked up as he closed the door behind him. "Ah, Colonel Northcutt, I was pleased to hear you were back and none the worse for wear." He raised his eyebrow. "I trust it was a productive trip?"

"Indeed, sir. And I'm ready to give you a verbal report."

Paterson motioned to a chair. "By all means. Tell me what you have." He thought a moment. "Were you able to recruit men who could form loyal companies?"

"I contacted two old friends, and another man who was referred by one of the friends. All three are ready—nay, eager—to raise companies: two would be foot and the third light horse. They know where there are pockets of people who remain sympathetic to the crown and are ready to act. They will make preparations and will be ready to form the companies when our campaign has begun."

"That is excellent, Barrett. We will direct them to become active after we have moved on Long Island and Manhattan and have a significant foothold on land beyond Staten Island. The light horse will be particularly useful."

"Quite true, sir. However, perhaps even more important to our cause, I met with a friend in Jersey—a man of considerable substance and intelligence who I know to be solidly loyal to the King and Parliament. He has both a house in Morristown and a plantation in the country to the west. He fought for the King throughout the French War here in America. I met with him at his country place, and I'm most happy to say that he has agreed to organize a web of well-placed spies, watchers, and couriers ready to serve our needs for information on the enemy's strength, fortifications, and troop movements. Markwood and I stayed at his plantation for the better part of two days, explained what was needed, and worked out the basics of his operations and a system of communications. I can tell you that he is at work recruiting his people as we speak."

Paterson put his hand to his chin and considered that for a while. "That is most encouraging news, Northcutt."

"I told him the first order of business will be to find the location and strength of all Washington's troop formations and the placement of his batteries for defending the harbor area. I presumed that would be the most urgent need."

"You presume correctly, sir. That's damned good work."

"I expect we will start receiving couriers with information within the next week."

"By God, Barrett, that would be very timely. We are working out plans for Long Island right now."

"I thought as much."

Paterson cocked his head. "If I may ask, who is this man?"

"I will tell you his name, but only on one condition."

Paterson raised an eyebrow. "Now, Northcutt, not to be too short with you, but who are you to set conditions?"

"Damn it, Paterson, it must be obvious that the man's name must be secret for his safety. He will be living in the shadow of the scaffold. My condition is that only you and Howe are to be aware of it, aside from Markwood and myself. That's more people than I would prefer, in any case."

The adjutant general stared at Northcutt for a long moment. "All right, you have it. So who is this gentleman?"

"His name is Clive Harfeld. He's a lawyer, well established in Jersey with many connections. He has no children, and his wife recently died.. I counted that as fortunate for our purposes when I found it out, for there will be no family complications affecting his performance for us."

"Yes, I daresay."

"Now you know his name, but from this day forward, we will not speak it outside this office. Instead, he has identified a *nom de guerre*, if you will, that we and his associates will use when speaking or messaging him." He paused, then continued, "That name will be 'Harkness.'"

"Just Harkness?"

"That's right. Rather thoughtfully, he chose it because it begins with the same sound as his actual last name. Easier for him to get right when speaking in a hurry."

"Yes, I quite see."

Barrett cleared his throat. "And there's one other thing: Harfeld asked for funding from the army to cover expenses. And I readily agreed to that."

"Damn it to hell, Northcutt, you weren't authorized to offer that. We didn't discuss anything of that nature."

Northcutt leaned forward in his chair and looked directly into Paterson's eyes. "Now listen close, James, here's the truth of it: You can't run a spy ring without money. Harfeld, like most Americans, is wealthy in land but not cash. And he's going to need hard money to pay for the travel and lodging expenses of himself and his associates. Couriers who bring us dispatches can't travel for free." He held up a finger. "And mark this: Some of Harfeld's spies, perhaps those in locations near the enemy's camps, will be in it for the money only, not some sense of loyalty. No payment, no information. And that's damn well a fact of life."

There was a long silence as the two men stared at each other across the desk. Finally, Paterson rose from his chair, paced a few steps, then turned and said, "All right, you've made your point. I'll take it to Howe. He'll have to authorize it."

"Good, Paterson. If he agrees, you've got yourself a spy ring." Northcutt rose and went to the door.

Paterson called out, "Wait a minute, Barrett. While you were gone, a couple of convoys arrived from Europe and one from Halifax. One of the European convoys carried British troops and the other the first increment of Germans." He paused. "We're having a reception to welcome the officers from all three convoys. You're invited, of course, as a member of the staff. Tomorrow afternoon, at six. There'll be a pavilion set up right here beside headquarters."

Hand on door, Northcutt turned back and responded with a broad smile, "I shall certainly look forward to it, James."

Then Paterson raised a finger. "Barrett, hold up. I just had a thought." He thought a moment, then continued, "Mrs. Loring and her children arrived on the convoy from Halifax. She's being established in a house up at the north end of the island."

Northcutt grinned. "How convenient for the General. Undoubtedly he will be taking many horse rides northward."

"It would pay to be *careful* with your words, Barrett. But be all that as it may, it happens that you could do Howe a great favor for the reception."

"And that would be, James?"

"You know Mrs. Loring from that incident in Halifax, when you had come up from Virginia with dispatches from Dunmore."

"Yes, you mean her medical problem."

"Indeed. The General was very thankful for your assistance. And your tactfulness."

"So what is this favor you want of me now?"

"I and the General would be grateful if you could escort Mrs. Loring to the reception."

Northcutt grinned knowingly. "Ah, yes, appearances and all that." He shrugged, still smiling. "It would be my great pleasure to escort the elegant lady for the occasion."

Colonel Alexander Tresh climbed the steps to the second floor of the Broad Street Inn and walked a few steps down the hall to his door. The Treshes had engaged a two-room suite for themselves and a single adjacent room for the Moulders in the large, comfortable inn with three floors in lower Manhattan, located a few blocks from Washington's headquarters.

As he entered, he saw that Catherine was sitting in a chair next to the window, a cup of libation in hand and a newspaper in the other. Several additional newspapers were on a table beside her. She looked up, anxiety on her face, and said, "Well, my dear, did your ride with Washington go well?"

Tresh put a serious look on his countenance and clasped his hands behind his back, not speaking.

Catherine impatiently straightened in her chair and repeated the question with more emphasis. "For God's sake, Alex, don't play games with me. How did you fare?"

Tresh broke his solemn look and, smiling broadly, said, "Now, Mrs. Tresh, you are looking at Washington's newest aide-de-camp, with the rank of colonel in the Continental Army. Washington said he would consider me as an unofficial inspector general of his army. He wants me to look into the various regiments and make suggestions to improve their efficiency." He shook his head. "And after looking at the army, I can tell you that it is a very necessary function. There is a lack of discipline, lack understanding how to lay out proper campsites, and lack of effective procedures."

Rising from her chair, drink still in hand, Catherine grinned. "Why Alex, that's excellent! Excellent for us!" She started pacing back and forth, lost in thought. "Just the kind of thing we have hoped for. But of course, it's only the first step." She took a sip of her drink. "I know you will do well advising him. But, as we have said often, the real goal is for you to get a *command*. An actual *field command*. That is the way to our goal." She stopped and took another pull on the cup. "A command and a chance for you to distinguish yourself on the battlefield."

"Well, dear, let's not get ahead of ourselves. First, I must secure Washington's confidence."

"Of course, I understand that. But we must never forget our purpose in coming here to America. We have staked all your money on it. We need what counts as wealth here in this country and that is *land*. And the only way we can obtain that is if you are rewarded for your performance in battle, like that other Swiss officer—that Henry Bouquet. You told me yourself he was rewarded with land for his great victory against the Red Indians at that place called Bushy Run."

"Yes, both Pennsylvania and Maryland granted him large holdings of land."

"Exactly: it made him instantly a wealthy man."

"But of course, my dear, he never lived to enjoy it. He contracted yellow fever and died on the way to his next assignment in Florida."

Catherine grinned conspiratorially. "Don't worry, dear, I won't let you be placed in danger once we've become landowners. I want to enjoy the benefits of being mistress of a large plantation, even if it is in some backcountry province."

"Now, my dear, we must not get ahead of ourselves. I must gain Washington's confidence and prove myself a valuable member of his staff before there will be the chance of a command." He held up a hand. "And speaking of that, we have a chance to begin that process two days hence. And you can play an important role."

An inquisitive look came over Catherine's face. "How may I do that?"

"There is to be a reception with prominent people of the city who are sympathetic to the patriot cause. Senior members of the staff are to attend, and

Washington specifically mentioned that you should come, since other women will be present. It will be our introduction to American society."

She smiled and cocked her head. "I shall be most excited to make acquaintances that can help us gain favor and prominence."

"Yes, Catherine, and you do that so well."

There was a momentary silence, then Catherine, moving on to another idea, said, "Today, Elise and I walked around the part of Manhattan close to the inn. It's a nice colonial town. There are some lovely shops, which I will visit."

Tresh sighed. "Yes, I'm sure you will make it your business."

"Well, I must have a distraction while you are out on your tours of the army. But listen, now: I found out something else in my travels. A place called *Fraunces Tavern* is just around the corner from here. And it seems that it is a favorite gathering place of the army's officers—not only the staff, but also the officers from the line regiments. It would be a good place for you to spend some time and mingle with the patrons. And many of the wealthy residents of the town dally there over a libation. It will make you well known and help you establish liaisons with important people."

"Yes, that makes sense, my dear. I shall make a point of visiting the place." He put his arm around her and said, softly, "You are always so conscious of matters like that."

Catherine shot him a knowing look, one eyebrow raised. She gave him a gentle kiss on the cheek. "The Irish runaway girl learned much while working in that salon in Paris. It was a place of both *pleasure* and *business*. You have no idea how many political alliances and agreements were made there by men of wealth and power."

Chapter Five

Armies in Waiting

Mary Fraser emerged from her tent into the late afternoon sun. She was dressed in her best gown. It was pale green, which blended well with her auburn hair. She had purchased it in May in Glasgow, just a few days before the regiment had sailed for America. It had last been worn a few days later when General Murray, the Proprietary Colonel of the Black Watch, had invited her to dinner in the regimental officer's mess just after she had been appointed Matron of the Hospital. But now, in late July, after weeks at sea onboard the *Prefect*, Glasgow seemed ages ago. She looked down at the gown and decided everything was in place. She settled down in a camp chair, which was located near her fire, and waited for Lieutenant Owen McDougal, her escort for General Howe's Reception.

She had only been there for a few minutes when the lieutenant arrived. McDougal, who was tall and lithe, was assigned to the colonel's company. Owen looked down at her as she sat in the chair. "Mary, may I say you look absolutely stunning this afternoon. Other officers shall be eyeing me quite enviously at the reception."

Mary looked up at the young man. "Owen, you are being quite the flatterer today." She rose and said, "Shall we go?"

McDougal took her arm, and they were about to walk off toward headquarters when a voice called out, "Hold on there, Owen! We'll walk with you."

Mary looked around to see three other young subalterns quickly striding toward them: Lieutenants Robertson and McCally and Ensign McGrath. It was

Robertson who had spoken, and now he continued, "I say, old chap, you don't mind if we join you on the way over, do you?" Then immediately he said, "You don't mind, do you Mary?"

McDougal looked at Robertson, irritation written all over his face, but immediately he realized that politeness dictated he agree. He said in a less than enthusiastic voice, "Suit yourself, gentleman."

Mary added, "Of course, we would enjoy your company."

The headquarters was only a couple of hundred yards from the camp, so they set off at a comfortable pace.

As they walked, young McGrath spoke up. "I hear that now that the Germans are here, the campaign shall begin very shortly."

McCally said, "Yes, the word is that the navy is building landing barges to transport men and rafts to transport horses and artillery from here to Long Island."

McGrath said enthusiastically, "Aye, it can't come soon enough for me. I'm tired of all this drilling and exercising that Stirling is putting us through."

Robertson readily agreed. "Indeed, it's time we go after the rebels and put them in their place."

Mary looked at the four young men around her. She realized that all had joined the regiment since it had returned from America in 1767. All their time had been served in peacetime, mostly garrison duty in Ireland. She thought of all the campaigns she had been through as a young child with the 77th and 42nd: Carolina to fight the Cherokee, Forbes Campaign against the French at the Forks of the Ohio, against the French in the West Indies, Bouquet's march to relieve Fort Pitt, and then the advance into the Ohio Country that ended the Pontiac War. She sighed to herself: These excited young men would soon learn the reality of war, of battles, and death. She looked over the four cheerful men walking with her and shivered as she realized the probability that one or more of them would meet their fate in the upcoming campaign.

They made their way through the tents of Howe's staff and arrived at the great canvas pavilion which had been erected close by the Rose and Crown. Mary said, "I don't believe I've ever seen such a large tent."

McDougal responded, "Indeed, Mary." He looked around and continued, "And many people have already arrived."

Mary remarked, "Yes, it's a mass of officers; I've never seen so many together."

Their other three companions nodded, and Robertson spoke up. "The word is that Howe is going to make some sort of announcement about the campaign and everyone wants to hear what he has to say."

McDougal looked over at the three unwanted men, a stern look in his eyes. "Gentlemen, there's a long line of officers waiting at the counter for drinks." He looked around. "And more people arriving all the time. Shouldn't you get in the queue if you want some libation?"

The three took his meaning, and excusing themselves, started on their way over to the serving line.

McDougal called out to young McGrath. "Charles!"

The ensign stopped and turned around. "Yes, sir?"

"Would you be so kind as to get something for Mary and myself, while I keep her company?"

"That would be my pleasure, sir. What would you like, Miss Fraser? Some wine, or I was told they also have punch. Which will it be?"

Mary gave him a grin. "Something a little stronger would be to my taste. Rum, if they have it."

"Yes, ma'am." Mary could see the youngster was a little startled by her request.

McDougal asked for rum also.

They stood talking for a few moments, and then a carriage, drawn by a smart team of bays, pulled up to the pavilion. An officer jumped down, then turned and handed down a well-dressed and coiffed blonde woman in her mid-twenties.

Mary immediately recognized the lady. She leaned over to McDougal. "Owen, that's Mrs. Loring. I met her at the ball in Halifax—the one right after we got there."

"Ah, yes. I seem to remember something about you being called away to help her with some sort of lady's medical problem."

Mary simply nodded, keeping her eyes on Elizabeth and her escort as they headed to the pavilion. Then her eyes moved to Elizabeth's escort, and she realized she also recognized him. She searched her mind for a name—then she had it. "Why, Owen, that's Colonel Northcutt, the officer who summoned me to help her. Later that night, he escorted me back to the *Prefect* in Halifax Harbor."

"Ah, yes, the gentleman seems familiar." He looked at Mary. "I hope he's not planning to steal you away tonight."

Mary laughed. "Oh, Owen, that's droll. Besides, he's busy with Mrs. Loring."

Then Mary heard someone speaking her name. "Miss Fraser! Mary Fraser!" She looked around to see that Elizabeth and Northcutt had stopped near where she and McDougal stood. Elizabeth was smiling at her. She extended her hand and touched Mary's. "I've often thought of how you helped me. It was so fortunate that such a competent nurse was available that night, and I was so indisposed as not to be able to properly thank you."

Mary flushed. "No thanks is necessary, Mrs. Loring. It was my honor to assist you with your problem."

There was an awkward moment when neither woman quite knew what more to say, and Northcutt quickly moved to fill the void. "Hello, Miss Fraser. It's good to see you again. I had not thought to be so fortunate so soon after Halifax."

"Nor I, Colonel. With you headed back to Virginia, I thought the odds of our meeting again would be most unlikely."

"Well, unfortunate as developments were in the Tidewater, it seems there is a silver lining after all, for events brought me to Staten Island to serve on General Howe's staff and allow us to meet again."

Mary smiled. "That's very gallant of you, Colonel Northcutt."

Barrett replied, "May I take it that you are still with the hospital of the 42nd, Miss Fraser?"

"Indeed I am. Our encampment is close by the headquarters here."

At that moment a young captain, an aide to Howe, approached them. "Good evening, Colonel Northcutt. Good evening, Mrs. Loring. The General has asked me to inform you that the German officers have just arrived, and he thinks you would like to meet them. I'm to escort you to join him." Then he quickly looked over at Northcutt. "And you also, of course."

Northcutt said quickly, "Mrs. Loring hasn't had time to get a refreshment. I'll obtain a drink for her and then join you presently."

Elizabeth looked over at him and said, "That will be so kind of you, Barrett. And remember, I'd like something substantial, not some weak ladies' punch."

"I quite remember your preferences, Mrs. Loring."

Elizabeth smiled and said, "Of course you do, Barrett." Then she looked over at Mary. "Miss Fraser, I've just moved into a house up at the northern end of the island. A place deserted by a rebel sympathizer who departed rather hastily when the army landed. Right now the place is full of unpacked trunks and such, but when we get things put together somewhat, I'll send you a note, and we can have tea together, by way of an overdue thank you for your assistance in Halifax."

"That would be my pleasure, Mrs. Loring."

"Oh Mary, please call me Betsy. Everyone else does, and I should like us to be on a first name basis."

Mary nodded and smiled. "Yes, Betsy."

Elizabeth said, "Good. It will be soon!" Then she turned to the aide. "Shall we go?"

Just as Mrs. Loring and the aide departed, Ensign McGrath arrived with their drinks. "Sorry it took so long, but some Dragoon officers had just arrived and were all getting their drinks."

Mary took her drink and said, "Not to worry, Jonathan, I just appreciated your kindness."

McGrath said, "Yes, Ma'am. Thank you. I'll just go over and join the others." He pointed to where Robertson and McCally were standing with several other subalterns of the regiment.

McDougal motioned toward the other side of the pavilion where the counter stood. "There, Mary: The officers of the 16th Light Dragoons. Look at their gaudy uniforms. They were designed by General Burgoyne himself, who raised them and was their first commandant. That's why, while they are officially 'The Queen's Own,' they are called 'Burgoyne's Beauties' throughout the army."

Mary looked where McDougal had indicated and saw a group of ten or twelve officers standing together. They had short red jackets with the blue facing of a royal regiment, white riding breeches, and highly polished knee-length riding boots. Their helmets, which had been placed on a table with the hats of the officers from other regiments, were distinctive: black with a red-dyed horse hair crest running from front to back.

And then she saw Nevin Haldane, cup in hand, talking with another cornet of the 16th. At the sight, a knot like a great fist formed in her stomach. Her eyes froze on the nephew of the man she had killed. At any moment, he could look across the crowd and recognize her. She suddenly realized how few women were in the assemblage and that her auburn hair made her stand out even more. She felt fear course through her body and instantly realized that she must do something to escape the reception.

She reached out and touched McDougal's arm and whispered to him. "Owen, this rum seems to have had a bad effect on my stomach, and I suddenly have a pain in my forehead. Regrettably, I believe I should return to my tent."

A look of puzzlement, then concern, came over the lieutenant's face. "Mary, is it so distressing that you must leave immediately? General Howe is about to speak. He will be talking about plans for the start of the campaign."

"Owen, I don't know why I feel so indisposed. Perhaps it is something I ate mixing with the rum, but it is urgent that I return to camp." She paused a moment. "You need not accompany me. I know the way."

"Of course I'll accompany you!" He put his drink down on a nearby table, then took hers and put it down. Then he gave her his arm and said to Northcutt, "Colonel, I apologize. We must take our leave since Miss Fraser is feeling ill."

Northcutt, who had been looking around, nodded and said, "Well, it was a pleasure meeting you, Lieutenant." He smiled at Mary. "And my great pleasure in seeing you again. I'm sorry you are feeling poorly." Then he motioned toward the counter. "Well, the crowd around the bar has diminished, and in any case I must fetch Mrs. Loring her libation. Good day to you."

It took just a few minutes for Mary and her escort to arrive at the hospital area of the encampment. Mary turned to McDougal and said, "Owen, I am so sorry to have caused you so much inconvenience. Please hurry back to the reception, so you won't miss what the general has to say."

McDougal nodded. "Yes, and I shall check on you after the reception and tell you about what he announces."

"That would be lovely, Owen."

The lieutenant turned and strode off. Mary pulled back the flap of the tent, went inside, and sat down on her cot. She took her straw hat off and then put her hands to her head as she tried to think what to do. She realized she was shivering despite the summer heat.

Suddenly a feminine voice interrupted her thoughts. "Na, Mary Fraser, what are you doing back here at the camp so soon after you just left? Surely that officer's gatherin' hasn't ended already?" She cocked her head. "And why are your hands shakin' so much?"

Mary looked up to see the tall, thin, angular figure of Kathryn O'Hara standing in the tent opening, one hand holding the flap aside. Kathryn was the wife of

Sergeant Archie O'Hara and had been Mary's closest friend in the hospital since the march to Fort Pitt in 1763.

Mary sighed and looked up. "Kathryn, something terrible has occurred. The nephew of the man I killed at Bonniecrest Manor has arrived with the 16th Light Dragoons. He was at the reception, and I had to leave before he discovered me."

"Ah, now, so he knows you by sight?"

"He was at the manor when his uncle tried to have his way with me." She sighed deeply. "The fact was, he was trying to court me, despite the fact that he's younger than I am. It had been planned for me to go riding with him before that terrible night occurred." She paused a moment, then continued, "After I was forced to kill Gerald, his son Dougal and Nevin pursued me across Scotland."

"Aye, I remember hearin' some of that from Bob Kirkwood when you and he came to Glasgow." Kathryn took a deep breath. "What are you going to do now? Will ye flee again?"

Mary didn't answer for a long time. Then she shook her head and said slowly, "I thought about it, Kathryn, but I can't do that. I owe so much to General Murray, Colonel Stirling, and Major McDonald. They protected me from the law and took me on as matron of the hospital. I promised I wouldn't leave the regiment until the rebellion was settled." She shrugged. "All I can do is find out where the 16th is camped here on the island and stay away from there, and hope fortune will keep me away from Devin's eyes."

Kathryn put her hand to her chin. "Aye, and remember, you have so many friends here. I'll let them know what be goin' on, and we'll keep a watch for officers of the 16th. And the truth is, it's a big army. When the campaign begins, it will be spread out, and the cavalry will be, as always, on scout at the edges of our army, so it's likely not to be near us. I'm sayin', you can be safe, less some trick of fate puts you right in this Nevin fellow's path."

"Yes, Kathryn, we must trust to vigilance and fortune. It's all we can do."

—∾—

Dusk was settling in the evening sky as Barrett Northcutt stood in line at the bar to get drinks for himself and Betsy. As he waited, Northcutt's mind wandered to thoughts of Mary Fraser. Upon first sighting her as he and Betsy had arrived, he had realized she was as devastatingly lovely as he remembered from when he had first seen her at the ball in Halifax. When Betsy had been escorted off to join the general, he had been gratified by the opportunity to spend some time with Mary and had been looking for a way to tactfully broach the idea of calling upon her. Before he could do that, she had abruptly declared she was indisposed. Now he couldn't get her sudden need to leave the reception out of his mind. The more he thought about it, the more puzzling it became. He was turning it over in his mind when it struck him that it had occurred just after McDougal had mentioned that the officers of the 16th Light Dragoons had arrived. And while the lieutenant had droned on about them, he had seen Mary's face suddenly take on a look of anxiety. It dawned on Northcutt that something about the 16th—or more likely someone in the 16th—was the cause of her anxiety.

Northcutt's thoughts were interrupted by a familiar voice. "By God, Barrett Northcutt! Didn't realize you were here in New York."

Northcutt turned to see his old friend, Colonel Thomas Stirling, standing by the bar. Next to him was another officer, who looked familiar, and then he realized it was the senior major of the Black Watch whom he had met in Halifax. With them was an officer in a German uniform, and Northcutt was startled to see he had a saber scar down the left side of his face. Barrett reached out to take Stirling's hand. "Indeed, I arrived some time ago from Virginia. Dunmore sailed back to England, and I am now on Howe's staff."

Stirling's face lit up. "Well, that's as good news as I've had. We should be able to put together a table for some cards, just like the old times when we were in Manhattan and you were advising the governor."

"Nothing would suit me better, Thomas," responded Barrett.

Stirling motioned to the major. "You remember Charles McDonald, my second, don't you?"

"Of course. Good to see you, Charles."

McDonald shook hands with Northcutt.

Then Stirling turned to the scarred officer. "And I have another old friend with me. This is Captain Ernst Wolff of the Hesse-Cassel Jaeger Corps. Ernst and I knew each other in Europe in the early days of the Seven Years War, when I was in Dutch service."

Northcutt shook hands with Wolff and then said, "I'm a bit embarrassed. I'm not familiar with the term 'Jaeger.' Perhaps you could enlighten me?"

Stirling laughed. "It's simple, old boy. Jaeger means *hunter* in German. And it's the name they give to their light foot. The principality of Hesse-Cassel has sent a battalion of them over here, and Ernst leads the fourth company."

Wolff spoke up in heavily accented English. "Ja, I have nearly a hundred men, all experienced woodsmen and rifle marksmen."

McDonald interjected, "Our friend Ernst can't wait to go up against some of the American riflemen."

Wolff smiled slyly. "Yes, we have heard great stories about these American hunters, with their great long rifles. We are quite eager to see if these woodsmen in their long frocks are as good as the legends one hears about them and to see if their marksmanship measures up to ours."

Barrett looked Wolff in the eye. "Captain, I witnessed Virginia riflemen in action in 1774 against the Shawnee and Mingo warriors. I believe you will find them worthy opponents for your men. They are indeed excellent shots and have mastered fighting in the bush."

Ernst Wolff smiled. "Well, sir, I relish meeting them on the skirmish line."

Stirling put his hand on the Hessian's arm. "My old friend, I expect you will soon get your chance." Then he looked back to Northcutt. "By the way, Ernst is a very good man with cards, so I say we have our four. I propose we get together one evening for a game."

At that moment the barkeep spoke up. "Sir, what would you like?"

Northcutt said to the others, "It's been a pleasure, gentlemen, and I eagerly accept the proposal for a night at the table." He pointed to the bar. "But I'm ordering for Mrs. Loring. And I'm sure she's getting impatient."

Stirling laughed. "Knowing Betsy, I cannot but agree. You'd best get on with it, Barrett."

Northcutt nodded to McDonald and said to the German, "Sir, a pleasure to meet you." Then he made his order.

A few minutes later, Barrett stood with Betsy Loring listening as General William Howe began his announcements. The officers of the army—British and German—stood gathered together as their commander began speaking. First he welcomed the German contingent and called for Lieutenant General Leopold

Philip von Heister, their senior officer, to join him. After a few complimentary words about the general, Howe launched into a discussion of the upcoming campaign. He went on for some time about the general elements of the plan, but then he paused and smiled for a moment, and Barrett realized that the important part of the talk was about to begin.

Howe cleared his throat and said, "And now, gentlemen," he paused momentarily, then added, "and ladies." He motioned toward the few women who were in the assemblage. "With the arrival of our German allies and the latest convoy of troops from England, we are nearly ready to begin action against these colonials. Of course, we need to give the new regiments some time to be integrated into our organization and get the horses of the 16th ashore and recovered from the rigors of the voyage. But I assure you, soon enough, we will move. Then, with the Navy's assistance, we will take to boats and barges and land across the harbor"—he pointed in the general direction of Long Island—"and confront the enemy with irresistible force."

There was a round of applause and calls of "Here, here!"

"Meanwhile, while we busy ourselves with training and final preparations, the Navy will entertain Washington with movements of ships around the harbor to confuse the rebels about our true intentions and ensure that they must disperse their forces among different possible landing sites. They will also be probing the rebel artillery positions." He paused as if considering his next words, then said, "I know you are all anxious to teach these misguided subjects a lesson about defying their King and Parliament. However, we must be patient for just a little longer. I vow to you that we will be ready to move in a few short weeks, not months."

Howe said a few more words, then concluded by wishing everyone luck in the coming campaign. Northcutt was just mulling all that had been said when he heard a voice speaking his name. He looked around to see that Paterson was approaching him.

"Barrett, glad to find you here." The colonel stopped by his side and spoke very softly. "Got good news for you. Had a word with Howe about that," he stopped for a moment and looked around to see who might be in earshot, then continued, "that *little project* you talked about to me yesterday."

"Indeed, James?"

"Yes, the General is enthusiastic. The, uh, *resources* you asked for will definitely be forthcoming. So you can get on with it."

Northcutt was ebullient. "Marvelous, James. Things will start moving immediately. I should have some news for you in a few days."

"That would be provident. You heard what the General said about the start of the campaign. Whatever you can develop before it starts would be appreciated."

At that moment Betsy tapped Northcutt on the shoulder. "Barrett, I don't want to disturb you and Colonel Paterson, but things are breaking up, and I'm ready to leave. Could you get the carriage?"

"Certainly, Mrs. Loring. That would be my pleasure."

In a few minutes they were on their way northward, passing regimental encampments one after another as they drove. With darkness coming on, the night was illuminated by the campfires in long rows along company streets. Betsy leaned over and remarked, "With all the fires, it looks so cheerful, even gay. Funny to think it is all part of war."

"Yes, Betsy, quite ironic when you think on it."

There were a few moments of silence as the carriage drove on, then Betsy turned to him, "Barrett, I need a favor."

"Whatever I can do, Betsy."

"It's about Mary Fraser. I do want to make friends with her. There are so few women here on the island. And after that night in Halifax, I feel comfortable with her. I've asked Mary to tea as soon as I can get the house organized, but it's a bit of a trip and it might be difficult for her. You are on the staff, can you help me by acting as my go-between with her and making sure that she has transportation to come and visit me now and then?"

"Why, that would be my pleasure, Betsy. I shall be glad to make all the arrangements whenever you want."

Betsy sat back in the cushions of the carriage. "I shall be so thankful, Barrett."

Northcutt looked off into the fields and army camps and felt excitement welling up inside. He thought, *Now, by God, I have an excuse to stay in touch with Mary!* It occurred to him that seemingly even providence was on his side in the pursuit of the beautiful Scots woman who had taken hold of his heart. *He would waste no time in visiting her on behalf of Mrs. Loring.*

—ɱ—

Wend Eckert, seated at a table in front of his tent, was going over some company papers. It was early morning on a sunny day, and a canvas fly had been rigged over the desk to shield him from its glare and heat. The company was encamped in a vacant lot near Washington's headquarters. Another vacant lot adjoined and that served as the camp of the Life Guard, which provided Washington's personal security.

Wend was lost in thought when Billy Wood interrupted him. "Cap'n, there's an officer here to see you. He be a cap'n like you and says he works for General Washington himself."

Wend looked up to see a tall officer in a well-tailored, immaculate uniform, standing beside Billy. His coat was blue with white facings. The waistcoat and breeches were also white, and he wore black gaiters. A black hat, with a blue and white feather, was tucked under his arm. All in all, it was quite elegant, much more so than the norm which Wend had seen in the army.

In the clipped accent of New England, the officer said, "Hello, sir. I presume you are, eh, Eckert? I'm Caleb Gibbs, commandant of Washington's Life Guards. I thought it was time to come over and introduce myself, seeing as you are going to be camped alongside us for a time." He cleared his throat. "Not to mention, I do have a spot of business with you."

Wend rose and extended his hand. "Glad to meet you, sir." He motioned toward a chair. "Have a seat."

Gibbs looked critically at the seat of the chair, brushed it with a pair of gloves he held in his left hand, and then sat down. Wend said, "I have some coffee at the fire, which is still warm."

Caleb held up his hand. "I've just had some *tea*." He smiled. "It happens we still have a small supply in the Guard."

Wend said dryly, "How *fortunate* for you, sir."

Gibbs nodded. "Indeed, sir. However, as I mentioned, I came on a bit of business. Colonel Grayson tells me that you are going to be here under Washington's direct command until he figures out where you'll be permanently assigned." He paused a second, then leaned forward as if he were imparting confidential information, "He implied they're waiting for a full Virginia regiment to arrive, and then you may become their light company."

"That's more than I know, sir. They just told me to set up camp here and wait for orders."

Gibbs laughed. "Well, now, I'm glad I could provide you some useful information. But to get down to business, it's been arranged for you to receive your provisions and other supplies through my command while you are here. So I thought to get a count of your company strength."

"That's easy. We have one hundred men, four officers, six women, and four children."

A look of mild surprise came over Gibbs' face. "Indeed, sir? One hundred—well, you are at full strength. Not that common in this army." He looked around and then said, "I see you have a number of horses with you. I would suggest that you combine your picket line with ours—we have a cavalry element. It will make it more efficient to fodder and grain them and keep their leavings in one place."

"That makes sense, Caleb. I'll have my first lieutenant make arrangements."

As he spoke, Donegal arrived and stood by, obviously wanting to talk about something. Gibbs rose. "I see company matters await you, so I will not take any more of your time at the moment."

Wend also stood up and said, "Captain, this is my company sergeant, Donegal."

"Ah, yes." Gibbs looked the Highlander over quickly and stared at the Highland bonnet for a long moment. "Send him over to meet my sergeant, Hollister. They'll need to work together."

Wend nodded. "Indeed."

"One other thing, Eckert. Tomorrow evening, there's a reception for Washington and his staff hosted by a certain Mr. and Mrs. Medford. The idea is to have some of the important people of Manhattan meet the officers. Grayson says that since you are right under Washington's command at the moment, you might as well attend the affair." He smiled slyly. "And Grayson says Washington wants an officer from Virginia there." He smiled. "I'll meet with you at six tomorrow and show you the way."

"Certainly, Gibbs. I'll be ready."

With that, the Guard captain turned and headed back to his own lines, taking a brisk salute rendered by Donegal.

Donegal leaned up against one of the posts holding up the fly and looked casually at the back of the departing Gibbs. "A bit stuffy, ain't he? Truth is, I've found officers of Guards in every army are snots."

Wend shrugged. "Well, he was a bit prim, but we shall have to work with him." Then Wend sat down and asked, "What's toward, Simon?"

"Ah, na, Wend, I've got the morning muster, if it please you."

"Give me a quick report."

"All's well, mostly. We got two men who say they're not feelin' well, so I gave them light duty. And young Patricia Carver is movin' along with her pregnancy. She's showin' more than ever, and her Jed says she's startin' to have the sickness."

Wend thought a moment. "Have Mrs. Flannagan look in on her. There's no woman knows more about bearing children in an army camp than her."

"Na, the thought had occurred to me on my very own." Donegal's face wrinkled up, then he said, "And another thing to tell you: Horner wants to take the day off. He wants to take care of personal business."

"What kind of personal business would Andrew have here in Manhattan?"

"Now just think about that, Wend."

Wend put his hand to his forehead. "Oh, damn!" He took a deep breath. "He wants to go try to find Emily Crider."

"You've got that right. He's heard that the esteemed Mrs. McGraw's wagons are camped out in a meadow on the edge of town and he's fevered to get there. Seems McGraw and her girls are quite popular throughout the army."

"Yes, and I expect Miss Crider has been very busy. I wish I could have dissuaded him from this."

"Well, you did get him to take up with Joseph Hornbeck's girl, that Frieda. She's got a pretty face and big tits, not to mention nice broad hips. A good German girl who will bear children easily. You even gave him leave to use Peggy's little chaise and horse to ride the girl around. Damned shame it didn't take."

Wend sat down in his chair and shook his head. "That girl disappointed me. She didn't know her business. Being courted by an up-and-coming tradesman should have thrilled her. I thought she would have wasted little time bedding Andrew in the hay, or the woods, or a loft somewhere. If she could have got herself pregnant, we wouldn't have to worry about Emily Crider, and Andrew would be back at Eckert Ridge, married off and working in my shop." Wend puckered up his lips in frustration. "Damn, damn, damn."

Donegal leaned against one of the posts supporting the fly. "So does Horner get his time off?"

"He's a contract gunsmith, not a soldier. I can't really control his time. It's just like Andrew to be polite about it. Of course he can go chase down Emily." Wend sighed. "I just hope he is not disappointed in how she is likely to have changed since he met her at Colleen McGraw's tavern back in Maryland."

"Well na, he knew back then she was a tart and that no kept him from getting sweet on her." He raised his eyebrows and grinned knowingly at Wend. "And he wouldn't be the first gunsmith I know of who married a woman who has taken money for providing pleasure."

Wend glared at his friend. "Damn you, Simon. Get out of here and send Horner on his way. And get the men busy on some serious drilling. They can use it after all the time on that ship and the march up here from Philadelphia."

Colleen McGraw sat at a table under the fly of her tent, going over the business returns for the last month. She was in an ebullient mood, for things had gone very well. *Very well*, indeed. There was admirable profit for the month. In fact, she reflected, there had been an excellent profit for the entire time since they had arrived in New York in mid-May. She was well on the way to recovering all the cost of investing in the wagons, horses, tents, and other material necessary to take her business on the road. She sat back in her chair and a thought struck her: *After all these sales, we must restock our goods again. I'll have to have Edna take inventory and make a list of what we need. Whiskey is a definite item; we've been going through that fast.*

"Colleen, I need to talk to you."

Looking up, Colleen saw her manager, Edna Farley, standing before the table. Colleen laughed. *It's as if she read my mind!* Pointing to the reports, she said, "Yes, indeed, Edna. I was just about to send for you. Looking at these returns, we've got to make a purchase of goods. We must take inventory quickly to understand what we need."

"Inventory be *damned*. Inventory is the last thing you need to have on your mind at this moment. There's something a lot more serious you need to deal with."

"More serious? Edna, what precisely do you mean?"

"I mean you're about to lose your prettiest girl, that's what. That young apprentice gunsmith from Virginia, that Andrew Horner, is here and is gettin' ready to take Emily away. They're down in her tent packing her things now."

Colleen sprang out of her seat. "Damn! Damn! Damn!"

"Yes, my thoughts precisely when I discovered them together." She cocked her head. "Remember we talked about this back when she got that letter from him, in April it was, just before we left Fredericktown? You wasn't worried 'cause you was so sure he'd think better of it or would take a long time to find her. Seems he works pretty fast. And I can tell you, lookin' at them together just now, they be serious about it. If you're gonna stop it, you better get down there posthaste."

"You're damn right I'm going down there! He's got another thing coming if he thinks he can just walk in here and take my best girl away. Not with all I've got invested in her."

She started off toward the tents where the women stayed. And then after a few steps she had a second thought. She stopped abruptly and turned on her heel to look at Edna. "No! I'm *not* going to them. *You* get down there and take Charley with you and make sure he's got a firelock." She gritted her teeth in anger and pumped her fist up and down. "And you bring them both up here to me. We'll settle this right here, *on my territory and on my terms.*"

Edna raised her eyebrows, then smiled and turned to go. She said, over her shoulder, "Charley and I will have them here shortly, if we have to drag them all the way."

As Edna hurried off, Colleen went back to the table and resumed her seat. She took a deep breath, then composed herself and quickly organized her thoughts. Finally, she practiced in her mind how she would handle the couple and what she would say to them.

She didn't have long to wait. In just a few moments, Edna appeared from behind a tent, followed by the young couple walking side by side, her son Charlie following behind with a fowling piece in the crook of his arm. Soon they were at her tent, and Edna pointed for the two to stand before the table.

Colleen remained seated, crossed her arms in front of herself, and stared silently at Horner and Emily as if thinking what to say. Emily had a look of trepidation on her face and had linked her arm with the young man. She was pressing up against his side as if to absorb strength from his presence. Horner's face exuded defiance, and a slight smile, perhaps betraying nervousness, was on his lips. Colleen continued her silence, to let the tension build.

Finally, Horner spoke up. "Good day, Mrs. McGraw. Good to see you again."

Continuing to stare at the lad, Colleen said, "Yes, Mr. Horner. I guess it's been seven or eight months since you and Wend Eckert and all those Virginia men were at my tavern in Fredericktown." She paused for a long moment, then continued. "So why don't you tell me why you are here in New York and in Emily's tent?"

Andrew pulled the girl even closer to him, if that was possible, and gulped. Then he stood as upright, holding his head as high as he could manage, and spoke in an assertive tone, "I'm here to get Emily and take her to my camp. We plan to get married."

Colleen looked at Emily. "And do you want to marry Mr. Horner?"

"Oh, yes, ma'am. I never felt like this about any other man."

Colleen nodded and said in an ironic tone, "Yes, considering what I employ you for, I dare say that's true." Then she put on as broad a smile as she could manage, raised her hands with palms open, and said, "Who am I to stop true love? Of course you two should marry, and you certainly have my blessing and all my hope for a long life together." She saw that Edna was looking at her with puzzlement in her eyes. There were expressions of ecstasy on the faces of the two young people before her.

After a moment, she continued, "But there's the matter of Emily's agreement with me."

Horner cocked his head and asked, "Agreement? What is that, ma'am?"

"When we left Fredericktown, all the girls agreed that they would work for me for at least a year." She looked over at the girl. "You *do* remember that, Emily?"

Emily's face went from joy to anxiety. "Yes, ma'am."

"And the reason for that was so that I could get my money back for all the things I bought for you for your job and so that I could make a profit. The gowns, the lady's underthings, stockings, the shoes. I spent a lot of hard cash on you. And of course, I have to feed you." She looked over at Andrew while pointing to Emily. "You wouldn't believe how much this thin little slip of a girl eats!" She shrugged. "But you'll find out once she's living with you."

"So like I said, you two can get married. But Emily has to continue working for me until the year's over."

Colleen was gratified to see the expression of shock that spread across Horner's face.

"But Mrs. McGraw, you mean she has to keep on," he took a deep breath, "keep on being with other men?"

Spreading her hands wide again, Colleen shrugged and said in a smooth voice, "My dear Andrew, that's what she *does*. And why not? I've known many a married woman who practiced the trade." She paused and let that sink in. "Of course, there's a way she wouldn't have to do that, and she could leave today."

Horner perked up. "How do you mean?"

"I mean, you could pay me the money she'd make over the rest of that year. I'd let her go in a minute for cash."

Both of the young people sagged. Andrew shook his head. "I used all the money I had saved to purchase a cart and horses."

Emily said, "Colleen, you know I don't have that much, even though I been saving my share of what the men pay."

"Then you need to fulfill what you promised me. It's a contract, like the lawyers talk about. In fact, if you try to leave this camp, I will go to a lawyer to protect my rights." She looked over at Andrew. "Now, you can come visit Emily when she ain't working. I give all the girls a day off every week." She looked between the two of them. "Emily can do whatever she wants on that day."

The two of them stood there, dejection all over their faces. Edna and Colleen exchanged smiles. Then Colleen thought of something. "Now, Mr. Horner, how did you get here and happen to find us? I recall you are an apprentice to Wend Eckert. How is it that he lets you travel all over the country?"

"I'm finished with my apprenticeship. I'm a free journeyman, practicing my trade to serve the army's needs. And I'm traveling with the Frederick County Light Foot Company. We just arrived, and we're camped down near Washington's headquarters. I found you 'cause everyone in the army knows where the Red Vixen is camped."

"Ah, yes, that's true enough. Our reputation has spread in the short time we've been with the army. Well, be sure to tell your captain and your friends in the company about us. We have everything a man would want that the army can't supply. And officers especially like us." Colleen leaned back in her chair. "And who does your captain happen to be? Perhaps he'd like to come by to meet me and see what we have to offer."

A mischievous smile came over Andrew Horner's face. He hesitated a moment and then said, "Why, my captain is Wend Eckert."

Colleen snapped forward in the chair and stiffened. "Eckert is here? Here in New York?"

"I just said so. Down in Manhattan, camped right next to Washington's Life Guard."

Colleen managed to keep a stone face to cover the shock of finding that Wend was in New York and, in fact, just a few blocks from where she sat. She thought for a moment on what to say. Then it came to her. "Well, you might remember me to Captain Eckert." She looked first at Emily and then to Andrew. "In fact, I just had a thought: Perhaps you should mention your situation to him and suggest he pay me a call to discuss things."

Horner looked at her questioningly. "Excuse me, Mrs. McGraw, I don't understand what you mean by that."

"It's not necessary, at least at this point. Just tell him what I said." She rose from her seat. "And I suggest you now go back to your camp or go about other business, if you have some. It's time for Emily and all the other girls to get ready for the evening's business."

Dejection spread all over Emily's face. Andrew looked at her. "I'll take you back to your tent before I go."

The girl nodded and said in a resigned voice, "Yes, I'd like that."

Without saying another word to Colleen, the two walked off hand in hand.

Edna stared at Colleen for a moment. "Well, I'd say you handled them well, at least for now. But I don't understand that last bit, the part about Eckert coming to see you."

Colleen sat down and leaned back in her chair. "My dear Edna, think on it. I consider that Wend Eckert owes me a debt."

"Yes, I've heard you say that in the past. It's about something that happened when you were both young."

"Indeed it is. Well, you know I *always* get paid what is owed to me. It may take a while, but one way or another, I always collect."

Edna laughed. "Yes, one way or another. Sometimes the 'another' is worse than the original."

"Yes. And now there's a chance I can finally collect Wend Eckert's debt over this little love affair between those two youngsters."

—m—

Clive Harfeld, walking with his friend John Parkinson, a prosperous merchant of Manhattan, strode up the walkway to the large mansion owned by Mr. Colby Selwyn Medford, which was located in lower Manhattan. He turned to his friend and asked, "John, are you sure it's not impolite for me to join you at this affair? I just called on you unannounced since I was visiting the city, and of course I wasn't on the invitation list."

Parkinson said, "Of course it's fine. Colby is my closest friend, and Carolyn is a gracious hostess. I dine with them frequently, and I play cards with Colby every week. They will be more than glad to meet you and have you join the reception. After all, this is supposed to be an opportunity for distinguished residents to meet and mix with Washington's staff and senior officers. Given your land holdings in Jersey and New York and the amount of business you do here in the city, you certainly qualify as 'distinguished,' if anyone does."

Shortly, they climbed the steps to the portico and came to the front doors, which were standing open and where a butler was waiting to greet arriving guests. Parkinson said, "Good evening, Charles. Good to see you."

The servant made a slight bow. "And you, sir. Just go right down the hall to the ballroom in the rear."

Soon the two stood at the entrance of the ballroom. It was crowded with military officers and civilians in stylish, well-tailored clothing, all holding drinks and standing in groups as they conversed. Parkinson leaned over and said, "Clive, the one in the corner with all the people gathered around him is Washington."

Harfeld responded, "My God, he's tall. The man qualifies as a small giant."

"Well, my dear Clive, that is only a bit of an overstatement." He leaned toward his friend and said in a low voice, "But one must admit that standing above other men does help enhance his presence and influence in both the political and military spheres."

As he was speaking, a blond-haired woman who Harfeld took to be in her early forties broke off from a cluster of people and, drink in hand, came toward them. Parkinson said, "Ah, here comes our hostess, Carolyn."

She held out her hand to Parkinson and exclaimed, "My dear John! I'm so glad you could come." She took his hand and then looked over at Clive. "And who is this gentleman you have brought with you?"

Parkinson put his hand on Harfeld's arm and introduced him, explaining, "Clive's a lawyer from New Jersey, here in Manhattan for a few days on business."

Carolyn smiled and said, "Welcome to our home, Mr. Harfeld, and I hope you enjoy the evening." Then a mischievous look came over her face. "Now, it happens that you two gentlemen can help me out. I know you would like to meet General Washington, but he's literally besieged by guests at the moment. On the other hand, General Charles Lee is standing almost alone over by that table." She motioned toward a corner of the room.

Harfeld's eyes followed her hand and saw a tall, rail-thin officer with a drink in his hand and a single other individual, an army captain, standing with him.

"So," said Carolyn, "allow me to take you over there and introduce you. If you entertain him for a while, I promise I'll come back and intervene to take you over to Washington when the crowd has thinned."

Parkinson laughed. "It would be our pleasure to help you out."

Carolyn took each by the arm and escorted them over to where Lee stood. As they approached, the general turned to look at them. The hostess said brightly, "General Lee, I have brought you some guests who are anxious to meet you." She introduced the two friends, then said, "General Lee has just arrived from Charleston in South Carolina to help defend us from the British. He commanded the forces that drove away the British expedition which attempted to take that city." Then she motioned to the captain. "This is Captain Eckert, of Virginia. He has just arrived in Manhattan with a company of light foot."

Then she said, "Gentlemen, I would love to remain and talk with you all, but alas, I must see to my other guests," and was gone, leaving the four of them.

Parkinson nodded to Eckert and said, "Nice to meet you, Captain."

"And I, to meet you two gentlemen," responded Eckert.

Harfeld thought he saw gratitude in the captain's eyes that they had relieved him from being Lee's only companion.

Then Parkinson congratulated Lee on the victory and asked, "To what do you attribute your success at Charleston?"

Lee clasped his hands behind his back and said, "It is, of course, sir, a question of experience, a factor which is sorely missing in most of our officer ranks."

Parkinson looked over at Harfeld, a puzzled look in his eyes, and asked Lee, "Could you amplify that, sir?"

The general shrugged and made a slight roll of his eyes. "It takes years of experience in the military to achieve successful results. I, for example, have spent twenty years in the British and other armies. I was, of course, initially commissioned into a British regiment and spent time serving in the Polish and Dutch service. There is no substitute for that, sir."

Clive bit his lip, then said, "So you think Continental forces suffer from a lack of that kind of experience?"

"Of course. Few officers have any experience leading large forces against European armies." Lee motioned to Eckert. "For example, the captain here has only fought tribal warriors on the western border. That has clearly not prepared him to engage regular forces."

Eckert spoke up. "Well, sir, I would point out that General Washington, at least, has years of experience. He raised and led the Virginia Regiment during the French War. He was on Braddock's staff and led his regiment during General Forbes' campaign to take Fort Duquesne at the Forks of the Ohio. There were French regulars in both of those campaigns."

Lee's face wrinkled up in what could only be taken as disdain. "I admire our Commanding General for his experience fighting Indians and French colonial troops on the frontier, but, sir, I must respectfully point out that he has never led troops in open-field battle against first-rate European regulars. I suggest that is a much different matter."

Harfeld found that answer very interesting. "So you believe that officers who have had that experience would be much better suited to command our army?"

A sly look came into Lee's eyes. He hesitated for a few seconds before answering. "Without a doubt. There are indeed senior officers in the army who have commanded regulars in Europe—myself and General Horatio Gates, for example. We both were commandants of battalions in action during the French War and other conflicts." He stopped again and waved a finger. "But, Mr. Harfeld, we must remember that command of the entire army is not just a matter of tactical skill. It is also a matter of political considerations. Our current commanding general was, of course, selected because, as a Virginian, his elevation to the office would help convince the southern colonies to join their cause with those of New England, where the insurrection began."

Harfeld noted that the general looked between his listeners with barely concealed defiance in his eyes.

Parkinson asked, "Well, sir, given your *great* experience, what are the chances of our forces successfully holding New York against the British? That is the question on everyone's lips."

"There is *no* question, sir. Our force will *never* be able to hold New York. The British are stronger, and their ability to attack at any point is provided by their navy. The plain truth is, the city shall be lost, sooner or later."

Harfeld noted a look of dismay in John Parkinson's countenance. "You are so sure, General Lee?"

"The fact is, we could not hold the place even with ten thousand more troops. Our presence here is, like Washington's appointment, a matter of political factors. Defending the city was necessary to achieve this colony's agreement to endorse independence." He took a deep breath and continued, "Were I in command, I would withdraw to favorable ground where we had some chance of meeting the British in more favorable tactical conditions."

There was a moment of silence, and Harfeld saw that Lee had a slight smile on his face. He said, "Well, General, have you made your views known to Washington?"

"Not only to Washington, but also in great detail to the military committee in Philadelphia on my way to join the army." He shrugged, "I must say, I feel my comments made a significant impression on some members of the Congress. I think once the failure of this campaign becomes evident, we shall soon see some changes."

Harfeld asked the obvious question, "And what are those changes?"

Lee waved his hand. "Let me summarize: Washington will dutifully attempt to defend the city." He shrugged. "However, the best outcome we can hope for once the British assault begins is a delaying action and orderly withdrawal in defeat. Then there will have to be a reconsideration of how the war is conducted."

Parkinson and Harfeld stood in shocked silence at the general's certainty and assertive outspokenness. Meanwhile, Lee stared at them, a knowing smile on his face, as if enjoying their reaction.

Harfeld asked, "Well, if this withdrawal is carried out, where would you engage in a battle with the British? How would you defeat them?"

Lee smiled. "Gentlemen, as I told members of Congress, I would not undertake to fight the British on the open battlefield. That would be meeting them on their own terms and would also inevitably lead to defeat." He looked at the two in turn. "I would instead disperse the Continental Army into small groups, use it to support the local militias in a war of raids and ambushes. In short, avoid open battle and bleed the British until they decide the game is not worth the price and time. Sooner or later, they must weary of the conflict and come to negotiations."

Harfeld was about to ask how he could be sure that it would not be the Americans who would tire of such a conflict when Carolyn's voice interrupted. "Well, General Lee, I have brought you someone I believe you know from your past."

The men turned to look. Harfeld saw Mrs. Medford had a couple in train. The man was in the blue and white uniform, which was different from the Continental Army. The lady accompanying him was a stunning raven-haired woman, taller than average with a graceful, willowy frame, and dressed in an elegant gown.

Carolyn said to the group: "Gentlemen, this is Colonel Tresh of Switzerland." She turned to Lee. "General, the Colonel says he served with you in the Polish army some time ago."

Lee looked at Tresh, and recognition came over his face. "Ah, yes. While I was on Leopold's staff. You were a captain at the time, commanding a company. We met at a reception when Leopold visited your regiment."

Tresh smiled. "You do have an excellent memory, sir, considering it was early in the Seven Years War—more than twenty years ago now. And shortly afterward, you returned to the British Army." The two shook hands, and then Tresh turned and introduced his wife. "Sir, allow me to present my lady, Catherine Tresh."

Lee made a small bow to Catherine and said, "A pleasure to meet such a lovely lady." Then he turned back to Alexander. "Colonel, I have just arrived from the Carolinas. May I ask what function you are serving here in our army?"

Tresh explained the advisory role to which Washington had appointed him.

Catherine then spoke up. "We have thrown our lot in with America. We hope to make it our home when the war is over and procure an estate."

Lee responded simply, "Well, a laudable goal, Mrs. Tresh."

Harfeld said, "Yes, very laudable, Mrs. Tresh, and I assure you we Americans would welcome such a distinguished couple." He cleared his throat and continued, "However, I must be candid. There is some danger for you. We Americans are in this war because we live here. However, if the British prevail, the officers of the rebel army could pay a price, and I might suggest that a professional officer from Europe who threw his lot in with them might be treated to even more severe consequences."

Tresh smiled and responded, "Well, then we must strive to ensure the British do not prevail."

Lee nodded. "Indeed, sir. But things are hanging quite in the balance at present."

Parkinson put his hand on Harfeld's arm. "Well, Colonel and Mrs. Tresh, assuming things work out in our favor, when the time comes for you to buy the land for that estate, you should get in touch with Harfeld here. Clive is a lawyer who also helps his clients find and purchase suitable property."

Harfeld reached into a pocket of his coat, took out one of his cards, and passed it to Tresh. "Yes, indeed, Colonel. Get in touch with me when you are ready to look for land."

Tresh looked down at the card. "Ah, I see that your office is in New Jersey."

"Yes, Colonel, in Morristown. I have a house and office in the town, and a plantation a few miles west. It is lovely country, and we would love to have such a distinguished couple in our state. But I have clients and land of my own in New York as well as Jersey. In fact, that's why I'm here in New York now—searching properties for a client. You may see me riding around the area for the next few days."

As he was speaking, their hostess rejoined the group. "General, I'm going to take these two gentlemen away from you. It's time they met General Washington."

Carolyn walked the two men over to where Washington stood, now talking with only three people: a colonel and a couple from the town. Then she performed introductions of Parkinson and Harfeld.

Harfeld had to admit that, up close, Washington was as impressive as seen from a distance. Harfeld was a tad above average height and had never been self-conscious of his height in groups of men, but the general's towering height was somewhat intimidating.

Parkinson brought the conversation to the war, saying, "General, I must say it is comforting to see all your soldiers in their encampments and the artillery batteries covering the harbor."

Washington responded, "Thank you, sir. I will tell you that we have disposed things as best we can, not knowing the enemy's precise intentions. When they become clearer, you will see redeployment of the batteries and foot battalions to more advantageous locations."

Harfeld decided to stir things up to see how Washington would react. "General, we were talking with General Lee, who people are calling the 'Hero of Charleston.' Permit me to be a little forward, but sir, Lee seems to think that defense of the city is problematic. He thinks the army should retire to ground more favorable and, in fact, not try to oppose the British and German regulars in open-country European fashion. Lee fears that it would lead to the destruction of the army. He favors resisting with small bands of mixed Continentals and militia against British outposts and isolated columns, capitalizing on the skirmish and ambush type warfare learned against the Indian warriors and French in the last war. What, sir, do you think of his proposal, which if I understand correctly, is in opposition to your ideas for the campaign?"

Harfeld looked closely at Washington's countenance to see the effect. He was in large measure surprised at the general's reaction, or more correctly, lack of one. He remained stone-faced, and Harfeld noticed only a quick flick of the eyes toward where Lee still stood, an almost imperceptible raising of the eyebrows, and a barely visible tightening of the lips.

After a moment, Washington made a small smile and said, "Mr. Harfeld, I always make it a practice of listening to the opinions of my senior officers and weighing the value of those thoughts in making decisions about the conduct of the war. General Lee is an intelligent and experienced military officer, perhaps the most experienced in our army. And he is *always* ready to share his thoughts, in great detail. As the campaign progresses, he knows I will consider his counsel." He paused, then said, "In the meantime, I repeat that, at the moment, we are most concerned with training the army and positioning its units in the most advantageous locations for countering our enemy's movements."

Harfeld looked into Washington's eyes. "A very thoughtful and diplomatic answer, General."

There was a pause in the conversation, and Parkinson interjected, "Perhaps we should refresh our drinks, Clive."

Harfeld nodded, they made their departing pleasantries with Washington and headed for the refreshment tables. Once there, Parkinson looked over at his friend and said, "Clive, that question to Washington was damned provocative."

Harfeld shrugged. "A lawyer's question—probing to see Washington's reaction. And it tells me a lot about the man. He was already aware of Lee's outspoken views but will not be distracted from his own plans." He smiled. "He will not let himself be bullied by Lee, the professional soldier with, if I may say, a very large ego."

Parkinson grinned. "You always were a rather aggressive fellow, Clive. But it was interesting."

Harfeld emptied his drink. "Yes, indeed it was. Now I have something even more interesting in mind. I'm sure you know somewhere here in Manhattan where gentlemen like us might at this moment be looking for partners at the card table."

"Most assuredly."

Harfeld leaned close to his friend and said conspiratorially, "Then let us slip out of here and proceed there posthaste."

The two men quietly left the mansion and headed for a tavern Parkinson knew a couple of blocks away. As they walked, Parkinson said, "I thought that Swiss colonel—Tresh—had a rather smashing wife. And much younger than himself."

"Yes, I can't but agree. He's a lucky man in that aspect."

Chapter Six

Careful Maneuvers

Following the reception at the Medford House, Wend returned to the company's bivouac just at dusk. He took off the heavy wool coat and carefully hung it in his tent, then sat down by the fire which Billy Wood had made at the front of the fly and poured himself a drink. He had just settled in when Donegal strode up.

"Na, did you have a swell time of it standin' around talkin' with all the rich mob?"

"It was as boring as you would expect, even more so because I got stuck in a corner talking with General Lee."

"Oh, na, you didn't enjoy that? Did you 'na like hearing from the Hero of Charleston, as they are calling him?"

Wend made a face and replied, "It turns out that the Hero of Charleston is a rail-thin, wasted-looking man with a huge opinion of himself." He waved his hand dismissively. "In any case, I could have missed the entire affair with no regrets. Now I just want to sit here and relax, and I'll not be late to my bed."

"Well, na', I hate to ruin your plans, but you've a wee piece of business to attend to a'fore you crawl into your blankets."

"Simon, it can wait 'til morning."

"You might be satisfied with that, and myself I'd have no objection, but Horner would 'na stand for it. The lad wants to see you posthaste, and he ain't in any mood to wait. It was all I could do to stop him from runnin' up here when word got out you were back."

Wend took a sip of the spirits. He sighed and said, "Is this about Emily Crider, for some reason?"

"Not for *some* reason, a right *serious* reason, leastways the way Andrew sees it. He found the wench right off, but there be a problem what is drivin' him crazy. He's boilin' like a pot a' water over a hot fire."

"Oh, let me guess: Has Miss Crider decided she no longer wants to settle down to life with a back-country gunsmith? Has she found that the city life and the gold she gets from providing pleasure for soldiers is more attractive and exciting? She wouldn't be the first girl who was seduced by it all."

"Ha! You damn well *wish* it was that. No, them two are still besotted with each other, and the girl wants to leave her business right enough and become Mrs. Horner. No, it's that Widow McGraw what is the problem. She won't let the tart go. Says she has to work off some money that's owed."

Wend shook his head then looked up at the heavens as if beseeching the Gods for deliverance. "That's Colleen, right enough. I should have thought of her pulling something like that."

"Well, you need to talk to Andrew tonight. He's beside himself thinkin' of little Miss Emily being just a few blocks away pleasuring some soldier. If you don't do something to cool him off, there's no tellin' what he might do."

Wend resigned himself. "All right, go fetch him, and we'll see why he thinks I can help him."

Donegal was back in a few minutes with the young gunsmith in tow. Wend looked at the wiry, light-haired young man who had been his best apprentice and now was rightly a fully qualified journeyman. Wend drained his whiskey, then said, "Well, Andrew, what is so urgent that we must speak tonight?"

"It's about Emily Crider. I found her, sir, with Mrs. McGraw. They're just on the edge of town."

"Yes, Donegal told me about that. I understand Colleen won't let her go. Please explain what she is demanding."

The muscles of Horner's face tightened in anguish. "The widow says Emily owes her service for a year, startin' last May, to pay off all the money she put into clothing and other female things. That means Emily's got 'bout nine months to go. Mrs. McGraw said that if I could buy out Emily, she'd let her go." He shook his head in despair. "But I used up all my money to get here, Mr. Eckert. It will take me months to earn enough money from the army, and she'll have to keep on . . ." His voice trailed off, and he stood silently looking at the ground.

Wend looked at the youth. "Andrew, I would lend you the money, but you know that after the loyalist attack on our farm in January, I'm pressed for cash. I have hardly any with me—I left it with Peggy. I'm sorry, I can't help."

"I didn't come here to ask for money, Mr. Eckert. But the fact is, Mrs. McGraw said I should ask you to come talk to her."

Wend sat up straight in his chair. "She wants me to see her about you and Emily? Why? What does she expect I can do?"

"She just said I should ask you to come see her. She wouldn't explain, but it seemed like she was sayin' maybe somethin' could be worked out." He took a deep breath. "Sir, I got to ask you to do it. If there's any chance of breakin' Emily free right now, we got to take it. And I know there's somethin' between you and that widow. Somethin' that goes back to when you were young like me and Emily." He looked at Wend and said in desperate supplication. "Sir, please just go up to her camp and see what she wants."

Wend rose from his chair and paced back and forth for a few seconds. "Well, first off, Andrew, I like to think that I'm *still* young. Thirty-two isn't old, you know." He thought for a moment, then said, "All right, Andrew. I'll go see her first thing in the morning."

Horner's face brightened. "Thank you, sir! I knew you'd try to help."

He turned to go back to his own tent, but Wend called out. "Hold up, Andrew, I've got some other news for you."

The youth turned around, curiosity written on his face. "News, sir?"

"Yes, at the reception, I spoke at some length with Colonel Grayson. I told him about you and that you were ready to provide gunsmithing service to the army. I pointed out that with your tool cart, you could move to the various battalions' camps to do your work. He was quite excited about it and said there was considerable need for your skills."

"Thank you for that, sir."

"Yes, but that's not all. Grayson said he would include news about your service in the next general orders going out to the whole army. That should get you some business right away." Wend paused and held up a finger. "And even more important, he said he would send over a quartermaster officer to work out a way for you to get paid for your work."

The young man's face brightened. "That's excellent, sir!"

"Yes, well you can thank me by being patient with the matter of Miss Crider while I go talk to Colleen. Meanwhile concentrate on your work."

Horner nodded. "I'll do that, Mr. Eckert." And with that, he headed back to his own tent.

Donegal leaned up against one of the poles supporting the fly. "Well, you sent him off as happy as could be, considering the situation. What the devil do you figure that Colleen has in mind callin' for you? She don't do anything 'cept for benefit to her."

Wend sat back down in his chair, reached over, and poured himself another measure of the whiskey. "Yes, she want's something, and I have an idea of what it is." He looked up at the sergeant. "And what she wants, Simon, is something I won't give her."

"Then what's the point of goin' up to her camp if it won't help out Horner?"

"Horner has always been loyal. Remember, back in March, he was all set to leave Eckert Ridge to find Emily, but he stayed after the loyalists' raid that burnt down the gun shop and other buildings. He postponed his own plans to help us rebuild. I owe him loyalty in return by seeing Colleen. Even if it doesn't amount to anything, it's the least I can do for him."

Donegal shook his head, then stared out into the darkness for a moment. "The Widow McGraw is a hard woman and I don't envy you having to bargain with her. But I wish you the best of luck for Andrew's sake. And he's goin' to be sorely disappointed if you can't work out something."

Wend grimaced. "You're damned right about that."

With that, Donegal pushed himself off the tent pole and headed back into the camp.

The open coach, pulled by a matched team of greys, moved swiftly along the road heading toward the northern end of Staten Island. The driver wore the uniform of the King's Loyal Virginia Legion. Accompanying the vehicle were two mounted outriders of the same regiment. Barrett Penfold Northcutt lounged in the forward seat of the coach, facing toward the rear seat, where, to his great pleasure, were seated, side by side, two charming ladies in a position where they could take in the view ahead.

Northcutt reflected on the contrast in appearance of the two women. Betsy Loring, with golden hair, was holding up a parasol to protect her creamy complexion. He was sure it would be the envy of any lady of quality in London or Paris. Seated beside her was Mary Fraser, with her deep bronze hair and a countenance burnished by a lifetime in the wind and sun. No parasol for Mary—she wore a simple straw hat. To Northcutt, there was no contest for his preference; he had decided Mary was his ideal at his first sight of her in the Halifax ballroom.

Betsy interrupted his thoughts. "Barrett, it's lovely being out for a ride on such a beautiful, sunny day. But I'm bemused by the great mystery about where you are taking us. I'm not aware of the detailed geography of the island, but I do know that there's not much further to go before we reach the shoreline of New York Harbor. Pray tell, what is all this about?" She turned to Mary, "Are you in on the plan?"

Mary Fraser shook her head and laughed. "He has told me nothing more than you. He simply showed up at my camp in the general's coach and said he was there to take me to join you for the afternoon. I assumed it was at your invitation for tea."

Barrett, enjoying the mystery, grinned broadly. "Ladies, as I told you, it is to be a surprise. But I will whet your appetite by saying that General Howe himself asked me to whisk you to a precise place on the northern coast of the island by a certain time, a time which is almost nigh. There is an event that will occur that you will find most edifying and entertaining, and something that you will someday be proud to tell your children and grandchildren that you witnessed."

In a matter of minutes, they arrived at the shore, and Northcutt had the driver pull up in a spot with shade trees and a good view of both the harbor and Manhattan across the water. Once they had stopped, he stepped down from the carriage and walked to the bank of the shore and, looking out onto the harbor waters, saw what he was expecting. He walked back to the rig. "Ladies, we are just in time for the show." He extended his hand to Betsy and helped her down, followed by Mary. Then he led them to the shore in the shade of a large tree.

Betsy exclaimed, "What a marvelous view! And across the harbor, we can see Manhattan quite clearly." She stared for a moment. "Well, it's not nearly the size of Boston, but it is substantial."

Mary said, "I spent considerable time there right after the French War. I thought it quite pleasant. Of course, I was a young child then."

Northcutt agreed. "Yes, I spent a decade there after coming from England. I readily admit that I am enamored of the place. Frankly, I prefer it to Williamsburg." Then he said, "But admiring the town is not what we are here for. Let me direct your attention to the waters just south of where we stand." He pointed with his right hand.

Betsy looked and then exclaimed, "Why, two warships! Quite near! And they're heading right up the harbor!"

Mary stared for a moment. "I learned something about men-of-war while coming across the Atlantic. They are sailing under shortened sail—their mainsails are reefed up, and their topsails and topgallants are being used to maneuver. They call it *fighting sail*. Are they about to attack something?"

Northcutt said, "Their progress is what we are here to witness. They are the forty-four-gun frigate *Phoenix* and the twenty-gun ship *Rose*. And what you are seeing is the very beginning of our campaign against the rebels. General Howe's brother, Admiral Richard Howe, has ordered them to sail past Manhattan and into the Hudson."

"Barrett," exclaimed Betsy, "I can see their gunports open and the cannon rolled out! Are they going to bombard the town?"

"Their mission is to draw out the defenses of the island, to see where their batteries are. They will certainly fire on the batteries, and there may well be some damage to buildings and residences. And once past, their job is to scout out the rebel defenses along the Hudson north of the town." He paused, then continued, "Moreover, their movement is also to confuse the rebels as to just what our intentions are. We know they expect us to land on Long Island, but sending ships up north may force them to disperse their strength to defend multiple possible landing sites. So, the ships' mission is both a reconnaissance and a feint."

They watched as the ships sailed onward. Northcutt went back to the carriage and pulled out a box from under his seat. "Ladies, while we wait for developments, please join me here for some refreshment." He turned and held up a bottle. "I have some fine product of the vine here for us."

Betsy laughed and walked back to where he stood. "Leave it to Barrett to think of everything."

Northcutt pulled a glass out of the box and poured her a measure of the wine, then did the same for Mary and himself. Then he held up his glass. "Ladies, to our fine lads of the navy! May they have every success in today's endeavor!"

The three touched glasses. As luck would have it, at that moment, the quiet of the afternoon was broken by the thunderous sound of cannon fire. All three turned to see flames and smoke erupting from the *Phoenix's* starboard side.

Betsy laughed. "Barrett, your timing is perfect!" She turned and walked back toward the shore to see the action better. "I can't see where the balls are landing!"

Northcutt said, "I believe that broadside was to test the range. It appears most of the shot has landed near the shoreline; I saw the splashes. But some dust did rise near the old fort down at the tip of Manhattan." He pointed to the derelict fortification.

Suddenly a few shots rang out from the Manhattan shoreline. Mary said, "There must be an American field battery there." She paused a second, then said, "I see the splashes of their shot; they are falling short of our ships." Mary considered a moment, then said in a professional tone, "Yes, I'd say the American guns are no larger than six-pounders." She waved at the two ships. "They seem to be staying close to the Jersey side. The American guns won't have the range to hit them, and in any case, the six-pound projectiles will not cause much damage if they did hit."

Betsy turned and stared at Mary. "My dear, you have learned so much from your time in the army. You have my admiration."

At that moment, *Phoenix* let fly with another broadside. Northcutt looked closely at the Manhattan shoreline. "They've elevated their guns. I can see more hits on and near the old fort and even beyond."

Quickly the American battery returned fire, but once again to no effect. Splashes appeared well short of the two ships.

Mary remarked, "In a few more minutes, they'll have passed the tip of Manhattan and be in the Hudson proper. I wonder if the Americans have more batteries further up the river?"

"Well, Mary, that's precisely what they intend to find out. Once clear to the north, they plan to note any batteries or troop encampments along the river." He thought a second. "And locate any good places for a landing if it becomes desirable to place troops on Washington's flank after the campaign begins on Long Island."

Northcutt refilled the ladies' glasses and then his own. "Ladies, it appears that they've passed into the river. I suggest we finish our wine and then drive back to Betsy's residence. Mary tells me she must be back to her camp for evening rounds." He waved to the three dragoons who were standing in a group at a discreet distance. "All right, lads, mount up. We'll be moving soon."

After dropping Betsy off at her house, the driver drove the carriage at a fast pace down to New Dorp and then on to the camp of the Black Watch. He pulled up right in front of Mary's tent, and Northcutt descended to hand her down.

As they stood before her tent, Barrett said, "Well, Mary, it's been my great pleasure to spend time with you this afternoon."

He was pleased to see she smiled warmly. She said in reply, "Well, the feeling is quite mutual, Barrett. I always enjoy your company." She smiled again and put her hand on his arm. "It was so thoughtful of you to include me in the outing, and I was so glad to visit with Mrs. Loring in a situation besides a medical problem. She is a very interesting person."

"Indeed, that is quite true." Northcutt paused a moment, preparing to carefully phrase the proposition he had been planning to make all afternoon. "After the action we saw today, the movement to Long Island and the campaign to drive the colonials out of the New York area will begin shortly. I am confident it will not take long; the rebels will not be able to stand up to our regulars. And when we have occupied Manhattan, if your regiment remains in the area for any length of time, I should like to take you to dinner. I know some fine establishments, and it would be my great pleasure to entertain you for an evening. I hope you would find that to your interest."

Mary looked up at him wordlessly for a few seconds, a look of faint surprise in her eyes. Then she smiled and quickly replied, "Why, of course, Barrett, I would be quite pleased if that could happen. In fact, I should look forward to it. It would be a nice reprieve from the routine of camp life."

Northcutt made a slight bow and said, "Have no doubt, my lady, I shall make it happen. In any case, I will be escorting you again to Mrs. Loring's residence in the near future." He turned and bounded up into the carriage, touched his hat to her, and said, "Until that moment." Then he motioned for the driver to take him back to his own camp. As it pulled away, Barrett felt a surge of euphoria like none he had experienced since he was a youth attending his first ball.

Colleen McGraw sat at the table in front of her tent, coffee cup in hand, taking in the fine morning, relishing the coolness before the climbing sun brought on the real heat of the day. Her tent was just a few yards off of the road into Manhattan and, as usual for this time of day, there was considerable traffic moving in both directions. Wagons and carts rumbled along, bound toward the town filled with farm products and other goods for the markets and shops. The same type of vehicles were coming out of the city, many empty, having delivered their loads. Occasionally chaises or carriages passed, and there were frequent horsemen—most often military messengers bearing orders or dispatches to the various brigade headquarters.

Colleen finished her coffee, put her cup down on the table, and rose from her chair in preparation for her customary morning turn around the camp. However, at that moment, she caught sight of a blue-coated officer riding along the road toward her. He was mounted on a sleek, long-legged, energetic black horse that pranced as it trotted along. She inspected the man's uniform and noticed that the facings were red, a color she had rarely seen in the army. Then she realized that something about the rider was familiar; she couldn't quite make out his face, but simply the way he held himself on the horse roused her memory. She stood standing, her eyes frozen on the man. Then, as he drew nearer, her heart first skipped a beat and then began racing in excitement as she realized it was Wend Eckert.

She took a deep breath, then thought, *My statement to Horner worked. Wend's coming to discuss Emily.* Colleen mentally cursed herself for her emotional reaction to the sight of him. She took a deep breath and thought, *For God's sake, calm down and steel yourself for hard bargaining.*

She quickly checked out her gown and ran her hands over her hair, making sure everything was in place. Then, sitting down in her chair, she assumed as serene a demeanor as she could manage.

Wend dismounted next to one of her big Conestoga wagons and tied the reins of his horse to the spokes of a wheel. Then he turned and walked with a deliberate step toward where she sat under the tent fly. Colleen looked hard to see if there was any anxiety in his face but could detect only his usual stony visage.

Wend came right up to the fly and took his hat off. "Well, Colleen, I certainly didn't expect to be in your company again so soon after that visit to Fredericktown last November." He smiled tightly, at the same time making a small bow. "But naturally it's always a pleasure to see you. And you look as lovely as ever. Life in an army camp seems to agree with you." He looked around at the wagons and tents. "May I say, you have an impressive outfit here."

Colleen cocked her head and put as seductive a look on her face as she could manage. "It is so good to see you, Wend." She moved her eyes over him with deliberate slowness. "I must say, encountering you in a captain's uniform is the last thing I would have imagined." She raised her eyebrows. "But it does flatter you." Then her face wrinkled up in puzzlement. "However, I had expected you would spend the war overseeing your shop and making firelocks for the army."

Eckert shrugged. "That's precisely where I *should* be, but events and pressure from the Committee of Safety in Winchester intervened. Suffice it to say that I am here in command of a company."

"Well, I for one am glad. It's always good to be in the presence of old friends."

The smile disappeared from Wend's face, and the muscles around his mouth tightened. "All right, Colleen, let's dispense with further pleasantries and get down to business. You damn well *know* why I'm here. Horner said you asked to see me in connection with his desire to marry Emily Crider. He told me that you wouldn't let her leave and get married because she owes you money."

Colleen put a look of distress on her face. "Oh, my, Wend, that's not *precisely* correct. I fear young Horner didn't explain it *quite* properly. Actually, I have no objection to them getting married. *None* at all. They can do it today, and I'll celebrate their nuptials." She grinned. "But it is true that Emily and all the other girls agreed to work for at least a year to compensate for all the money I had to spend to dress them. I've outfitted them in lovely clothing. And beyond that, I need to get my profit out of their work. Any lawyer would tell you they made a contract with me, even if it ain't written down." She shrugged and smiled even more broadly. "So the two can get married, but Emily will have to continue on with me until the year is up, which is nine more months."

Wend stared at her for a long moment. "Colleen, you are a heartless woman."

"Damn it, Wend, it was a fair bargain I made with them. And I've carried out *my* part. They've never dressed so well or had better food and drink in their lives. And I damn well deserve my due from the bargain." She stood up and put her hands on her hips. "And I *always* get my due!"

"Ah, yes, Colleen, I've certainly learned that."

Colleen held up a finger. "But there is a way I'll let her go right away. That's if she—or the two of them—comes up with money to pay me off."

"You know Horner doesn't have any money."

"Yes, he told me that yesterday. And I know Emily doesn't have enough, though she's made some from her work." She gave Wend a knowing look. "But it occurred to me that perhaps you could loan Horner and Emily the money." She held out a hand palm up. "I'd let her go in a minute. I 'spect I could find another willing girl here in Manhattan." She sighed. "But not like Emily. Her good looks draw in the men better than any of my others."

Wend shook his head. "That's not possible. Earlier this year, Lord Dunmore's loyalists raided my farm. They burned many of the buildings down. It cost me everything I had to rebuild it. Beyond that, I'm in debt to many of my neighbors for helping out with the restoration. I've come here with hardly two coins to rub together. That's part of the reason I had to agree to raise a company for the army."

Colleen said in a sweet voice, "I'm so sorry to hear that, Wend." She rose from her chair and put her hand on his arm. She moved around until she was behind him and put her hands on his shoulders. Then she whispered into his ear, "But there is one way I would let Emily go and no money would have to change hands." She paused to let that sink in. "You could do it by repaying an old debt. You know you owe me for saving you from those men who wanted to kill you, back in the tavern near York, in 1764, when I was a nineteen-year-old tavern maid. You were fleeing from that renegade trader Richard Grenough's men. You had just found out about all the gunpowder he was getting ready to trade to the Indians. So you came into the tavern and took a seat at a table, hoping to hide. Then those two men came in, pulled pistols, and attempted to take you away, claiming you were a thief for breaking into his warehouse. They said they were taking you to the sheriff, but I knew you'd be dead within the hour. And I lied to them, and everyone in the common room; I said that you couldn't have done it because you had just come down from being in bed with me." She paused again and then asked, "You haven't forgotten that, have you?"

"Damn it, Colleen, of course not."

"Well, you know I did that because I was so taken with you, one of the few foolish moments in my life. And then, after they were gone, I said you could pay me back by sleeping with me that night in your room."

"Yes, and we spent the night together."

"No, only *part* of the night! You left me before dawn while I was in deep sleep, dreaming of having you one more time in the early morning. I even said that just before we fell asleep."

Wend sighed deeply. "Colleen, we've gone over this before. I left you because I feared those men would come back to grab me while we were asleep. I worried that you might be hurt, or worse, if that happened."

"Well, they didn't come. And I woke up to find you gone. And I was deprived of morning sex with you. Every woman knows that men are at their best in the morning, and I certainly understood that better than others." She smiled tightly then whispered, "So I have always considered that you didn't fully pay your debt to me. It is still owed." She looked at him for a moment, then continued, "And I always collect in the end. No man leaves me without paying in some way. But I'll give you a sweet deal: Pay your debt now, and I'll release Emily immediately."

"For God's sake, Colleen, you know I can't do that. I won't betray my wife and family."

"There are married men who come here and do that with my girls every day." She slid her hands up to his shoulders, pulled herself close, and spoke, whispered into his ear: "It could be very discrete. I know an inn down in Manhattan, the Britannic Crown. We could have supper in a private dining room, then spend the night in one of their comfortable rooms. No one would be the wiser, and no chance of word getting back to your wife." She pressed her body up against his. "One night's pleasure for both of us, and you could be free of debt to me, and a young couple could start their new life."

"I'll not do it! Andrew is like a son to me. We've been through a lot together, and I'd do *almost* anything for him. But that's a step too far."

Colleen dropped her hands, then went back and resumed her seat. "Then Emily can damn well work off her debt right here."

Wend stared at her for a very long moment. Then he said, "All right, Colleen, there is a way I can pay for Emily's freedom. In barter, not cash."

"Oh, my dear Wend, and what might that be?"

"I suspect you must maintain a supply of spirits to sell to your customers. And here in New York, what with the war and the blockade, you must pay a high price for it."

Colleen cocked her head, put her hand to her chin, and looked at him with puzzlement in her eyes. "What are you proposing? Get to it."

"You know I distill whiskey, in partnership with my friend Simon Donegal."

"You are still doing that, even with the war on?"

"Of course. The war is a great opportunity because of the British having cut off the supply of rum. Everyone wants whiskey instead. Donegal has a hired man running his distillery." Wend raised a finger. "So here is my proposal: I'll arrange for a wagon load of my whiskey to be delivered to you at no cost. That's a damned generous offer, worth more than nine months of Emily's service. You just release her now, and I'll send word to Eckert Ridge for the spirits to be delivered."

Colleen leaned back in her chair and laughed. Then she said, "No deal, my dear Wend, at least not the way you are proposing it." She thought a moment. "How long would it take for you to get the whiskey here?"

"A month, six weeks at the outside, what with the time for a letter to get to Winchester and for a wagon to make the trip up here."

"I'll think about it. In any case, Emily works until it arrives. There's no deal until I have spirits in hand and know the quality."

Wend was about to respond when the thunder of loud explosions interrupted him. The noise was coming from the direction of Manhattan. He turned toward the sound, and a startled Colleen jumped up out of her chair.

"For God's sake, what is that, Wend?"

Another series of explosions erupted. He looked at her. "That's cannon fire! Coming from the direction of our batteries down at the tip of Manhattan, right at the harbor." He thought a moment. "The British must be trying something—maybe an assault."

He was interrupted by more cannon fire, this time not as loud, as if from a greater distance. He looked at Colleen. "That's further away. It could be British fire coming from ships in the harbor bombarding our positions."

Suddenly more cannon fire erupted. "That's our batteries again." He turned to Colleen. "I must go immediately and rejoin my company. We are close to the harbor, and headquarters may call on us to support the artillery."

Without saying more, he ran to his horse, mounted, and was off at the gallop in the direction of Manhattan.

Colleen stood up and stamped her foot in frustration. Then, arms crossed in front of her, she stood and watched the only man who had ever taken her heart ride off toward the sound of the guns.

—~—

With the noise of the cannonade spurring him on, Wend galloped Sonny all the way to the company's campsite. He arrived to find that Newkirk had the men under arms and ready to move. He pulled up the horse and looked down at his first lieutenant and Donegal, who stood alongside him.

"What's the word, Reese? Do we have any orders?"

Newkirk shook his head. "Nary a word." He pointed toward the camp of the Life Guards. "But right after the cannonade started, they formed up and marched off."

Wend looked over at the Guard camp. "I assume that means Washington is on the move from his headquarters."

Donegal spoke up. "But sure and they was tight-mouthed about it, if they knew anything. Wouldn't spare us a word. So we figured we just ought to be ready, 'case somebody at headquarters remembered we was here."

Wend thought a second, then said, "Keep them ready to march. I'm going down to the harbor to see what's going on." He paused, then continued. "Donegal, get Billy Wood mounted. I'll take him along as messenger."

"That will be easy enough. We got the riding horses saddled." He strode off to get the corporal.

Wend said to Newkirk, "I'll send back word if it looks like we might have any business. I thought that the British might be trying an assault, but if that was the case, I think we would have already been called to action. And we'd have seen other troops moving."

The lieutenant nodded. "I was thinking the same thing. Maybe they're just probing our artillery defenses to see their strength."

Wend looked around to see Wood approaching on his mount. He waved to him, "Come on, Billy, let's do a little scouting." Then he led off toward the harbor.

In a few minutes, they arrived at the tip of Manhattan. Wend looked out in the harbor and immediately recognized the source of the problem. Visible were two three-masted ships flying British colors. They were north of the island, heading into the Hudson. To get there, they must have sailed past Manhattan and fired at the Continental batteries emplaced to protect from a seaward attack, and the Americans had then responded.

Billy called out, "Mr. Wend, take a look over there! There's a building been hit!"

Wend turned his gaze to where the lad was pointing and saw that he was right. A medium-sized house had taken a ball, and one side had collapsed. It had just happened, because dust was rising.

Wend looked around and saw Washington, Grayson, and a number of staff officers mounted and contemplating the ships. Several had glasses to their eye. Wend considered approaching them, but finally decided it would be presumptuous to join them uninvited. Instead, he headed for the nearest battery, which was adjacent to the remains of an old fort. He saw a very young captain standing to one side, telescope in hand, following the ships.

Wend dismounted and walked over to where the youthful officer stood. He was somewhat below average height, of slim build and swarthy complexion, with a handsome, narrow face featuring striking blue eyes and light red hair.

Sensing his presence, the officer took the glass from his eye and looked over at Wend with a speculative look.

Wend touched his hat to the captain. "Good day, sir. I'm Captain Eckert of the Frederick County Light Foot. I thought to find out what all the firing was about." He grinned. "And you appear to be a man involved in the matter."

The captain looked at Wend and then up at Billy Wood. He pointed to the private. "Ah, yes. You would be from that company of shirtmen who are bivouacked just up the street, next to the Guard. Seen your men walking about."

"That's correct, sir."

The artillery captain stuck out his hand. "Hamilton, sir. Alexander Hamilton of the New York Artillery, but you can call me Alex. It's easier and much less formal." He motioned toward the battery of six guns. "This is my company."

"So you did some of the firing."

"Actually, most of it is from our side. Our first time firing at enemy targets." A look of frustration passed over his face. "Regrettably, not to much effect. With the wind as it is, the damned Britishers were able to hug to the other side of the harbor, essentially out of our effective range. All we did was put balls into the water near them."

Wend held out his hand toward the far shore. "We don't have any guns on the Jersey side?"

Hamilton gritted his teeth. "No, damnation!" He turned to Wend, a fierce look in his eye. "But it's not for lack of asking! Colonel Knox, the artillery commander, damned well wanted some over there, and I pointed it out to the staff myself." He shook his head. "But the army just doesn't have enough guns, and what we do have are spread thin. A lot of them are with the forces down on Long Island, and what's left are parceled out trying to defend Manhattan and other places where the British might try to assault. There are so many places to defend, and we just don't know where they're going to attack." He pointed across the harbor. "If we had a battery over there, we could have made it very hot for the English to sail through."

Wend looked back to the ships. They were continuing northward in the river. "What do you think their purpose is?"

Hamilton thought a moment. "I expect it's a probing action, checking out the geography and the state of our defenses." He paused a moment. "Or possibly a diversion to get our attention while they're up to something else. Maybe they want us focused on this while they undertake their movement to cross over to Long Island from Staten Island or to wherever they're going to make their first landing." He looked down at the British fleet in the lower harbor. "One thing's sure; they've massed enough force here now to start the ball."

Wend nodded. "Yes, I think you are right. It will begin soon." Wend said good-bye to Hamilton and walked over to where Wood held the horses.

"Come on, Billy. We're going back to the company. The action is finished here, and there's no business for us." He smiled at the young man he had known for so long. "But have no doubt, things will heat up soon. Very soon."

Part II

Autumn of Despair

Chapter Seven

The Game Begins

Colonel Barrett Northcutt, coming from lunch at the officer's mess, found Markwood at the table before the tent which served as their office, poring over some papers. "Well, George, what is it that you find so absorbing?"

The captain looked up. "It's damn well going to absorb your attention also." He held up a paper. "A courier delivered a packet of information from Harfeld—er, I mean Harkness. It was dropped off at the outpost at Shoreham then brought here by boat." Markwood dropped the sheet of paper and waved his hand over the packet. "In just a few days, he's done an amazing job."

"Amazing? What precisely do you mean?"

"He's been in Manhattan. He intermingled with senior officers of the rebel army." He turned and grinned at Northcutt. "Including the head rebel, Washington himself."

Northcutt stood, shocked into silence. Finally he recovered enough to say, "The devil you say!"

Markwood laughed. "It appears Harkness actually *is* the *Devil*." He spread the papers out on the table. How he got all this, I don't know." He pointed to one piece of paper.

"My God, Markwood! It's a map of where all Washington's troops on Manhattan are located."

"Yes, and it gives an estimate of the numbers." Markwood looked up from the table and turned to Northcutt. "But here's something rather personal you'll want to know immediately: That gunsmith Eckert and his company are on Manhattan, encamped near Washington's headquarters and as of now, under his direct command." Markwood stared at his colonel for a moment, then continued, "Harkness reports that his company is the first of the Virginia troops sent to join the army."

Barrett gritted his teeth. "It appears I shall never be shed of that man." Northcutt stopped to think, then said, "But in a sense it is fortunate: With any luck, we may have the opportunity to wreak vengeance on him for what he did to our regiment at Mobjack Bay."

"Indeed, sir. That would be most savory."

Barrett sighed. "But that's for the future. Right now I must get this information to Howe—this *very* afternoon. Pack it up, and I will go see Paterson directly." He looked at Markwood and gave him a meaningful smile. "George, Harkness has presented us with a coup. This will give Howe a great appreciation for what our spy network can achieve and it will cement our influence here on the staff. And that cannot help but enhance our fortunes, particularly when the rebels are defeated and the spoils of victory are to be distributed."

Northcutt watched General William Howe's face as he stood at a table in his office, looking over Harkness' map of Washington's troop dispositions. He had already briefed the general on most of the spy's report, and Howe had been elated at the extent and depth of the information.

Howe looked up at Barrett. "Damn, sir. This is all extraordinarily valuable. Your man has done a marvelous job." He thought for a brief moment, then asked, "Now, Northcutt, you say that over a third of Washington's nineteen thousand men are militia? And their training is very poor?"

"Indeed, sir. But Harkness evaluates that the training of all of the rebel force, including the so-called regulars of the Continental regiments, is quite poor. Their drill is rudimentary, and there is no standard throughout the army." He waved his hand. "But that doesn't mean they can't fight effectively in certain situations, as when they are behind stone walls or in the bush."

Howe sighed and nodded. "Yes, we saw that well enough at Concord and

Bunker Hill. And regardless of their lack of discipline, some of them are effective skirmishers and dangerous marksmen."

There were a few moments of silence, and then Barrett spoke up. "There's something else Harkness reported. It may prove useful." He held up a sheet of paper. "There appears to be a serious difference of opinion between Washington and his second in command, General Lee, about how to use their army."

Howe stared at Northcutt and raised his eyebrows. "Oh? And just how so?"

Barrett looked between the commander and the adjutant general. "Washington is attempting to build an army that is essentially a replica of ours. He intends to fight in traditional style."

Howe held up his hands in a questioning gesture. "And why is that controversial, sir? It seems necessary if they expect a chance for victory."

"I would agree, sir. But General Charles Lee, who is in fact a veteran of the King's army, opposes that idea. He believes they will never be able to stand up to us using formal tactics. He is urging that the rebels fight as partisans, using militia supported by small detachments of Continentals. He wants to avoid any stand-up battles—essentially a war of ambushes, skirmishes, raids."

Howe shot a look at Paterson. "I quite see. This Lee is thinking of a war of attrition—an attempt to wear us down over time." He shrugged. "That will keep us busy, but it won't produce any victories. And they'll never be able to outlast us. The war will simply die out over time as the rebels lose enthusiasm."

Northcutt nodded. "Yes, I believe you are quite right, General. But the point is, this Lee is a strong advocate for his strategy and has some persuasive arguments. He could develop a following among senior officers to resist and impede Washington's plans."

Howe said, "I take your point." Then his forehead wrinkled up in thought. "Paterson, back at the start of the French War, there was a colonel named Lee—commandant of the 44th Foot. I wonder if this chap is any relation."

Paterson put his hand to his chin and stared into the distance for a moment. "Indeed, sir, you are correct. I know this Charles Lee. He is the son of the colonel you mentioned and started his career as a subaltern in the 44th, but transferred to the 103rd during the French war. Rose to the rank of major but went on half-pay when the regiment was reduced after the conflict. Then he spent many years in foreign armies, particularly in Portuguese regiments." Paterson grinned. "As I recall, the fellow is very opinionated and more than a bit arrogant. Not always correct, but always certain of his views, and doesn't hesitate to tell you about it."

Northcutt said, "That would seem to be the persona of this fellow." He cleared his throat. "The reason I brought this up is that I believe this Lee may perform some service for us."

Howe gave Barrett a sharp look. "You mean as a spy for us?"

"No, sir. Not as a spy. Here's my point: I believe it is certain that we will drive the rebels out of New York in defeat. And when that happens, their confidence will be broken. It is quite likely that their senior leaders will begin bickering over the cause of the defeat, and this man Lee may attempt to contest Washington for command of the army."

Howe raised a finger. "Ah, yes, I see what you are getting at. He may conspire with other officers and perhaps intrigue with their damnable Continental Congress to replace the disgraced Washington."

Northcutt smiled. "That is my thought, sir. He would claim that only his superior experience could rescue their cause."

Howe walked over to his table and sat down, a thoughtful look on his face. He remained quite still for long moments, staring into the distance. Finally, he looked at Paterson and then at Barrett, a tight smile on his lips. "Gentlemen, this is good news, and we must move to take advantage of it. It's time to expedite our move on Long Island. We must hurry the completion of the landing barges." He motioned toward his adjutant general. "Get a message to my brother Richard that we must meet posthaste to discuss getting our men across the harbor and to set a firm date. And invite all the lieutenant generals to the meeting as well."

Paterson nodded. "It will be done, sir."

Howe nodded and looked at Northcutt. "If the enemy leadership is conflicted, we must do everything we can to increase their acrimony. And giving them a hard knock, a ringing defeat on the battlefield, will certainly achieve that end. And, in fact, may spur the collapse of the rebellion." He smiled. "Barrett, you have indeed brought us welcome news and a pathway to early success." He paused and said, "Get in touch with your man, this Harkness, and encourage him to do everything he can to gather more information."

Barrett grinned. "I can assure you, he is already at it, sir."

Howe leaned back in his chair. "Gentlemen, we now have our forces fully gathered, we know there is some dissension among the leadership of our enemy. If we strike hard, I believe we can look forward to having the whole of this unpleasant business over by the end of the year."

Paterson nodded. "Indeed, sir! And most importantly, His Majesty's Government will be quite pleased at such an outcome. And, dare I say, pleased at the general who orchestrated it."

—\~—

Wend walked through the company camp to where Andrew Horner had his tent and wagon. As he approached, he saw that the gunsmith had set up a bench and was at work.

"Well, Andrew, it looks like you have found a way to keep yourself busy."

Horner motioned to his bench. "Indeed, sir, I've already got work." He pointed to a musket laid out before him. "It's from a Connecticut battalion. They sent me several muskets that need work of various kinds, mostly repair of their locks—weak springs and triggers that need adjustment. But there's one with a cracked butt." He pointed to a pistol laying on another table. "And an officer dropped that pistol, and the lock needs to be repaired."

Wend nodded. "Just the kind of work I would expect you to get." He paused and said, "But I've got a little job for you to do, one you might find more exciting."

Horner looked up. "More exciting?"

"Yes. It concerns you and Emily." He dropped a sealed letter on the workbench. "That letter is to Peggy, back at the farm. It's a request for the distillery to send us a full Conestoga wagon of whiskey barrels, as soon as possible and as much as they can get into it."

"Sir, I don't understand."

"I made a deal with Colleen McGraw: trading whiskey for Emily's release."

Andrew jumped up. "That's wonderful, sir! When will she be free?"

Wend put his hand on the lad's arm. "Rein yourself in. Unfortunately, not until the whiskey is in Colleen's hands."

The youth looked crestfallen. "But, sir! That could be weeks! Maybe months."

"I figure six weeks, but lad, it's better than nine months."

Horner sat breathing heavily in disappointment.

Wend pointed to the letter. "But that's where you come in. Take the letter and find the fastest way to get it to Winchester. You're a smart lad. Nose around the town and see what kind of post service there is or someone who's going south. Perhaps coach service to Alexandria, and then it could be sent on from there. It's obviously in your interest, so I suggest you drop your work for a while and get to it."

Horner rose from his chair, took off his apron, and grabbed his hat. He picked up the packet from his bench. Looking at Wend, he said, "This letter will leave New York today."

And with that, he was off toward the main business area of Manhattan.

A grinning Wend watched him go and then headed back toward his tent.

Wend Eckert stood leaning with his back against the wall in the center hallway of Richmond Hill House. The headquarters building was bustling with activity as staff officers came and went on business. Eckert had been summoned by Grayson and had hurried over from the company's encampment, but now he had been cooling his heels for over a half-hour, with the adjutant general's door closed. The military secretary, who sat at a desk near the front door of the mansion, had informed Wend that Grayson would see him as soon as he finished meeting with another officer. Ever since the messenger had requested he report to headquarters, his mind had been busy wondering what it was all about. He sighed deeply and crossed his arms in resignation.

No sooner had he done so than the door to Grayson's office swung open, and an officer came out and hurried down the hall to the front doors. Momentarily, Grayson came to the doorway. "Ah, there you are, Eckert. Come in and shut the door behind you."

Grayson went over to his desk and sat down. He began writing something on a piece of paper. Wend came and stood silently before the desk, waiting for him to finish.

While still writing, Grayson said, without looking up, "Well, I guess you are wondering why you are here."

"Naturally, sir."

"Well, Eckert, we've made a decision about an assignment for your company."

Wend perked up. "Sir, the rumor is that additional forces are to be sent down to Long Island in anticipation of the British landing. Is that where we're going?"

Grayson put his quill down on the desk and looked up at Wend, a small smile on his face. "Well, I can tell you that rumor happens to be true. We're sending several battalions down there as reinforcements—troops able to stand in the battle line. But it happens that we have adequate light foot down on the island, most notably a Ranger battalion of Connecticut, Rhode Island, and Massachusetts men under Lieutenant Colonel Thomas Knowlton. He's a veteran of bush warfare in the French War and other Indian hostilities."

Wend was bemused. "If we're not going to Long Island, where are we bound? Are you assigning us to be the light company of a battalion here on Manhattan?"

Grayson leaned back in his chair and smiled broadly. "You're not so lucky. No more leisure time here in the town. You're marching North."

Wend was stunned. "North? I don't understand."

Grayson rose from his desk and walked over to a table which had a large map spread out. "Come on over. I'll show you."

The colonel pointed to Manhattan, then ran his finger northward along the Hudson River to a point where the symbol for a fort was drawn in. "That's Fort Washington, about nine miles north of where we stand. It's a fortification built so that its artillery can prevent movement up the Hudson in case the British should make the effort." He looked at Wend. "Well, with two ships—a frigate and a twenty-gun ship—moored above Manhattan, they might try it." He pointed to a spot on the Hudson. "That's where they lie, and they've been sending out boats to scout out our defensive positions." He shrugged, "They passed our harbor batteries a few days ago."

"I saw that, Colonel. I went down and watched after the cannonade began."

Grayson cleared his throat. "Well, here's the point: That action demonstrated that having guns on one side of the river won't stop the British. So after some consideration, we've decided to build another fort on the far side of the Hudson, just opposite Fort Washington. There are high bluffs there, called the Hudson Palisades. Guns at the top can fire down on any vessels trying to ascend the river."

"Is that where you are sending us?"

"Indeed. Washington has ordered General Hugh Mercer—a Virginian like yourself, and a good friend of Washington's—to build fortifications there. We consider it so important, we're sending him artillery from our limited quantity. In fact, he's already on the site with some men."

Wend was shocked. "So we are to become fort builders? Sir, I've been training my men to be skirmishers, scouts, bush fighters. In just the short time we've been here, I've marched the company out to open country three times to practice skirmishing and for my musket men to drill in rapid firing. I would submit, with pride, that there are none finer in the army for that type of fighting. We will be far more useful here when the time comes to meet the British on the battlefield than as laborers in a bloody rear area!"

Grayson shot Wend a look of irritation. "Calm yourself, Captain Eckert. There's no argument that you have a fine, well-trained company. We've known that since your arrival. The fact is, we are *not* sending you to become laborers. Mercer has militia for that purpose. We're sending you to patrol the area around the fort, particularly along the bluffs, to keep watch for any movement by the British on the river or the outside chance that those ships may land marines for some kind of raid. Washington himself conceived the need for you to be there. And I can say there will be another task for you, which Mercer will explain when you arrive."

Wend took a deep breath. "My apologies for speaking hastily." Then a thought hit him. He pointed to Fort Washington. "I can see a road up to that fort. But how do we get across the river? Do we cross down here, like we did when we first arrived, or is there some way up there?"

"It happens there's a ferry right there at Fort Washington—Bourdette's Ferry. And that's the best place for you to cross. With the British getting more active by the day with their ships and boats, crossing here in the harbor is becoming hazardous. So you'll march on this side of the river and cross when you get to Fort Washington. I'm told the ferry is small, so it will take the better part of a day to get all your men, horses, and wagons across." He turned to Wend. "So dispatch is important. When can you march?"

Wend shrugged. "It's rather late in the day. Is tomorrow at dawn soon enough?"

Grayson laughed. "Quite all right. And by the way, Washington is sending a personal letter to Mercer, if you would be so good as to carry it."

"Of course, sir."

"We'll get the letter to you this evening." He walked over to his desk and seated himself. Then he looked up. "Well then, Captain Eckert, you have your orders. Godspeed, sir."

—ꟽ—

It was early morning when Lieutenant Geoffrey Fairfield mounted the steps to Washington's headquarters and strode into the center hall. He stopped before the captain at the reception desk and announced himself. "Grayson called for me."

The captain didn't bother to look up from an orderly book in front of him. "Yes, Fairfield, I was told you'd be coming. You took a bit longer than expected. But in any case, it happens that Grayson's free right now, so go on in."

Geoffrey walked the few steps along the hall to the Adjutant General's door, knocked, and then swung the door open. Grayson looked up and said, "Ah, Fairfield. Come right in." He leaned back in his chair and added, "Took you a bit longer than we anticipated."

Geoffrey shrugged. "Yes, it's getting harder to slip across the harbor, what with the British running more boat patrols. We had to come by night in a small rowing boat."

"Indeed," responded Grayson. "That's one of the things I wanted to talk about." He motioned to a straight-backed chair in front of the desk. "Sit down. We have a lot to discuss."

Fairfield took his seat. "Sir, I'd like to report that there's a lot of movement on Staten Island: regiments marching, companies and battalions drilling hard. Watchers on the island tell us the British are hard at work building landing barges. Barges that can hold an entire company at a time."

Grayson nodded. "Yes, we have our own spies on Staten who tell us the same thing. Their navy is gathering boats from the ships in the fleet, and sailors are being landed, one presumes to man those barges you mentioned. The indisputable conclusion is that they are about to start the campaign—and do it in days, not weeks."

"That's my supposition, sir."

"Well, Fairfield, the point is that once they land on this side of the harbor, almost undoubtedly somewhere on Long Island, the campaign is going to get very fluid. Lots of movement throughout the environs of New York." He paused, then motioned toward him. "That's where you come in. We're going to need as much cavalry as possible to keep track of what's going on. We need your troop on this side of the harbor as soon as possible for scouting and courier duty."

Geoffrey bit his lip. "Sir, what about watching events on Staten Island?"

"We are sending a staff officer to organize the local militia to do that—admittedly that will be less than optimum—but it won't matter as much once the British make their move. Staten Island will empty out and simply become a supply station."

Fairfield nodded. "So what are your orders for me then?"

"First, I don't want you going back across the harbor. Too much chance of the British intercepting you. We'll send a courier by an upstream ferry to get the word to your second in command to break camp at the current bivouac and march upstream. Now, there's a good ferry right where Fort Washington sits on the east side of the river, and we're building another fortification on the west bank. Your men and horses can cross there, then come down this side of the river. I've arranged for you to camp close to headquarters, next to Washington's Guard. That way you'll be near at hand for communications purposes."

"I'll ride to meet my troop at Fort Washington tomorrow."

"Good. Once you get them down here and settled, you need a couple of days riding the area to familiarize yourself with the various villages and other landmarks." He handed Fairfield a rolled up paper. "Here's a rough map of the vicinity."

They discussed matters for a few more minutes and then Grayson dismissed Fairfield. He found Bloom waiting at the headquarters steps. He asked, "Well, Trumpeter, did you see Mrs. McGraw?"

"Yes sir, Lieutenant. She said she would love to have dinner with you tonight."

A thrill ran through Geoffrey's body. Clearly, this night there would be no interruptions, no urgent call to duty. His only mission would be the siege of Colleen McGraw and finally breaching the wall she had erected around her very beautiful body. "Well, Bloom, let's go hire that carriage and then it's off to the inn to make arrangements. And afterward I shall go escort the lady to what must certainly develop into an enchanting and satisfying evening."

—w—

Colleen McGraw was making her morning rounds of the Red Vixen Sutler Company. She had just passed the tents of the girls, who were sleeping late because they had had a busy time of it the last evening, when she heard someone calling out her name.

"Mrs. McGraw! Mrs. McGraw!"

She stopped and looked around to see Edna Farley's son, Charlie, approaching at a fast walk, waving frantically at her. "What is it that's got you so excited, Charlie?"

"Mother says to come to the north end of the camp. Come right now. There's something you should see."

"Well, Charlie, what is it?"

"It's that *Horner* fellow. The one what is after Emily Crider. He's setting up camp right next to us."

Colleen felt a flash of anger course through her body. "You're damned right I'm going to see what's happening."

It took them less than a minute to arrive at the northern side of the sutler company's encampment, where stood Edna, hands on her ample hips, watching as the young gunsmith worked at erecting his tent. He had already unhitched his horse from a good-sized cart and staked it out to graze.

Edna looked around and said, "He just arrived a few minutes ago. Looks like he's planning to settle in."

Colleen gritted her teeth. "If I have anything to say about things, it's likely to be a lot shorter than he's got in mind." She walked over to where Horner was busy. "Good day, Mr. Horner."

The lad turned and looked at her, then smiled broadly. "Why, Mrs. McGraw, it's good to see you again."

"May I ask what you are doing?"

Horner stopped work and looked around, then motioned with his arm to take in his wagon and the tent. "I should think that would be rather obvious. I'm setting up camp."

Colleen stifled the anger she felt rising within. "And why in this particular spot?"

"Now Mrs. McGraw, I should think that would be rather obvious. First, I'm a gunsmith and there are lots of firelocks around this very spot." He swept his arm around to take in all the regimental encampments in the area. "And second, and most important, this is close to Emily."

Colleen said with in a severe voice, "And just *who* said you could set up shop in this spot? This area is under the control of the army."

"Why, ma'am, I have the permission of the Quartermaster General himself. A letter of authorization, all signed and sealed. I'm an official contract gunsmith for the army. Would you like to see the letter itself?" He shrugged. "But I 'spect it's probably just like the one you have to run your business and stay with army."

He had her there. "Well, why don't you move up the road? You can take care of your work just as easily up there, and you'll be in the very center of the army encampment. Your presence here is going to be a distraction for Emily." She smiled meaningfully. "As you know, she is *much* in demand."

Horner beamed. "Why, Mrs. McGraw, I intend to be a *very great* distraction for Emily—every chance I get, right up to the time Mr. Eckert's whiskey arrives and she leaves your company."

Colleen was stunned. "Wait a minute! There was no formal agreement about that whiskey. Wend took off to see about the British bombardment before I gave him my answer!"

"Well, ma'am, Wend sure thinks you made a deal. He just sent off a letter two days ago tellin' his wife to send a big wagon load. It should be here in a few weeks."

"You tell Wend to get back up here and talk to me about this. I'll not be bound by a deal I didn't agree to."

Horner shrugged. "Be sort of hard, Mrs. McGraw. Wend ain't in Manhattan anymore."

"Not in Manhattan? Where the Devil is he?"

"Near ten miles north of here and on the other side of the river. He and the company are part of the garrison of a new fort General Mercer is building. It's up on the high bluffs right across the Hudson from Fort Washington." He held up a finger. "But, Mrs. McGraw, I think you are going to take that deal about the whiskey and be happy about it. I did a little checking around in the last couple of days. There ain't much of it here in Manhattan. Lot's of taverns and inns trying to figure out how to get some or invest in making it, but it's going to take a lot of time. There's getting to be a shortage of hard spirits because the British have cut off the flow of rum. It seems to me Wend's offering you a bargain you can't refuse. So I'm gonna stay right here and do my business and keep Emma company every chance I get. I recall you saying I could do that long as she kept working for you."

Colleen stared at Horner for a long moment in frustration. Then she stamped her foot and exclaimed, "Andrew Horner, you are a damned cheeky bastard!"

Cocking his head, Horner laughed and said, "That ain't the first time I've been called *cheeky*. But I got to tell you, Mrs. McGraw, I don't take kindly to being called a bastard, 'cause sure as there's a God above, my Ma and Pa were married when they had me. Truth is, if you was a man, I'd take that smile off your face right now."

Colleen stamped her foot again but said nothing immediately. She stood glaring at Horner while he stared back with a grin on his face, which further infuriated her. Finally, she shook her finger at him. "Horner, I can't stop you from camping and carryin' out your trade in this spot. But I'm warning you: Don't you interfere with Emily doin' her work. You understand?" But she didn't wait for an answer, instead spinning on her heel and stalking off to her tent, followed by Edna and Charlie.

Horner stood watching them go, still with a broad smile on his face. When they had disappeared behind a row of tents, he returned to his work of setting up camp, got his work table out of the cart, and began organizing his tools.

After arriving at her tent, Colleen poured herself some whiskey, sat down, and stared out at the road to let her temper cool.

Edna arrived shortly thereafter. "Now, Colleen, are you going to take Eckert up on that offer of whiskey?"

"I damn well don't want to give up on keeping Emily. If I go along with it, she'll be gone in weeks."

"Well," Edna responded, "you may want to think about that. I've been looking around the city to see where we could replace our stocks of spirits, and I got to tell you, it ain't gonna be easy. That lad was right about a shortage. I can't find someone who can sell us any real quantity of either rum or whiskey. Ale, wine—yes, they got it. But not hard spirits, 'cept in tiny quantities and at a price too dear for us. And we'll be lucky if the whiskey and rum we got will last the month."

The proprietress of the Red Vixen gritted her teeth and vehemently exclaimed, "Damnation!" and then downed the rest of her drink in one swallow. She stared off into the distance.

Edna crossed her arms in front of her large chest. "Colleen, listen to me: Right now, it's easier to replace Emily than it is to get our hands on whiskey in New York. I think you better take Eckert's deal. And I'll start looking for a new tart right now. I've no doubt that in this town or in the army there's plenty who'd jump at the chance to work for you."

Colleen shook her head. "I don't see that we have any choice. But I hate the thought of writing to Wend and telling him we accept the deal."

"I don't think you need to do that, Colleen. The way Horner was talking, Eckert already considers it a done thing and has ordered the whiskey. All you got to do is wait 'til it gets here."

Colleen was considering that thought when her attention was distracted by a horseman on the road riding in their direction. She sat up in her chair and looked closely. "Edna, that's one of Fairfield's South Carolina dragoons. I wonder what he's doing out here?"

"I'll guess he's carrying a message from the lieutenant. Probably wants to make another try at bedding you."

Colleen shot her manager an irritated glance but said nothing.

The dragoon was indeed bound for them, for he pulled up in the road at the front of the tent, dismounted, and strode toward where they waited. Touching the visor of his helmet in casual salute, he addressed Colleen. "Mrs. McGraw, I'm Trumpeter Bloom, come from Lieutenant Fairfield with a message for you." He reached into his coat, pulled out a small, folded piece of paper, and handed it to her.

Colleen opened the note, read it quickly, and nodded to Edna. Then she said, "Tell Mr. Fairfield that I gladly accept."

"Yes, ma'am. The lieutenant said he'd send a carriage for you round about six tonight, if that suits you."

"It suits me very well. And tell him I look forward to a pleasant supper at the inn with him."

Bloom touched his helmet again and said, "I shall convey your answer to the lieutenant, and I bid you good day, ma'am." And with that, he went back to his animal, mounted, and rode off in the direction from which he had come.

Edna stood watching him go, arms crossed. Then she turned to Colleen and said, "You are fixin' to head into danger. I'm sayin' Fairfield's in no mood to take no for an answer after all the time and money he's put into you, unless you are ready to give him what he wants."

Colleen didn't answer at once. Instead, she sat, eyes unfocused, head cocked, thinking about it. Finally, she took a deep breath. "Well, this *may* be the time, my dear Edna. After that naval bombardment, there are all sorts of stories floating around New York that the British Army is ready to move."

"Yes," nodded Edna. "Everybody's sayin' that. What has that got to do with lettin' Fairfield bed you?"

"For the same reason I entertained the Sheriff of Frederick County, Maryland. The fact is he may be helpful to us. When the fighting does start, I expect things are going to happen fast. The army will move rapidly to counter the British, and who knows the outcome. If things go badly, we may have to get out of Manhattan on short notice. Geoffrey works directly for Washington—he can provide the information we need on where to go or when to run if it comes to that. If I keep him happy and close, we'll get that information. Otherwise, we may be caught unawares."

Edna gave her a knowing look. "So you may not be back tonight."

"We'll see how it develops." Colleen made a crooked smile and waved a hand in resignation. "In any case, he's good-looking and certainly smells more pleasant than that sheriff."

—∞—

It was just after noon, and Colleen was in her tent, with the flap closed, getting ready for her evening with Fairfield. She was laying out the clothing she planned to wear when she heard Edna Farley call to her. "Mrs. McGraw, there's someone here to see you."

She opened the tent flap and stepped out under the fly to see a young captain in a blue uniform with buff-colored facings standing with his hat tucked under his arm.

Edna introduced him. "Captain Coleson, this is Mrs. McGraw."

The officer made a small bow and said, "Good afternoon, ma'am."

Edna cleared her throat, then explained, "Mr. Coleson is an aide to General Lee."

Coleson nodded. "Indeed, ma'am. In fact, I'm here on business for the General." He looked at Edna. "Of a private and quite personal nature."

"Anything you want to say to me, Mrs. Farley can hear. She is my manager." She motioned to a chair. "Please be seated." She sat down herself.

The captain took a chair, and Colleen asked, "And what, sir, is this business you speak of?" She could see that Coleson was showing signs of nervousness and discomfort.

He took a deep breath and said, "Well, ma'am, the fact of the matter is that General Lee is looking for some companionship." He bit his lip and continued, "Companionship of the female type, if you know what I mean."

Colleen shot a quick glance at Edna. "Ah, yes, Captain. I completely understand."

Coleson said, "We—the General and his staff—have only recently arrived in the area from the South, but we are informed that you have some of the loveliest and accomplished young ladies in Manhattan in your employ."

Colleen felt playful. "We would most sincerely agree with that sentiment. But if I may ask, where did you happen to get that information? I like to know who is recommending our services."

"Well, confidentially, I spoke with some officers on General Washington's staff."

Smothering a laugh, Colleen said, "Well, indeed several on the staff have favored our ladies." She shrugged. "When would the General like this companionship?"

"He was thinking of this very evening, if that were convenient."

"Captain, we can certainly manage that." Colleen gave him a sweet smile. "Now, I should ask, what is his taste in women?"

"He likes them younger than himself, and he does have a predilection for blonde-haired girls."

Colleen put her hand to her chin. "Well, my dear sir, I daresay all my girls are quite younger than the General. In any case, I believe we have just the girl for him. She is just twenty with a comely countenance, willowy figure, and has the finest golden hair you'll ever see." She glanced quickly at Edna and then back to Coleson. "Her name is Emily, and I'm sure she will more than satisfy General Lee's desires."

"Mrs. McGraw, I believe the General will be well pleased. Now, can you arrange for her to be at our headquarters, which is at the house next to Washington's, this evening?"

"That would be our pleasure. As a matter of fact, I'm traveling down to lower Manhattan tonight and she can ride with me in the carriage." Colleen thought a moment. "And how long do you expect her to stay?"

"Oh, the General likes to have them for the full night. He has considerable, err, *stamina*."

"Well, then, we shall arrange for her to be picked up early in the morning. For discretion, I suggest just before dawn and before the army is stirring."

Coleson smiled. "I was just going to suggest that myself."

"Well, sir, we do have some experience with matters of this nature."

"Indeed it would seem so, Ma'am. Then it would appear that things are settled."

"Except," said Colleen, holding up a finger, "for *one* matter. One *very* important matter: the question of payment."

"Ah, yes. Well, the General usually takes care of that himself at the end of the engagement."

"I'm not sure who he has been dealing with, but my Emily is not going anywhere until we have settled the payment amount."

"Well, Ma'am, in that case, please advise me of your price."

"We shall put it in writing, Captain." Colleen took a piece of paper and wrote a figure on it.

Coleson looked at what she had written. "I'm not particularly experienced in these matters, but that seems quite stiff, Ma'am."

"That price is for my best girl's services for a full night, for her transportation, and of course, discretion in the matter. The fact is, she would make that amount by servicing several men here tonight. My girls are always *quite* busy." She shrugged. "I suggest you take that to the General and let me know by courier if that amount is not satisfactory."

Coleson rose and put on his hat. "As you say, we shall inform you only if the General does not agree." With that, he turned, went to his horse, mounted, and rode off back toward lower Manhattan.

Edna looked at Colleen sternly. "Sally Croft would have served the General's taste as much as Emily. And Sally would have treated it as a lark. You know that seeing her going off to service a general on his first day here is certainly going to disturb Horner."

"That, my dear Edna, is *precisely* my intention. I want him to see for himself what the reality of her life is and has been. Perhaps it will give him second thoughts about marrying a tart."

Edna raised her eyebrows. "Or mayhap it will make him even more determined to spirit her away from this life."

Colleen thought a while, then shrugged. "Well, we shall see. In any case, tell Emily to get into her most flattering gown, powder her face pretty, and make ready to join me in the carriage when it arrives. And instruct Charlie to take one of the wagons to pick her up tomorrow at dawn."

—ɯ—

James the waiter ushered Geoffrey and Colleen into the private dining room at the Britannic Crown Inn and helped them take their seats. Then he took their order for libations and departed to fetch the drinks.

Colleen gave Fairfield an impish smile. "Why Jeffrey, you've arranged everything just as it was the last time, when we were so abruptly interrupted. Same inn, same time, same dining room, same server. How thoughtful and charming of you."

"I wanted to take up precisely where we were before."

Colleen replied in a coquettish tone, "Including the well-appointed bedroom with wine?"

Geoffrey raised his eyebrows in surprise. "So, you found out about that?"

"The serving man mentioned it to me, and I asked to take a look."

He shrugged. "Well, I always knew you were a clever one, my dear. But yes, I thought after dinner it would be nice to have a private glass of wine in a cozier setting."

"Well, Geoffrey, you know where I stand on that; it depends on how cozy you intend for things to become."

Fairfield was thinking of a proper comeback when the waiter returned with their drinks and took their dinner order. With the thread of conversation broken, he changed the subject. "The young lady—Emily, I believe—who rode with us to General Lee's headquarters was quite pretty. But I dare say she looked none too happy. She stared straight ahead and hardly spoke a word save for a greeting." He smiled knowingly, "Although I dare say spending the night with Lee cannot be a happy prospect."

Colleen replied, "No one said she was going to see the general himself. There are many officers at the headquarters."

Geoffrey made a small laugh. "Now, Colleen, you may feel it necessary to be discrete, but it is common knowledge that Lee pays for his nocturnal companionship. Have you ever laid eyes on him?"

"I've never seen or met him."

"Then you would know why he pays for his pleasure. Lee is a singularly unattractive man, with a body lean as a fence post and an angular face only a mother could love. He's unmarried and likely to remain so, as I believe no man would choose to subject his daughter to such as Lee. In fact, he surrounds himself with a pack of dogs for companionship. Your young lady will have quite a job keeping a pleasant face as she does her work."

"Emily is both pretty and accomplished at being pleasing with a man, whatever his attributes. I have every confidence that whoever she is with tonight will find her pleasant and pleasurable company." She took a sip of her drink and diverted the conversation away from the general. "What has brought you to Manhattan on this occasion? I should have thought you would be very busy watching the British on Staten Island, what with the campaign about to start."

"Actually, I'm here because of the campaign. My troop is being brought over from Jersey to act as scouts and couriers when the British have landed. The men and horses should be ferried across the river tomorrow, and then be here a short time afterward. We'll be working right under Washington himself. I flatter myself that he has great confidence in me because of our work in watching the British on Staten." Fairfield was gratified to see that what he had said seemed to make a great impression on Colleen. She raised her eyebrows, put her drink down, and leaned toward him.

She asked in a serious tone, "So you will be aware of all the movements of the British? You will also have to know where our army will be going?"

"Of course, by necessity. In fact, I shall know many things about the British even before Washington himself."

Fairfield was thrilled at Colleen's reaction. She leaned over the table, reached out to put her hand on his and said in an admiring tone, "I'm so proud of you, Geoffrey! It's incredible that an officer so junior has been selected to perform such a critical role in the army. And no doubt your friends in South Carolina will be mightily impressed when they find that their troop has become Washington's eyes and ears."

"Well, Colleen, we shall have to see how things actually work out."

At that moment, the door opened and their waiter entered, assisted by another man, carrying their dinner. When the two had departed, the couple had a leisurely meal accompanied by pleasant conversation. Fairfield thought Colleen had never been more personable. Presently the waiter brought sweets, which they both downed enthusiastically.

When they had finished, she looked up at him, a satisfied smile on her face. She sighed and said, "Geoffrey, what a pleasant meal. This was such a good idea."

"Thank you, my dear."

"And you know," she said in a sweet, provocative voice, "all this good food has put me in a mood which would greatly appreciate the comforts of that room and bottle of wine."

Feeling exultant, Geoffrey rose to his feet and helped her out of her chair. It was clear that he was about to realize the fulfillment of his long—and costly—quest. "Well, my dear, then we shall let nothing stand in our way to that delightful pleasure."

—~—

The sun was well up when Fairfield's carriage dropped Colleen off at her tent at the Red Vixen camp. She took off her hat and dropped it on the table under the fly. She was about to enter the tent to change when Edna Farley arrived. She had a sly smile on her face. "So you finally did it." It was a statement, not a question. "So how was it gracing the sheets with our gallant young southerner?"

"He knows his way around a woman's body, but he's not as good as he thinks he is." She shrugged. "All in all, it certainly wasn't unpleasant." Colleen gave Edna a knowing look.

"Well, Colleen, most men ain't as good as they think."

Colleen laughed. "That's true enough, but always make them believe they are." Then she asked, "Did Emily get back all right?"

"She's here. Not happy—sulking, I'd say. Told me nothing about her night—just said she needed sleep and walked right to her tent."

Shrugging, Colleen said, "She'll be all right." Then she thought of something important. "Did Lee pay her in the amount we agreed?"

"Indeed," responded Edna. "She brought it with her."

Then Colleen thought of something else. "We need to have a meeting. Get Charlie and Elijah Lynch here, besides yourself. I've some things to tell you all that

I learned from Fairfield." She walked to the tent and pulled back the flap. "Give me a quarter hour to change clothes."

In a few minutes, the four of them were seated around the table. Colleen went right to the point. "Last evening, I learned a lot from Lieutenant Fairfield about what's going on with the army and what we may have to face when the British land." She looked around at all of them. "Things are not likely to go well for Washington's men, so we have to be ready to move, and move smartly, when things start to happen."

Elijah Lynch, the master of the horse and head wagoner, looked puzzled. "And just how are we going to know when we got to get movin'?"

"We'll know, Elijah, because Lieutenant Fairfield of the Palmetto Light Horse has pledged to keep me informed of what's going on and, most importantly, when it's time to move to a safer location."

She motioned toward Charlie and said, "You're going to have to do some scouting for us." Then she looked back at Lynch. "Elijah, get him a good horse."

"Aye, that will be no problem, Mrs. McGraw."

Colleen turned back to the lad. "Charlie, if we have to get out of the way of trouble, Fairfield tells me we should go north, toward Fort Washington. So I want you to scout out the lay of the land in that direction. Particularly, make a map of all the roads so that we'll know the best way to go in the face of changing conditions, and note places where we could camp." She held up a finger. "And this is important: If things really go bad, we may have to get across the Hudson. So ask around and find out where all the likely ferries are."

"Yes, ma'am," the lad responded. He reflected a moment and added, "I 'spect that's going to take a few days."

Colleen nodded. "Yes, so take along enough provisions for you and your horse. And I'll give you some coin in case you need it." Then she turned to Lynch. "Elijah, we've been camped here for many weeks. The horses have been in the pasture. Check them and your wagons and harness. I don't want to be kept from moving by an unexpected problem, like a wheel hub which needs greasing."

Lynch looked irritated. He said, in a pained voice, "Mrs. McGraw, there ain't nothin' wrong with my horses or the wagons. We'll be ready when the time comes."

Colleen ignored the edge in his words and put her hand to her chin. "And make sure we have a good supply of grain for the animals. Get out and purchase it now. It may be hard to find and much more expensive once the battles begin."

In the same irritated voice, Elijah said, "Yes, ma'am."

Then she turned to Edna. "If we have to move fast, getting enough food for our people may be impossible. I want you to try to find a way to get barrels of salt meat, like the army uses, beef or pork, whatever you can get your hands on." Then another thought hit her. "Since we've been here, a lot of material has been taken out of the wagons so we could get at it easily—chests and barrels on the ground for convenience. Check around the camp, and pack everything we don't use every day back into the Conestogas."

Edna's face wrinkled up. "That's goin' to make it harder to get things done and provide for the customers." She raised her hands in supplication. "Colleen, aren't you bein' a little hasty about all this?"

Colleen smacked her hand down on the table. "Now listen to me, all of you: We've got fourteen people here at the Red Vixen. I mean to keep everyone safe, and my intuition tells me that we will have to move in great haste when the campaign begins." She gave everyone at the table a fierce glance and repeated, "I tell you, I want to keep the people safe!" An even more determined look came over her face. "And then there's the little matter of *my* bloody investment in all this!" She swept her hand around to take in everything in the camp. "My whole fortune, everything I've worked for all my life, is here, and I'm damn well not going to give the British a chance to take it away!"

In the late afternoon, Andrew Horner was deeply occupied with the repair of the lock and trigger mechanism of a musket. The quartermaster of a Pennsylvania regiment had brought him several that needed various types of repair, and the entire lot provided for work that would take several days to complete. Then he was pleasantly surprised by the arrival of Emily. Without looking closely, he said, "Good afternoon, my dear. I'd hoped you would pay me a visit."

He was puzzled when she didn't answer. He looked up to see her standing, arms crossed in front of her chest, with tears running down her cheeks. His joy at her presence disappeared. Dropping his tools, he jumped up and took her into his arms. She immediately broke into sobs, her whole body shaking.

"What's wrong, Emily? What has you so upset?"

She took a deep breath. "Oh, God, Andrew, I feel so dirty, so spoiled. You know how many men I have been with. I get through that by thinking of other things while they have their pleasure. But last night, with this General Lee, was the worst of my life."

"My God! Did he mistreat you? Did he hit you?"

She shook her head. "No, it wasn't like that. It wasn't *physical.* It was the way he regarded me—like I wasn't human, like I was nothing but a tool, a machine with no purpose except to satisfy his desire. Other men at least make an effort to be friendly and sort of romantic, but when I came into his bedroom, Lee hardly looked at me, just told me to undress and then waved me to the bed." Her body shook all over. "He never slept during the night; he took me over and over again like he had a hunger which couldn't be satisfied."

Andrew hugged her close, trying to console her, but her sobs only got worse.

Then she took a deep breath, and her face displayed agony. "But the worst part was the dogs."

Andrew looked into her eyes. "Dogs? I don't understand." Then an ugly thought struck him. "He didn't . . . He didn't make you . . .?"

"No, no, it wasn't like that—not *with* a dog. But he does keep a big pack of the beasts. They live with him, sleep with him. And they smell." She shivered all over. "And, oh Lord, he smells like them. But even the smell wasn't the worst part. It was that they were all around us as he took his pleasure. They were staring at us, they were in bed with us—watching and panting and snorting and drooling as he had his way with me. Then, when he was resting, the dogs would lie down with us."

Andrew kissed her on the cheek. "It must have been terrible for you. But there's only a short time, and you'll be free. The whiskey will be here."

"But Colleen said she hasn't agreed to take that. She's crafty. She'll find a way to keep me working."

"I think she doesn't have any choice. There's no good whiskey around here. We'll soon be free of her and together forever."

But instead of being reassured, Emily broke down into the heaviest sobbing so far. "But Andrew, how can you be so sure of your love of me? How can you still want to marry me, knowing what I've been doing? I'm a soiled woman and always will be. And many people know what I've done. They'll hold us in shame. They'll ridicule you for living with me. How will you bear to be seen with me?"

Andrew held her tight, gave her a long embrace, and stroked her hair.

When her sobbing had somewhat subsided, he said, "Emily, it's a big country. After the war, we'll get a fresh start where people don't know us. It won't be the first time people have gone to a new place to leave their problems behind. Donegal and Joshua Baird have told me the story of how Wend Eckert himself left Pennsylvania to make a new life after he became a wanted man for taking revenge on a gang of renegade traders. And he prospered and is one of the most respected men in Frederick County."

"But he doesn't have a wife who was a whore. That's not something he had to overcome."

"Emily, don't despair. We'll go so far no one will know or guess. There's a need for gunsmiths everywhere. We'll do well, build a comfortable house, and have many children. And you can put all this in your past."

She looked up at him, hope in her eyes. "Do you really think we can do it?"

Andrew grinned down into her teary but still beautiful eyes. "Together we can do anything."

She raised her lips and kissed him. "Oh, I so want to believe it."

Suddenly a female voice spoke up with a sarcastic tone, "Well, that's all very romantic, like one of those European fairytales: *young love will conquer all adversity.*"

Startled, they turned to see Colleen McGraw standing a few feet away, hands on hips. She looked at each of them, then said, "I'm sorry to cut this little festival of love short, but it's getting late and Emily has to get ready for work. Men will be arriving soon."

Anger welled up in Andrew. "Mrs. McGraw, as far as I can see, the only thing you believe in is profit. But other people have a different view of life, and they have a right to pursue their dream."

"Yes, well you'll have to make your plans another time." She waved at Emily. "Get to your tent and prepare yourself."

Horner stepped forward until he was close to Colleen. "She's not working tonight! Not after what she went through last night. I don't know how much you heard, but that damned general worked her to exhaustion and then made her lay down with dogs! Stinking dogs! Dogs, do you understand? No, I'll not let her work tonight." He paused, then continued, "Look at her. Can't you see she's exhausted and in despair? She'll not be good company for any man tonight. Your customers won't be satisfied. They'll want their money back."

Colleen looked closely at Emily and back at the enraged Horner. Then she was quiet for a long moment, mulling his words. Finally, she said in a stern voice, "All right, she can rest tonight. We'll probably not be very busy. But mark my words: There's a big party for some officers tomorrow night. She must be ready to sing, keep them good company, and satisfy their desires. Do you understand that, my little Miss Crider?"

Emily wiped the tears from her eyes. "Oh, thank you, Colleen. I promise I'll be ready. I'm just so very tired right now."

Colleen shot Horner an angry look and then, without saying another word, stomped off toward her tent.

Andrew stared after the departing woman. "What a despicable person she is. All she thinks about is enriching herself—enriching herself from the labor of others." He looked over at Emily and was surprised to see her shaking her head.

"Andrew, you're right about most of that, but you must try to understand. She's had a hard life. Her father deserted the family, and her mother became a drunkard. They lived in desperate poverty. Finally, she sold Colleen into bondage as a tavern maid to get money for herself and her drink."

"That may be true, but, my love, I don't understand how you can bring yourself to be so charitable toward her. Look at what she is doing to you."

"Andrew, she rescued me from a situation almost as bad as hers had been. My family was killed by a raiding party during Pontiac's War. I survived only because I was able to hide in the woods. Then neighbors helped me get to my uncle's house back east, but that turned out bad. He started to take an interest in me, and his wife sent me away—to be a tavern maid just like Colleen. But the proprietor considered me his property and started having his way with me almost at once. That's where Colleen found me—he was looking for girls for her place in Fredericktown in Maryland. She visited the tavern and took to me right away. She sat me down and explained what she wanted girls for and what I would be doing. But she said at least I would be getting paid for it and someday would have enough money to leave whoring and make my way in the world. She said I would have nice clothes and enough food to eat and that she would make sure the men treated me right. I didn't have to think much about it: It was a better life than I had lived since the Indian attack, and besides, I knew I was considered a spoiled woman. It took me only a few seconds to agree. So she paid the tavern owner some money and took me to her own place. And she was right; for the most part I've lived better since then." She shivered again. "But last night was too much. I can't do this much longer."

Horner hugged her tight. "And it won't be much longer. Mr. Eckert's whiskey will be here soon, and you can leave this business forever. We just have to get through the next few weeks."

Emily closed her eyes and nodded slowly. "Yes, I'll steel myself and keep Colleen pleased. But I will be counting the days until I," she paused, "*No,* until *we* will be free."

Chapter Eight

Matters of Intelligence

Clive Harfeld entered the tea shop off Broad Street and, looking around, soon saw what he was seeking—a table in a nook of the room which would afford privacy. That would be necessary for the conversation he planned. Walking over to the table, he placed his hat on a chair and seated himself in another facing the front of the shop where he could see the door. Soon the proprietor came over to ask for his order.

"Some finger cakes if you will, and a pot of tea with two cups."

"Sir," said the owner, looking at Harfeld with a puzzled expression, "you must understand we have only coffee. The blockade, of course."

Harfeld stared at him for a prolonged moment, then allowed a knowing smile to spread over his face. "Now my dear sir, you have the look of a clever man. And with that in mind, I would suggest you have a private supply of tea in this shop. I assure you I am quite willing to pay the exorbitant price you would ask for a pot of it. Confidentially, I'm having a *very* special guest and know that *she* would most greatly appreciate it."

The shopkeeper looked around furtively and, seeing no one else close by, replied with a sly grin, "Indeed, what you mention would be quite dear. And I would ask that you not advertise the fact that I have a certain amount in stock. I keep it for a very special clientele."

"Of course, my dear sir, I will keep it in the strictest confidence and would be greatly pleased if you would henceforth include me in that select group."

"I will brew a pot and be back presently, sir."

Harfeld took the watch out of his pocket and checked the time. He had just finished when the door opened and his guest entered the shop. She stood just inside, closing her parasol and glancing around for him. It struck him that Catherine Tresh was one of the most handsome women he had had the pleasure to meet: the thin, high cheek-boned face, deep blue eyes, raven hair, which she, at the moment, wore put up but in a manner which nicely framed her head. She wore a very flat, medium-brimmed straw hat which could only have stayed on her head with the help of pins. He noted she was taller than average with a willowy frame that was accentuated by a tight-fitting, medium-blue, low-cut gown which exposed a tantalizing amount of cleavage. Seeing her, Clive could not but feel a surge of arousal. He had not been with a woman since Adele had passed and now he suddenly realized what was missing from his life and found himself thinking of what it would be like to have this enchanting woman in his arms. But he forced himself to dismiss the thought and focus on the business at hand.

He stood up and waved, and she smiled and came toward him.

Catherine said, "I'm so glad we could meet so soon. And this is a lovely little shop."

"It's my pleasure, Mrs. Tresh." He grinned. "And of course, it is business. But it's always a good day when you can combine the two."

He helped her take her seat, and she looked up at him. "Of course, you are right about that, Clive. And I am so eager to learn about the possibilities of property in this area."

"Well of course, we shall get into that, Catherine. But first, I have a bit of a surprise for you."

She cocked her head and smiled. "I love surprises. What is it?"

"It wouldn't be a surprise if I told you in advance." He looked to see the proprietor on the way with a tray. "But it is arriving at this very moment."

The shopkeeper set the teapot down, followed by two cups and saucers and small containers of sugar and cream. "There you have it, sir. Shall I pour?"

Clive looked at Catherine and winked. "No, it will be my pleasure to serve the lady."

When he had left, Catherine looked at the pot and said. "I admit that I am having some trouble getting used to this coffee here in America. Would that tea were available."

"Well, Catherine, I'm pleased to fulfill your desire."

She looked down at the pot again, leaned forward, reached out, and lifted the lid. A look of pleasure appeared on her face. "My God! It is tea! Clive, however did you manage it?"

"The shopkeeper and I have conspired. The promise of a bribe induced him to produce some of his personal stock."

Catherine smiled seductively. "I shall always be indebted to you."

He poured her a cup of the tea and said, "Well, we should indulge ourselves now, for soon enough I am certain there will be no tea available in New York at any price." He held up a finger, then continued, "Unless the British should win the forthcoming battle. Then it's safe to say tea will be plentiful in the city."

Catherine looked down at her tea, a serious look on her face. "Well, if that is the outcome, I shall certainly be somewhere else." She looked up at Harfeld. "Shall we discuss the matter of land? You promised to help me understand where property suitable to our needs might be found."

"And my dear lady, what are your needs?"

"We would like a country establishment, but one near a sizable town for the conveniences it would offer." She reflected a moment. "The New York City area is pleasant, with many amenities, but I fear the country around it is well settled and perhaps beyond the reach of our purse."

Harfeld said, "That is an important factor, Catherine. I hate to be indelicate, but what is the extent of your resources?"

"We have a moderate-sized amount of capital. It is based on an inheritance the Colonel received from a distant relative." She hesitated a moment, then said, "One of the reasons we came to America is because we understood land would be much cheaper here than in Europe." She took a sip of tea, then continued, "Another reason is that we hope for some recompense from the new government for Alexander's services with the army, once true independence is achieved—perhaps in the form of a land grant of some type."

Clive held up a finger. "There may be some validity to that. However, I would advise that any land you receive from a new American government would likely be in the western border country, or even beyond, in the Ohio Valley, which is truly wild territory."

Disappointment showed in Catherine's eyes. "Oh, dear. That would not do at all. I fear we may have to retreat on our expectations."

"Well, my dear, not necessarily. Such land, even in remote regions, is still a useful asset. It can be sold to a speculator to raise cash, to settlers for the same purpose, or, more usefully for you, could be traded for property in the settled regions. That, combined with the resources you have in hand, could add up to the assembly of a comfortable estate."

"Why, Clive, in the space of a brief minute you sent me into the depths of despair and then raised me up in hope. I begin to see how our dream may be realized." She picked up one of the tea cakes and took a bite. "Now I recall you saying you lived in New Jersey. What is it like there?"

"Well, my lady, I live in Morristown. It's about a day's journey to the northwest of Manhattan. It's a pleasant and fair-sized town, where I have my practice in a house there. And of course, my plantation is located a few miles to the west of town." He thought a second, then continued, "Actually, Morristown and the region around it rather reflect the kind of area you seem to be interested in. There is still considerable open land, suitable for agriculture, to the west of town that was purchased by speculators. I have a good friend who has considerable acreage held for eventual sale, and he is only one of several. You and the colonel might well consider looking at it once the war is settled."

"We shall certainly consider it—why, we could end up as neighbors! That would be very pleasant,"

Harfeld smiled. "Indeed it would, Catherine. But of course, for you it is all dependent on the outcome of the war, or might I say, a victorious outcome of the war."

He watched as a cloud passed over her countenance. "Yes, you are right about that. And from everything Alexander tells me, the outcome is quite in doubt."

Harfeld feigned surprise. "How so, my dear?" He put a hand to his chin and furrowed his brow. "I admit I am quite ignorant of military matters, but I see we have many troops here in Manhattan and more on Long Island, which seemed reassuring to me. What are the Colonel's concerns?"

Catherine took a sip of tea, then leaned forward and spoke in a soft voice.

"Alexander is quite shocked. There is no standard drill system for maneuvering on the battlefield. Most regiments have a mixture of weapons—muskets, fowling pieces, and New England smoothbore hunting guns. Few have bayonets. That is crucial, for many battles are settled in the end by determined use of the bayonet." She took a deep breath. "But Alexander has just discovered what he thinks is the biggest problem."

Clive cocked his head and whispered, "And just what is that, Ma'am?"

"Most regiments in the army itself—they're calling it the Continental Army now—are enlisted for only a year. And most of them enlisted after Lexington and Concord, for the siege of Boston. And thus most of those men are due to leave in the late Summer and Fall."

"You mean in a few weeks or months?"

"Yes. The simple truth is, unless there is heavy recruiting of new regiments, or men can be persuaded to re-enlist, the greater part of the army will be gone by the end of the year. Washington will only have a few thousand men left, and even many of those will depart early in the new year."

"You are saying that the ability to continue the war may evaporate."

"Yes, Clive. Alexander says even as Washington is making plans to campaign against the British here in New York, he must devote much time sending letters to governors of the states to raise troops, and he is constantly beseeching Congress to support the effort."

"Well, Catherine, I must say that is very sobering."

"Yes, I would say we must depend on the favor of Providence if we are to prevail."

At that moment, the door of the shop opened, and a woman dressed in maid's clothing, carrying several sacks of food, entered. She looked around until her eyes fixed on Catherine. She immediately approached their table.

Catherine looked around. "Ah, Elise. I see you have finished your shopping at the market."

"Yes, Ma'am. I was able to get everything."

Catherine turned to Harfeld. "Elise is my maid. We need to get all this back to our rooms." She gave him an appreciative smile, and continued, "But I'm most thankful for all the advice you have given me today. I'm sure the Colonel will have some questions. Perhaps we can talk again soon."

Clive stood up. "Mrs. Tresh, nothing would please me more. I visit Manhattan frequently and will let you know when I am in town."

"That will be my pleasure, Clive." She turned to the maid. "Come, Elise, let us be off."

Harfeld watched as they left the shop. When they had gone, he pulled out one of the cigars that Northcutt had given him and looked for a way to light it. He didn't have to worry. The proprietor came over, burning taper in hand, and helped him get it lit.

"Now, sir, that was a lovely lady you met with. I hope everything went the way you desired."

"Everything went perfectly. And she greatly appreciated the tea."

"Well, then it was my pleasure, sir." He nodded and went back to the counter.

Clive Harfeld exhaled the smoke and watched it swirl away and finally dissipate. He thought, *Indeed, things had gone as well as he could possibly have hoped with Mrs. Catherine Tresh. And he would have an important bit of information for Barrett Northcutt, who in turn would take it directly to General Howe.*

The aide stood at attention in front of the commanding officer's tent and said, "General Mercer, this is Captain Eckert reporting for duty with his company of light foot."

The general, reading correspondence at his table under the shade of a canvas fly, looked up at his aide, and then glanced at Wend. He smiled and then motioned toward a vacant chair next to his writing table and said, "Come, take a seat, Captain. We need to talk." He pointed to the paper before him and said, "I'll be with you in just a minute." Then he went back to reading.

Wend sat down and looked over the officer he was going to be working for. He saw a man of medium height, chunky build, with a round face, dark hair, and a ruddy complexion. As he read, his face was a study in concentration.

Finishing up, Mercer put the paper aside and looked up at Wend. "Well, Mr. Eckert, Washington sent me a letter with some information about you." He grinned. "It's good to have a fellow Virginian with me."

"Indeed, sir. I feel the same. I understand from Colonel Grayson that you and General Washington are friends."

Mercer smiled. "Quite correct. George and I are old comrades. We met during the Braddock Expedition back in '55 and were fortunate enough to survive. We also marched together with Forbes on the campaign to take the Forks of the Ohio in '58. He's often stayed at my house in Fredericksburg on the way to or back from Williamsburg." He motioned toward Wend. "I see you are from near Winchester. I have a friend from Scotland there: Angus McDonald; we fought at Culloden and afterwards realized the colonies were our best choice in the aftermath."

"Indeed, I know Angus well. His plantation is just a few miles from mine. My wife and his are thick as thieves."

Mercer laughed. "I understand what you mean: women do develop very close friendships." Then he asked, "Have you ever been to Fredericksburg?"

Wend responded, "Just once, on my way down to the Tidewater to fight Dunmore. I thought it was a rather nice town."

"It is indeed." He thought for a few seconds, then continued. "Now, Washington says you fought with Bouquet in the Pontiac War and served in the Dunmore campaign back in '74. And that our Governor Henry has a very high opinion of you and your men."

"Well, sir, perhaps I should be flattered, but then there are some who would say that a recommendation from Henry is a very dubious asset."

Mercer sat back in his chair and laughed heartily, then wiped his face as if to clear tears from his eyes. "Quite on point, sir!" There was a pause, then he asked, "Has your company all arrived?"

"They're in the process of crossing on the ferry. It will take several loads. I came ahead to report in and to learn where we should bivouac."

"Yes, my adjutant, Colonel Harper, will give you that information." Then his face took on a serious expression, and he asked, "What did they tell you about your assignment here?"

"Grayson told me that you are building this fort to complement Fort Washington in order to prevent British ships from ascending the Hudson, and that we were to patrol the river bluffs to warn of any raiding or scouting by the British."

"Well, Eckert, that's correct as far as it goes."

Puzzled, Wend responded, "As far as it goes?"

"Captain, let me speak quite confidentially. It may surprise you to know that Washington expects to lose the forthcoming battle to the British."

"I had heard that opinion expressed before."

"Well, we must be prepared for that outcome, and that is part of our job here." He leaned forward and spoke in a quiet voice. "These two forts will have an important function besides stopping British ships. They are intended to be a strong point for the army to gather and rally after a likely retreat from New York—a last line of defense, if you will, while Washington determines a course of action for the future."

Wend said, "I understand, sir. But if I take your earlier words properly, there is something we are to do here besides watch the river and the cliffs."

"Quite correct, Eckert." The general rose from his chair and walked to another table under the fly. "Join me here, sir."

Wend stepped over to stand beside Mercer. Laid out on the table was a map of New Jersey.

"Eckert, you are to keep this in strictest confidence except for a limited number of people in your company who need to know. For your information, I have been tasked by Washington to plan for a retreat of the army if it becomes necessary." Mercer pointed with his finger to a point on the map. "This is where we stand." Then he slid his finger along a southwesterly line to a river. "It is likely that we will retreat through New Jersey to Pennsylvania and take refuge behind the most significant natural barrier available—the Delaware River."

Mercer looked over at Wend and raised his eyebrows. "Your task is to scout out the route to the river, find the best places for us to cross—and of paramount importance—locate all the boats along the river and mark their location so we can use them to assist our crossing and keep them out of the hands of the British."

Wend studied the map and thought for a long moment. "Sir, if I may speak directly, it seems more like a job for light horse than light foot. There will be a lot of ground to cover, and men on foot will be at a great disadvantage in attempting to perform this task, particularly moving up and down the river to mark where boats are located."

Mercer sighed. "You are spot on, Eckert, but we don't have cavalry available. Now, I would expect that, coming from the Valley, you have a significant number of men who can ride."

"Sir," Wend responded, "I have many men who were essentially born to the saddle, both officers and soldiers." He shrugged. "We do have a few horses in the company which are suitable for riding."

"Yes, and I've rounded up about another dozen. They're not cavalry horses, but they are trained to the saddle. I would expect you would be able to put together a small troop adequate for this business."

"General, if you've got the horses, we've got the men for this service."

"Excellent, Captain. Now get your men settled in camp tonight, and then come back tomorrow, and we will discuss what is needed in more detail."

—ʊʊ—

The aide announced Wend to General Mercer, who looked up from his desk under the tent fly. "Ah, Eckert! 'Morning to you. Can I assume you have your company all settled? Is your campsite suitable?"

"Indeed, sir. Quite adequate."

Mercer nodded. "And who are these other gentlemen?"

"Sir, may I introduce Lieutenant Shay O'beirne and Ensign Edward Childers. I brought them along because I propose they lead the missions which we discussed yesterday and thought it would be appropriate for them to join our discussion."

"Good idea, Eckert." Mercer looked at the ensign sharply and said thoughtfully, "Childers—the name sounds familiar." His face wrinkled in concentration. "Ah, I have it. There was a fellow named Childers in The Valley, who had a big landholding south of Winchester." He held up a finger. "*Langston* Childers was his name. Met him while Washington was commanding the Virginia Regiment at Fort Loudoun in '56. Are you related, sir?"

Edward grinned "Quite closely related, sir. He is my father, and the plantation is called *Greenfields Manor.*"

"Ah, yes, now I recall. Well, remember me to Langston when you next correspond with him." The general turned to Shay. "And you, sir, are you also from The Valley? Do you have a place in Frederick County?"

O'beirne shook his head. "Actually, General, my only *place* is in a military company. I've not had a proper home since I left my sainted mother's side in Ireland these twenty years ago."

Wend spoke up. "Lieutenant O'beirne is a professional officer who has served in many armies of Europe, sir. We are fortunate that he chose to join our ranks in the cause of Virginia. I consider it fortunate to be able to rely on his experience." He motioned in the general direction of Mercer's map table. "And I believe he is well suited to lead the mission that we discussed yesterday, sir."

Mercer said, "Well, then your services are most welcome, Mr. O'beirne." With that, he turned toward the table. "Gentlemen, shall we discuss the work which lies ahead of us?"

The four gathered around the table that displayed a rough map of New Jersey and the eastern part of Pennsylvania.

The general pointed to the map, then moved his hand around to several towns. "I propose a series of patrols to become familiar with potential routes of withdrawal from New York State. The first would be to develop good knowledge of the roads to Pennsylvania and the towns and villages along the various roads which the army might travel. On the most direct route, the King's Way, we have Hackensack, Aquackanock, Newark, Elizabethtown, Rahway, New Brunswick, and Princeton. Along roads more to the norht are the towns of Morristown, Basking Ridge, and Spankstown, and others." He looked around at the others. "We need to know what defensive positions they might offer to hold off or delay the British, what provisions might be available in each, what facilities are available for both bivouacs and the places to shelter our wounded and sick."

O'beirne looked at the map. "If I may say so, sir, that's going to take a lot of time."

Mercer looked up from the map. "Lieutenant, that's why we're getting started now. The assessment of those towns is only the first step. Once we've done that, we'll look at the location of ferries and fords of the Delaware, to see where it is best for the army to cross. And then we must focus on the location of boats."

They all stared at the map for a moment. Then Mercer spoke again. "And Mr. O'beirne, in all your travels, it will be important to make contact with local militia leaders. I have corresponded with William Livingston, the newly elected Governor of New Jersey, regarding the availability of militia. He has been most cooperative." He waved his arm to take in the camp and new fortifications around them. "You will have noted that virtually all the troops here under my command are Jersey militia, the exceptions being your company and the artillerymen." He smiled as if reflecting on a private joke. "As a matter of fact, Washington has given my command the rather theatrical name of 'The Flying Camp of Militia,' in that we are the main force in Jersey and must be ready to march to counter any British incursion." He pointed to the south. "In fact, a detachment of my command is watching the British who are ashore at Shoreham, just across from Staten Island."

All three nodded.

Mercer continued, "Now, Mr. O'beirne, you need to inquire about the militia in the various areas for two reasons: first, we need to know what armed assistance might be available in holding back pursuing British. The second is because they can help us determine what Loyalist strength there is in this part of Jersey. Our information is skimpy, but we have heard of the existence of loyal militias and partisan gangs. There are also bands of thieves which have sprung up to steal foodstuffs and horses to sell to the British."

O'beirne raised an eyebrow. "And of course, my General, you don't want us to let on that we are planning for a retreat."

"Indeed, Mr. O'beirne. It would inspire a loss of confidence in our cause."

"With all respect, sir, the good citizens are going to be a bit curious about patrols riding along the roads and nosing around their towns, asking questions. Just what are we supposed to tell them?"

Mercer nodded. "A good point, sir. Of course, you can say that you are there simply to check out the readiness of militia for service with the main army. Perhaps another story will be to say you are working for the quartermaster general, looking for a good supply of provisions for the army in New York." He shrugged. "It's not particularly clever, but it's the best I can think of. In any case, I'm sure they've seen troop detachments moving through their countryside." He smiled. "And perhaps an experienced Irish officer like yourself can work out a more convincing story."

A gleam appeared in Shay's eyes. "Indeed, sir. Perhaps I can at that."

Mercer picked up a rolled up paper and handed it to Wend. "That's a copy of this map drawn up by one of my aides for your use." He waved toward the table. "Mr. O'beirne, I expect you to fill in notations with as much detail as you can manage. With each trip you make, we should get a clearer picture of the countryside."

"Right, sir."

"Now, Eckert, talk to my adjutant general—he will tell you where to pick up the horses we have allocated for your use." He pondered a moment. "When do you think your men can depart?"

Wend looked at O'beirne. "I don't see why they can't leave first thing in the morning."

The lieutenant nodded. "We'll be ready if the horses are."

—~—

Northcutt sat cooling his heels in Colonel Paterson's office, his briefing package on his lap. There was a council going on in Howe's office next door that included the senior officers of the army as well as the commanding general's brother, Admiral Richard Howe, commander of His Majesty's ships and vessels on the North American station. The Admiral's nickname was "Black Dick," in light of his naturally dark complexion, further aggravated by years of sunbaked service at sea. The meeting had gone on for over an hour, and Barrett's impatience was rising.

Then the door swung open and Paterson stood there, hand on the knob. "All right, Northcutt, please come in." He grinned and said, "It's time for your little show."

Barrett stood, checked his uniform, and then walked through the door and looked around the room. Seated at a table, besides the Howe brothers, were the lieutenant generals of the army: Sir Henry Clinton, newly arrived from the failed expedition to take Charleston, Charles Lord Cornwallis, and Earl Hugh Percy. A Hessian lieutenant general was also present, and Northcutt realized it must be Leopold Von Heister, senior officer of the German contingent.

Northcutt was used to meetings with important people, but he had to admit that the thought of briefing this assemblage of high-ranking officers had had him nervous since the previous afternoon when he had received Paterson's note requesting his presence.

Howe said, "Ah, yes, gentlemen. Here's Colonel Northcutt of my staff, and former advisor to Lord Dunmore. Some of you may remember him from when he briefed me last Spring on the conditions in Virginia at the time."

Cornwallis spoke up. "Yes, I remember quite well. Very succinct and informative."

Howe said, "Indeed it was. And now Northcutt has been seconded to my staff from the regiment he commands." He looked at the officers. "In point of fact, Northcutt, who has considerable experience in the New York and New Jersey region, is managing an information-gathering web of spies and watchers. And he is now about to provide you with some very important information about the rebel forces which you will of course understand must be kept most confidential." He nodded to Barrett. "Please proceed, Colonel."

Northcutt opened his leather case and pulled out a folded map. He spread it out on the table in front of the generals. "Here we have the disposition, as of a few days ago, of Washington's army." That immediately got their attention. The generals leaned forward to examine the map more closely, and Cornwallis even rose from his chair and moved to where he could see better. Northcutt pointed out that the rebels had about 12,000 men on Long Island and most of the remaining 7,000 bivouacked in and around Manhattan. He added, "And a few hundred at Fort Washington, about ten miles northward on the east bank of the Hudson." He thought a second. "Oh, yes, and it appears that they are constructing another fortification on the western side of the Hudson opposite Fort Washington. The troops there appear to be mostly militia."

The admiral commented, a knowing grin on his face, "It seems that the Americans learned something from the cruise of the *Phoenix* and *Rose* up the river past Manhattan."

Northcutt replied, "Indeed, sir. We've spotted some of their heaviest guns moving northward, probably to be emplaced in this new fort." He gathered his thoughts for a moment, then said, "We also have some indication that Washington, after some hesitation, has decided we are most likely to strike on Long Island and is moving to reinforce his force there with five or six battalions."

Clinton nodded. "Well, I should say that is rather obvious, despite any feints we make. I'm just surprised he's not making a stronger reinforcement."

Howe said, "Henry, he's clearly hedging his bets by keeping a mobile reserve on Manhattan. He may fear us striking in two locations in rapid succession."

There was a nodding of heads around the table. Howe motioned toward Northcutt. "As important as all this information about troop dispositions is, the colonel is about to brief you on something far more important—something that may well affect the speed with which we can win this war."

All heads turned toward Northcutt. He cleared his throat. "Gentlemen, the agent who has gathered all this information for us, some by himself, some through a web of spies he is recruiting, has just provided us with news which I believe is most important." He paused for effect. "This agent has established a relationship with a member of the household of one of the senior officers on Washington's staff."

Cornwallis stiffened. "The devil you say! You mean you have an informer on Washington's staff?"

"The person in question does not know they are informing but has no hesitation in conversing with our man and thus unknowingly provides us with useful information."

"So just what," responded Cornwallis with a touch of skepticism in his voice, "is this most important news?"

Northcutt chose his words carefully. "Just this, gentlemen: The condition of Washington's army is very fragile. Most of his regiments were recruited in the weeks right after Concord, during the early days of the siege of Boston." He paused and looked at the faces all staring at him. "Now, as you are well aware, our soldiers, both British and German, enlist for long service. Twenty years is the norm. But the Americans have enlisted most of their regiments for one year only." He paused to let that sink in. He could see them making calculations in their minds.

Howe interrupted. "The point is, most of Washington's regiments' term of service will be over in the course of the next few months—certainly by the end of the year."

Percy had it quickly. "By God, that means his army could disintegrate before our eyes if they are not able to reenlist the regiments or enlist new ones."

Cornwallis added, "And any new regiments he recruits will be green—untrained, inexperienced."

Northcutt raised a finger. "There's another factor which makes the situation even more grave for Washington: Almost a third of the men he can muster are militia, and their enlistment is for three *months—ninety days* only, gentlemen. After that, they can't be kept in service unless they volunteer. And we can rest assured that most of these farmers, shopkeepers, tradesmen are going to want to go home to tend their business."

Howe nodded to Northcutt. "Thank you, Colonel. Your agent—and his watchers—are doing good work for us." Then he looked around the table at his subordinates. "Now, gentlemen, it's up to us to make plans which take advantage of Washington's problem. My thoughts on this are as follows: First, our overwhelming goal must be to put this insurrection down as rapidly as possible. We have the largest part of the King's army here with us, in addition to our allies from Germany." He nodded to Von Heister. "So all this is costing a great deal of the government's treasure. Second, we need to show the rebels that they are no match for our regulars and that there is no hope for victory. In other words, we must send them into despair, which will lead to their regiments giving up and going home when their time is over instead of reenlisting. It could even cause large-scale desertion. So, in the coming campaign in the New York area, we must as early as possible give them a hard knock, or series of hard knocks, to encourage that feeling. Third, once they have been driven out of New York, we must continue to push them hard, giving them no chance to regroup, or, if you will, catch their breath. If we do all that, I believe we will see Washington's army dissolve by December, for all purposes ending the rebellion."

Clinton interjected, "And if Washington's army is defeated, we can occupy wide areas of New York and New Jersey. We shall have cut off New England from the middle and southern colonies. We must remember that Massachusetts and the adjoining colonies are where this insurrection was hatched. I maintain that once this division is accomplished, the middle and southern colonies will reconsider their position and likely lose enthusiasm for the war."

Howe said, "Yes, Henry, I quite agree. A significant objective has always been to split the hard-line northern colonies from the others."

Cornwallis put his hand to his chin. "Yes, that's true and a necessary predicate of victory. And I completely agree that the key to an early conclusion of this game is the collapse of Washington's army." He looked at Northcutt. "Colonel, if your information is correct, by December or January, we could be dealing only with small centers of resistance and isolated bands of fanatical partisans. And the populace, which in any case I believe to be quite divided in their support for this war, will likely turn on them. And then we can begin the work of apprehending the ringleaders: Washington, Henry, Adams, this Jefferson fellow, and the rest of them and make them face the consequences of their actions."

Howe cleared his throat. "We all seem in agreement about the prospects for early victory and the course to achieve it. Now let us get down to concrete plans."

He looked to his brother. "Richard, when will the navy be ready to move us to Long Island?"

The admiral thought for a long moment, the eyes of everyone upon him. Finally, he said, "Construction of the landing barges, which will hold about seventy-five men each, is nearly complete. We have organized the boats and sailors of the fleet to assist in the movement, and they can be ready and in place to embark your soldiers within a few hours of a signal from my flagship." He shrugged. "Tell me the day and the place you want to land, and we will be ready."

Howe smiled and motioned to Paterson. "Put the chart on the table, sir."

Paterson went to a table in the corner and returned with a large chart of Staten Island, Long Island, and the harbor waters between. He flattened it on the table before the generals.

Howe pointed to a beach area on Long Island. The men all rose and gathered around. Howe smiled mischievously and said, "Richard, not *the* place, but actually *two* places." He pointed to the map. "This is Denyse's Ferry. There's a good dock and flat beach to make debarkation easy. We'll land there first." Then he moved his finger a little southward. "A few hours later, we land at Gravesend Bay—a wide inlet, once again with favorable beaches." He looked at his brother. "Is it feasible?"

With no hesitation Richard Howe said, "Nothing would be easier, William." Then he added, "I'll have waters off those places surveyed to ensure we know the depths and types of bottom."

William Howe looked at his brother generals. "Well, the date will be one week hence. That will give us time to designate the troops that will be used, make final organization arrangements for our divisions, and plan their movement to the boats. Does that meet with everyone's approval?"

No one demurred.

Howe clasped his hands behind his back and said, "Then, gentlemen, the die is cast, and the game is on."

Chapter Nine

Eckert Ridge

Peggy McCartie Eckert, dressed in a pale blue gown, her raven hair put up, and carrying a straw summer hat in her hand, descended the stairway to the center hall of the main house at Eckert Ridge. Once in the hall, she heard someone moving around in the parlor and looked in to see Wilma Wood, the matron of the African family that served the Eckerts, dusting and tidying up the room.

"Wilma, I'll be leaving for Glengarry Plantation soon. Can you have Liza bring me some coffee? I'll be out on the porch."

"Yes, ma'am. Jacob Specht was just here and he said he'd be bringing up your chaise from the stable in 'bout a half hour."

Peggy nodded. "That will be just right for me to leave." She pushed through the front door and took a seat in one of the chairs on the porch. She noticed that there was plenty of activity in the gunsmith workshop across the drive from the house. Her oldest child, Bernd, now an apprentice, sat at the rifling machine, which was outside the actual shop under a lean-to roof. He was sitting at one end, busily turning the mechanism to put grooves in a rifle barrel. Inside, she could see the journeyman manager of the shop, William Hecht, talking with Wend's son Johann and the two newest apprentices, Hardt and Schmidt, who had been taken on to help with making muskets for the army. She knew Hecht and the entire shop crew were working hard to get an increment of 100 muskets ready for shipping to Williamsburg for the new regiments being raised.

At that moment Liza arrived with the coffee and put the tray on the table next to her chair. Peggy spooned some sugar and cream into the steaming liquid and took her first sip. She leaned back and relaxed. Then she casually looked down the front drive. She was surprised to sight a horseman on Ashby's Ferry Road who turned into the drive and started up the slope at a trot. She squinted hard and realized it was David Hill, the post rider. A sense of anticipation swelled up inside her with the thought that maybe he would be carrying a letter from Wend.

In a few minutes the rider arrived at the porch, and Peggy took the steps down to the ground to get the mail. Hill grinned at her and said, "Got a few things for you, Mrs. Eckert!" Without dismounting, he handed down what looked to be just a couple of news journals rolled up and tied with twine. Then he was off back down the drive.

Disappointed, Peggy took the steps up to the porch and settled into her seat. She took a sip of coffee, then broke the twine holding the rolled-up newspapers together and was surprised to see a folded packet drop out, landing on the porch floor. She had to stretch to reach it. Then she realized it was a letter. She quickly broke the seal. Scanning the words, she was thrilled to find it was indeed from Wend. Peggy read the opening paragraph with a smile on her face, then suddenly she stiffened, sat up, and reread the second paragraph, a look of concentration on her face. Her nearly full coffee cup forgotten, she jumped up, ran down the steps, and then walked briskly along the drive toward the central part of the farm and then turned north on a path to walk past the farmhands' bunkhouse, known as The Barracks, and headed for the distillery.

She walked in the door, her nose immediately full of the pungent smell of hot spirits. She glanced around and quickly saw who she was looking for: Thomas Brown, the distilling master they had hired to run whiskey production in Donegal's absence. She called out, "Mr. Brown, I need to talk to you!"

The other workers turned to stare, spurred by the urgency in her voice. She motioned toward the door, and the Scotsman followed her outside.

Brown, looking somewhat perturbed, asked, "And na', Mrs. Eckert, what is so urgent?"

Peggy waved the letter and said, "I've just got this from Mr. Eckert. He says there is great opportunity to sell whiskey in New York. He wants a full Conestoga load of kegs sent to him as soon as possible." She motioned back toward the distillery. "How soon can you have such an amount ready?"

Brown's face wrinkled up in concentration. He put his hand to his chin. Then he frowned and said, "I dunna know about this, Mrs. Eckert. The batch I'm makin' now is promised to several taverns and inns around the valley. And then we got to clean the distilling vats a'fore we can get started on a new batch." He shook his head. "But that ain't nothin' compared to the real problem: We need more rye and barley grain. We used up most everything we had from the farm here, and I sent off a message to Widow Callow. I know she's had a good crop of it. But I don't know if she's got it all harvested. Got to find that out a'fore I'll ken when we can start distilling." He shrugged. "Anyway you look at it, it's gonna be a piece of time 'till we can get that amount finished."

Frustrated, Peggy bit her lip. Then she said, "I'll get in touch with Edna Callow myself and try to get things moving. Meanwhile, get this batch done and out the door as soon as possible. Then get ready for a big batch."

At that moment, Specht arrived and interrupted them. "Mrs. Eckert, I've got your rig ready. It's in front of the house."

Peggy took a deep breath and said to Brown, "Tom, do the best you can. And I will talk to Edna posthaste." Then she turned and followed Specht back to the house. The chaise was ready for her, with Boots in the harness, tossing his head and stamping a front hoof, impatient to be off. The medium-sized bay, with white boots on three of his four legs and a white blaze on his face, was young and high spirited. Peggy loved driving both Boots and the lightweight chaise and was a familiar and much remarked sight around the roads of Frederick County and Winchester.

Peggy went up to the porch, drained her coffee in one gulp, picked up her hat, and pinned it in place. Then she went down to the chaise, where Jacob handed her up to the seat, then gave her the reins. She thanked him, slapped the reins on Boots' back, and they were off down the drive at a fast trot.

Wilma, who had come out on the porch as Peggy drove off, looked down at Jacob. She shook her head and said, "That woman drives like the devil is on her heels. Someday she gonna hit a big rut or somethin' and take a powerful spill."

Specht looked as the mistress of Eckert Ridge raced down the drive. "She does like to fly. But I'll say this: She can handle a horse."

And with that, he headed back down to the stables.

—ꝏ—

With the sun directly overhead, Peggy Eckert turned the chaise off the Winchester Road into the drive of Glengarry Plantation. Surrounded by gardens, the imposing two-story mansion stood at the end of the drive. As Boots trotted along the well-groomed roadway, she could see the carriages of the other women who would be in attendance at lunch were already in the park next to the house.

Peggy pulled up in front of the porch, and one of the grooms came running to help her down and park the chaise. "Good day, Mrs. Eckert. All the other ladies are already inside."

"Thank you, Henry. I've pushed Boots pretty hard on the way over. Please get him some water and grain."

The groom ran his hand along Boots' back. "Yes, ma'am. He did work up a lather. I'll sure 'nuff take care of him."

Peggy hurried around the rig and started up the front steps. As she stepped onto the porch, Anna McDonald came out the front door.

"Oh, Peggy, we were afraid something had kept you from coming. We were about to sit down to the table! But I'm so glad you made it."

Peggy gave the mistress of Glengarry a quick hug. Anna was her best friend in Frederick County. It was a natural pairing: Anna was about the age of Peggy's younger sister Ellen, and both had risen from backcountry origins to a level of comfort and social prestige that neither had ever anticipated in their youth.

Peggy apologized. "Something came up just as I was about to leave, and it took some time to deal with. But I kept Boots flying all the way here."

Anna took Peggy's arm. "Well, let's go join the other ladies. And I have a lovely dinner ready for us all."

Arm in arm, they strode into the front hall and then into the parlor, where the other members of what wags at the local taverns called the "Ladies Committee of Frederick County" were assembled. Anna called out, "Well, now that Peggy's here, let's go right into the dining room. Alice has our meal ready to serve." Everyone rose from their chairs and followed their hostess across the hall into the McDonald's large dining room, which was well appointed with elegant furniture that had come from England itself. Anna took her seat at the head of the table. The rest of the ladies took their long-accustomed places around the table. Jean Moncure Wood, wife of James Wood, their representative at the legislature, took the seat at the other end. As Anna's close friend, Peggy sat to her right. Sarah Marsham Childers, wife of Langston Childers—whose plantation was the largest in the county—sat to the hostess' left. Patricia Smith, wife of the County Sheriff, Charles Smith, sat next to Peggy. Finally, Jane Rutledge, wife of the County Lieutenant, David Rutledge, took her seat next to Sarah.

Then Alice and the kitchen staff promptly served the meal and wine, all of which had been strategically staged on the sideboard. After everyone had taken their first bites, Anna put down her fork and said, "Well, now, I have some news."

Peggy cocked her head. "Good Lord, you're not with child again? You just had baby John in January!"

Anna laughed. "No, it's not that kind of news." She motioned to the sheriff's wife. "Actually, Patricia and I have news together."

Patricia cleared her throat. "Charles is resigning, effective immediately." She looked around. "He's been sheriff for over five years and wants to begin clearing that large landholding we have out to the western foothills. He wants to get it ready for planting. It's going to be a big job. He won't be able to dedicate the time needed to function as sheriff as well."

Jane Rutledge said, "Well, we'll need a new sheriff."

Anna responded, "That's the other part of the news. The Committee of Safety has asked Angus to be the sheriff until the next election, and he has agreed to do it." She looked around the table. "And confidentially, after some further consideration, Angus has decided to run for sheriff when the present term is over."

Sarah Childers said, "Now, Anna, I can't think of a better person to be our sheriff. He has all that experience with the militia."

All the others nodded their agreement, and Anna beamed at the compliment to her husband.

Then Jean Wood smiled. "Well, I've just got a letter from James at Williamsburg. And there's some news about the war. The Virginia regiments that were raised earlier in the year are getting ready to march." She looked around the table. "Some will be going to join Washington with the main army, but others will be going down to the Carolinas to help defend Charleston and Savannah." She turned to Peggy. "They're hoping that more muskets will come in—they are still short of what they need."

Peggy straightened, sighed, then said, "Jean, we're doing the best we can. William Hecht and the apprentices are working as fast as possible. We'll be sending 100 muskets to Williamsburg very soon."

Jean smiled. "My dear, I'm sure you are all working as fast as you possibly can." She paused and said, "There's also news from Washington. He's written to the Governor and legislature that even more regiments are needed. It seems that the terms of many of the men he has are about to expire. So the military committee has taken that up and are looking for where the men can be raised." She paused again and looked around the table. "And James thinks they will be requesting a full regiment from here in the valley. That means eight companies, each with as many men as they can recruit."

Patricia Rutledge exclaimed, "That will be a lot of men, more than we've ever sent at once, more than we sent in '74 to Lord Dunmore's War in the Ohio Country."

Peggy looked at Anna. "If a regiment is raised from this area, I think Angus would be likely to be named its commander. After all, he is presently a major in the militia, and he led our battalion to the Ohio Country under Dunmore. No one has more experience."

The others nodded their agreement.

Anna took a deep breath. "Angus is a good soldier, but frankly, I like him as sheriff more. I'd prefer he be around the house with all our young children. Anyway, he's just turned fifty, and I shouldn't like to see him facing the rigors of the field." Then she grinned. "But my desire may matter little in the matter. Frankly, I think he would jump at the chance to organize a regiment. He's still anguished at the loss at Culloden thirty years ago, and he would welcome the opportunity to confront the King's forces again."

The other ladies nodded, and there was a silence as they addressed their plates. Peggy took the opportunity to speak up. "I also have some news. I got a letter from Wend today. You'll be happy to know that our company spent the last few weeks after they arrived directly under General Washington. Now they've been sent to work under General Hugh Mercer, who is building a fort north of New York City itself."

Jean Woods looked up from her plate and said, "Oh, James and I know Hugh quite well. We've visited with him in Fredericksburg." She looked around the table. "He's a doctor, and his apothecary shop is right on the main street."

Patricia said, "Well, at least our men are working under a Virginian."

"Indeed, Wend is quite happy about it," she smiled. "But there's more news.

Wend wants me to send a wagon of our spirits up to New York. They say there's a great shortage in the town because of the British blockade."

Sarah Childers shot Peggy a knowing look. "A wagonload should produce a nice profit for you, my dear."

Peggy nodded but responded, "That's true enough, but I thought about something else on my way over here, and that's why I brought it up: As long as we are sending one wagon to the company, perhaps we can send a second with things the men need. Wend mentioned that some men's shoes are wearing out and not enough are available in New York. And it occurred to me that maybe we could send some more hunting shirts. They're linen, and everyone knows how fast they wear out. And there must be many more things that they need."

Anna nodded her head vigorously. "Oh, Peggy, that's a marvelous idea. We can organize the women of the county to make up what is necessary, just as we did when the company was formed."

"Indeed," said Peggy. "I was planning to hire a Conestoga from Abbey Morgan, and we might as well send two."

Sarah Childers' eyes brightened. "I have some things to send to Edward. Perhaps we could make room in a wagon for things from the men's families."

Peggy nodded. "Of course, Patricia. We'll make it known to the county, and the families can drop packages off at the farm."

At that moment, Alice came in with a tray of sweets, and soon the ladies were busy working at their desserts. But the planning for providing supplies to the company continued, with excitement growing as they talked.

Finally, Anna looked around the table and saw that all had finished. She smiled broadly. "Now, ladies, I suggest we continue this conversation over a game of Goose."

Jane exclaimed, "I thought you'd never get around to that!"

They all laughed, then the "Ladies Committee" rose together and happily paraded across the hall to the parlor, where a table had been set up with the gameboard to enable them to pursue their favorite afternoon diversion.

—m—

Right after breakfast, Jacob Specht brought the mistress' chaise to the front porch of the main house with Boots between the shafts, prancing with eagerness to be off. Peggy immediately emerged from the front door, dressed in an everyday gown, scarf, and bonnet. Wilma came out with her and Peggy said to the African woman, "I'll have my visit with Edna Callow and be back in time for the midday meal," and then quickly went down the steps to the chaise.

Specht handed Peggy up to the seat and she took the reins. He warned, "Boots is full of it today, Mrs. Eckert. Not even fazed by the workout you gave him yesterday. You'll have to hold him in a little."

Peggy laughed. "I've no intention of holding him in. I want to get to the Callow place in time to catch Edna before she goes out to check the fields." And with that, she slapped the reins on the bay's back and Boots went right to the trot. Specht stood shaking his head as he watched them fly down the drive.

Widow Callow's substantial farm was just over two miles south of Eckert Ridge and lay on the eastern side of the Ashby Ferry Road. Her husband had been the captain of one of the eight independent companies of foot that the Crown had maintained in the colonies prior to the start of the French and Indian War. Henry Callow had died in that war, leaving Edna to manage the property. Having spent decades as an army wife, she was a smart, tough, and no-nonsense woman who ran the property with as much efficiency as any man, directing her stable and field hands personally.

In less than a half-hour after leaving Eckert Ridge, Peggy had the chaise turning into the entrance drive to Callow Farm. The white frame house was of simple one-floor design, with only a set of three stone steps up to front door in lieu of a broad porch. Pulling the rig up directly in front of the door, Peggy stepped down to the ground and ascended the steps to the door, giving it a few sharp knocks. In a minute, it was opened by Edna's cook, Paulette.

"Hello, Paulette," said Peggy. "I'm here to see your mistress."

"Mistress Edna, she be down at the stable. That mare, Princess, done dropped her foal this mornin'. She be see'in after it. I'll go fetch her for you."

Peggy held up her hand. "No need, Paulette. I know the way. I can talk with Edna down there just as well as here."

Making her way down to the stables, Peggy soon found Edna and one of the hands standing by a box stall. Inside was a large mare with elegant lines, licking a new foal laying in the hay. "Well, Edna, you've got yourself a handsome looking foal. Is it a colt or a mare?"

Edna looked around, gave her neighbor a wave, and said, "It's a colt, by God! And a strong one at that."

He grinned. "Came out very easy. Princess did it almost by herself." Then she asked, "Are you here on business or just to visit?"

Peggy said, "We need to talk. Why don't we go outside for a moment?"

Edna nodded and led the way out to the stable yard. "So, what's on your mind?"

Peggy said, "Rye and barley grain. I got a letter from Wend yesterday. He wants a wagonload of whiskey sent to him posthaste. There's a great opportunity for selling it at a profit in New York, where they're running out of spirits, what with all the men from the army and the British blockade. And we've used up most of our supply of grain in the current distilling run, which is all promised to local merchants. We need the grain we arranged to buy from you as soon as possible to get started on another batch."

Edna waved in the general direction of her fields. "We've harvested a little bit and got it into the shed, but those rains we've been havin' held things up. When the fields dry out in a day or two, we'll get started again."

Peggy bit her lip. "I'll send wagons down tomorrow to get what you've harvested so far. And when the time comes, I'll send a crew down to help speed with the harvesting. We can take the grain directly off the fields. We've done it before." She looked at her friend. "That is, if you agree."

Edna shrugged. "I've no hesitancy, but you must be in a powerful hurry."

"Wend said we need to get it there fast, to take advantage of the shortage."

Edna pointed to the house. "Well, that's settled. Let's go up to the house, have some refreshment, and visit a bit. I haven't been in to Winchester for a while, and I'll wager you've got some news of what's going on."

"Indeed, I was at Glengarry yesterday. There's lots of news."

Together the two friends walked back up to the house.

As they walked, Peggy told Edna about the other parts of the letter and how the "Ladies Committee" was going to send more hunting shirts and shoes in a second wagon.

Edna stopped walking and turned to Peggy. "That's all good, but you forgot the most important thing."

"What do you mean, Edna?"

"Just think a little. Winter's coming on. I'm bettin' there are few men who have overcoats."

Peggy exclaimed, "My God, you're right. We didn't think of that."

"In the British Army, each company had eight overcoats, or watchcoats, as they called them. They were for the men when they were standing sentinel duty out in the wind or rain. Most times, their wool uniform coats were enough, particularly if they were moving around or sitting by the fire, or asleep, when they had blankets." She raised a finger to Peggy. "But our boys only got linen hunting shirts. They're going to need overcoats to keep warm in them northern winters."

Peggy took a deep breath. "But how do we get overcoats in time? That's not something that's easy to sew. It takes a tailor."

Edna said, "There's bound to be old unused coats around the county. They won't be uniform, but they'll serve to keep the men warm. Somebody's just got to find a way to round them up."

"You're absolutely right. We've got one or two sitting around." She thought a moment. "I'll get in touch with my friends and they'll contact others. We'll get as many coats as we can and send them along."

They turned and headed for the house again.

Later, after a pleasurable morning with Edna, Peggy drove up the drive to Eckert Ridge, just before noon. She was satisfied they would be getting the needed grain in just a few days. While driving, she had done a rough calculation of what kind of profit they could make out of a Conestoga full of whiskey kegs and the likely amount was most gratifying. And it would come in handy. They still had significant debts from the rebuilding of the farm after the Loyalist raid in the early Spring. The money would also make it more comfortable meeting the normal monthly running costs of Eckert Ridge.

She pulled up in front of the house and one of the hands came running to take Boots and the chaise. Peggy had worked up a good appetite and looked forward to dinner with the children—Johann, Bernd, Elise, and Ellen. As she walked into the hall, she noticed a folded letter on the table next to the front doors. She picked it up and saw the address:

Mrs. Elizabeth McCartie Eckert
Eckert Ridge Farm
Ashby Ferry Road
Frederick County, Virginia

In the dining room, Liza was setting up the dinner food on the sideboard. Peggy stepped in and, holding up the letter asked, "How did this get here? The post rider isn't due to come by again until later in the week."

"Yes, Ma'am, it weren't David. It was someone I ne'er seen before. And he wasn't on no regular saddle horse. No Ma'am, he was ridin' what looked like a Conestoga wagon horse."

Bemused, Peggy asked, "What did he say about why he was delivering the mail?"

"Oh, yes, Ma'am, I sure 'nuff asked him that very question. He said he was in a tavern at Winchester and mentioned he was comin' this way, and some man he ne'er seen a'fore asked him to drop this letter here." She shook her head. "That's all he said, then he just turned his animal around and rode back down the drive."

"Thank you, Liza. I'll be in the parlor. Call me when dinner is served."

Peggy walked into the parlor and seated herself in a wing chair before the fireplace. She unfolded the paper and began reading, and after just a few words she felt a shock run through her body, her heart begin racing, and a knot form in her stomach. For a long moment, she sat staring straight ahead, frozen in her position. Then she slowly put the paper down on the side table beside the chair, rose, and went over to the liquor cabinet. She took out a cup, filled it with whiskey, and downed the entire amount in one gulp. Then she refilled it and went back to the chair and read the letter for a second time, her anxiety increasing with each word.

Presently, she heard Bernd and Johann coming in from the shop, and the noise of steps on the stairs in the hall signaling the descent of the two girls. Then in a minute Liza came to the parlor door and said, "Mrs. Eckert, we be all ready for the dinner."

Peggy, without looking at the servant, answered, "Liza, I've changed my mind about eating. Go ahead and serve the children without me."

Astonished, Liza asked, "Are you sure, Mrs. Eckert? You want me to bring you a tray in here?"

"No, I'm fine. Just take care of the others."

Peggy sat for a few more minutes, staring into the distance. Then she drained the whiskey cup, got up, and walked to her sewing room, which was adjacent to the parlor. She went over to a chest, pulled open the lowest drawer, and took out a cloth bag closed at the top with a drawstring. Opening it, she poured out the contents onto her work table. The gold, silver, and copper coins clanked as they landed on the wooden surface. Then with great concentration, she counted the coins. When she had finished, she sighed deeply, then returned them to the bag and replaced it in the drawer.

Then she sat down at the table, put a hand to her forehead, and remained motionless for a long time, breathing deeply. In a moment, tears began to roll down her cheeks.

—m—

Early on the second morning after the unsettling letter arrived, Peggy drove the chaise down the drive from Eckert Ridge and turned northward on the Ashby Ferry Road. A half hour later, she arrived at Battletown Crossroads and turned eastward on the Winchester Road. Just before noon she pulled up Boots in the stableyard of the Golden Buck Inn at Winchester, to give the horse rest. Although she had no appetite, she ordered luncheon as a reason to spend time in the common room. With the food, she ordered a whiskey to fortify herself for what lay ahead.

She had just finished ordering when she heard a familiar voice from behind her. "Why, Peggy, what brings you here today?"

She looked around to see Jean Wood, accompanied by Mary Haley, mistress of a plantation to the west of Winchester. "Why, I just made a quick trip to town to get material for hunting shirts, as we discussed at Glengarry. I wanted to get started right away." She motioned to the two. "Won't you join me?"

The two ladies sat down and ordered their luncheon. The next hour was stressful for Peggy as she labored to make small talk while mentally contemplating what she must do following the meal. She also forced herself to eat, for otherwise her companions would have found her behavior puzzling. But after what seemed an interminable amount of time, she smiled and said, "I fear I must go now to pick up the linen if I'm to get back to Eckert Ridge in time for supper." She made her goodbyes, then hurried out the door to the yard, where Boots and the chaise waited. She slipped a small coin to the yard boy and then was off.

After leaving the Inn, she turned right to go east on Market Street until coming to Piccadilly Street, and then turned southward. In just a few minutes she left the town behind and was surrounded by forest land. Soon she crossed the bridge over

Town Creek. After the bridge, the road turned into a mere wagon track. Presently, she came to Abraham Creek. Reining in Boots, she carefully rolled through the shallow ford and immediately saw what she was looking for: A wagon pulled up in a clearing beside the creek. The wagon had a canvas cover, and on the side was painted the words, "McColley's Fine Leather Goods."

Peggy turned the chaise off the road and pulled up just short of the wagon. No one was visible. She sat waiting, not sure what to do. Then a short, stocky, thick-waisted man with reddish brown hair, in his early thirties, came out from behind the wagon.

Suddenly he saw her and stopped in his tracks. Then a disdainful smile formed on his face. The man slowly walked over to the chaise, his smile getting broader as he approached. "Well, well, our own little Peggy McCartie of Sherman Valley." He shrugged, "Or I guess I should properly say, Mrs. Elizabeth McCartie Eckert?" He put his hand on his hips and, clucking his tongue, continued, "My, my, now ain't Sherman Mill's favorite tavern maid prospered? You moved from Pennsylvania to Virginia ten years ago and done right well. Yes, indeed. All decked out in a gown fit for a proper lady of the gentry, fine straw hat on her head, driving an elegant little carriage with a high-stepping bay horse." He put his hand on Boots' flank and said, "But all in all, it's nice to see an old neighbor after all these years."

Peggy responded, "Stop it, Howie McColly. I'm in no mood for mock pleasantries. Let's cut to the business at hand: Why are you doing this?"

"Now Peggy, naturally I want the money. My business keeps body and soul together, but I'm not puttin' much aside." He turned and waved at his wagon. "And truth is, my rig is old and pretty rickety. I'm needin' a new and bigger wagon, and a younger team. Yes, ma'am. Some extra money would sure help out." He shrugged. "But that ain't the biggest reason. I'm goin' to enjoy getting back at you and that Dutchman husband of yours who done wrong to my friend Matt Bratton. We grew up together and was close as this"—he held up his hand with two fingers tight together. He shook his head. "You was engaged to him and then you left him for that Dutchman. And then Eckert attacked Matt right there in your father's tavern, beatin' him with a heavy stick till his face was broken and crooked, permanent-like. And he was never quite right in the head again. I watched it happen, held back by that bastard Donegal so I couldn't help him."

"You left out the fact that Matt was calling me a bitch and a whore right in front of everybody in the common room. Wend was just defending me."

McColley laughed and waved his finger at Peggy. "Matt weren't sayin' anything what wasn't true. Lock, stock, and barrel. Everyone knows you was givin' pleasure out in the stable to every travelin' peddler in the Cumberland Valley. Anyone who would give you a coin or even just a nice scarf or gown. Yeah, you was doin' it for whatever you could get."

Anger flaring up inside, Peggy leaned forward in her seat and started to speak, but McColley cut her off.

"But that isn't the only reason I'm here. I hold that you and that Dutchman husband of yours killed Matt. He and that merchant Matt worked for, that Richard Grenough, were known to be traveling through here on their way to Williamsburg, heading there so Grenough could get paid for work he did for Dunmore in that war against the Shawnee in the Ohio Country. Spring of '75 it was—just over a year ago. And neither of them has ever been seen once they passed through Winchester headin' south. They just disappeared. Ain't no answer 'cept Eckert did it. Everyone in Sherman Mill knows he held Grenough responsible for the death of his Ma and Pa and brother and sister at the hands of them Mingoes. Yeah, I ain't got no doubt he done it."

Peggy, having calmed herself somewhat, said in a steady voice, "Howie, you're making this up."

McColley stared at Peggy for a long moment, a sly grin on his face. Then he laughed again and said, "Well, it don't matter. What you need to know is all I have to do is spread word around this place about your whorin' yourself back in Pennsylvania and this fine life you and Eckert made for yourself will be over. Yes ma'am, I saw that big place you got yourself when I dropped off that letter, that fine plantation with a great white house with the wide porch in front, stables and grain sheds and whiskey still, and that gun shop with all the apprentices. And in every tavern, people around the county here all singin' the praises of you and your husband, the captain of their army company. They be proud of you now, but they find out about your past, they'll shun you like them lepers they talk about in the Bible. All them gentry will never talk to you again. No more tea parties at their grand houses. They'll treat your children like trash." He paused and nodded at her. "You probably will have to move on—leavin' behind all you got."

Peggy almost spit at him, but controlled herself and simply said, "You bastard."

"The only bastard what concerns us is that oldest son of yours." McColley cackled, then continued, "Yeah, Peggy, I know about that too, sired by Bratton, treated like his own by Eckert. You want that boy to know where he really came from? That he ain't really an Eckert? And of course, that wouldn't help you much with your friends in the gentry if they found out you had a bastard son." He raised his eyebrows. "So I figure you got a lot of reasons to hand over the money I'm askin' for." He held up a hand. "You got it with you, like I wrote?"

Peggy made no move to comply. Instead she asked, "How did you find out where we lived?"

McColley shrugged. "I been travelin' up and down the Great Road sellin' my wares. Last year I was here in time for a court day. I was set up in the square next to an iron monger called Rhys. We was talkin' and havin' some ale together when I saw you across the square, passin' the time with some elegant women." He sighed. "I had had a goodly amount of ale, and my mouth was loose, and after I got over the surprise of seein' you, I told him about Eckert and you comin' from Sherman Valley and about your tarting yourself in your father's stable."

"Damn you to hell, Howie."

A reflective look came over McColley's face. "Now I think on it, I ain't seen Rhys along the road this year. Wonder where he be?"

"He's in Hell. You'll see him there when you go to your rewards."

"He died? Young healthy fellow like that?"

"He died at the end of a noose. Hung as a spy for Lord Dunmore."

McColley raised his eyebrows. "Well, these be dangerous times." He reflected a moment, then continued, "Any rate, you thought you was in the clear, particularly when that Irish lieutenant in your husbands' company chased me out of town." He laughed. "That was the second time I told someone about you. Sometimes I can't keep my mouth shut, especially after some spirits."

"Shay O'bierne chased you out of town?"

"Ha! Don't play dumb with me. Sure and he told you. I blabbed about you to him over ale at the counter in that Golden Buck Inn. Then he took me out to the yard, sayin' he wanted to buy some of my goods and then threw me up against the stable wall and gave me the worst beating I ever had. Then he forced me to drive out of the county under his pistols and told me never to come back." He raised a finger. "But after that was when I vowed on revenge. And it struck me that the best way was to get money from you. Yeah, vengeance and profit goin' hand in hand. Finally I started usin' my mind instead of my mouth. I realized soon as the company had gone off to the army I could come back and start bein' paid for my knowledge about you."

Peggy shook her head. "You are pure scum, Howie McColley. Everybody in Sherman Mill knew you were a piece of stinking dung. The only reason anyone took account of you at all was because you were part of Bratton's band of toughs."

McColley scowled and his face turned red. Then he laughed and said, "Well, now, you're talkin' like a tavern tart again." Then he put out his hand. "But no more bantering words. You got the money I asked for?"

Peggy reached down to her purse and pulled out the small drawstring coin bag. She threw it to the ground. "There. It's not as much as you asked for, but it is all the coin I have."

"Now you expect me to believe that?"

"I don't care what you believe. We get paid for our work on muskets for the state by a letter of credit. That won't do you any good. And what hard coin we receive from the whiskey sales is used to run the distillery and pay our debtors. We owe a lot because of the cost of rebuilding after Lord Dunmore's loyalists raided us last year." She pointed at the bag. "So that's all you get."

McColley bent over, picked up the bag, emptied the contents into his hand, and counted the coins. Then he shrugged. "That will do." Then he made a sly face. "It will do 'till *next* year."

Peggy felt a surge of fear run through her body. "What do you mean—next year?"

"Now Peggy, you didn't really expect this was all going to end right here today? Fact is, I get down this way every year. I'm going to expect Eckert money each time I come. So next summer, you can just plan on makin' another payment. You got plenty of time to put it aside."

Peggy felt a great knot form in her stomach and thought she might throw up the food she had eaten at the inn. She took a deep breath and waited a moment for her stomach to settle. Finally, through gritted teeth, she asked, "Are we finished here today?"

McColley stepped back from the chaise. "Yes, my dear Mrs. Eckert. We're finished 'till next year."

Without saying more, Peggy slapped the reins down on Boots' back, swung the chaise around to the road, passed through the ford, and headed toward Winchester at the trot.

McColley stood watching her go, then held up the coin bag, shook it to hear the coins jingle, and smiled broadly.

—m—

Peggy pushed Boots to speed through Winchester rapidly, not wanting to run into any of her close friends who might wonder why she was coming from the country below the town. When she finally got onto the road to Battletown Crossroads, she brought the animal down to a walk to let him cool down. She needed devote little attention to the horse who had pulled the chaise over this stretch of road many times. She had often joked that he knew the way home from Winchester by himself.

At first she remained very agitated and angry from the encounter with McColley. But after riding for what must have been at least a half hour, she had calmed down enough to think rationally, and in her mind started to go over the implications of what McColley had said.

There had been several surprises. The first was that it had been McColley who had told Rhys about her past. The ironmonger, on the day before his hanging, had told Reverend Thruston and James Wood the story of her being a prostitute. Later that day, they had run into Wend at the Golden Buck and had told him what Rhys had said, expressing with great indignation that they did not believe the story—they thought it was just something the Welshman had made up as a vindictive measure of revenge on the Eckerts before his death. That had been a scare for Wend and her, but nothing had come of it. For weeks she had been worried about that—had they told their wives or anyone else confidentially? She had looked carefully at both Jean Wood and Beatrice Thruston to see if there was any change in their demeanor around her and had paid great attention to their words to detect any knowing remark. Eventually, she had been satisfied that they either hadn't learned of Rhys' story or were ignoring it. But it was sure that they would remember Rhys' claim if McColley started spreading word around Winchester.

A more shocking revelation was that McColley had told Lieutenant O'beirne about her past. It was gratifying that the Irishman had driven McColley out of town and had subsequently kept the information confidential. She took a deep breath. But the fact was that another person now knew about her youthful indiscretions. Too many people were becoming aware of her secret, which increased the likelihood of someone eventually letting it out.

As the chaise rolled eastward, she continued to fret about all the implications of McColley's visit. Then it occurred to her that she must write Wend and inform him of what had transpired. He must immediately know about McColley's threat to inform on her. Beyond that, there was the surprising new information that McColley had guessed that Wend had killed both Grenough and Bratton. She started to form the phrases she would use in the letter. But after a few minutes, a thought struck her: *Wend has enough on his mind, leading the company in action, taking care of the men—without being burdened by this new problem.* She sighed. No, she couldn't write him about this. She must keep it to herself until Wend returned after the company's time was up. Then, at the proper time, she would inform him, and together the two of them would work out what could be done to deal with Howie McColley.

The principal residents of Eckert Ridge sat around the dining room table in the westernmost house on the farm, the residence of Joshua Baird and his common-law wife, Alice Downy. This included—besides the Bairds—Peggy, Thomas Brown the distiller, Wilhelm Hecht the gunsmith, and Jacob Specht, the master of the horse. It was five weeks after Wend's letter had arrived asking for a shipment of whiskey, and Peggy had called the group together to determine progress toward fulfilling that request. The group was waiting for one more participant, Abigail Morgan, whose hauling company would supply the necessary Conestoga wagons and drivers for the trip.

Presently, they heard the sound of hooves and wagon wheels on the drive. Peggy went to the door and saw that it was indeed Abbey, who was just dismounting from a small farm wagon. She called out, "Good to see you, Abbey," and continued in a friendly way, "What held you up?"

Abigail, who was in her early forties, walked toward the house. "I got good reason to be late. I ran into Harry Wills along the road. He got some news of the war. There are some big things happenin' up North."

"Well, come on in and share it with us all." Peggy held the door for her friend. "Sit down and give us the details."

Abbey took a seat at the table, and everyone looked at her expectantly. She gathered her thoughts for a moment and then said, "Well, I ran into Harry on the road just as I was leavin' our place. He was commin' down from Battletown Crossroads. He waved and pulled up his horse beside my wagon." She looked around. "A rider came into town with news. It ain't good. Seems the British have given Washington a beating." She put a finger to her lips as she concentrated. "At a place called Long Island, which is just south of that New York place. There's a river between them. Anyhow, the British and those Hessians was sittin' on a place called Staten Island, just across the harbor from this Long Island and the city, the part they call Manhattan. One day afore dawn they took to boats and landed on Long Island at daybreak, afore our men could do anything about it. They landed a lot of troops and outnumbered the men Washington had. Well, our boys fought pretty well, holdin' out against them—Harry said for three days. But then the British found a secret way around to the rear of our line and where they wasn't expected. Washington had to pull back in a hurry. And it looked like they was gonna' trap our men with their backs to that river between Long Island and the city, and they would have to surrender."

Joshua said, "So what happened? Did our boys have to give up?"

Abbey shook her head. "No, they got away back to New York. Seems there is a regiment made up of sailors and fishermen from somewhere in Massachusetts. They got a'hold of a lot of boats and they carried the whole army across the river back to New York City in one night. Washington was lucky there was a rainstorm and then heavy fog, so the British navy couldn't interfere with their crossing. If they'd been able to come in with their big guns, they could have smashed up those boats and it would have been all over for our army."

Alice sighed. "They were real lucky." She looked around the table with a grim expression. "But any way you look at it, it was a big defeat."

Abbey nodded. "Yes, they got away, but Harry said they had to leave a lot of stuff behind. They lost cannons, horses, and provisions, and powder. It all fell into the hands of the Redcoats."

Hecht said, "That puts them in a bad situation. It will be hard to replace."

Abbey responded emphatically. "That ain't the worst of it. Harry said the word is they might not be able to hold the main part of New York—that place called Manhattan. The Royal Navy can land troops any one of a number of places, and Washington can't defend them all. It looks pretty hopeless."

Brown sat up straight in his chair. "Now, Mrs. Eckert, with all this goin' on may-hap we shouldn't be sendin' all that whiskey up north. How do we know where the army will be? Where will Mr. Eckert and his company be? And will he even be able to take care of or sell this whiskey? We put all this effort into three runs of distilling—which we be still working on—and we might just be settin' up for a big loss. Maybe we should keep it here. I can sell it here in the valley and make a lot of money."

Peggy set her jaw. "Wend and his men aren't in the place where all this is hap-pening. They're to the North of there." She paused and raised her finger. "And we're not just sending whiskey. We're sending clothing and shoes and other things our men will need, particularly with the cold weather coming on. I'm not backing down."

A perplexed expression crossed Brown's face. "Aye, ma'am, I understand. But there's no tellin' what will be goin' on and how dangerous it will be by the time they get there—and 'there' might be somewhere else pretty soon. Fact is, they could find themselves runnin' into the British if our army has to quickly retreat. And then all we would have done is give the British a present of first rate spirits." He shook his finger. "And them British soldiers would also appreciate all the shirts and coats and shoes you're sendin' along."

Abbey Morgan made a stern face at the distillery man. "Thomas, I'm sendin' my best two waggoners—Jake Cather and Elijah McCartney. They been travelin' the road a long time, in peace and war. They'll be keepin' up with what's goin' on as they travel. They'll get the word from local people." She looked over at Peggy. "Our boys gonna' need them coats and shoes. I say they go. And with winter comin' on, the whiskey will be useful too."

While Brown had been talking, Joshua had risen from his chair and stood staring out a window. Now he turned and walked back to the table. Peggy could see he had a crooked grin on his face and a gleam in his eye. "Yeah, I say send the wagons. But they'll stand a better chance with three men—two to drive and one to scout."

Peggy's face wrinkled up into a look of anger. "Oh, damn. I should have guessed you'd try to find a way to go on this trip."

Baird put out his hand toward her. "Now, Lass, it just makes sense. I can ride ahead and see if there be any trouble 'long the road and make sure we know where the army really is. Yes, ma'am, just like Thomas said, we need to be sure we don't run into any Redcoats in an unexpected place." He shrugged. "And if there is trouble, three rifles are better than two."

Peggy leaned forward in her seat. With heavy sarcasm she said, "Like you three could fight the British Army all by yourself."

"No," replied Joshua, "I ain't aimin' to do that. But we could sure brush off a cavalry patrol or light foot picket. Yeah, it just makes sense for me to go."

Alice laughed. "Give it up, Peggy. He's been walkin' around here in a mood for the last fortnight. I couldn't figure out what was goin' on in his mind, but now we all know. He was lookin' for a way to go on this trip and get away from the farm and us women. And he ain't been on the road since he got back from helpin' drive out Lord Dunmore." She shook her head. "Anyway, if he's made up his mind, there ain't nothin' we can do to keep him out of this."

Abbey Morgan looked at Peggy. "You know, I'm puttin' two wagons on the line for this trip, and I wouldn't like to lose them. We all know that Joshua's got a nose for seein' when trouble lies ahead. I vow I'd rest easier at night if he was along."

Joshua grinned at her. "Bless you, Abbey."

A frustrated Peggy changed the subject. "Thomas, when will your last batch of whiskey be finished?"

Brown stared out the window for a long moment, then answered, "It will be in the kegs end of next week. And that's pushing it. And then it ought to be aged at least a few days."

Peggy frowned. "It will age on the road north." She sighed. "We're going to be weeks later than Wend desired. I hope it will be in time. He was planning to sell it in New York, but with the word we just got from Abbey, the only army that might be in New York by then is the British."

Joshua laughed. "He'll be able to sell it wherever our army is encamped. Mostly he'll sell it to the sutlers, and let them make money from the troops."

Peggy turned to Abbey. "You heard Thomas. We'll load the wagons when the whiskey is finished. Can you have them here then?"

"Sure enough. They just came back from Fredericksburg." She asked, "You gonna have all that clothing ready by then?"

"I've got a shed nearly full of things which have been dropped off. There's more being collected in a room at the Golden Buck—I'll send Jacob with one of our wagons in a few days to pick that up. And Anna's got more at Glengarry. We'll have it all here in time to load." She thought a moment. "We need to get those wagons off immediately once Thomas gets the whiskey loaded."

Abbey waved her finger. "It won't be me who holds things up. My men, horses, and wagons will be ready when you got everything collected."

Joshua stood up. "Jacob, let's go look at Beau. I want to make sure he's in top shape. And I want to take a spare along for a trip like this—always want to have one fresh. Let's look through the herd."

Specht said, "I got just one for you. Let's go bring him in from the pasture and you can look him over."

The two men headed out. Brown and Hecht also left to get back to work.

Alice looked around at the other two women. "Now that it's just us three girls, how about some coffee while we think about getting all that stuff which has been donated here in time and bundled up to fit in the wagon." She stood up and smiled. "And I've got an entire apple pie that I've been hiding from Joshua, else it would have been gone yesterday. I figure we'll get our fill before I let him know about it."

There were laughs all around as Alice rose to get the pie and coffee.

On a warm day in late September, Peggy stood watching as the teamsters Cather and McCartney finished hitching the six-horse teams to the two great Conestogas. With her were Alice Downy and Abbey Morgan. The last week had been busy. The teamsters had brought the wagons over the week before and then taken their teams back to the Morgan place until time for departure. Brown and his men had loaded each of the blue-painted vehicles with half of the kegs of whiskey bound for Eckert. Then they had topped each off each with clothing and shoes which had been gathered from all over the county and had been delivered in small wagons and carts. Then, earlier in the morning, Abbey had accompanied her two drivers and their teams back to Eckert Ridge.

The three ladies stood talking when Joshua and Specht came from the direction of the stable, leading two horses. Baird led a tall, long-legged, powerfully built bay hunter named Beau that was saddled and ready for him to ride. The other, a slightly smaller black called Partner, was unsaddled. Specht tied it to the rear of what would be the second wagon in line.

Joshua, his long rifle on a sling over his left shoulder, walked over to the group of women, a broad grin on his face.

Alice laughed. "Look at him, he's excited like a little boy goin' on his first hunt. He can't wait to be away and on the road."

"Well," replied Joshua, "it's a good day for travelin' and we should be away." He looked up at the sky. "Wish we could have been goin' down the drive right after dawn. It'll be noon in about two hours and we need to make the most of what's left of the day. I want to get north of Winchester on the Great Road afore we have to camp for the night. With luck we'll reach Shepard's Ford on the Potomac tomorrow by dusk and be across the next mornin'."

Specht, who had been standing with Cather and McCartney, called out, "Mrs. Eckert, there be riders comin' up the drive. Three of them."

Everyone turned to look. Joshua shaded his eyes, then said, "It's Angus and Anna. And McLeod is with them. Must be comin' to see the wagons off."

Peggy said, "They've come in a hurry, if Anna is riding. She usually prefers the carriage."

Very shortly the Glengarry people arrived. They pulled up at the hitching rail in front of the big house. Angus dismounted, and Evan McLeod, a long-time family retainer who had fought at Culloden with Angus thirty years before, threw down and hurried to help Anna down from her sidesaddle.

Once dismounted, the three hurried over to the group beside the wagons.

Peggy waved and said, "We weren't expecting you, but it's nice of you to come see the wagons off."

Anna responded, "We weren't planning to come, but we got some news. News of the war! Joshua will want to know about it."

Angus added, "Yes, a fast courier came into town late yesterday carrying dispatches from the army. As sheriff, I got word of it early this morning."

Joshua took a step toward the McDonalds. "Well, don't keep us a' guessin'. What is this news?"

Everyone gathered around. Angus said, "Washington and his army have evacuated Manhattan—that's the main part of New York. He's withdrawn to the north of the city." He shrugged. "By now, the British will have crossed the river which separates Manhattan from Long Island and have occupied it."

Baird asked, "Where is our army?"

"As I said, Washington has formed a defensive line north of the city. It's open country. I'm told there are two forts there, which will form the back-up for our troops."

Peggy nodded. "Yes, and the last I heard, Wend is at one of them—the one that is on the New Jersey side. It's called Fort Lee."

Angus thought a minute, then said, "That's the way things stood when the courier left the area days ago. A lot could have changed since then."

Brown, the distiller, shook his head. Anxiety was written all over his face. "I've been sayin' for weeks that this is a fool's mission. We're sendin' weeks of work on this whiskey to dangerous country. We can sell it in Virginia for a great profit and no danger."

Peggy shot the Scotsman an angry look. "I'm giving Wend what he asked for. And the men need this clothing, especially the shoes and cold weather coats. Damn it, they're going."

Joshua said, "Now I'm full out in agreement with that. We'll just have to head up into Jersey and find out where the army is when we get there."

"Yes," answered McDonald. "It could be anywhere by then. Further up to the north, or in New Jersey. There's no telling. You'll have to be careful. By then the British could also be in Jersey. You'll have to watch out for hostile patrols."

"Hell, Angus, that's what a scout is for. And that'll just make it more fun."

The Highlander gave Baird a tight grin. Then he looked around at the gathering. "There's other news from the courier. Pretty grim news." He looked at all who had gathered around. "Washington's army is shrinking. Over 1400 men were lost—killed or captured—during the battle on Long Island. And there are numerous regiments whose time is up and are going home. And worse, after the defeat on Long Island, some men are simply leaving the cause—deserting." There was a bitter tone in his voice.

There was a silence as they all considered that. Then Alice said, "We just got to trust in the Good Lord and the justice of our cause. And we owe it to all the people of the county that contributed this clothing for our men." She walked over to Joshua and gave him a hug. "Much as I hate it, you have got to go. Best get started now."

Angus said, "Joshua, I'll ride with you the first few miles—till we pass Glengarry." He turned to McLeod. "Anna wants to stay here and visit with Peggy for a while. Escort her back to the plantation when she's ready."

Peggy said, "Yes, Anna, by all means stay here for a while and we'll have coffee and you can relax after your trip over here."

"That would be my great pleasure, Peggy!"

Peggy motioned to Baird and the teamsters and said, "Godspeed to all three of you."

The rest of them made their farewells, and Joshua swung up into Beau's saddle while Cather and McCartney took their reins in hand, slapped them down on the horses' backs, and started down the drive with the brass bells on each horse tinkling merrily. Joshua took off his hat and swept it around in a gesture of farewell and then spurred the powerful hunter forward to take the lead of the little caravan. McDonald had mounted and shortly had his horse alongside Joshua.

The rest of them stood watching in deep silence as the caravan made its way down the drive and turned north on the Ashby Ferry Road, heading north to Battletown Crossroads and thence to Winchester and the Great Wagon Road. Everyone among them understood that the wagons loaded with kegs and clothing represented both their fortune and the comfort of their men.

When the caravan disappeared, the watchers broke up. Peggy, Anna, and McLeod went to the big house, Specht and Brown back to their work, and Alice and Edna started walking back to the Baird's house.

Alice looked over at Edna as they walked. "Have you noticed anything different about Peggy over the last few weeks?"

Edna made a thoughtful face, then shook her head. "No, but I ain't around her as much as you are. What are you thinkin'?"

"Peggy doesn't seem her usual self. Don't laugh much and that twinkle in her eyes ain't there, like she always had had since I known her, these ten years. Like somethin' is botherin' her."

Edna shrugged. "I 'spect it's all the worry about getting' the wagons ready to go. She's been working with all the women around the county and carryin' the load on her shoulders to get things organized. And she's been worried 'cause it took weeks longer than Wend expected. Now that the wagons are off, I wager she'll brighten up."

"Perhaps you're right." She shrugged. "Time will tell." She pointed to Edna's wagon and team. "Before you go, why don't you come to my place and get fortified for the trip home? And I mean something a little stronger than the coffee Peggy is serving Anna."

"Now, Alice, you know I won't turn that down."

Chapter Ten

Dangerous Days

"Mrs. McGraw, this is the spot I recommend for the campsite." Charley Farley stood with Colleen and Elijah Lynch, surveying the terrain. They were just a few hundred yards east of the Hudson. He pointed southward. "Fort Washington is just over a quarter mile away, and this here creek that feeds into the river will provide good water. And there's plenty of pastureland for the animals." He pointed to a semi-wooded area. "That'll be a place for the camp itself; it's nice and flat, shade from the trees, and big enough to spread out the wagons and tents for the women's privacy."

Colleen turned to Lynch. "Elijah, how do you feel about it?"

Lynch nodded. "It will do. That's good grass for the horses, and I'll set up a picket line just over there near the creek." He looked down at the fort. "And I guess we can't find a safer place to camp, what with them earthworks and cannon standin' between us and any British who approach. And we'll sure have plenty of warnin' if they do advance in this direction."

Colleen grinned, and a gleam came to her eyes. "Yes, and there's a couple of thousand men in and around the fort—plenty of business for us. That will sure be welcome; we haven't made a farthing since we had to pull out of Manhattan."

Charley said, "The word I have from talkin' to officers at the fort is that most of the army will be comin' this way as they retreat."

"Excellent!" replied Colleen. "I think we couldn't find a better place, at least for the present." She turned to the youth. "Charley, ride back down the road and bring up the wagons. Elijah and I will lay out the camp."

Two hours later, with evening coming on, the four big Conestogas and the two smaller wagons had been parked in the best places, and the tents had been raised. The girls were busy moving their belongings into their tents.

Andrew Horner, who had followed Colleen's caravan, was busy setting up his tent and workbench. Fires had been lit, and the cook and her assistant were preparing the evening meal.

It was near dark when Sally Croft startled the whole camp by shouting, "Look, look! There's a big fire." She was pointing toward the southern horizon, then she ran to the edge of the camp to get a better view. The entire company ran to join her. What they saw was a massive amount of smoke rising into the evening sky.

Edna Farley said, "My God, it's Manhattan! It's burning. I can see the glow of flames!"

Sally exclaimed, "Is it the British? Did they fire it?"

Horner, standing at the edge of the crowd, said, "No. One thing's sure, it ain't the British. They want the place as their headquarters. That's the whole point of their campaign." He shook his head. "If it's anybody doing it on purpose, it's our army, trying to deny the British the comfort of the town."

Lynch rushed to agree. "Aye, that's my guess. Our boys fired the place before they left."

Horner shook his head. "Actually, I don't think Washington would order the burning of one of our own towns. He wouldn't punish our own people, and more importantly, wouldn't want to get them angry at the Patriot cause. And the army's had enough time to remove its provisions and stores, so it wasn't done to deny them to the enemy." He thought a moment. "It might be some of our troops going rogue, acting on their own, or it simply could be an accident. It's been a dry summer up here, and a cook fire could set a house or tavern afire and spread rapidly."

There was a burst of conversation as others speculated on what might have caused the fire. Colleen leaned over to Edna, who was standing beside her, and said quietly, "Much as I detest that young man, I think he's right. Neither army would want to destroy the town. There's no gain for either side."

After a while, the people began to go back to their work in the camp, but Colleen and Edna remained behind momentarily. Colleen turned to her manager. "Tell Elijah to have one of the small wagons hitched and ready to go after breakfast tomorrow morning with someone to drive me. I intend to pay calls on the commander of the fort and the troops encamped around it to let them know we are ready for business. It's time to start bringing in money again."

"I'll have it all ready for you," responded Edna.

Colleen considered a moment, then continued, "And have Charley ride south tomorrow to see where our main army is and try to find out what's happening." She pointed to Fort Washington. "It seems safe here, but we must be cautious and remain ready to move."

Edna nodded. "He'll ride at first light." Then she looked back at the camp. "I think supper is ready, and it's going to be welcome after a long day."

Together they walked back toward where the cook was setting the table at Colleen's tent.

—∞—

The afternoon sun was low on the horizon when the mounted patrol approached the town of New Brunswick, nestled on the western bank of the Raritan River. O'beirne held up his hand to call for the halt, and the other six—Ensign Childers, Corporal Schreiber, and four riflemen—pulled up their horses on the eastern bank where the road descended to a ford.

Childers thought a moment. "This river would be a good place to hold the British for a while in a retreat. We could delay them by placing artillery to cover the ford."

"Correct, Edward," replied O'beirne. "But it would also take some foot soldiers to protect the guns. Else the British would have light foot take positions in cover and pick off the gunners, and eventually there would be an assault through the ford."

The lieutenant looked around. "It's near dusk. Edward, we'll stay the night here. Let's go across and find a place to encamp at the outskirts of the town." He leaned over to be closer to Childers and whispered, "And I've got the name of a militia captain from Mercer's list that I'm to speak with to get information on local conditions." Then he turned to the men and waved them forward. Soon the horses were splashing through the shallow waters of the ford.

Soon they trotted through the main street of the town. With evening coming on, shops were closing, and men and women were on their way home. Some stopped to stare at the detachment. Childers saw a group of young boys standing on one corner watching the soldiers. What he didn't notice was that once the patrol had passed by, one of the youths, a boy no more than ten, detached himself from the group and ran off along the street and then turned and disappeared down a side road.

Ten minutes later, they had found a small clearing surrounded by woodland and some pastureland. A narrow creek ran alongside the open space.

O'beirne looked over at Edward, "Well, lad, we'll not find a better place than this to stay the night. And it's close to the town, where I can make inquiries to contact that militia captain." He turned to Schreiber. "Well, Corporal, this is our camp. Go ahead and find the best place for the tents, the picket line, and cook fire."

The corporal nodded. "Right, sir."

The Irishman pulled his horse into the grass beside the road and slipped to the ground, the others following suit. He said to the ensign, "Once we get things set up, we'll walk back to town and take our supper at a tavern. I saw a snug, well-kept place as we rode by." He winked at Edward, "And I would welcome a well-cooked spot of supper not made from army rations."

Childers grinned. "You'll not get the slightest objection from me."

A half-hour later, the two officers arrived at a tavern that bore the sign, "Jolly Times Ordinary." O'beirne pointed to the sign. "Now that's a promising name if I ever saw one."

Childers responded, "Indeed, sir." He opened the door for Shay, and the two entered.

The tavern was clearly popular, for the common room was well populated with men taking their ease at tables or standing at the counter, loud with talk and laughter. As they entered, the place quieted down, and virtually all heads turned to look at the officers attired in their Hunting shirts and leggings. O'beirne ignored the stares and scanned the room. Then he motioned toward a corner table not far from the hearth. "Well, lad, that's as snug a place as we're likely to find, given the crowd in here."

The two walked over and sat down. They had no sooner taken their seats when a perky, petite blond came to the table, tray in hand.

"Hello, gentlemen, my name is Joy."

O'beirne smiled and said, "Well, now, your mother picked an apt name. You certainly are a joy to behold."

The girl rolled her eyes. "Now, soldier, you'll have to do better than that. I've been here for three years, and I get that all the time."

Shay laughed. "All right, lass, I'll work on it." He raised a finger to his chin as if deliberating. Then he said, "But it's also clear she could have called you Cheeky."

"I've been called that too." Joy cocked her head and looked over the two of them with speculative eyes. "It's not often we get soldiers in here. And *shirtmen* at that. Where are you from? The Pennsylvania backcountry?"

Edward answered, "No, not likely. I'm from Virginia. A place called Frederick County in the Great Valley."

"Indeed? You've come a far piece."

Childers motioned toward his companion. "On the other hand, Shay here is from Ireland, but he's been soldiering in Europe for years."

Joy's eyes narrowed. "What's an Irishman doing here fighting with the Americans?"

"And why not, lass?" responded Shay. "What's wrong with an Irishman fighting for liberty from the King?"

The girl shot O'beirne a defiant look. "I don't mind saying that Irishmen are not my favorite people. My family left Scotland and went to Ulster to avoid the King's religion, but then the Irish gave us grief and trouble, which is why we came to the colonies." She gave Shay a hard look. "Truth is, I hear there are many Irishmen among the Redcoats."

O'beirne gave her his best smile. "Now, my dear Joy, that's being quite unfair. You have to take each man on his own merits. We can't let the way some people in Ulster treated your family keep us from being friends. And more than one lass has told me that I'm not hard to look on, and they found my company very charming."

Joy's face took on an amused smile. She looked at Shay for a long moment and said, "You seem to have rather a high opinion of yourself." Then she tapped her hand on the tray. "Well, I must get back to business: What can I get you two gentlemen?"

Shay replied, "We're here for supper, but we'll start with drinks. You got any rum?"

The girl threw back her head and laughed. "You must be dreaming. Rum's long gone. And we had some whiskey, but we're out of that now. What we got is wine and ale."

Shay and Edward looked at each other and said "Ale" at the same time.

Joy said, "All right, I'll get you the ale and then take your order for the meal. You can think on it: we got a choice of roast duck or venison tonight."

O'beirne said, "We'll save you trouble. We'll just take the venison."

"All right, I'll tell the cook." And with that, she was off, her body moving in a way that showed she knew they were watching.

O'beirne looked over at his companion. "Ah, now my fine lad. A right saucy young lady and not hard on the eyes."

"Yes," responded Childers, "and she knows she's good looking."

Shay laughed. "Now lad, I've long held that a lass who knows she's got a curvy body and knows how to use it is a pleasure to behold and to keep company with."

Just then the door swung open and a tall man wearing a gray overcoat and a cocked hat entered. He stood in the doorway, his eyes sweeping around the room. Then they stopped when they saw the two officers. The man went up to the counter, bought a tumbler of ale, then turned and walked toward them.

He stopped at their table and said, "My name's Harwood. Jacob Harwood. Captain of the county militia."

Shay stiffened. "I'm O'beirne. Lieutenant O'beirne of the Frederick County Light Foot. And this is Ensign Childers. It happens you are the very man I'm here to see on behalf of General Mercer."

"Aye, I figured that." He pulled out a chair and sat down.

"Now how the Devil," asked Shay, did you know we were here?"

Harwood took a quick sip from his cup. "A few days ago I got word from Governor Williams you was comin'. And it happens I have a group of young boys who keep their eyes open; they watch who comes through here. One of them came runnin' to me tonight, sayin' some army shirtmen came ridin' through." He shrugged. "I figured it might be you." He sighed. "This is the third tavern I looked in on. Should have figured you'd go to this place, it's the nicest in town."

"Indeed," replied O'beirne, "I saw that while riding through this evening." He looked meaningfully at Joy, who was working at the counter, and continued, "And it seems to have exceptional interior scenery, if you know what I mean."

Harwood glanced at the counter and nodded. "Indeed I do. That little wench pulls in a lot of business for this place." Then he turned back and said, "But on to business. The Governor said you would want information on the local militia."

"Quite right, Harwood. What can you tell me?"

"I can tell you there are some very good companies and some that are poorly organized and with few men. My company from the area south of New Brunswick is eager and well trained. We have about fifty men who can be counted on."

"Good," said O'beirne. I'll note that in my report. Now what about others in the area?"

"All right, here's the story." Harwood listed several companies in the surrounding territory and explained their condition. Then he held up a finger. "But there's something else you should know."

Shay raised his eyebrows. "And what might that be?"

"There's a lot of Tory militia—men who remain loyal to the King." He leaned forward. "There likely are near as many of them as there are Patriot militia." He thought a second. "The entire expanse of Jersey is like a patchwork quilt: Patriot and Tory militia existing side by side." He shrugged. "It reflects the way people think about their politics."

"I'm not surprised," responded O'beirne. "It's that way all over the colonies."

"Well, then you'll not be surprised by this: There's a lot of men who were for the Patriot Party, good Whigs, mind you, who were out in the streets back in July, celebrating that Declaration of Independence. But now they see the British takin' Long Island and drivin' Washington and his men out of New York and they think Jersey may be next. So they are wavering in their loyalty. They don't want to be on the wrong side if the British army gets here."

Shay put his hand to his chin. "I'll be sure to relate that to General Mercer. It will be of great concern to him."

"There's somethin' else that should be of concern to that general of yours and to Washington himself. There's a lot of thievery goin' on, spurred by the British."

Shay straightened up in his seat. "What do you mean by that?"

"Just what I said. The British on Staten Island landed in Jersey at Shoreham and they be asking for supplies and payin' in hard coin."

Childers said, "Yes, we're familiar with that enclave. Farmers selling their crops to them."

Harwood looked at the Ensign, then back to O'beirne. "Well, now it's more than farmers. There are bands of men, a mixture of whites and some runaway African slaves that are stealing goods from farms, travelers, even stores and sellin' it to the British. And they're stealin' horses—it seems the British need them for their cavalry and for their transport wagons." He raised his hands. "The militia is doin' what it can to stop these Partisan bands—that's what they're callin' them—but they move fast and there's no way of predictin' where they'll strike next." He raised a finger and added, "And they are well armed and getting brazen." He leaned forward. "I hear they attacked some wagons takin' supplies to our army last week."

Shay and Edward exchanged looks. O'beirne said, "You're right, Harwood. Mercer needs to know about that."

They talked for a few more minutes, then Harwood drained his ale and stood up. "Well, I've given you everythin' I got, and I'll be gettin' on home. Perhaps I'll see you again. The Governor said you'd be patrolin' this area often enough."

O'beirne nodded. "Indeed, we will. And thank you for coming to see me."

With that he turned and departed, waving at acquaintances as he went.

Shay looked over at Edward. "Well, my young Ensign, it's time for you to return to camp, make sure everything is well, and then turn in. We'll be having a long day tomorrow."

Childers raised an eyebrow and asked, "You're not coming with me?"

"Not right away. I have some other business to conduct here."

Edward's face broke into a sly look, and he glanced up at the counter. "Could we say some *Joyful* business?"

"Perhaps, young sir. But it is for you to ponder as you return to camp. I shall be along later."

"I would dare to say much later, if you are lucky."

"You are a cheeky one, Ensign Childers, with a certain lack of respect for your elders. And luck has little to do with it. Don't wait up for me." Shay motioned toward the door. "Now off with you and leave me to my business."

After Childers had departed, Shay caught Joy's eye. He raised his mug and turned it sideways to show that it was empty. The girl nodded and shortly brought him a replacement. She looked around and said, "What happened to your friend?"

"Well, my dear Joy, a young lad like that needs a full night's sleep, so I sent him off to camp."

"And you Irishmen don't need as much?"

"At my age, sometimes a busy night can be as refreshing as a full night's sleep."

Joy put her tray under her left arm and put her hand on her right hip. "And what kind of busy night did you have in mind?"

"I thought perhaps of taking a room and proving to a certain Ulster lass how charming and, shall I say, *satisfying*, the proper Irishman can be."

Joy's eyes narrowed, and a sly smile came over her face. "That endeavor might cost you more than the price of a room."

O'beirne shrugged. "Well worth it for the opportunity to change a pretty lass's opinion."

A crisp, businesslike tone came over her voice. "Closing is in about an hour. If you're still here and have the room and hard coin, something might be arranged." She turned and sauntered back to the counter in a most provocative way.

With his horse at a gallop, General Hugh Mercer rode up to Washington's headquarters at Harlem Heights. One aide only accompanied him. The army headquarters had been moved several times since the withdrawal from Manhattan in mid-September and was now at the spacious, imposing house of a certain Roger Morris. The white mansion had a two-level portico graced by four columns. Mercer saw that the area around the house was a beehive of activity as staff tents were being struck and wagons were being loaded with baggage. Clearly, thought Mercer, another move was in the offing.

The general dismounted, threw the reins to his aide, and went up the steps into the front hall, where a captain was seated at a table. The officer looked up and, recognizing him, said, "Sir, I'll take you to Colonel Grayson immediately. General Washington is waiting for you." He stood and motioned for Mercer to follow.

The aide knocked on a door, swung it open, and said, "Colonel, General Mercer is here." He turned to the general. "Please go in, sir."

Mercer pressed past the aide and saw that Grayson was busy stowing his papers in leather cases. The colonel looked up. "Well, General, you made good time getting across the river and riding down here." He put down the case in his hands and walked to a door, which he knocked on once and then entered, with Mercer following behind him.

Washington was standing in front of the hearth, staring into the flames, his hands clasped behind him. He looked around and his face lit up. "Hugh, I'm damned glad to see you." He waved to a chair by his desk and then said, "Grayson, shut that door. I want no other ears listening."

All three men sat down. Washington said, "Hugh, I don't have to tell you that things are not going well. Our losses are mounting. We've been driven out of Long Island, forced to abandon Manhattan, and Howe has maneuvered his army so that we have had to withdraw northward or be trapped against the river."

Mercer responded, "General, I think you are too rough on yourself. There have been some successes. They were precluded from advancing after making several landings and forced to return to their boats. And not long ago you drove back the Black Watch and German Jaegers here at Harlem Heights."

Washington shook his head and sighed. "Those actions have been minor and no more than temporary checks on Howe. He continues to maneuver in an attempt to trap us and force surrender of a large portion, if not the entirety, of this army. His navy has given him an exceptional mobility, and we shall have to be nimble and lucky to prevent his success." He looked over at Grayson. "Does Hugh know about the latest British move?"

"No, General. I brought him straight to you."

Washington looked at Mercer. "Hugh, late yesterday we got word of another British advance. I sent out General Putnam with Fairfield's South Carolina Light Horse and Knowlton's Rangers to investigate. He has just sent a message that a strong British force of thousands is advancing toward the village of White Plains. It's near twenty miles to the northeast of here, and it houses a depot containing a large amount of our stores and provisions. We must hold that town to prevent Howe from capturing the supplies and trapping us here against the Hudson."

Mercer contemplated a moment. "Indeed, and if they do capture that town, Fort Washington itself will be in danger, and we will lose the ability to prevent the Royal Navy from ascending the Hudson."

Washington nodded. "That is precisely why we must make a stand at White Plains. I have set the army in motion—it is essential that we get there before Howe and establish a strong defensive line. I'm moving my headquarters there overnight."

Grayson looked at Mercer. "That's what led to us calling you here in such a hurry. We cannot predict the outcome of such a battle and must prepare for any eventuality, particularly a need for retreat."

Giving Mercer a direct look, Washington said, "Your idea to withdraw through Jersey is becoming more relevant every day. I must ask you the progress you have made in your planning." He bit his lip and sighed. "Our men have fought as well as could be expected, but Howe has been deliberate and relentless in pushing us back." He stopped and stared into the distance. "New York is inevitably lost. We must now think of interposing the army between the British and what likely will be their next objective, the seizure of Philadelphia."

"Yes," added Grayson, "frankly, the lads have become dispirited at the series of defeats. We lost 1400 at Long Island, and since then many have deserted. And of course, we are losing units every week due to the end of enlistments. We started this campaign with 19,000, and we are pressed to muster 14,000 now, counting those with us here and outlying detachments."

Mercer looked from Washington to Grayson. "Let me say this: Eckert's men have been busy. We now have a detailed map of routes to the Delaware and the terrain that would constitute good defensive positions. We are presently working on locating all the boats available along the relevant area of the river. But, General, there are a lot of them. We'll need the help of militia and the governments of both New Jersey and Pennsylvania to find them all and keep them from British hands."

Washington turned to his adjutant general. "William, get off dispatches to the governors telling them what must be done and to cooperate with our officers. They must act immediately."

"I'll do so as soon as we are in our new headquarters."

Washington turned back to Mercer. "I must now ask you to add to your endeavor. You are to scout out the ferry locations northward along the Hudson to facilitate our crossing into Jersey. All your efforts will prove useless if we can't get the main body of our troops across expeditiously."

Mercer nodded. "I quite understand. I'll get back to my headquarters immediately and set things in motion to identify the best places for you to cross." He got up and asked, "Is that all you need for tonight, sir?"

Washington held up a hand. "No, General, you need to rest before you ride again. Sit and talk with me a few moments."

Grayson rose. "With your permission, General, I'll get back to packing up my papers and then check on preparations for the staff to march."

When they were alone, Washington beckoned to the hearth. "Come, Hugh, join me in front of the hearth and have a drink."

Mercer pulled up a pair of chairs while Washington went to the sideboard and poured libation into two glasses. "Here, Hugh, take some of this—it's very good whiskey and it will help keep you warm for the ride back."

Mercer took a sip. "My God, George, where did you get this? It's fine stuff."

"You'll be surprised to learn it comes from our very own Virginia captain—Eckert himself." He turned and smiled to his friend. "He and that company sergeant of his distill the stuff on their farm near Winchester. My staff found out about it and obtained a small amount from the sergeant some time ago. I've been hoarding it."

Raising his eyebrows, Mercer said, "You were right about this fellow Eckert. He's a damned good soldier and"—he held up the glass—"obviously a skilled man of business. His company may well be the best in the army, and they've done fine service for us mapping out Jersey and working with the militia."

Washington sat down and took a deep breath. "Hugh, you were so right about the need to be ready for a withdrawal. I only hope that we can make the Delaware an effective barrier against the British."

"George, the boats are the key. Right now, Eckert's second lieutenant is leading a patrol to map the location of the most useful boats along the river." Mercer laughed. "He's an Irishman—a real Irishman—not Ulster Irish. And I also get word that he's intent on despoiling every pretty tavern maid between the Hudson and the Delaware."

Washington laughed out loud, something that Mercer hadn't seen him do since Long Island. He wiped some tears from his eyes, then said, "Hugh, are we sure it is possible to despoil a tavern maid?"

Now it was Mercer's turn to laugh. "A very good question, George. But womanizing aside, O'beirne is a professional—a very experienced mercenary—and he gets the needed information one way or another." He thought a moment. "But we can't collect all the boats by ourselves when the time comes. I was very serious about getting the help of the governors."

"Indeed, I understand. I'll keep after them." Washington took a sip of his drink, sighed deeply, then slapped his other hand down on the arm of his chair in frustration. "Damn, Hugh, a few weeks ago we had a fine army of nearly 20,000 men. Now we have less than 14,000, and we are losing more every day." He clenched his fist. "It was a mistake to try to defend New York City and the local territory." He bit his lip. "I should have been more insistent with Congress after the declaration. We should have withdrawn to a more defensible position after that."

Mercer turned and put a hand on his friend's shoulder. "George, you must not berate yourself. You could have done nothing. Congress was adamant." He put a hand to his chin as he thought of more to say. "George, there's an old saying, 'You have to lie down in the bed you make.' But that's not true for soldiers. We have to lie down in the bed made by the bloody, conniving politicians. So all we can do is try to deal with the problems they have handed us." He drained his drink and stood up. "I'm going now. As soon as I get back to Fort Lee, I'm sending out Eckert to find the best place for you to cross the Hudson. If you can just hold them for a few days at White Plains and Fort Washington, we'll get clear away with the army, cross Jersey, and be ready to recruit and reorganize once we get across the Delaware. Pennsylvania will be a new start."

Washington stared silently into the fire for a long moment. Then he looked up at Mercer. "Hugh, I most fervently hope you are right." He stood up and put his hand on Mercer's shoulder. "God be with you, my friend."

Alexander Tresh hurried up the steps of the small house located a short distance from Washington's Headquarters, pushed open the door, and walked into the parlor, where Catherine sat, relaxing with drink in hand.

"Alex, you're late, but we've waited supper for you." With an irritated tone in her voice she continued, "And Elise has cooked a marvelous meal—the aroma has been tantalizing me for an hour." She rose from her chair. "And now tell me what the Devil is going on? There's been a lot of movement of troops and wagons—is that why you are so late?"

"You are quite right, Catherine. The British have a new push on. They're headed for a village called White Plains twenty miles north of here. We have a major depot for provisions and military stores there, and it seems Howe is intent on capturing it. Washington is marching to counter him." He stopped and thought a moment. "And if Howe is victorious there, he will have a good chance of trapping our army."

"So we will be moving to this White Plains?"

"Not *we*, my dear, but only *I*. I'm afraid we're going to be separated for a while. I just encountered General Mercer, who commands at Fort Lee on the other side of the river. He had been conferring with Washington. I am informed the two are old friends and confidants. In any case, we talked, and he has agreed to provide you shelter while I am riding with the army. We must hurry through supper and then pack our trunks and get them loaded onto the cart. At first light tomorrow, Moulders will escort you and Elise across the river on the ferry at Fort Washington and get you settled at Mercer's headquarters, then return to join me."

Catherine drained her cup. "Alex, I would rather be with you. For God's sake, why can't we all go to White Plains? Surely I will be safe with the army."

"My dear, the truth is that I am not sanguine about the outcome of this battle. Howe is massing his forces—he means to strike a hard blow. And let me be honest: While Washington's men have had some success in skirmishes, they have not done well at all in formal battles. Look what happened at Long Island. The army lost many men and barely escaped across the East River. Quite frankly, I see the chance that our army will be broken at White Plains and forced into a disorganized retreat." He gave Catherine a hard look. "And I cannot state this too strongly: Hessian soldiers are known to treat women harshly when encountering them in that type of situation."

Catherine's face tightened, her eyes wide. "I take your meaning."

Alexander continued in a deadly serious tone, "I have seen it firsthand, and I assure you it is not pretty."

Catherine stamped her foot impatiently. "All right, all right, Alex! You've *made* your point. I'll go to General Mercer. We'll be ready to move at dawn." She sighed, "But I don't have to like it."

Tresh put his hands on his wife's shoulders and said in a tender tone, "My dear, we will reunite as soon as possible. But meanwhile, I will be much more comfortable with you on the other side of the Hudson."

"Yes, Alex. But at least we can have some semblance of a normal supper. Let us not keep Elise waiting any longer."

—※—

Colleen was enjoying her supper under the tent fly, sitting close by the fire to dispel the chill of late October. The last month in their location near Fort Washington had been reasonably profitable, if not as spectacular as the days in Manhattan. But she felt a sense of disquiet as she ate, for earlier in the day they had heard rumors that the British were astir after being quiet in their camps around the occupied city for over a month. She had immediately sent Charley Farley to find out what was happening.

She had just put her plate aside and lit her pipe when she saw Charley coming up the road from the fort, pushing his horse hard. He rode right up to her tent and threw himself down from the saddle. "Mrs. McGraw! Ma'am, it's true! The Redcoats are on the march."

Colleen exhaled. "And just how do we know this?"

"Ma'am, I got it from Lieutenant Fairfield himself, who's with General Putnam's column. He's watching the British. And it's a big force—made up of both Redcoats and Hessians."

"All right, Charlie. Now for the important question: Where are they supposed to be heading?"

"Mrs. McGraw, it looks like they are going toward a place called White Plains. It's a little village, but it's got an army depot—a depot with military stores. But this is what's important: it's about twenty miles northwest of here." He paused to catch his breath. "Washington's army is moving—marching from Harlem Heights down below the fort to try to keep Howe from taking this White Plains place."

"How much of the army is Washington taking—and what about Fort Washington? Are they abandoning it?"

"Mrs. McGraw, it looks like Washington's taking the whole army, 'cept for some men in the fort here. Some brigades are already marching. But I knew you'd want to know about the fort, so I stopped by there. Some of the garrison is joining the main army, but at least a thousand are staying to man the defenses."

Colleen thought that over. "I don't understand: Fort Washington will be isolated." Then a shock ran through her body. "Why, we could soon be south of both armies. We could end up behind the British lines! That is, if we just sit here."

"Yes, Ma'am, that's true."

"Charlie, go get your Ma and Elijah right away. We need to make some plans."

Pipe in hand, Colleen rose from her chair and went into her tent, retrieving the map Charlie had made during his scouting expeditions. She brought it to her table and spent a few minutes studying it and soon made her decision. In a moment Charlie returned with Edna and Elijah.

Edna spoke out as she arrived, "So General Howe is stirring the pot, is he now?"

Colleen nodded and waved at Charlie. "Give them a quick summary of what you told me."

Charlie did so in a few minutes.

Elijah said, "I'm guessin' you're planning to move."

Colleen spoke up. "That's right, Elijah, there'll be no discussion. We need to get out of here." She turned to the youth. "Charlie, tell us everything you know about Peekskill."

"It's a small village, right on the river where a couple of creeks join it. It's a hard day's journey north of here, traveling on the river road. The river there is pretty wide, but there's a busy ferry—King's Ferry, it's called. Like I said, the village itself is small, but there's a lot of tradesmen and other business in the area. I recall an ironworks, coopering, a couple of blacksmiths, and others. And there are lots of farms around it." He pointed to the eastern side of the town. "Lots of open country for us to set up camp."

Colleen nodded. "And most importantly, it will be well north of White Plains. We can watch what happens there in safety and be ready to cross the river if things go bad for our army." She turned and looked at her managers. "Well, that's it. Start packing. We're leaving here at first light tomorrow morning. Charlie will ride on ahead and find a good campsite at Peekskill. The way I see it, there's no time to waste—the armies could be fighting as soon as tomorrow and make it difficult for us to travel." She waved her hand around the camp. "So let's get moving."

Chapter Eleven

Withdrawal to Jersey

Captain Wend Eckert, with Sergeant Simon Donegal at his side, rode down the sloping road toward the river, heading for the ferry landing on the western bank of the Hudson. The landing was just south of the village. The leaves were turning in the late October chill, giving the wooded hills on both sides of the river a colorful appearance. Behind the two friends rode four more men of the company, their rifles slung over their shoulders. One of the men led a pack horse. As they approached the river, Wend could see a sign at the landing proclaiming, "King's Ferry. Peekskill."

In the distance, they could see the ferry approaching. It was large, and several wagons were aboard. Donegal commented, "Well, that's as big a ferry as I've seen in this part of the country." He looked over at Wend. "Na, are you proposing to cross over?"

"Indeed, Simon. Besides the ferry, I want to see how many other substantial boats are available in the area in case Washington decides to cross at this point. The more boats, the faster the army can cross, and if the British are at his heels, speed may be critical." He pointed to the other bank. "There's supposed to be a militia outpost over near the village. They should be able to tell us what we need to know, or at least help us find out."

An hour later, they disembarked from the ferry and rode toward the village. They soon found the military encampment. Pulling up in front of the single sentry, Wend asked for the officer in charge. The sentry, dressed in a brown frock coat and breeches, eyed their hunting shirts curiously and said, "Aye, sir, I'll find the captain. It might take a few minutes."

All six men of the patrol dismounted and waited on foot. Presently, a man in a green coat and gray breeches came toward them, followed by the sentry. The sentry pointed to Wend and whispered to the man in green, who then looked at Wend and said, "I'm Captain Josh Hardisty." He stared curiously at their hunting shirts. "You wanted to talk to me?"

Wend nodded. "Indeed, Mr. Hardisty. I'm Captain Wend Eckert of the Frederick County Light Foot, here at the orders of General Mercer at Fort Lee. You *have* heard of him?"

Hardisty's face went blank, but he said hesitantly, "Er, yes, I *believe* so."

"We're here to check on the suitability of this location as a possible place for Washington's army to cross the Hudson. There's a battle in the offing to the south of here, and it might prove expedient for our men to cross into Jersey here in the wake of the action."

Hardisty shrugged, then pointed in the direction of the ferry. "Well, you just came across on King's Ferry."

"Captain Hardisty, what I need to know is if there are a number of large boats in this vicinity—boats large enough to carry significant numbers of troops, artillery, and wagons."

The captain looked puzzled for a moment, as if he had never contemplated that question. Then his face lit up. "Now you mention it, there are some good-sized boats 'round here. The iron works has got a number that are used to bring in ore and transport their finished iron. And Vanderhill, the cooper who's got a shop right down by the water, uses boats and some flat barges to carry in lumber from a sawmill upriver and then transport his barrels. Yes, sir. I guess you could say we got a fair number of boats 'round here."

Wend said, "That sounds promising, Hardisty. Could I ask you to show me where these boats might be located, so that I can determine the actual numbers and their suitability?"

Just then Donegal tapped Wend on the shoulder. "Na, my dear Captain, you might just want to take a moment and cast your eyes down to the south at the road comin' down the hill to the river."

Irritated at the interruption, Wend responded, "Hold on a minute, Donegal."

He was about to turn back to Hardisty when he saw what Donegal was looking at. He exclaimed, "Damn! It's Colleen and her whole bloody caravan!"

Donegal grinned. "Aye, just like that bad penny they talk about. Pops up just when you ain't expectin' it."

Hardisty looked at the caravan. "Yep, it appears that's Mrs. McGraw's sutler company. There was a young fellow rode in here earlier sayin' they'd be arrivin' and askin' about a good campsite." He pointed to a flat meadow surrounded by trees. "I said that would be as good as any. There's a creek flows beside it down to the river."

Donegal said playfully to Wend, "Na, you gonna' go over and have a chat with Colleen? Sure and she'd love to talk with you about whiskey and Horner's tart."

Wend frowned. "I don't suppose I can avoid it, but after I see about the boats." He turned back to the militia captain. "I would be obliged, sir, if you could show us where these boats are located."

An hour later, having satisfied himself that there was an abundance of boats in and around Peekskill, Wend and his party rode back down to the ferry and then to a spot near the Red Vixen Camp. He gave the others the word to settle in, water their horses, light a fire, and make coffee. Then he headed for Colleen's camp, where he could see her personal tent had already been set up. As he walked up to it, the Red Vixen herself pushed open the flap of the tent and came out, carrying a cup in her hand.

Colleen looked up to see Wend approaching, and surprise spread over her face. She called out, "What the devil are you doing here? Last I heard you were down at Fort Lee, twenty miles down river!"

Wend thought for a second, then responded, "General Mercer is using us for patrols along the river."

Colleen cocked her head and a skeptical smile came over her face. "No, you *are not* on a routine patrol, not with a big battle going on down at White Plains. I say you're here to check out the suitability of places for Washington to cross if Howe whips him." She raised an eyebrow. "Go ahead, tell me I'm wrong."

Wend sighed. "All right, you've got it right. And obviously you've come here for safety and to be ready to escape if Washington retreats."

"That's right. Based on what I've seen since the British landed on Long Island, Howe's regulars are going to send Washington's men packing. And I want to be ready to move in whatever direction is best." She motioned to a chair. "But meanwhile, we have some serious business to talk about."

Wend settled in the chair and played dumb. "And what would that be, Colleen?"

Running her hand through her auburn hair, she responded, "You damn well know we had a deal about some whiskey: Emily for a wagonload of spirits." She cocked her head. "You said it could be here in a few weeks. So where is it?"

Wend grinned. "I wasn't really sure that we had an agreement. You weren't sure you wanted it, or that you would let Emily go. As I recall, that's where you left it when we were interrupted by the Royal Navy."

Colleen stiffened in her chair and slammed her cup down on the table. "Are you telling me you don't have any whiskey on the way?"

"Now Colleen, are you saying we *did* have a deal?"

Colleen's face muscles tightened. "Yes, damn you, we had a deal, and I need whiskey. We ran out three weeks ago, and there's none to be had for any price here in New York. You get me that whiskey and that damned Horner can have her." She sighed deeply. "Do you have it?"

"Not exactly, Colleen."

"What the hell does that mean? It's been weeks since we talked, and you said it wouldn't take long to be here."

"Look, Colly, there was a problem. The distilling master on my farm had just finished a big batch of whiskey promised to local taverns and used up most of the grain. It took a long time to get more and properly prepare it for the vats. You understand how that could happen."

She laughed bitterly, "What I understand is that you said the whiskey would arrive soon. That was many weeks ago. I think you're making all this up."

"The fact is I got a letter from my wife ten days ago saying a load of the stuff is on the way—it left the day she wrote the letter. So it could be here anytime now, depending on road conditions. Damn it, I've been acting in good faith." He pulled up his shirt, removed a folded piece of paper from his breeches, and handed it to her. "Here, if you don't believe me, read this—it's the letter I told you about. Look at the first few lines."

Colleen snatched it from his hand, opened it, and quickly scanned it. Then she looked up and smirked at him. "Very romantic at the end. Did it arouse you?"

"For God's sake, Colleen, do you have no shame? You weren't supposed to read that part."

"Now my dear Wend, *shame* is an emotion I dispensed with a long time ago. I realized it's of no use whatsoever." She handed the letter back. "All right, I believe what you said about the spirits. I'll tell dear Miss Emily that her release is imminent."

"If you know it's coming, Colleen, why not let her go now? Why continue forcing her to be with other men?"

"Wend, she'll go when I have that whiskey in hand, no sooner."

"I see that sympathy is another emotion you have dispensed with."

"That went even before shame."

"Well," he replied, "at least you are honest with yourself."

"Always, my dearest Wend." She glanced over at soldiers at their fire. "Are you staying the night here?"

"No, Colleen. With Washington engaged, or soon to be engaged, we must get back and report to General Mercer about the crossing places. Washington may need that information very soon."

The words were barely out of his mouth when there was the sound of galloping hooves coming down the road toward the river, and in a few seconds a horse bearing a young lad appeared. He rode right up to the tent where they sat. Before even dismounting, the youth called out, "Mrs. McGraw! The battle's over! Howe's men flanked Washington's line, and our boys are pulling back."

Colleen stood up. "Charlie, get off that horse and give me the details. Which way are they headed?"

Charlie slid to the ground and looked over at Wend, then turned to Colleen. "I'm not sure Washington knows where he's going to end up. Word I got when I left was that he had withdrawn a short distance to get reorganized and Howe was occupying the village. But there was no doubt if Howe moved forward again, they were going to have to retreat." He took a deep breath. "And while I was on the road, I saw there be men leavin' the army—leavin' on their own."

Wend said, "You mean deserting, discouraged by the loss."

"Yes, sir. Most of them. But I came across a whole battalion that was goin' home. They said their enlistment was almost over and they didn't see much use in stickin' around. Officers and men all marching back to their homes in Connecticut."

Colleen turned to Wend. "Well, it sounds like you better get back to your General Mercer posthaste with what you know about the crossings."

Wend sat for several seconds turning things over in his mind. Then he shook his head. "No, that would take too long. I must take it upon myself to go straight to Washington. I must ride from here to find him." He looked back at the village and ferry. "I'm going to recommend he cross here, if withdrawing to Jersey is what he intends. This is the best place I've found."

Colleen said, "You may have trouble finding him, if the army retreats rapidly. And you don't know the countryside or the roads. And night's coming on."

"You're right." He looked hard at her for a moment, then he turned to Charlie and a smile appeared on his face. "But the lad does. He can be my guide."

Colleen laughed in his face. "Are you jesting with me? Why should I let Charlie go with you?" She pointed toward his horse. "Besides, the animal is worn out."

"I can get him a fresh horse, Colleen." He put his hand on her arm and looked her in the eye. "And it's to your interest that the army get across the river to safety. If Howe traps the army and destroys it or forces Washington to surrender, you are out of business." He gave her a wicked smile. "Unless you plan to start serving the British. And I don't think a woman who is half Ulster, half real Irish would find that palatable. She wouldn't want that kind of money."

Colleen stared back into his eyes, her face muscles tight and her jaw sticking out. Finally, she took a deep breath and said, "All right, he can ride with you." She looked at the youth. "But only if he says he's up to it. The lad's been up day and night for a long time."

Charlie looked at Wend. "I'm all right—I'll show you the way to the army."

Wend nodded. "Good—get yourself something to eat and I'll arrange for you to use one of our horses." Then Wend turned back to Colleen and motioned toward her tents and wagons. "But you don't want to stay here. You need to get across the river now—this very evening."

"But dusk is coming on. The ferry is going to shut down."

Wend said, "You may be running out of time. Bribe the ferryman if necessary, but get across. If the army starts arriving while you are still here, the troops and artillery and supply wagons are going to take priority—you could find yourself stranded. And I think it may be a close thing, if Howe is in hot pursuit of Washington."

He turned to Charlie. "I'll be back with horses in a short time, and we'll ride immediately."

—∞—

Wend and Charlie Farley rode out of Peekskill as dusk was turning to night. Eckert had sent off a courier to Mercer with a dispatch informing him what he intended to tell Washington. He had also sent a note to the militia captain, Hardisty, informing him of the situation and requesting that he marshal all available boats near the ferry landing. He sent Donegal along with that note to make sure the captain would carry out the plan.

Several hours into their ride, they began to encounter deserters. Most were alone or in small groups, but on one occasion they came across a full company, including the officers, resting beside the road. Wend queried the captain, who said they were from Massachusetts and that their time would be up in a few weeks. The captain added that, in any case, he considered the war lost, so he and his men could do more good back home.

It was two hours after midnight when, with exhausted horses, they encountered the pickets of the main army. Charlie said, "They're much further north of the village than I expected. I wonder if Howe is pushing them hard?"

Wend answered, "I've never known Howe to be aggressive in the aftermath of a battle. Perhaps Washington wants to get a safe distance between himself and their lines."

They rode up to the picket, and Wend asked the officer in charge where headquarters was located.

The man waved southward. "Just a short distance down the road. In tents—you won't miss it because they are the only tents that have been pitched."

They rode on for about a quarter of a mile and sighted a cluster of tents. Wend saw a tent larger than the others with an officer he recognized to be one of Washington's aides sitting beside a fire in front of it. He dismounted and walked over to the officer.

"Sir, I am Captain Eckert, serving under General Mercer. I have important information and need to see Colonel Grayson immediately."

The young captain looked up, eyeing Wend's hunting shirt. "He's in a meeting with Washington and some other generals, making plans for tomorrow. You can talk to him when they're done." He pointed to another fire with several officers sitting around, capes over their shoulders. "You might be able to get some coffee over there while you wait."

Wend felt a surge of anger and impatience. Tired as he was, he thought about grabbing the man's collar and yanking him to his feet. Instead, he leaned over close to his face. "Now listen, this lad and I have just ridden through the night for fifteen miles. I've got a message directly from Mercer, which will be critical to the army's movements. Grayson and Washington will want to know about it immediately. If you value your *ass*, sir, you will get me the adjutant general *now*. And if you don't, I'm going to walk right in there myself. So go fetch Grayson."

The officer took a deep breath and stared at Wend with hot anger in his eyes. But after perhaps fifteen seconds, he pushed himself up. "All right, but you better know what you are talking about, or I'll see that you rue this moment."

"Just go, Captain."

Wend stood there, crossing his arms against the night chill. But it was only a short minute until the flap of the tent flew open and Grayson strode out. He spied Wend and said, "Eckert! You've got a message from Mercer? Give it to me immediately."

Wend walked over to the colonel. "Actually, sir, that's not *exactly* correct."

"Not correct? You're not here because Mercer sent you?"

"No, sir. I was scouting out places for the army to cross the Hudson. But then I heard of the battle and that you were retreating. I thought it urgent to get the information to you directly, instead of sending it through Mercer. So I came on my own authority."

Grayson motioned toward the tent with his hand. "Eckert, you better come with me right now." He spun on his heel and re-entered the tent. Wend couldn't resist shooting a smirk at the aide before following.

Once in the tent, Wend was startled by what he saw. The interior was sparsely lit with a few flickering candles, most burnt down almost to their base. Washington sat behind a small writing table in semi-darkness. Looking around, Wend saw that most of the senior generals of the army were present—some standing, some in camp chairs, three actually sitting on Washington's cot. Another two sat on the ground, one of whom seemed to be nodding off. *In fact,* Wend thought, *everyone here looks sleepy-eyed.* Lee stood in one corner, arms crossed in front of himself, a rather sour look on his face. He had just finished talking to Washington, who was staring at him, as if getting ready to reply. Wend noticed two of the ever-present dogs lay at his feet.

Paterson broke the silence. "General, Captain Eckert of Mercer's command is here. He has some information regarding crossings of the Hudson which you may find relevant."

Washington turned and said, "Very timely, Captain Eckert. We are discussing the army's future movements in the face of Howe's imminent advance. Back at Harlem Heights, I requested that General Mercer investigate potential crossing locations. I take it you are carrying that information from him?"

"Not precisely, sir." Wend took a deep breath and looked around the room. "I was ordered by the General to investigate ferry locations and make a recommendation to him. As of today, I had gone as far as Peekskill. Then I heard about the battle and your retreat from the village."

Lee interrupted in a snarky tone, "More properly, Captain, the army was *driven* out of White Plains."

Wend ignored Lee. "And I decided on my own initiative to come here directly with the information I had gathered in the expectation that time would be of the essence."

Washington raised his eyebrows, then said, "All right, Captain, what information do you bring?"

"Sir, I investigated several ferry crossings, but in short, I believe that the King's Ferry at Peekskill is the most favorable location for the army to cross."

Lee straightened and took a step forward, a scowl on his face. "Why, I know the map. Peekskill is over fifteen miles from here, and as you say, time is of the essence. Howe may well be on the move at first light—just a few hours from now. I am aware of several crossings much closer."

All the officers in the tent were staring at Wend now, but it was Washington who spoke. "Indeed, Mr. Eckert, why Peekskill?"

"Because, sir, unlike the others, in addition to the ferry itself, there are numerous boats which can be used to expedite the crossing. And not only boats that can carry men, but there are flatboats that will accommodate the army's horses, guns, and supply wagons. That's because there is an ironworks and a coopering establishment in the village. In short, we can cross much faster at Peekskill than at any other location, and there is much less chance of a part of the army being caught on the eastern banks of the river. So, if I may say so, it is worth the longer march to facilitate a faster crossing."

"Sir, may I speak?"

Wend looked around and saw the voice was from one of the men on the cot—a stout colonel.

Washington nodded. "Yes, Colonel Knox, proceed."

"The captain's right, sir. We'll get the guns over much faster with barges. They should be able to take more at once, along with the caissons."

"There's another factor, General Washington." Wend saw that it was General Greene who had spoken up.

Washington waved at him. "Yes, Greene. What is that factor?"

"If we do march northward, instead of toward one of the nearer ferries, we may distract Howe from Fort Washington. And I say we need the guns of both Forts—Washington and Lee—to make it harder for the Royal Navy to come upriver to oppose our crossing. Their heavy guns could destroy any attempt to cross, and with heavy loss of life and equipment, I might add."

There were nods all around the room, and Wend saw the slightest nod of Washington's head. The commanding general looked over at Lee. "Charles, do you agree with that assessment?"

Lee cleared his throat. "I'll not deny that some good points have been made."

Washington took that for agreement. He stood up and looked around the tent. "All right, gentlemen, here is how we shall proceed. The main body of the army will march for Peekskill at first light. General Lee will command the rearguard with Sullivan's division. He will have a dual function: first, to delay Howe's advance, if in fact he moves aggressively, and secondly, to perform a distraction. I want you to remain in New York for a time, so as to force the British to worry about their northern flank. And if you see an opportunity to strike them effectively, you have that option. That might cause them to delay crossing and thus prevent a close pursuit for some time."

Lee smiled and responded, "I quite understand what you desire and welcome the opportunity for independent action."

Washington turned to Greene. "General, your point about holding Fort

Washington has merit. You will lead about two thousand men and reinforce that fortification. You will hold it as long as possible and then be ready to withdraw the garrison to Jersey via the local ferry when the situation demands it."

Washington looked at Grayson. "Get word to Glover. Tell him we will need the services of his Marblehead fishermen to get across the river just as when we evacuated Long Island. Have him send an officer to headquarters, mounted and ready to ride to Peekskill."

Grayson responded, "I'll send a messenger to Glover immediately."

Washington smiled at Wend. "Captain, you have done us excellent service this day, but I must ask more of you. You must show Glover's officer to Peekskill so he may help get the boats ready and the crossing organized." Then he looked at Grayson again. "Glover and his regiment must be the first to march so they can be ready when the army arrives."

After staring into the distance for a moment, Washington continued to Grayson. "Where is Fairfield and his troop of light horse?"

Grayson responded. "Half the troop, under his ensign, is watching the British lines. Fairfield, with the other half, is here in camp, ready for service."

"Good," said Washington. "Get word to them to prepare to ride and have Fairfield himself come here to headquarters for instructions." He looked at Wend. "Fairfield and his men will also accompany you, and he will detach men at various places to provide guidance to the units of our army as they march and make sure they take the correct roads."

The general stood staring into the distance, and Wend realized he was trying to think of any other necessary actions. Then he addressed the entire assemblage. "Gentlemen, I'm sorry that there will be little rest for any of you this night. Return to your commands and prepare them to march."

Eckert walked out of Washington's tent with the adjutant general. Once outside, Grayson called out to the aide beside the fire, "Captain Ralls, send a messenger to summon Lieutenant Fairfield. We need him immediately." Then he motioned toward the fire. "Sit down and rest, Eckert. You've done hard service tonight, and you have much more before you. You can probably rest for an hour or two; it will take at least that long to get Glover's man here and for Fairfield to get his troop ready to ride."

Wend saw that Charlie was already beside the fire, seated on the ground with his head down on his chest, apparently asleep. Wend sat on a log beside the fire, grateful for the warmth of the flames. Shortly, Ralls was back and had a pot and a cup in his hand. "Here, Eckert, I've got coffee if you'd like it."

Wend nodded, took the cup, and drank the strong black liquid. Ralls went off to help Grayson draw up orders for the different divisions of the army to move. It took a couple of minutes for him to finish the coffee, then he crossed his arms and stared into the fire.

The next thing he knew, Ralls' hand was on his shoulder. "Eckert, the cavalry troop is ready to ride. Colonel Grayson wants to talk to you."

Wend looked up. There was a faint tint of light in the sky. He looked over at Charlie, who was still asleep. He looked up at Ralls. "How long have I been sleeping?"

"The better part of two hours, Eckert."

Wend pulled himself up to his feet and shook off his sleepiness. He looked around and saw Grayson at his writing table beside his tent, poring over a report. A dragoon officer, dressed in a short gray coat and white breeches, stood there with his back to Wend. He asked Ralls, "Is that the South Carolina lieutenant?"

"Indeed, sir. He just came to report his men are ready."

Wend walked over to where the two officers were talking. "Good morning, Colonel. I understand it's time to ride."

"Indeed, Eckert. It will soon be first light. The army is stirring and getting ready to march. You'll need to start now to get out ahead of the columns." He motioned to the dragoon officer. "This is Lieutenant Geoffrey Fairfield of the Palmetto Light Horse."

Wend turned and saw the man's face for the first time and stood speechless, transfixed in shock. *My God, it's Geoffrey Caufield, the highwayman!*

Grayson continued on, "Mr. Fairfield has performed most effective scouting work for the army. He's from Charleston, if I remember correctly."

Fairfield showed no reaction to seeing Wend. Instead, he smiled and said smoothly, "Actually, the family plantation is located in the low country across the harbor from the city, several miles up Wando Creek. We call it *Wando Landing*, to be precise. A lovely place, if I do say so myself."

Grayson said, "Yes, I'm sure it is." He looked at Wend. "Captain Eckert is a Virginian, from the Shenandoah Valley near Winchester."

Fairfield looked at Wend and responded, "Ah, yes. I gathered he was from the backcountry. The hunting shirt and all."

"Well," continued Grayson, "you two can get acquainted on the ride north. We'll be watching for your guides along the way, Fairfield."

"I completely understand what you desire, sir." Then he looked questioningly at Wend, "Now, sir, are we ready to ride?"

"Yes, as soon as I and my guide, a lad who knows the roads, get mounted."

Grayson sat back down at his table. "Then off with the two of you and Godspeed."

Two hours after dawn and three hours after leaving army headquarters, the troop came to a small stream that crossed the road. Wend pulled up and turned to Fairfield. "My horse and Charlie's need to rest at least for a little while. They've been ridden hard yesterday and the day before. I suggest we stop here to water and rest the animals for a short time. We're well in advance of the army."

Fairfield looked around. "I have no objection, as long as we stay ahead of Glover's vanguard. We'll light a fire and make some quick coffee."

After securing the horses to a picket rope and loosening their girths, Wend caught up with Fairfield and, pointing upstream, said, "We need to talk. In *private*."

A sly smile came over Fairfield's face. "Of course, Captain. Whatever you please."

Wend led them about fifty feet along the creek until they were out of earshot. Then he turned around and said, "And now, Caufield, you are going to tell me how the leader of a crew of thieving highwaymen became a South Carolina lieutenant named Fairfield and the head of a troop of dragoons. Is this legitimate, or some sort of trick you are playing on the army?" He took a breath. "Though I can't for the love of God understand your motivation."

"Now old chap," Fairfield grinned, "you will of course recall that I told you we were bound for Carolina that night I saved your life. That night in the camp beside the Shenandoah River when we came upon that irascible fellow Grenough and his henchmen just about to finish you off."

"I don't need to be reminded of that night."

"Well, my dear Eckert, I assure you everything is quite legitimate. I have a signed commission from South Carolina's most admirable Governor, John Rutledge."

Wend looked up at the morning sky, then asked, "And how the devil did you manage that?"

"Why, a very young widow, who just happens to be a distant relative of the governor, suggested to him that I might be the very person to raise a troop of light horse for service in the South Carolina forces."

"This is beginning to become clear. Knowing you, Caufield, I assume the widow is quite handsome and very willing."

"Eckert, I assure you that *any* widow who is the mistress of a large rice plantation on the Ashley River with over eighty Africans in service and who also owns a comfortable house in Charleston, is quite beautiful to behold." He smiled mischievously and then continued, "And, by the way, I must insist you refrain from using the name *Caufield,* even in private. We wouldn't want you to slip up in front of our brother officers. It might prove quite awkward."

Wend said, "So I am to assist you in your lie?"

"You damn well owe me your life, Eckert. Don't jeopardize my future."

"I'll play along unless you start playing tricks and going back to your old profession under cover of army service."

Fairfield laughed. "There's no need of that. I told you, my goal has always been the life of a gentleman."

"And what about this place, Wando Landing, you spoke of—does that even exist?"

Grinning broadly, Fairfield said, "Well, it *should.* And indeed, there's a lovely spot at the head of navigation on the Wando where we camped for several days on our way down to Charleston. It would be perfect for a graceful plantation mansion."

"How long do you plan to carry on this charade? Surely you understand you can't keep it up forever?"

"Now my dear fellow, of course I can. The widow I spoke of is enthusiastically planning for nuptials upon my return. I assure you that my military reputation in Charleston burns bright. We performed excellent service when the British attempted to land in the Low Country, keeping track of their movement and providing courier service between the disparate units of the army. And you should have seen the size of the crowd who gathered to see the troop off when we departed to become the state's sole unit in Washington's army. Everyone of any importance in the city was present." He grinned broadly. "I look forward to the life of a respected gentleman of Charleston's society."

Wend motioned toward where the troop was making coffee. "I see that one-eared scoundrel of yours, Quinn, is still with you. What about the other one—Freddy McRae?"

"Of course *Sergeant* Quinn is with me. And *Sergeant* McRae also—he's presently with Ensign Middleton down with the rearguard of the army. I would remind you that both have years of service in the King's Irish Dragoons."

Wend put his hands on his hips. "Well, Lieutenant Fairfield, it appears that I have to work with you, at least for the present. But I'll always know who you really are and won't trust you for one minute. Let me make this clear: If I see or get word of anything that makes me think you are going back to your old ways, I'll expose you to the army command. Do you understand that?"

Fairfield laughed in his face, then said, "You know, Eckert, Quinn always said I made the wrong decision back on the Shenandoah. He thinks we should have let Grenough kill you, or that we should have done the job ourselves." He paused and looked directly into Wend's eyes. "I'm beginning to think he might have been right."

The two of them stared at each other for a long moment, then Wend said, "I think I'll have some of that coffee, then we should ride. We need to get to Peekskill so Glover's men can get the boats organized."

Fairfield raised an eyebrow, a sly grin on his face.. "As you say, Captain." Then he headed back toward the campfire.

—m—

"Come in and sit down, Eckert." Mercer sat a camp table inside his headquarters tent. "And make sure the flap is closed behind you. That November wind is damned cold."

Eckert did as he was told and settled down before the general. He pulled his old gray army overcoat, which a certain Corporal Kirkwood of the 42nd Foot had managed to pilfer for him from quartermaster stores at Fort Pitt thirteen years ago, tightly around him. "You are sure right about this chill, General."

Mercer acknowledged with a nod, then said, "Thanks for the good work in the matter of Peekskill. The army got across in fine shape. Washington's on his way here to make his headquarters in the tavern down by the ferry. The rest of the force that crossed with him will bivouac here at Fort Lee." He picked up the lighted pipe from the table by his side, took a puff, then continued, "And now, it's time for some new orders for you and your company."

"New orders?"

"Yes. Your men patrolling the Hudson bluffs will be relieved by militia. It's time to prepare for a movement through Jersey. Once your men are relieved, I want you to move your camp to Hackensack, just a few miles to the west. It's on the main road we'll probably use, so that you can be ready to march on short notice. Your company will be our guides and provide other services for the movement. O'beirne and Childers have scouted out the roads and know the best locations to set up for rearguard actions, if that proves necessary." He exhaled smoke from the pipe and, looking directly into Wend's eyes, added, "And I have every belief that will be required."

"Aye, sir. I'll make preparations to break camp immediately. It will be good to have the company together again, except for Lieutenant O'beirne and the men of his latest patrol."

"Yes, he went out last week and should be back soon, with the locations of boats on the Delaware. I understand the Pennsylvania and New Jersey militia are helping him with that task." He took another draw on his pipe.

Wend assumed they were done and started to rise from his chair. "If that's all, I'll get back to camp and start things moving."

"Eckert, stay where you are for a moment. I have more for you."

"Yes, sir." He dropped back down into his seat. "What would that be?"

Mercer sighed. "Two things. First, there's a situation I want you to help with. As you may be aware, Mrs. Tresh is here. She came over for safety just before White Plains."

"Yes, General. I've seen her at her tent, and of course, I and my officers are familiar with both she and the colonel. They traveled with us when we joined the army."

"I'm aware of that. That's one reason for what I'm about to ask. But here's the point: if we do have to retreat, it will be in a hurry, and I'm responsible for her safety. She's the only lady of a senior officer with the army at the moment, so I want you to take her with you to Hackensack and then keep her with you during the retreat."

"Yes, sir. I'll talk to Mrs. Tresh on my way back to my own camp and have her start preparations to travel. But you said there were two things?"

Mercer nodded. "Yes, something important. There is a troop of South Carolina light horse with the army. They've been doing good work in scouting and providing couriers."

Wend said, "Yes, sir. I'm familiar with them. Lieutenant Fairfield and part of the troop rode with me from Washington's headquarters to Peekskill."

"Excellent, Eckert. Well, the fact is that the entire troop is on the way here. When they arrive, I'll be sending them up to Hackensack. Washington has decided that they'll be put under your command for the present. Light horse will be of great assistance to you in scouting and serving to help guide the army. And with both of you being from the southern colonies, you should be able to work well together."

Wend felt a shock run through his body. Being in daily contact with Fairfield was the last thing he wanted. But he kept a straight face, looked at Mercer, and simply said, "I'm sure that will certainly prove an interesting experience, sir."

Clive Harfeld sat in the coffee shop on Broad Street, some of the proprietor's precious tea in front of him, waiting for Northcutt. He didn't have long to wait—the colonel showed up just a quarter hour after his own arrival. Harfeld waved his friend to the table and said, "Sit down, Barrett. I've got some libation here you might enjoy."

Northcutt looked around the shop and said, "A very pleasant shop. It gives you warm feeling."

"Yes," agreed Harfeld. "I've been here several times. And luckily, it's just outside the area that was burned by the fire."

"Indeed, sir." Northcutt took a chair and looked at the pot. "By God, Harfeld, you've got tea!"

"Yes. The proprietor and I are in collusion. Help yourself, Northcutt."

Barrett smiled and poured some of the liquid. "Well, Clive, I assume you have some information for me since it was you who called this meeting."

"I do indeed. My web of observers is getting larger and developing some good information. Naturally, my coverage is most effective in Jersey, and that's what I'm here to talk about. It happens something is going on there." He raised a finger. "The rebels are up to some mischief."

"What makes you think that, Clive?"

"Well, as background, Washington has put a general named Mercer in charge of militia units in New Jersey. He's from Virginia. Perhaps you know him?"

"Yes, he's a physician from Fredericksburg. I met him in Williamsburg. He's a smart fellow and very close to Washington."

Harfeld raised his eyebrows. "Now that makes sense." He paused, then said, "Well, our General Mercer is running patrols up and down the roads of Jersey, all the way to Pennsylvania. And this will interest you: They are made up of officers and men from that Virginia Light Foot Company—the one led by your acquaintance Eckert."

"That is interesting. But more to the point, what are these patrols for—what are they doing?"

"The officers in charge are spending time with rebel militia officers and, at the same time, mapping out various roads and geographical features. One of my men got a quick look at a map they were making—just for a few seconds, but he got the gist of what they are doing. And here's something of even greater interest: The latest patrol is going along the Jersey bank of the Delaware River, apparently checking out boats."

"Damn! It's obvious—Washington is planning a retreat into Pennsylvania." He thought a second, then said, "Perhaps Washington is making preparations to shield Philadelphia, where their Continental Congress meets. It's their de facto capital."

"Yes, Barrett, I rather thought the same thing myself. And it also occurred to me that we are getting well into November. It seems likely that Washington is getting ready to go into Winter Quarters. The Delaware could be a natural barrier against our potential attack."

Northcutt put his hand to his chin. "Both things could be true. Washington could go into an encampment across the river but in a location where he can move rapidly if we threaten Philadelphia."

There was a silence as the two men considered Northcutt's words. Then Harfeld said in a soft voice, "You know, Barrett, people are wondering about the pace of the campaign. Many on our side are wondering why Washington's army still exists. He was allowed to escape across the East River after the Battle of Long Island, and now Howe didn't pursue Washington after White Plains. For God's sake, after a significant, hard-hitting victory, he didn't press the Rebels as they withdrew Now the main body of their army has made it across the Hudson."

Northcutt leaned forward and said, "I know there are many people asking those questions. What you have to understand, Clive, is that Howe is very conscious of the need to conserve the lives of our troops. He was very affected by the bloody toll at Bunker Hill. You also must remember that he and his brother Richard are also designated as peace commissioners. The crown still hopes a long period of hostilities can be averted and that a negotiated settlement can be achieved sooner rather than later. As part of that, Howe has hesitated thus far to inflict excessive casualties on the Americans because it might lead to embitterment and a resistance to come to terms."

Harfeld leaned back in his chair and said thoughtfully, "There may be some reason to believe that. I can tell you that with these successive defeats of Washington's army, enthusiasm for the rebel cause and the war is waning in many of the population. They don't want to end up on the wrong side when we prevail."

"There you have it, Clive. Howe will, in the main, continue to proceed with caution on the battlefield until he determines that reconciliation is impossible." He raised a finger. "And there are other military considerations that lead Howe to proceed slowly. The first is that Washington left behind sizable forces on this side of the Hudson. One is a strong force of 6000 or more men under Lee that is hovering to the north, possibly waiting for any opening to strike any outlying portion of our forces. A second, and rather puzzling situation, is at Fort Washington. For some reason, instead of evacuating when the rebels retreated from White Plains, the place has been reinforced to a garrison of over 3000 men, enough to be a bother if some sortied forth, perhaps in coordination with Lee's division."

"All right, Barrett, I see that Howe is facing some complications. But perhaps the best way to conserve men and to relieve oneself of all these considerations is a hard strike on the rebels that will sow discouragement in the ranks and lead to the disintegration of Washington's army." He leaned forward. "Remember, we know that enlistments are expiring and that there is already significant desertion. Why not encourage it with strong action?"

Northcutt smiled and said, "Patience, my dear friend. I can relate that you will see a strong strike very soon." He paused a moment for effect. "Howe is determined to capture Fort Washington and, if possible, its entire garrison. That will eliminate nearly a quarter of Washington's present force, and the shock of such a loss will possibly accelerate desertions among the colonials."

"Barrett, I look forward to such an undertaking."

Northcutt drained his teacup. Then he leaned forward again and asked, "Meanwhile, what about that lady whose husband is on Washington's staff with whom you have developed a relationship? Has she provided any more information?"

Harfeld sighed. "No. Regrettably, she is currently within the camp of the garrison of Fort Lee and inaccessible to me. However, I have sent her a letter to keep myself in her mind. I offered my services if she finds herself in difficult circumstances." He waved a hand. "That's the most I can do at this moment."

"That's a good idea. At least keep the channel open." Northcutt pulled out his watch and looked at the time. "Regrettably, I must leave you now." He grinned, "Speaking of ladies, I must visit one momentarily."

Harfeld raised his eyebrows. "Ah, my dear Northcutt, have you found some young woman who arouses your interest? It is about time you thought about that; you're not getting any younger."

Barrett laughed. "There is a certain lady who has my attention, but this is not the one, Clive. I am going to see an elegant woman, but it's Mrs. Loring."

A knowing grin spread across Harfeld's face. "Ah, yes, Howe's golden-haired doxy. What business do you have with her?"

"She's just moved into a house that one of the colonists abandoned when the city was evacuated. Howe wants me to see how she is doing and if she needs any assistance in getting settled." He shrugged his shoulders. "Since becoming involved in a sensitive medical event back in Halifax, I seem to have inherited the duty of performing discreet liaison with her for the general."

"Well, that could be some bother. However, at least it keeps you in good favor with Howe. That can't be a bad development."

Northcutt winked at Harfeld and said dryly, "My dear friend, obviously that had occurred to me."

—∞—

Wend stood near the company's horse picket line in the Hackensack encampment, where he had come to check on his mount, Sonny. The young, long-legged, muscular hunter was descended from the tall, black mare Wend had ridden for many years, and who now spent her time in the pasture at Eckert Ridge. Billy Wood was at work grooming the horse as Wend watched.

Wend heard a familiar voice call out, "Eckert! We need to talk."

Wend turned to see Geoffrey Fairfield standing a few feet away. The troop had ridden into camp a couple of hours ago and set up their bivouac. Now Fairfield, who had a piece of paper in his hand, raised it up and exclaimed in an angry tone, "What the *hell* is the meaning of this? Is it your doing?"

Wend pointed to the paper and put a puzzled look on his face, although he was confident he knew what it said. "What specifically is *that*? Perhaps you could enlighten me."

"Damn it! It's today's general orders for the army, which I just received. And the third item on the list says that the 1st Troop of the Palmetto Light Horse will be subject to the command of Captain Eckert of the Frederick County Light Foot. Effective immediately!"

Wend raised his eyebrows and said in the calmest voice he could muster, "Ah, yes. General Mercer mentioned it to me."

"Mercer told you? What's he got to do with it? My troop has been under the direct command of Washington since we joined the army."

"Well, Geoffrey, actually it was General Washington's idea that he passed on to Mercer, who you should understand is now acting as his deputy. He thought that we would both be more effective if we worked in concert, since we are both involved in scouting and other special activities. I must admit, it does sound logical."

"Logical, hell! Cavalry under the control of infantry makes no sense."

Ignoring Fairfield's words, Wend continued, "And Washington thought we would be compatible, since we're both from the southern colonies. Certainly you can see some logic to that." Wend stared at Fairfield for a moment. "And since I'm a captain and you're a lieutenant, naturally I was put in command."

Fairfield said nothing, simply glaring at Wend.

Wend added, "And there seems to be some consideration in high places that perhaps more mature supervision would help the efficiency of your troop." *Of course no one had actually said that, least of all Washington, but Wend couldn't resist the temptation to twist the knife a little bit.*

"God damn it, Eckert, I'll not stand for this! You've got another thing coming if you think you can lord it over me! This isn't going to end here!"

"Fairfield, you can take your objections to the General in the future and you'll have my blessing. But right now, this army is in a lot of trouble, and we've been tasked to play a key role in getting it safely across the Delaware. So I expect you to take orders and get your job done, and you can do your complaining later."

"You bastard, Eckert."

Wend ignored Fairfield's words and cleared his throat. "And since the order putting you under my command has now come out, here's my first guidance to you: It makes sense to consolidate all our horses on the same picket line and share the feeding and grooming chores. It will be more efficient and make better use of the grain and hay, since the army's supplies are so limited. Also, I think we should consolidate the officers' mess. I should tell you our Melinda is a marvelous cook." Wend gave Fairfield a mischievous glance. "Don't you think that will be most beneficial? That way we'll have six officers dining together. It will be more efficient of food and make for increased conviviality at meals."

Fairfield's face was a study in rage. He opened his mouth as if to say something, but Wend didn't give him a chance to speak. He just said in a peremptory tone, "Please have your Ensign Middleton speak to my Ensign Childers, who handles the messing arrangements for us. The two youngsters can work out the details."

And with that, he turned and walked back to his tent, leaving Fairfield sputtering behind him.

Chapter Twelve

A Matter of Horses

With light fading, the two Conestoga freight wagons rolled along the New Jersey road northeast of the town of Princeton, the brass bells on the horses' harnesses jingling with every step. Joshua Baird, who had been scouting ahead, rode back and pulled Beau around so that he was riding beside Jake Cather as he walked alongside the lead wagon.

Leaning over in the saddle, Baird said, "I've found a likely place for us to camp tonight. Nice little clearing beside the road with a small creek running nearby. It will take you 'bout a quarter of an hour to get there."

"Can't be soon enough," replied the teamster. "Been a long day, and my legs are feeling it."

"Well," replied Baird, "these long days are almost over. We're getting close to the army, by my reckoning." Then he rode out ahead to lead them to the campsite.

Later, after dark, when the horses had been tied to a picket rope and grained, a fire built, and a stew of salt beef cooking over the flames, all three men sat waiting for the meal to be ready. Each had a cup of whiskey in hand, the reward for the day's journey.

Elijah McCartney looked up from his drink and asked, "Sure 'nuff we must be getting near the end. Trouble is, we don't know exactly where Eckert's company is."

Joshua said, "I talked to some people at that last village. Seems the army, a good part of it anyway, has moved into New Jersey near a certain Fort Lee. Best I can make out from what they told me, it's about two more days' journey. Once we get to the army bivouac, we can start askin' around about where our boys are."

Jake looked over at Elijah and then back to Joshua. "And I'm hopin' like Hell that the company is on this side of the river. It will be a real pain to have to make another ferry crossing. We done enough of that already on this trip. It's been one damn river after another."

Joshua agreed. "Yeah, you got it right; the other side of the river is where the British are. We don't want to get caught over there if things start heatin' up. I damn well hope we don't have to cross into New York to find Wend."

Cather, who was tending the pot, lifted a spoon to sample the stew and announced, "This stuff is ready. Hand me the bowls."

The three hungry men spent the next few minutes devoid of conversation while devouring the stew. When all had finished, Jake gathered up the bowls and utensils and said, "I'll wash these all out down at the stream, then check the horses. I'm planning for an early night of it."

Joshua responded, "You'll get no argument from me. And I say we get out of here with first light in the morning." Then he got up and put some more wood on the fire to keep it going through the night. "It's gonna be a cold one. I'm puttin' on a coat besides my blankets."

The three all finished the evening with a pipe, and soon after, they were bundled up in blankets and coats, lying in a close circle around the fire, deep in sleep, as attested to by the heavy breathing and snores.

It was well after midnight when they were startled awake by the noise of loud whinnying at the picket line. Not one horse, but the whole lot. Jake sat up, rubbed his eyes, and exclaimed, "What the Devil is going on?"

Joshua said, "Mayhap some varmint animal is stirring them up."

Jake threw off his blankets and stood up. As he did so, they all heard the sound of men's voices shouting, "Ha, ha!" followed by the sound of many horses' hooves beating in the night.

Elijah shouted, "Jesus Christ, someone's stampeding our horses!"

All three picked up their firelocks and headed for the picket line.

They arrived to find—*nothing!* All the animals were gone, with the noise of pounding hooves and the shouting of the thieves fading into the distance. All three men stood staring into the night for a long minute, shocked into silence by what had just happened.

Elijah let out a string of curses, then said, "God damn our bad luck! Running into horse thieves! I been a wagoner for fifteen years, and never even heard of anything like this."

Joshua stood silent for a moment more, then replied, "Actually, we're lucky. Those thieves missed their chance."

Jake looked at Joshua with abject puzzlement on his face. "We're lucky? What the Hell do you mean?"

"I mean those thieves didn't look in the wagons and realize what we are carrying. There's a hell of a lot more money in the whiskey than in horses. If they had seen those casks, it would have made a world of sense for them to kill us in our sleep and take everything. That's why fortune was on our side."

Elijah laughed. "Except we ain't got no horses and no way of getting more. None of us is carrying 'nuff money to replace the teams. And if we did, findin' trained Conestoga teams near at hand ain't likely."

Joshua answered. "Those horses are goin' to end up somewhere around here. And a herd of fourteen got to leave some sign that I could follow and be seen by people along the way, wherever they're heading. But I need a horse to do it." He stared into the night. "Sure and there's a town up the road, no doubt just a few miles ahead. I'll walk there and get a horse, one way or another." He looked back at the wagons. "But first I got to fill my canteen with whiskey."

Jake asked, "Whiskey? Not water?"

He pointed to the wagons. "I'll barter a keg of the whiskey for a horse. The spirits in the canteen is proof we got good stuff."

In a few minutes he had his kit together and slung his rifle over his shoulder. He turned to the other. "You two stick to the wagons 'till I get back, no matter what. And keep your firelocks close at hand."

And then he was off, traveling northward along the wagon track, walking briskly into the pre-dawn darkness despite the limp in his left leg from the old Bushy Run wound.

—᪥—

After walking for nearly three hours, Joshua welcomed the morning twilight that revealed a sizable town ahead in the distance. As he approached, signs soon identified it as New Brunswick. While traveling, he had been working out in his mind how he would proceed in getting a horse and had made a plan. But to achieve it, he needed information about the town. And of course, the best place to get that was a tavern. Soon enough, walking along the town's main street, he came to a likely looking establishment with an inviting sign which proclaimed it the "Jolly Times Ordinary." Baird pushed his way through the front door and saw that at this early hour, the common room was sparsely populated with just a few men taking their breakfasts. The smell of food emanating from the cook room was tantalizing, but he knew he hadn't time for eating. Joshua went up to the bar where a pretty blonde girl was working and asked to see the proprietor.

The girl didn't immediately answer. Instead, she stared at him for a few seconds, then asked, "Would you happen to be from Virginia?"

Puzzled, Joshua said, "Aye, Lass, that I am. Now, how would you have guessed that?"

"Because, sir, we don't see all that many hunting shirts in here. And someone from Virginia I've met recently has one that looks just about like yours." She smiled and said, "He's a soldier from the Frederick County Light Foot."

Shocked, Joshua said, "Not only am I from Frederick County, I know most of the men in that company by name. Who the devil is it you speak of?"

A broad grin spread over the girl's face and she flushed. "Oh, yes, he's a *devil* indeed. He's an Irishman named O'beirne. Lieutenant Shay O'beirne."

Joshua, rolling his eyes, said, "I should have guessed." Then he continued, "What would O'beirne be doing here?"

"He has been traveling this part of Jersey to work with the militia for the army. In fact, he was just here a few days ago, heading down toward the Delaware. I 'spect he'll be back with his men any day now, riding back up to Fort Lee."

Baird cocked his head. "Fort Lee—is that where his company be?"

"Indeed, sir. It's right on the Hudson River."

"And how far from here is it?"

"Why, I'd say a two day ride, supposin' you had a strong horse and you pushed him hard."

"Thank you, Miss. And what's your name?"

"Joy, sir."

"Well, Joy, would you find the proprietor for me now? I have some important business to discuss with him."

The girl was back in a moment, with a balding, chubby man in a grease-stained apron which had once been white. He smelled strongly of the cook room. He said, "I'm George Watkins. I own this place. And it's a mystery what business you might have with me, just a'fore dawn."

Joshua introduced himself, then asked, "How much rum or whiskey do you have on hand?"

Watkins' face wrinkled up. "What kind of jest is that? There's been no spirits of that kind around here for weeks. All we got, just like everyone else, is ale and wine."

Baird grinned broadly and handed the man his canteen. "Take yourself a wee gulp of that, George."

Watkins' eyes narrowed. He pulled the cork and raised the canteen to his nose. Then his eyes opened wide and he quickly took a sip and swallowed it. Then he stared down at the canteen and asked, "Now where the hell did you get that? That's damned good stuff."

"It's from Virginia. And I've got two wagon loads of it stranded five miles south of here."

Baird thought the tavern keeper's eyes would pop right out of his head.

"Stranded? What do you mean by that?"

"We was campin' by a stream that crossed the road and after midnight a band of thieves stole all our horses: twelve Conestoga Horses and two fine Virginia hunters."

Watkins shook his head. "I'm not surprised. Been a lot of horses stole around here recently. The British are wantin' horses for their cavalry and supply wagons and payin' top price in hard coin. They got a place where they're buying horses and farm produce near Staten Island. Likely that's where they're takin' your animals."

Joshua said, "Well, I intend to track down these thieves and my horses. But I need a horse to do that. Fact is, I'm willin' to trade a keg of whiskey for a horse." He looked at Watkins and raised his finger. "So here's my deal to you: You hire or buy me a horse and you get a keg. That's far more than the value of a horse—you'll make a good gain on the trade."

Watkins cocked his head. "Yeah, that's good, if you really got that whiskey. How do I know you ain't lyin'?"

"It won't take long for you to send someone down to check what I'm sayin'. But we got to do it fast, so's I can get on the trail of those thieves."

Watkins looked at Baird speculatively. "You goin' after them all by yourself? There had to be a gang to take all those horses and herd them. That ain't good odds, mister." He thought a moment, then took his apron off and threw it onto the counter. "Come on, let's go to Harwood's livery stable and see about a horse. His place is on a back street to the south, just a short way from here."

"Now," exclaimed Joshua, "you're talkin', Watkins. Let's go—time's a wastin'."

As he walked out from behind the bar, the proprietor said, "It doesn't hurt that Harwood is the captain of our local militia company. It might be he could arrange some help for you."

They arrived at the stable in just a few moments. It was at the eastern edge of town and included a large, fenced yard and a sizable stable where Joshua could see numerous horses grazing. As they approached, a tall, broad-shouldered man with thinning hair, who looked to be nearing forty, appeared in the entrance to the stable. When he saw them, the man smiled and said in a jocular tone, "Now Watkins, what has got you out of your cook room so early in the morning? Your patrons are gonna' be callin' for their food and drink."

Watkins pointed toward Baird. "This here man's got a problem and needs help. In particular, he needs a horse, which is why we are here."

Harwood looked at Joshua, then asked, "Are you from that Virginia Light Company?"

Watkins answered, "He be from Virginia, same place as O'beirne and his men. But he's leadin' two Conestogas loaded with whiskey that was goin' to the army. But the thieves got their horses."

Harwood's face wrinkled up as he thought through what Watkins had said. Then he said, "Yeah, sure and it was those Partisans. Takin' horses for the British."

Joshua cocked his head and asked, "Partisans? Never heard that word before. Who the hell are Partisans?"

"Heavily armed bands of brigands who profess to be loyal to the crown. They've started to attack plantations and steal from travelers. And they make money by sellin' what they steal to the British Army."

Watkins said, "Baird here is promising me a keg of his whiskey if I buy a horse for him. He's set on goin' after the Partisans."

Harwood stared at Joshua, then sighed. "Goin' after them by yourself? Not likely, Baird. There's too many of them and they're well armed. It ain't just a couple of thieves who got your horses. You'll need a party of men for the job."

"Now where," asked Joshua, "am I goin' to get men to go with me, Harwood?"

The tavern proprietor motioned toward Watkins. "Like I said, he's the captain of the militia, and this sounds like a job for your men, Jacob. Maybe you can get Baird's horses back and put an end to this band of renegades at the same time. Sure, they've been terrorizing the whole county. It would give the people a reason to respect the militia, which can't hurt."

Harwood put his hand to his chin and a sly look came to his face. "And it's certain the Governor would appreciate the man who got rid of this partisan band." He stared into the distance for a few seconds then turned to Joshua. "All right, Baird, we're goin' after these renegades. I'll call out some men I know who can mount themselves. While they're comin' in, we'll get those wagons of yours up here to my stable. We can't leave them sittin' down in the country—the thieves might go after their cargo. I got two two-horse teams here—they ain't proper Conestoga horses, but they're good solid draft animals. We'll take them with us when we go down to your camp, and your teamsters can get the wagons up here. It will be slow with only two animals for each wagon, but it's just a short distance and pretty flat country and they ought to be able to do it." He shrugged. "Then we'll go after those partisans."

Joshua said, "There was enough moonlight for me to see they was headin' east. Watkins here says the British are buyin' horses over by Staten Island near New York."

Harwood nodded. "Yeah, it's at a place called Shoreham. That's probably where they're taking them. But we'll know for sure once we can scout their trail in the light of day." He turned to Watkins. "Take Baird here back to your place and feed him. I'll bring my men and teams up there when we're ready and then we'll head down to the ford where his wagons are. It'll be a couple of hours."

Baird smiled. "Now that sounds good. I'm obliged to you, Harwood." He turned to the tavern proprietor. "And I could sure use some food and a bit of rest for my legs."

—∞—

Northcutt walked briskly through the camp, the late afternoon noises and smells of the army all around him. Cook fires were burning and the smell of meat stewing wafted through the air. Women stood gossiping as they tended pots, soldiers were sitting around mending clothing or cleaning their weapons. Arriving at Howe's headquarters, he noticed the aides of many general officers standing around a crackling fire, warming themselves against the November cold and a biting breeze. A young aide, bundled up in a watch coat, sat in front of the large tent which was used for meetings and Paterson himself stood by the tent flap.

The adjutant general called out, "There you are, Barrett. Come right in—everyone is assembled, and you are first up to give them your intelligence assessment."

"Sorry I'm a little late, James. I just got a communication from the field, and I thought it best to read through it before my performance!"

"Quite right, Barrett," replied Paterson, and opened the flap for Northcutt.

Once inside, he saw that the top leadership of the army was present, informally chatting with each other. Besides Howe were the three lieutenant generals of the British Army—Clinton, Cornwallis, Percy—and the lieutenant general of the Germans—Von Heister. Northcutt was surprised to see several more junior officers in the tent: Colonel Thomas Sterling of the 42nd, Captain Wolff of the German Jaeger Corps, and a Hessian colonel he didn't recognize. He thought, *I wonder why they are here?*

His thoughts were interrupted by Paterson's words to Howe, "General, Northcutt's here, so we may begin the meeting."

Howe, who had been talking with Von Heister, looked up and said, "Ah, yes. Good to see you, Barrett." Then he stood and said, "We'll start with an appreciation of the Americans' situation by Colonel Northcutt of my staff. I can tell you that he has established, in a very short time, a web of spies and watchers who keep us informed of the rebel movements."

Northcutt walked to a table that had been placed near one wall of the tent and laid out his briefing papers. He looked at the assemblage and said, "The General is too kind to me. Our web is almost totally due to the efforts of a remarkable man, who for purposes of confidentiality chooses to simply be known to us as 'Harkness.' In addition to controlling his group of watchers, he easily moves through the lines to personally observe the activities of the colonials and provides us with much useful information."

The audience nodded their agreement, and Northcutt dove into his briefing. "Gentlemen, as you are aware, we are here, with the preponderance of the army, before the series of earthen works and artillery positions that the rebels call Fort Washington. The fort is manned by a force of 3000 men under the command of their General Nathan Greene, a former Quaker from Rhode Island."

Cornwallis, holding a cigar in his hand, exhaled smoke and interjected, "For the life of me, I cannot fathom why they have kept so large a force before us with their backs to the river. What purpose could they possibly have? Why have they not evacuated to the other side?"

Northcutt nodded. "As you understand, sir, they have built another work, called Fort Lee, on the bluffs directly across the river. Since White Plains, Washington has concentrated his main body in the vicinity of that fort. The fact is, they are under the impression that the guns of the two forts will prevent our navy from going up river."

Howe spoke up. "Which idea is pure poppycock, gentlemen! Richard says he could push a couple of frigates through there any time we desire. Their guns are far heavier than the rebels have in the forts." He shook his head. "I cannot understand why the rebels fantasize the forts would stop us."

Cornwallis responded, "Well, I say we can take it as conclusive evidence of Washington's tactical naivety."

There were expressions of agreement from the other generals. Then Howe said, "We'll get back to Fort Washington shortly." He motioned to Northcutt. "Colonel, continue with your briefing."

"Besides the troops with Washington on the western side of the Hudson, there is a strong force hovering to the north on this side of the river. Harkness said it is under General Lee. It is a division of at least five thousand men and obviously in a position to cause us concern. Clearly Washington has placed it there so that we must watch our flank and maintain significant forces there to counter it. To date, Lee has made no aggressive move, and we have it under continuous watch by cavalry detachments." Northcutt smiled. "Including, I might say, a mounted company of my own regiment, the King's Loyal Virginia Regiment."

Barrett reached down and picked up a sheet of parchment. "That summarizes the position of our forces and those of the enemy. Now I have some information that just came into my possession today—a dispatch from Harkness." He looked around at the officers. "We have previously discussed the precarious situation Washington faces regarding his troop strength—expiring enlistments of regular troops and short term militia. Well, Harkness' people have reported that the exodus of regiments has begun. Several have been seen marching back toward their home colonies." He looked around again. "But that is not the most important thing in Harkness' report. In the aftermath of White Plains, it is clear that there is growing disenchantment among Washington's rank and file as well as some of the officer class." Northcutt looked down at his paper. "In the days after the recent battle, our observers saw large numbers of individual soldiers leaving on their own accord—*deserting*, gentlemen. And here is what I find striking: They even saw whole bodies of troops under their officers—company and battalion strength—marching off before the expiration of their enlistments." He smiled and looked around again. "Gentlemen, the evidence is clear: Washington's army is wasting away. Harkness tells me that Washington probably has no more than thirteen or fourteen thousand men at hand, and the number is undoubtedly decreasing daily." He paused for effect and then said, "Let me summarize: There are 3000 men before us at Fort Washington, say 5000 with Lee, and that leaves only something on the order of 4000 at the most on the heights of the Hudson with Washington himself."

All the generals sat, contemplating what he had said. After a few seconds, he said, "There is one more matter to consider: It may well have a bearing on what Washington is contemplating for the near future."

Clinton looked at him. "I daresay, how can you claim to be inside Washington's mind?"

Barrett raised a hand. "I don't claim that, sir. All I can do is speculate based on the enemy's actions. And at a personal meeting with Harkness just a few days ago, he informed me that the enemy is conducting a series of mounted patrols along the main road down through New Jersey—the King's Way, if you will. These patrols are mapping the territory between Washington's position at Fort Lee and the Delaware River." He paused to let that sink in.

Percy said, "I see what you are getting at, Northcutt. Perhaps Washington is planning a withdrawal in that direction."

Cornwallis had been sitting with his hand on his chin, thinking. He looked up, "That would clearly put him between us and Philadelphia. I say he's preparing to defend that city where their congress is meeting."

"Yes, sir," Northcutt responded. "That's one of the possibilities."

Cornwallis's face wrinkled up. "One of the possibilities? And what, say you, are the others?"

"One other, General, given the lateness of the season, is that Washington is contemplating going into Winter Quarters across the Delaware River somewhere in Pennsylvania, in a position where he could shield Philadelphia while spending the winter recruiting and rebuilding his army."

Clinton laughed. "Gentlemen, I submit that if we are sufficiently aggressive and play our cards right in the next few weeks, the only place Washington and his ragtag army will spend the winter is in a prisoner camp."

The senior officers of the British force all broke into smiles and outright laughter.

When the laughs had subsided, Northcutt turned to Howe. "Sir, that concludes my presentation."

Howe rose from his chair. "Thank you, Barrett. As usual, you have provided us with most valuable information and intelligent insights." Then he paused and looked around at his lieutenants. "Gentlemen, let us now discuss our course of action over the next few days." A look of reflection came over his face, and then he began speaking. "Let me begin by saying that I am quite aware that in some quarters I am being criticized for my conduct of the campaign—that we have not pressed hard enough against the rebel forces and have not pursued them vigorously after defeats on the battlefield."

Northcutt, watching Howe closely, saw his eyes flick in the direction of Clinton, who everyone knew was one of the most severe critics. Clinton was staring into the distance, avoiding eye contact with the army commander.

Howe resumed speaking. "I believe you all know why we have operated with a calculated amount of restraint. We wanted to give the colonials a chance to reflect on their dangerous path and come to terms with us. That is in line with the commission given to me and my brother by the crown. The other reason is simply conservation of our highly trained soldiers, of which Britain has relatively few." He paused and took a deep breath. "But the time for that is over." He paused for effect.

Northcutt could see all the officers in the tent looking at him with great concentration, waiting for what would come next.

"Gentlemen, in the next few days we will begin the disassembly of Washington's army. He has blundered by disposing it into three segments, none of which can support the other. The first step will be right here—the reduction of Fort Washington and the capture of the men who are holding it." He motioned toward Stirling and the German colonel. "That is why you are here. I intend to demonstrate to the rebels the destructive effect of an assault by determined, veteran regular soldiers. You will lead your units in the attack on the outer works of the fort—trenches manned by their infantry."

Looking directly at Stirling, he said, "Thomas, the entire army knows your regiment is without parallel in use of the bayonet. The assault the 42nd made in 1759 at Ticonderoga, in the face of massed artillery and well-protected French foot, is legendary." He turned to the German colonel. "Colonel Rall, German Grenadiers are known and respected throughout Europe for their skill and determination in the attack with cold steel."

Howe looked over at Von Heister. "And your general has assured me that your regiment is the very best in the assault of all his battalions."

Rall responded. "We shall demonstrate that fact to you and to the colonials, General."

Howe turned to Wolff. "Captain, I should imagine that you are wondering why you are here, when we are planning a massed attack with the bayonet against a fortified position."

Wolff stood up, heels together, body stiff, but with a broad smile on his lips. "Sir, with respect, I have no doubt why you have invited me here. You expect me to lead the assault with my Jaegers—to advance in skirmish disposition using whatever cover is available, under the artillery bombardment you will assuredly order, to within rifle shot of the trenches. Then we are to suppress the foot soldiers manning those positions with accurate rifle fire to reduce their ability to engage the advance of Stirling and Rall." He raised his eyebrows and looked around the gathering of senior officers. "Am I not correct?"

Howe grinned. "Quite correct, Captain. And I admire your confidence."

Wolff responded, "My Jaegers and I have been eagerly awaiting the opportunity to engage these American back country rifle hunters who have such a reputation for marksmanship. We look forward to showing them we are their match." He looked around the room and added, "My men will be happy when I tell them of their assignment."

Howe clasped his hands behind his back. "Well, gentlemen, that's what is toward. On the morrow, Colonel Paterson will issue detailed orders for the movement on Fort Washington." He scanned the gathering. "I take it there is no argument?"

Clinton spoke up. "Certainly not. This is precisely what is needed. I am certain we will reduce the fort with little trouble."

No one else spoke up. Howe said, "Well, gentlemen, that should do it for this evening. Return to your divisions and begin your preparations. And good luck to you all."

Northcutt stood waiting as the senior officers departed, followed by the unit commanders. He was about to leave when Cornwallis, who had also hung back, came over and said to Howe, who had seated himself at his camp table, "William, may I have a word with you?"

Howe looked up. "Of course, Charles."

Northcutt turned to leave, but Cornwallis said, "Colonel Northcutt, stay for a moment. This may concern you."

Cornwallis turned back to Howe. "William, I want to discuss a tactical option with you—to wit, what follows our reduction of Fort Washington." He gathered his thoughts and then continued, "You have said you want to pursue the destruction of Washington's army at the earliest opportunity. Well, I believe we should, as soon as possible, attack the main body of the rebels at Fort Lee."

Howe squinted at Cornwallis and asked, "And just how would you achieve that? He is protected by a wide river and high bluffs."

"That is precisely why we have an opportunity. They won't be expecting us to attack them quickly after we take Fort Washington. They will expect us to take time to recover and reorganize afterwards. But I say we bring all the landing boats of the navy up river and, under cover of night, transport an attack force across the river. I am told by locals hereabouts that there are numerous trails by which the bluffs can be ascended. Actually, we have some loyal colonists who have offered to be guides. A dawn attack on the rebels would have a chance achieving complete surprise and result in a rout."

Howe leaned back in his chair, a look of contemplation on his face. Then he looked up at Cornwallis. "Charles, it occurs to me that what you are proposing is in large measure a repeat of James Wolfe's surprise attack on Quebec in '59."

"I'll not argue that, William. But in fact, the situation is very similar, as is the chance we shall attain the same result as Wolfe—a victory over an unprepared enemy."

Howe rose from his chair, reached for a cigar from a box on his desk, walked over to the stove and lit it. He took a deep pull on the cigar, then exhaled. That done, he began pacing back and forth between the walls of the tent. Cornwallis and Northcutt watched in silence. Finally, he stopped and pointed his cigar at Cornwallis. "Charles, you make a good case. It would be risky, but it offers the chance of knocking Washington's main force out of the picture."

"Indeed a risk, sir, but the potential reward is commensurate—an early end to this wretched rebellion."

Howe nodded. "All right, Charles. We'll make the attempt. I'll send a message to Richard to move his boats upriver posthaste but keep them out of sight until the night we are ready to move. You select a contingent from your division to make the attack and develop a detailed plan for the movement and the attack itself." He thought a moment, then looked at Cornwallis with a broad smile on his face. "But I must advise you of this: Success will in large part depend on the man you select to lead the ascent up those bluffs and the initial attack at the top. He must be ready to push his men to get up rapidly before the enemy knows they are there. Any hesitation or other kind of delay could lead to discovery and defeat."

Cornwallis laughed aloud. "I will not even think of ignoring your advice, sir," Cornwallis responded. Then, a grin still on his face, he turned to Northcutt. "Colonel, that brings us to the reason I asked you to remain."

Barrett replied, "What is it you desire of me, General?"

"Just this, Northcutt: Knowing the disposition of Washington's troops in and around Fort Lee would be invaluable in our attack. Is it possible that your web of watchers could obtain us that information in a timely fashion?"

Northcutt bit his lip, then said, "It may be possible. The problem is getting word to my operatives, particularly Harkness, who controls the organization operationally. He is always on the move, but we have set up procedures for contacting him in situations like this. I will do my upmost to get a coded message to him. If we can contact him in time, I am confident he will obtain the information you need."

Cornwallis beamed. "Excellent, Northcutt." He turned to Howe. "You can rest assured, my assault force will be ready when the time comes."

"Well," said Howe, "then we are finished here. Thank you both."

Cornwallis and Northcutt took their leave and departed the tent together.

Once outside, the general turned to Barrett. "Colonel, please keep me personally informed about the progress of obtaining the information you find about the enemy's disposition."

"Of course, sir."

Cornwallis stared into the distance for a moment and then said softly, in a confidential manner, "Northcutt, I have a personal reason for wanting to wrap up this war most expeditiously. Just a few days ago, I received a letter informing me that my wife, dearest Jemima, has become quite ill. I'll spare you the details, but her ultimate well-being is in question. In short, I am most desirous of returning to England as soon as possible."

Northcutt said, "I will do everything in my power to ensure you have the intelligence you need, My Lord." Then he asked, "But if I may ask a personal question?"

"Certainly, Colonel. What is it?"

"Back there in the tent, when you and General Howe were discussing the selection of the man to lead the climb up the bluffs and the assault itself, there was some undercurrent that puzzled me, as if there was something between you and him that I didn't understand. If it's not too personal for me to ask, what might that be?"

Cornwallis laughed. Then, a smile on his face, he put his hand on Barrett's shoulder. "Of course you would be puzzled, my dear Northcutt, you are new to the army. The fact is, the man who led the climbing of the cliffs at Quebec and the spear point of the army's movement onto the Plains of Abraham was a certain Lieutenant Colonel Howe—William Howe, to be sure. So, of course, he would take care to instruct and caution me on the selection of the officer to lead the forthcoming assault."

The sun was just below the horizon in the east and was projecting just enough light to make for morning dusk. Baird and Harwood, dismounted and hiding in a grove of trees, stared at the row of horses tied to a picket line less than one hundred fifty yards away. Not far from where the animals stood was a campfire with a group of men lying and sitting around it. One of them was heating food in a pot suspended from a tripod above the fire.

Joshua nudged the militia captain. "See that tall horse at the left end of the picket line? That's my Beau. So it's sure enough we got the right bunch of men in front of us."

Harwood replied, "Well, we're just a mile or two from Shoreham Ordinary, where the British got their outpost. They'll probably finish breakfast and head on in soon." He shrugged. "Or maybe they'll send someone in to fetch the British and do their business right here."

"Don't make no difference." Baird looked over at the captain. "We ain't goin' to wait. We'll deal with them now while they're eatin' and doin' all their mornin' stuff. We got seven men all told, and I only see five of them around that fire. Why don't you bring up your men on foot, real quiet-like?" Then he thought of something. "And make sure they check the loads and primin' in their firelocks."

Harwood nodded. "All right, it won't take but a few moments." Then he was gone, keeping the grove of trees behind him as he went back to where the militiamen waited in another patch of woods.

They arrived in less than five minutes. Baird, speaking in a whisper, addressed them, "Now look, we're goin' on in to surprise those bastards. I've figured a path that will keep us behind trees and brush until we're near to them, so keep right with me." He looked at Harwood. "Once we get close, we'll hide in the bush and wait while you send two of your men to make sure the horses are secure. Then we'll rush their camp." He looked at them one by one. "Now here's somethin' to keep in mind: They ain't expectin' us and they ain't got their firelocks right at hand. But if they try to go for them, there can't be no hesitation. You got to be ready to pull the trigger. We ain't like the sheriff tryin' to apprehend a bunch of thieves to take to the jail. They go for their guns, we gotta' shoot first. Everyone good with that?"

Harwood spoke up. "He's right—they go down if they resist. They're desperate men. It's our lives against theirs."

Joshua looked up at the sky, then waved them forward. "All right, let's go. We want to creep up on them while there's still this mornin' gloom to help hide us." With that, he led out, rifle cocked and in hand, toward the partisan position, moving carefully to take advantage of the bush and trees along the way. He looked at the Jersey militia as they advanced, and thought, *Damn, you can sure tell they're town folks not used to moving carefully through the bush.* He sighed mentally and hoped they wouldn't give themselves away.

Despite his worries, they made it undetected to perhaps thirty or forty yards from the fire. Joshua stopped and signaled with his hand to Harwood, who in turn waved two of the men to work their way around so that they could cut the partisans off from the horses. Then they waited quietly to give them time to get into position.

Joshua looked over at Harwood. "All right, let's move in quickly now!" He jumped up from his cover and ran across the remaining distance. He could hear the others rushing with him. In a few instants he was at the edge of the camp. Suddenly one of the partisans turned and saw him and screamed a warning to his mates. The man reached down, and Joshua saw him grab a horse pistol and start to cock the hammer. Joshua quickly aimed and fired; the pistol fell out of the partisan's hand, and he reached up with his other hand to grab his shoulder, then he went to his knees, screaming in pain, blood oozing through his fingers.

Joshua dropped his rifle and pulled both pistols from his belt. Then he called out, "None of you bastards make a move, or we'll serve you like him!" He waved to the militiamen and continued, "You be surrounded by armed men who would love to put a ball in any one of you!"

The partisans froze in their positions. Joshua stepped closer and, pointing to the wounded man, said, "Now you all get on your knees beside him and keep your hands in the air where we can see them." Then he turned to Harwood. "Have your men pick up all their firelocks and pile them up well out of reach."

The partisans hurried to gather around the wounded comrade, whose right side was now covered with blood. Joshua saw that there were three white men and two Africans.

One of the partisans asked in a surly voice, "What are you going to do with us?"

Joshua waved a pistol at the man. "We damn well ought to send you to hell, but all we want is them horses you stole." He thought a second and, grinning, said, "And now that I think on it, all the other horses you got—sort of payment for all the trouble you put us through."

Harwood called out to his men, "Let's get those horses off the picket line. Lead them back to where our horses are. Joshua and I will keep these bastards covered while you do it." Then he waved to the pile of discarded weapons. "And take as many of these as you want and throw the rest into the fire."

One of the partisans shouted, "You'll not get away with this! We know where you are from, and we'll come for you!"

Harwood looked at the speaker and said, "You won't come for a while, not without horses. And there'll be a full company of militia ready for you if you show up. I wouldn't try it if I were you."

Then suddenly a new voice, surprisingly in a strong English upper-class accent, called out, "Now, my fine gentlemen, they won't need to chase you down to your town or fear some rustic militia, because you'll not be going anywhere except to a British Army prison camp, and those horses will soon be the property of His Majesty's 16th Light Dragoons."

Every head turned in the direction of the voice, and what they saw was a red-coated dragoon officer holding two pistols. With him were seven more red-coated cavalrymen, also holding pistols. With them was a man not in uniform, armed with a fowling piece and a pistol in his belt.

One of the partisans dropped his hands and rose to his feet, and looked at the man dressed in civilian clothes. "Well, Jamie, you got back with the army just in time."

It was the dragoon officer who answered. "Yes, arriving just in time to save the day is a cavalry *specialty*. Actually, Mr. Clark was leading us here to take charge of the horses when we heard a shot and thought it might be prudent to hurry to the camp and approach on foot." He smiled and waved at the partisans. "It would now be most appropriate for you to get on your feet and take the weapons from all these colonials." He grinned. "I don't think these gentlemen will make any objection. And when you've finished and have them under guard, we'll get organized to take these animals over to Shoreham." He turned and looked over the horses on the picket line and spoke to the man who had come with him. "Now, my dear Mr. Clark, those look like a fine lot you have brought us, particularly that long-legged beauty at the end of the line. I should think one of our senior officers would love him as their mount. He's as good as anything I've seen here in the colonies."

The partisans were just moving to disarm Joshua and the militia, when suddenly another voice loudly interrupted. "Now, all you lads just freeze where you are, and I'll have the dragoons drop their pistols, if you please."

All heads snapped around to see the source of this command. It was a tall, lean man, dressed in a hunting shirt similar to Joshua's. And as they looked at him, everyone saw more shirtmen emerging from the bush, all armed with rifles and pistols.

The British officer, still holding his pistol, looked around and said, "It seems New Jersey is sprouting shirtmen like flowers in May."

The shirtman who had spoken stared at the British officer for a few seconds, then grinned and said, "Well, I'll be damned if it isn't Banastre Tarleton, dressed up in the coat of a dragoon cornet. Not quite what I would have expected."

The British officer's face turned into an expression of puzzlement. "Now, sir, are we somehow acquainted? I confess I don't recollect being introduced to you."

"We've never been introduced, Tarleton, but I was in the crowd of onlookers who watched you lose more than 200 quid at a gaming table in the Cocoa Tree Club in London one night almost two years ago. I must say, you took the loss with good grace."

Tarleton shrugged. "Well of course. It was what a gentleman should do." He paused a moment. "Might I have your name?"

"Shay O'beirne, Lieutenant of the Frederick County Light Foot, at your service, sir."

Joshua, impatient with all the polite upper class banter, spoke up. "And damned glad we are to see you, O'beirne. Though I can't for the life of me understand how the Devil you happen to be here."

"No coincidence, old fellow. We arrived in New Brunswick a few hours after you and Harwood's merry band rode out. Watkins at the Jolly Times told me all about the situation. It immediately occurred to me that you might need some reinforcement."

Harwood said, "And thank God you did."

O'beirne looked around. "Well, be that as it may, we can't dally here all day. Corporal Schreiber, collect all the weapons from our dear friends of the 16th Light Dragoons and add them to the pile."

Tarleton spoke up. "I shall surrender only to an officer, not some common soldier."

Shay made a short laugh. "My pleasure to oblige you, sir." He pointed to Childers. "The Ensign here, Mr. Childers, will take your sword and firelocks. He is every bit the gentleman you are, being heir to the largest plantation in Frederick County."

Edward spoke up. "Shay, just to clarify, I'm the *second* son, so I'm not the heir of Greenfields Manor."

Tarleton looked over at Childers and said dryly. "Mr. Childers, I'm also the second son, so I *quite* understand your situation."

Edward walked over and relieved Tarleton of his pistols and sword. Meanwhile, Schreiber had collected the weapons from all the others.

O'beirne looked over at Harwood. "Well, Captain, if you and your men will collect the horses from the picket line, we'll be on our way." He hesitated, then a smile came over his face. "And by the way, send someone to find all the dragoons' horses. Prize of war for us."

In a few minutes, the horses had been gathered up and the weapons of the partisans and dragoons either in the possession of the militia or disposed of in the fire. Tarleton asked, "Well, Mr. O'beirne, it seems we are your prisoners. What provision have you made to transport us?"

"No provision, Mr. Tarleton. We're not taking you with us. Too much damned trouble. You will have to walk back to the depot at Shoreham Ordinary." He shrugged. "And I must say, that won't be very comfortable in those stiff cavalry boots." He winked at the British cornet. "But of course, the most *uncomfortable* part will be when your compatriots in the regiment find that you have lost your horses."

Tarleton glared at O'beirne with pure hatred in his eyes. "Sir, you have won the day. But the time will come when my retribution shall be exacted on you and all these despicable shirtmen of your company. You have my personal vow on that."

One of the men had brought up Shay's horse, and he sprang up into the saddle. Then he pulled the horse around so he faced Tarleton. "Cornet, I look forward to the day, should it actually arrive, when we face each other with arms at hand. I rather doubt you will prevail. But until that day, sir, I bid you farewell and better fortune than you have suffered today."

And with that, he and all the Americans rode off, bound for New Brunswick with a herd of over thirty horses.

Part III

Retreat in the Cold

Chapter Thirteen

Disaster in the Morning

The aide emerged from Cornwallis' tent and waved to Northcutt. "The General will see you now." Then he held open the tent flap for Barrett to enter. Cornwallis was sitting at a writing table placed not far from a stove which was fighting manfully against the November cold.

The general looked up. "Well, Northcutt, I hope this means you've been able to develop some information on the rebel positions across the river."

Northcutt said, "Indeed I have. But first let me congratulate you on the tremendous success in the assault on Fort Washington today. Virtually the entire garrison of 3000 captured, along with many guns. A signal victory sir, which has taken almost a third of their effective force off the game board."

"Yes, and that charge of the Highlanders and Ralls' German Grenadiers will certainly put the fear of God in the rest of the rebel army." He shrugged and said, "Shame their General Greene wasn't present. Capturing him would have been the plum of the day. He waved his hand. "But now, on to current matters. With Fort Washington reduced, I believe our assault of Fort Lee is quite urgent. We must keep the colonists on the run." He raised his eyebrows. "So what is the position of the enemy's force across the river?"

"Sir, my informants report that the situation has changed from what we perceived a few days ago. The main units of the rebel army have moved to the town of Hackensack, which is actually about five miles east of Fort Lee. There are about 2000 men in and around the fort, but it seems they are mostly militia under General Mercer."

Cornwallis exclaimed "Damn! We'll be landing at a cove north of Fort Lee, where there's a narrow but useful trail up the bluffs. But that's five miles from Fort Lee itself, which is a long way to go if we want to surprise them, but Hackensack is another five miles further. With luck we'll route Mercer and his militia, but Washington's main force will be alerted and ready to either fight or retreat." He rose from his chair, picked up a cigar and lighted it, and took a deep draw, a speculative look in his eyes.

Barrett took the opportunity to raise a finger and say, "Actually, we do still have an opportunity to strike a decisive blow. A blow that might be even more effective than if we were able to surprise Washington's Continentals."

Cornwallis took the cigar out of his mouth and looked at Barrett inquisitively. "Now what the Devil do you mean by that? Explain yourself, Northcutt."

"Sir, Washington's Continentals have left Fort Lee, but there is something very important still there: to wit, a major cache of supplies. In fact, the main storeyard of the army. Barrels of salt meat, flour, and grain which constitute the core of their winter rations. Also a multitude of canon shot, massive supplies of powder and lead for musket cartridges. Crates of blankets, shoes, and clothing. They are trying to move it, but are having trouble getting wagons and teamsters."

The general's face lit up. "By God, that is a prize. Seizing their supplies would indeed be almost as debilitating as capturing the men. It will be hard for them to go on, particularly with winter almost here."

"Precisely, General. And it's there for the taking, given militia's hesitancy to fight regulars in the open field."

Cornwallis went to his cot, picked up a gray overcoat and donned it. Then he quickly put on his hat. "Come along, Northcutt. I'm going to see Howe and insist that he get those landing barges up here posthaste. This is moment we've been waiting for—the opportunity to strike a decisive blow. We must cross the river before the Rebels are able to move those supplies."

Catherine Tresh sat before a fire in front of her tent, a heavy coat pulled around her. Even so, she was still feeling the chill of the November evening. It seemed like she hadn't really been warm, even in her blankets at night, since leaving the house at Harlem Heights weeks ago. She was on the edge of the army's bivouac in the fields near Hackensack. Washington's troops had been arriving from Fort Lee for the last two days, brigade by brigade. Now virtually all the Continentals with the commanding general were encamped nearby. She sighed, picked up the book she had been reading, and tried to muster some interest.

Then she heard a horse approaching and looked up to see her husband pull up in front of the tent and dismount. Catherine put the book down and rose from her chair. "My God, Alex, it's been days. And I've been sitting here not knowing what's happened with you." She looked him over, then exclaimed, "Why, you haven't shaved for days! That's so unlike you. What's going on?"

Tresh walked over and took a seat next to the fire. After staring into the flames for a minute, he looked over at Catherine. "My dear, there's been no time for shaving. I've been with Washington trying to organize the army for withdrawal through New Jersey. But yesterday I watched a terrible, needless disaster occur: Fort Washington has fallen. Fallen, and all the men of its garrison, 3000 all told, have been surrendered. Some of the best battalions in the army."

"How is it you could you watch? The fort is across the river."

"I was standing on the bluffs above the Hudson along with Washington, his staff and many of his generals, including Greene, who supposedly was in command of the fort. It all happened in plain sight. There was some preliminary cannon bombardment by the British artillery, then an irresistible bayonet charge by Highlanders and German Grenadiers on the earthworks in front of the fort. The Americans simply could not stand against the assault; they fled into the fort, and in a short time it was clear that resistance had ended. Presently the flag was lowered and we knew it was over."

Catherine didn't know what to say so she remained silent while Alex shook his head in despair "This is like the finale of a concert. A concert of disaster. First, defeat at Long Island and most of the army nearly lost, saved only by the ability of a regiment of sailors who managed against all odds to evacuate our forces. Then Washington forced to evacuate Manhattan. Later, defeat at several small skirmishes and White Plains. Now the loss of Fort Washington and its garrison. Frankly, my dear, the only reason the army has survived so long is because of the sluggishness of Howe in capitalizing on his victories." He looked up and stared into the distance. "And I am at a loss at why he has hesitated to follow up after each of these victories and strike a decisive blow. Had he done so, inevitably Washington's army would have been destroyed." He turned to Catherine. "The puzzle is, William Howe had an excellent reputation for aggressive leadership as a battalion commander during the French War here in the colonies. I cannot fathom his lack of alacrity now."

Catherine put her hand on her husband's arm. "Alex, why did they not abandon Fort Washington and evacuate the troops to this side of the river before the British had invested it? There was plenty of time after White Plains to do so."

"Washington wanted to do just that. However, General Greene, whom for some reason Washington invests considerable trust, thought the fort could be held. He advised that it needed to be kept to help keep the British navy from being able to go up the river." He shook his head. "I actually advised Washington confidentially that consolidating the army was more important." He raised a finger. "And I was not the only one." He leaned closer to Catherine. "In truth, this is only the latest of the blunders Washington has made during this campaign."

"Alex, this is the first time I have heard you say that of Washington."

"Well, as a foreigner, I have felt it necessary to hold my tongue. After all, I owe my position to him. But it is becoming obvious that despite his experiences in border warfare, Washington has much to learn about maneuvering armies in the field."

The two sat quietly for a while. Then Tresh said, "And I am not the only one saying that about our commander." He looked meaningfully at his wife. "There are many in the army who are grumbling about the state of affairs and blaming Washington. And General Lee is surreptitiously stirring the pot. He's been discussing the situation with various officers and writing letters to other generals criticizing Washington's ability. I don't know if this is true, but I have heard gossip that he has written to members of Congress expressing his feelings. His position is that, given his experience in the British army, he could do much better as army commander."

"My, God, Alex; does Washington know about this?"

"I don't know. I have kept everything I have heard to myself and not been in any way committal in talking with other officers. But keep this in mind: At the moment, Lee actually commands the largest segment of the army. He has upwards of

5000 men, whereas I doubt if Washington at this moment could muster 4000 with him. And he is losing men to desertion and expiring enlistments every day."

Catherine thought for a moment, then said, "If what you say is true, this rebellion could be nearing its end. The army might simply fall apart."

"I am afraid, my dear Catherine, that is a distinct possibility."

"Alex, perhaps it is time to think of ourselves. To admit we made a mistake in joining this cause."

"My dear, what are you saying we should do?"

"Just this—maybe it is time to leave the army. You are simply a volunteer. They have no hold on you." She paused, then explained, "By leaving now, we may be able to avoid any repercussions from the British if the rebels surrender or are conquered. We came here to improve our fortunes. But we must, above all else, save what we do have. It's not a terribly lot of money, but it might get us a moderate estate, upon which we could build."

Tresh crossed his arms and sat silent for a minute. Then he said, "My beloved, I have been a professional soldier for a long time. I have never left a cause for which I volunteered until things had come to a final resolution. And I won't start now, not as long as the colonials have some chance of winning or at least coming to an equitable settlement with the crown. Washington's plan is to retreat across Jersey into Pennsylvania where he might gain some breathing time to rebuild his army. We should at least wait to see if that proves viable. Let us re-evaluate the situation once the army has crossed the Delaware."

Catherine rose and paced before the fire for a moment, hands on her hips. Then she looked at her husband and said, "I'm not sure this is a moment for loyalty. Frankly, I doubt we have that much time." She turned and briefly went into the tent, returning with a piece of paper in her hand. "Alex, I got this letter from that lawyer, Mr. Harfeld, who is prepared to help us find property. Most of it discusses land available here in New Jersey." She looked down at the letter. "But he mentions that there is growing sentiment among people that the colonial cause is a failure and increasing hesitancy to support Washington and his army." She looked at her husband. "If that is the case, if the people aren't supporting the rebels, this war may in reality be over. Washington and his generals may be doomed men who simply refuse to admit it."

Catherine was about to say more when Tresh raised his hand to stop her.

"Captain Eckert is approaching." She stopped pacing and turned toward the approaching officer.

Eckert stopped right in front of the fire and touched his hat to Catherine. "Ma'am." Then he turned to Tresh. "Good day, Colonel. I just got word that you had arrived at the camp. I've also been informed by courier from General Mercer that Fort Washington has fallen and I came to see if you had more details about what happened."

Tresh quickly related the story of Fort Washington's fall to Wend. After he finished, Wend made some calculations, then said, "So, after losing the men at Fort Washington, the army would be lucky to muster 10,000 men, between here and Lee's division."

"That is correct, Captain. And you know the situation with expiring enlistments."

Wend replied, "Yes, but I am told new regiments are coming in from different states. For example, from Virginia, where they were held up because of Dunmore's action."

"Yes, Mr. Eckert. The question is, will they arrive in time? Or will Howe move quickly to attack?"

Wend nodded. "A good point, Colonel. Thank you for your information." Then he turned to return to his tent.

Tresh called after him, "Let me walk with you as you go."

Once they had gotten out of earshot of Catherine, Tresh said, "I have something personal to discuss."

"Certainly, sir."

"It's about Catherine. I know she's been in your care here at Hackensack by request of Mercer. He has also told me that your company will be leading the withdrawal to Pennsylvania."

"Yes, that's my expectation. In fact, General Mercer has just ordered me to be ready to move."

"Indeed, sir. And that leads me to beg a favor. I would ask that you keep Catherine with your company during the retreat. One cannot predict how orderly the movement will be and what danger the enemy will present. I should like her to be as far from any pursuit as is possible."

Wend said, "I understand your concern, Colonel. It happens that I am already acting to protect my women and children and the company baggage by sending them ahead under the protection of a small squad of soldiers. They are leaving early tomorrow. Have your wife and her cart ready and she can go with them."

Tresh smiled. "I am indebted to you, Eckert." He extended his hand, and Wend shook it. "I assure you Catherine and her maid will be ready."

—m—

Lieutenant Owen McDougal strode in the dark of night through the camp of the 42nd Foot. The campfires had mostly burned down to embers and the men were in their tents or in their blankets around the coals. Just a little to the north he could make out the earthworks of the captured and empty Fort Washington, the 3000 prisoners already having been marched off to a prison camp. Soon he came to his objective, the two rows of tents forming the regimental hospital. When he arrived, he saw a blazing fire between the rows with the thin figure of Surgeon Potts sitting in a chair in front of the flames. He was bundled in a watch-coat and had a mug of tea in his hands. McDougal could see exhaustion in his eyes, the lids drooping.

"Good Morning, Wendell," said Owen. He saw the surgeon's eyes slowly open fully. "You look like you've had a hard time of it since the end of the battle."

"Yes, but not as hard as some of them in there," he motioned to the tents with his head. "We've had to extract several balls and do three amputations. And treat a couple of bayonet wounds. Those are the fellows who had a rough time."

"Ah, yes," responded McDougal. "Poor chaps." He looked reflectively at the hospital tents. "But actually I'm here about Ensign Charles McGrath. He's in my company, and the captain asked for me to drop by and see how he's doing." He shrugged. "Cheer him up a bit if he's awake."

"You're a bit too late, Owen. Ensign McGrath passed away an hour ago."

A look of shock came over the lieutenant's face. "I didn't realize it was so serious. A damned shame," said McDougal. "He was a cheerful lad and a stout fellow. Did well leading his men on Long Island and the landing at Kips Bay. And when they were carrying him off to hospital today, he seemed strong and was quite cheerful."

Potts responded in a tired voice, "He took two rifle balls. One broke his arm just below the shoulder. The other was in his chest. We did our best—amputated the arm and extracted the other ball. I thought he had a chance at survival. But it was all just too much shock for his body on top of the original wounds. He didn't have the strength to take it. Mary sat with him as he faded and was holding his hand when he slipped away."

"It must have been hard on Mary to deal with that."

Potts took a deep breath. "Yes, but one thing I have learned about her: She is as much a toughened soldier as any long serving officer or sergeant." He looked up at McDougal and continued, "She is hard as nails when needed and soft as your mother when that is the appropriate emotion. She doesn't shy away from sitting with a dying man and helping him make the final passage. Frankly, I don't know how she bears it."

"Indeed, Wendell, she is special."

Wendell Potts looked up from his seat and locked eyes with McDougal. "Owen, I'll say this: When General Murray and Colonel Stirling and Major McDonald met with me back in Glasgow, I admit that I was quite hesitant about accepting her as Matron. Ferguson—the surgeon she served under during the French War—advised me against her. He said she had been insubordinate." He shook his head. "But I've seen none of that. Instead she's become my right arm."

McDougal hesitated, a moment then said, "The whole officer's mess admires her and personally, I made up my mind about her long ago." Then, "Do you mind if I see her for a moment?"

The surgeon shrugged his shoulders. "No, not at all. It might be good for her to see someone who isn't wounded or dying. Go right in—I believe she's in the third tent up the line."

Owen went to the tent and opened the flap. Mary and the tall, wiry, horse-faced nurse Mrs. O'Hara were standing on either side of a young private, who was awake and obviously in some pain, his eyes on the two women. They were working together to change a dressing on his side above his right waist.

Mary was speaking, "Michael, I've put a new, clean dressing on the wound. Now Kathryn and I are going lift you up by your shoulders so we can wrap some bandaging around you to hold it in place. And just to prepare you, it's going to hurt some as we do it. I can tell you from experience: I took a wound much like yours at a place called Bushy Run, thirteen years ago, but I can still remember the pain every time I moved."

The man looked up at her, surprise in his face. "Sure and that's the truth of it, Miss Fraser? A ball in your side? Na' you must have been but a child."

"God's truth, Michael, I was just fifteen years old. And it nearly killed me. But I survived and you have my word you'll do the same."

The private smiled. "Na, don't worry about me, Ma'am. If I could stand the ball when it hit, Miss Fraser, sure and I can take the pain while you're doin' your work. Just get on with you have to do."

Owen stared at Mary—she was dressed in a ragged old blue gown, a white, blood stained apron covering from her chest down three quarters of the way to the hem of her gown, a cloth inelegantly wrapped around her head, but with strands of her shiny auburn hair escaping and laying down across her forehead. A trace of dried blood was visible on her left cheek. But disheveled as she was, McDougal found her as appealing and attractive as the first day he had seen her six months ago. Then she had been standing by the road as he lead his recruiting party past the Highland manor where she was the governess for three children. He had stopped to talk with her and had immediately become smitten, but at the same time reconciled that he would never see her again. Then, miracle of miracles, she had suddenly arrived at the regimental depot at Glasgow and General Murray had appointed her the matron of the hospital.

As he was reflecting, Mary looked up and saw him and her face quickly broke into a warm smile. A surge of affection and desire flashed through his body as his eyes met hers. She said nothing but turned back to the patient as she and O'Hara finished bandaging his waist. When they were done, she said a few more words to the private, then came to join McDougal.

"Hello, Owen. I'm glad you came safely through the day. I know your company was in the first element of the assault."

"Yes, God was with me today. But of course, young McGrath was not so lucky. I came here to see him, but Potts say he passed earlier tonight after you treated his wounds."

"Indeed, he just faded away."

McDougal's face took on a grim look. "Can I see his remains? We'll send men to pick him up later. The company will take care of the burial. Our way to honor him."

"Yes, of course. It's over here, Owen." Mary picked up a torch, lit it from a nearby fire and walked past all the tents to where a number of blanket covered bodies lay. She approached one of the blankets and said, "I'll hold the light for you to look." McDougal knelt and pulled the blanket back, revealing Charles' face. He stared for a long moment and then said, "He was hit just as we were beginning our advance. Quite a ways from the earthworks."

"It was long range rifle fire, Owen. He was hit with balls from two marksmen almost at the same time."

McDougal gritted his teeth in anger. "Those damned Yankee riflemen aren't soldiers, they're assassins."

Mary responded passionately with a stern tone in her voice. "Owen, this is *not* Europe where it's considered bad form to shoot directly at officers. War is *brutal* here. Those back country riflemen seek out officers as their first targets and take pride in their shots, as if they were taking game in the bush. I listened to them bragging about how they 'bagged' Indian sachem's and French officers during the last war." She leaned over so their faces were close. "Now do this for me: You must talk to the other subalterns in the mess. Tell them to strip all the braid and fine buttons off their coats—get rid of anything that identifies them as an officer. Even better, wear a private's clothing into battle. She pointed down at McGrath and said, "If you do that, perhaps Charles' death will count for something and preserve the lives of some others."

"All right, Mary. I'll do it for you and for young McGrath's memory."

It was still dark at the picket station five miles north of Fort Lee on the bluffs towering four hundred feet above the Hudson and Lower Closter Landing. Several militiamen lay in blankets around the embers of a fire, sleeping as best they could in the cold November night aggravated by a steady drizzle of rain. Presently, one of the soldiers threw off his blanket and got to his feet. Slipping into his shoes, he went to a nearby wood pile and tossed some split logs onto the campfire, which quickly flamed up. Then he prepared a pot of coffee and put it in the hot coals at the edge of the fire to boil.

Momentarily, a man who had been standing sentry duty at the very edge of the cliffs came out of the darkness, a blanket tightly wrapped around his shoulders.

He lay his musket down and called out to the man at the fire, "It be time for Harry to relieve me." Then he leaned close to the fire to warm himself. "Damn, it's been cold and windy and wet out there above the river." After a few moments he walked up to one of the sleeping forms, nudged him with his foot. "Come on, Harry, get your ass out of the blankets. You're always late."

The man who was tending the coffee said, "Anything goin' on down on the landing, Jacob?"

"Naw, same as always. Quiet as a damned churchyard."

Another form stirred and got up from his blankets. He looked at the sentry and said, "Now, what the Devil are you doing here, Brown. You're opposed to stay on post 'till relieved."

"Hell, Lieutenant, if I did that, I'd never get relieved. As usual, Harry's din't get up in time. He'll be on the post in a few minutes. It's not like anything is goin' to happen."

The lieutenant shrugged and asked the man by the fire, "Is that coffee ready, Hart?"

"Be a few minutes, Lieutenant. Just put it on." Then he pointed to a canvas sack. "And I'm fixin' to put some bacon on the fire."

The oncoming sentry, Harry, said, "Lieutenant, can't I wait till the coffee be ready?" He looked around. "Nothin stirring—just like all the time we been here."

"All right, but you damn well get on sentry post soon as you had a few sips. If anything's goin' to happen, it would likely be right after dawn."

Suddenly a voice, in precise English, but with a heavy foreign accent, boomed out of the darkness. "My dear sir, you are quite incorrect about that. In war, many things happen well before dawn, in the dark of night. As is the situation just now."

A figure appeared out of the darkness. His appearance was like nothing the militiamen had seen before. His coat was forest green and he wore white breeches. On his head was a black cocked hat. His face was high cheek-boned and narrow, with a thick mustache above his lip. But the most startling feature was a long thick scar that ran down his left cheek from the eye to the cheekbone. Also startling were the pistols he held in his hands.

The man shouted, "Come on in, my lads!" And immediately the militiamen realized they were surrounded by men dressed in green uniforms, all holding short-barreled rifles on them.

The militia lieutenant said, "Who the devil are you?"

The man touched one of the pistols to his hat in a rakish kind of salute. "Why, I am Captain Ernst Ludwig Wolff of the Hesse-Cassel Corps of Jaegers. And you, gentlemen, are obviously my prisoners. I suggest you all raise your hands and keep them where we can see them. We want no unpleasantness so early in the day."

Once all the militiamen were on their feet and gathered into a group with their hands in the air, Wolff turned to an officer and said, "Go tell that British colonel he can bring up his battalion of light foot now." He turned to another man. "Give the signal to the boats on the river that all's clear up here on the bluff."

The Jaeger found a stick of wood, lit it from the fire, walked to the edge of the bluff and waved it back and forth."

While that was going on, a steady stream of British soldiers began to come out of the now lessening gloom, hurrying past the picket station into the open area beyond. Some were in short red jackets and white breaches, others in Highland kilts. Officers and sergeants began calling their men into formation. Presently a British lieutenant colonel appeared and stood beside Wolff, who touched his hat to him. "Well, sir, everything's clear and we can begin the march on Fort Lee when you are quite ready."

The colonel smiled. "Indeed, my dear Ernst, we shall have the entire brigade up here on the plateau and ready to advance by dawn. I dare say we shall soon present the Yankee renegades with quite a surprise."

Wolff went over to the fire, picked up a cup, and filled it from the pot. "My dear Colonel, would you care a bit of coffee while we wait? I can assure you that it is quite freshly brewed."

"General, we are having a *damned* hard time getting a sufficient number of wagons." Hugh Mercer waved his hand in a sign of resignation. Nathaniel Greene bit his lip, then said, "Please clarify what problems you are having. Surely there are many vehicles in a settled part of the country like this?."

Besides the two generals, also present in the headquarters tent were the adjutant generals for each man's staff as well as one of Greene's aide de camps, who was taking notes. Mercer responded, "Nathaniel, there are plenty of wagons and carts in the area. But the populace is very hesitant about providing their services.

First, they can't be sure when they'll be paid. Second, they don't know where they'll be bound or how long they'll be needed. But most importantly, they're afraid of what's going to happen in the near future. They've seen the enemy consistently victorious and they expect the British to be in New Jersey soon. There is widespread fear of retribution if they are found to be connected with our cause." Mercer waved in the general direction of the supplies piled up outside the fort. "As it is, we've only been able to get about a quarter of the stores on the road south."

"Well," Greene responded, "Clearly we don't have much time left. Sooner or later Howe is going to cross the river."

Colonel Howard, Greene's adjutant general, seemed somewhat more optimistic. He said, "Luckily, Howe's been lethargic in following up after his successes. So we may have some time to correct the problem." He looked around the room. "But the fact is, these supplies are critical for sustenance of the army. If I may make a suggestion it is time for use of our requisition power to obtain the necessary transport."

Greene put his hand to his chin. "Howard, I fear you are right. These stores must be moved soon and I see no alternative."

At that moment, there was the noise of men shouting outside the tent. Then one of Greene's aides burst through the tent flap. With him was a disheveled soldier, gasping for breath.. Without pause the aide said in a panicked voice, "General, the British are here!" He turned to the soldier. "Tell them!"

The young soldier was both winded and tongue-tied at being in the presence of so many senior officers. After gasping for a few moments more he was able to speak, "Sirs, we was on picket just off the river road 'bout two miles north of here. Just finishin' breakfast. And suddenly, we see soldiers commin' at us. Skirmishers and light foot and behind them Redcoats and them Hessians." He took a deep breath. "Thousands of them! Don't know where they came from. It was quiet all night. But they're headin' this way fast." He took a deep breath. "We scattered, some of the men ran into the bush on the other side of the road. Me and a few others took off runnin' on the road fast as we could go. Some of the men dropped along the way, they was so exhausted." He looked around at the officers. "I tell you, the enemy are commin' fast, almost at the run. It's sure they'll be here any time now!"

Mercer looked at Greene. For the first time in his life he realized the truth of the old expression, "white as a sheet"—Greene was a perfect example, pale and frozen in shock.

Now the aide was speaking again. Looking at Greene he said, "General, I sent Captain Thompson on horseback to ride north on the road to get a feel for the actual size of the enemy force and their composition."

Greene literally shook himself to action. "Yes, yes, that's good." Then he turned back to the soldier. "Thank, you, private, For your information."

The aide took the young soldier outside. Then, before anyone could speak, there was the sound of a galloping horse arriving and the aide stuck his head back in the tent. "Sir, Thompson is back!"

Greene seemed to shake himself and then strode out of the tent, followed by all the others. Mercer saw the captain throw down from his horse and turn to all the officers gathered at the front of the tent. His face was ashen.

"Sir," exclaimed Thompson, "It's true! The British advance is less than a half mile from here. I got to the top of a small rise and could see it all. Jaegers and Light Foot in the advance, skirmish fashion. Coming almost at the run. And behind them at least two brigades of foot. British Redcoats and Highlanders and Hessian Grenadiers!" He cupped his hand. "Listen! Listen! You can hear them coming!"

Mercer stepped out some distance from the tent, and listened. *My God!* There it was, faint but clear: the sound of drums, fifes, bagpipes coming from the North. He looked around at the soldiers in their camp, many now standing still and listening also. Then he looked at the piles of stores and over at the fort with all its precious heavy guns. He felt a lump like a fist form in his stomach as he had the sudden realization: *There's no time, the British are going to get it all.*

Greene's aide, Howard, exclaimed, "General, we must hurry to form a line of defense! There's little time! Shall I give the order?"

Greene took a step toward the direction of the British advance, staring into the distance as if thinking hard. Mercer hurried over to his side and spoke softly, "Nathaniel, we have less than 2000 men here, and all of them, except for the artillerymen, are raw militia. They'll never stand against an attack of hardened Redcoats and Hessians. And if they didn't run, they'd be cut to pieces. The most we can do is save the men: We must spike the guns and retreat immediately—fall back to Hackensack where Washington's main force is. That's the only place there's a chance of stopping them."

"But, but ..." responded Greene. Then he sighed and stared to the North for a moment, teeth clinched. Finally he turned and called out to his aides, "Spread the word to all commanders: Retreat! Leave everything! Every man take his pack and firelock and personal accouterments and head down the road to Hackensack. We must join with Washington's force!"

Mercer immediately turned to his adjutant general. "Hurry, Sperry! We must get back to our tent and pack my papers and maps—if British officers see them they will know our precise plans. We will lose everything else, but our personal things can be replaced. Let's run!"

As they headed toward their headquarter tents, he could see the militia running for the road. There was no order to the retreat, just a mob of officers, men, camp women, and children with fear on their faces, moving as fast as they could. Many were outright running. In their wake were abandoned tents, pots hanging over fires, carts, and every other sort of camp fixture.

Mercer arrived at the headquarters tent to find his aides at work. All were gathering up what they could and one was leading the saddled horses up from the picket line. Mercer hurried into his tent, followed by Sperry. Together they began packing the critical papers into saddlebags and leather cases. When they had finished, they distributed the bags to the aides to carry on their horses. Soon all had left the tent and Mercer was alone. Then he went to a chest beside his bed and grabbed two things: a bag of coins and the packet of letters from his wife. Stuffing them into pockets, he ran out of the tent.

It was just in time. He looked to the north and saw a skirmish line of men in green coats just a couple of hundred yards away and coming fast. Suddenly there was the brassy sound of a hunting horn playing the foxhunting chase call. He thought, My God, *they're taunting us like the quarry in a morning of sport.*

Then an aide handed him the reins to his horse and said, "Sir, we must not tarry! General Greene rode out some time ago." Mercer mounted and the entire staff rode off at the trot, bound for the Hackensack road. They were the last to leave. Just ahead of them on the road Mercer saw the artillerymen who had spiked the guns, some riding on horses, the others running alongside.

Mercer and his aides rode at the trot along the road, passing much of the disorganized mass of men and camp followers hurrying to reach the succor of the army position at Hackensack. They had gone what he judged to be two miles when one of his aides called out, "General, there's a line of men across the road ahead. Right where that creek and trees are." He followed up by adding, "And they're in hunting shirts."

Rising in his stirrups to see better, Mercer stared at the tree line. It was true: Some kind of position had been established, stretching in a wide line that crossed the road and extended on each side for considerable distance. Then it dawned on him, and he said aloud, "Why, that's Eckert's company! What the devil are they doing here?"

As he spoke, he saw a horseman on a tall, black hunter emerge from the tree line and ride toward them. Almost immediately he realized it was Eckert himself. The captain rode some distance forward then pulled up the horse and sat waiting in the road. As they approached, Eckert touched his hat. "Sir, my men have taken positions in the bush on both sides of the ford. We can contest the enemy's advance, at least for a while, if you feel that's necessary."

Mercer waved at the company. "How do you happen to be here?"

"I had the company exercising skirmish tactics in the fields to the east of Hackensack. We encountered a courier from Greene who told us what happened at Fort Lee before he rode on to Washington's headquarters. I took it upon myself to hurry the company forward."

"Damned good decision, Eckert. How many men do you have?"

"General, I have my own company, with about ninety men present. O'beirne and his patrol are still gone, and there's also the Palmetto Light Horse, about twenty-two men. I've got them dismounted in reserve behind my line."

"You have only ninety men in line? It looks longer than that."

"Sir, we have nine of what I call fields squads, or sections if you will. Each of about ten men. There in what I call an interrupted line—there are gaps of about twenty or thirty yards separating the squads, which have established good positions in the cover of the bush. That makes the line far wider than a company would normally cover, almost the like a battalion, but the squads are close enough to support each other with rifle and musket fire. We worked this out for a situation like today, where, as light foot, we might be ordered to delay an enemy while our main force formed it's lines."

The general raised his eyebrows and nodded. "By God, I see your plan. Well-conceived, sir."

At that moment, the hunting horn sounded again, faint in the distance. Eckert's face wrinkled in puzzlement. "What's that, sir? It's not a cavalry trumpet; I've never heard quite that sound before."

Mercer smiled. "You have a powerful looking hunter, there, Eckert. But I take it you've never rode to the hounds?"

Wend laughed. "General, it's not likely any of the gentry of Frederick County would invite a gunsmith to a foxhunt."

Mercer realized his indiscretion and said, "Ah, yes, I quite understand. Well, what you are hearing is a brass horn used to rally the hunt riders and taunt the fox."

Eckert grinned. "And this morning we're the fox?"

"Precisely, Eckert." Then he turned and looked toward the rear. "There is something like a full division of the enemy behind us, both British and German. Jaegers and Light Foot are the advance guard. It's the Hessian Jaegers who are using that horn. You are to hold your position until you see no more of our people coming along the road. Then slowly fall back to the army's bivouac at Hackensack, where I'm confident Washington is preparing defense lines. If the enemy is coming so fast that our retreating men are endanger of being overtaken, do what you can to hold the enemy's advance force in check long enough for our people to get clear."

"I understand, sir." Then Eckert smiled and said in a wry tone, "It happens that I come from Jaeger stock myself—before my ancestors became gunsmiths. So if we engage the Hessians, it will be something of a family affair, General."

Still looking back toward the enemy, Mercer replied, "Yes, indeed it would. But I hope you'll not need to fight today. Avoid it, if possible. I don't want you taking serious casualties, because we're going to need your company for the withdrawal." He nodded to Wend. "Good luck to you."

And with that, he motioned to his staff and they rode off toward Hackensack.

Wend Eckert sat his horse in the road, looking toward where the enemy would appear. And as he sat there, he heard the brassy sound again, this time it was closer and the notes clearer.

The 4th Company of the Hesse-Cassel Field Jaeger Corps advanced along the Hackensack Road in open skirmish line. Their formation straddled the wagon track, with half the company of nearly 100 men walking in the open fields on either side. Ernst Wolff walked some twenty yards behind the line, with the trumpeter close beside him. They were the advance guard of the British force moving to pursue the rebels from the Fort Lee garrison.

Suddenly Lieutenant Johann Trautnetter, who was in the skirmish line and in charge of controlling its movement, held up his right arm in the air, signaling the halt. He turned and briskly walked back to join Wolff. "Captain, it appears there's a Yankee defense position in that line of trees ahead of us. I see shirtmen at various points in the bush on either side of the road. Most likely the colonist have rallied enough to form some sort of rearguard."

Without saying anything, Wolff reached into his coat and pulled out a brass telescope, opened it, and put it to his right eye. He inspected the tree line carefully, then took the glass from his eye and snapped it shut. "You are quite correct, Johann. They look like riflemen, several companies at least, maybe a full battalion. They are in the trees along a creek."

"Ja, Captain. Shall we advance and test their strength? We have been waiting for the opportunity engage some of their riflemen. Then men are quite eager for it. This is our opportunity!"

Wolff stared at the enemy position for a few seconds then sighed. "No one is more eager than I. But we don't want to start something we can't finish and at the moment we don't have any support available. The Yankees may have rallied and have a force behind this line. In any case, Cornwallis will need to know about it and make the decision if he wants us to advance further at this point." He looked at the lieutenant, "Johann, go back to the fort and find the General. Tell him what we have in front of us and ask him if he wants us to press matters. And if he does, I recommend he forward more light foot to support us."

"Ja, my Captain!" Trautnetter turned and started heading toward the fort.

Wolff called out to his company, "All right lads, settle down and rest. We'll be here for a while!"

To Wolff's surprise, they didn't have long to wait. In just a few minutes he saw a few mounted men approaching and was astonished to recognize Cornwallis himself on one of the animals. another horse carried one of his aide de camps with Trautnetter mounted behind him. Soon the party had arrived and the Jaeger lieutenant slipped to the ground. Cornwallis and the aide remained mounted. Wolff walked up to the general, saluted, and said, "My Lord, if I may be so bold, where did you get that horse? It seems it should be pulling a cart, not being the steed of a general officer."

Cornwallis threw his head back and laughed. "Wolff, you are an impertinent one, but you are damned right about the animal. The colonists left these behind. My horse and those of my staff are being ferried across the river later today." Then he waved toward the tree line ahead. "Tell me what you have here in front of you."

Wolff explained the situation in as much detail as he could, then said, "We can advance and press them skirmish style to test their strength if you desire, sir. But given their apparent numbers, I would request the presence of supporting troops as a precaution."

Cornwallis stared at the enemy line for a moment, then said, "No, Captain. We'll not press them at this moment. My force is still being ferried across the river, and those who formed the attack this morning need rest and reorganization. So we shall go into camp this evening and be ready to catch up with the rebels in the morning and drive them then." The general looked at the tree line again and a broad smile came over his face. "I have to admit, the enemy seems to have a strong position here. And in any case, each of your Jaegers is worth ten of the rebels and I should not like to lose any of them in a simple probing action." He looked down at Wolff and smiled. "And in my opinion, the rebels are likely to depart on their own accord any time now."

Wolff said, "Yes, My Lord. Dusk is coming on. Shall we go into bivouac here and keep watch on the enemy?"

Cornwallis replied, "Indeed, sir. And at first light tomorrow, once all our brigades, artillery, and transport have arrived, I will bring up the full division. For your information, Captain, General Howe has just sent me a dispatch giving me the order to pursue Washington and his ragtag relentlessly to their destruction." He turned and stared at the tree line for a long moment. "And right here at dawn tomorrow the chase shall begin."

With that, Cornwallis turned his horse around and started back toward Fort Lee.

Chapter Fourteen

The Bridge at Aquackanock

The gaggle of officers stood around a table in Washington's office at his headquarters—the house of Peter Zabriskie on Main Street in Hackensack. It was the morning after the loss of Fort Lee, and on the table was Mercer's map of New Jersey. Washington and the others listened as Mercer pointed out the route he recommended for the retreat to Pennsylvania.

Mercer slid his finger along a road that led in a southwesterly direction. "I recommend we take the King's Way all the way through Jersey to Trenton, a town on the Delaware. There is a ferry right at the town. There are other ferries in the vicinity, so that we can cross at several points. We also will gather as many boats as possible to speed the crossing into Pennsylvania."

Greene asked, "And what have we done to keep the British from following us across the Delaware?"

Mercer raised a finger. "Actually, General, quite a bit. We have sent patrols down to the river to map the locations of all boats we can find. As it happens, the latest patrol is still in the field. But we have also contacted Pennsylvania's governor, who has pledged to send row galleys of his state navy up the river to help ensure no boats remain on the Jersey side and to use their guns to break up a crossing if the British were to build boats or rafts or transport them from another place."

Greene nodded his agreement.

Then Mercer pointed to a town just a few miles away from where they stood. "This is Aquackanock and presents the first opportunity to slow the pursuit. The river is deep there and crossed by a bridge. If we withdraw to the other side and demolish the bridge, a small force could delay the British for a significant time."

Colonel Tresh, who had been looking at the map with the others, pointed to several roads in the north, which ran from Haverstraw on the Hudson through Morristown and Basking Ridge and then on to the Delaware. Then he looked at Mercer. "General, are these roads suitable for movement of a large force?"

"Indeed, Colonel. What are you getting at?"

Tresh scanned the room. "As a volunteer from Europe, I have been hesitant to make comments about the movement of the army, but I would now like to make a suggestion. Specifically, I believe it's time to recall Lee and his division. With the British on this side of the river, his original function of diversion has little value, and, given our decreasing strength here, it makes sense to consolidate our force sooner rather than later." He pointed to the map again. "Lee and his men could cross at Haverstraw and march to join us in Pennsylvania via the northern route. That would force Howe to split his attention between the two elements, and if needed, Lee could come south to reinforce us." He thought a second. "There is also the danger that the British could cut him off from us if he stays in New York."

Grayson, the adjutant general, nodded and said, "I agree. Our strength diminishes every day. We're losing two regiments today to expiration of enlistments, and there is a constant rate of desertions. We cannot muster 4,000 men here while, at last report, Lee had about 5,000. We'll need every man available when we reach Pennsylvania."

Washington stared into the distance for a minute, every eye on him. Then he said, "Yes, I agree—it is essential that we consolidate our forces. We must summon Lee." He motioned to Grayson. "Prepare a dispatch."

At that moment, a junior aide entered the room and whispered something to Grayson. Immediately the adjutant general turned to Washington. "Sir, Captain Eckert is here. He has information on the enemy's movements. Shall I have him come in?"

Washington responded, "By all means."

The aide departed, and momentarily Eckert entered.

Grayson said to the assembled officers, "Captain Eckert's company, with the South Carolina light horse troop attached, has been watching the British advance." He turned to Eckert. "Sir, what is your report?"

Wend took a deep breath, feeling the eyes of all the gathering on him. "We held our position behind a creek about three miles along the road from here until dawn. I lit camp fires to simulate a battalion-sized unit and kept them bright through the night. The British advance party consisted of a company of Jaegers on our front, but just before first light, we heard the noise of additional troops moving to their support. It sounded like several battalions. At that point, assuming they would assault our position early in the morning, I withdrew my company and got them on the road for here. I left Lieutenant Fairfield and half his troop to watch and report on the British movement. Then I rode ahead of my company with the other half-troop of cavalry to report the situation. It seemed clear to me that the British are heading here in force."

Washington replied, "Thank you, Captain Eckert." He turned to Grayson. "Based on the events of yesterday, we know the enemy force greatly outnumbers the men we have here. We must leave this vicinity posthaste and begin the withdrawal to Pennsylvania. Please issue the orders immediately to break camp and march for Aquackanock."

Grayson said, "I will, sir, but there's something else Mercer and I have been discussing, related to our withdrawal, that I need to bring to your attention."

Washington raised his eyebrows and said, "Please do so, sir."

"We have a very large number of sick men in camp, who are of no use if it comes to a fight. They will find it difficult to keep up with us. We also have a large number of women and children present. Both the wounded and the camp followers will slow us down at a time when haste may become necessary. They will also encumber us when we cross the Delaware. I believe we need to send them to a place of refuge at the earliest opportunity."

Washington sighed. "I fear you are correct. But where do we send them?"

Grayson replied, "I've been working that out with Mercer." He waved to the general. "Please describe your plan."

Mercer moved back over to the map. "There's a good road from Newark to Morristown, off to the northwest. It appears, for the present, that Morristown is not a British target. I propose that once we have some space between us and the pursuit, we can assemble a convoy with wagons to transport the sick, wounded, and camp followers. We would send surgeons with them. It's likely to be safe there, at least for the present, since the British will most likely follow us."

Grayson added, "Once we're across the river and into quarters, we could arrange for them to rejoin the army."

There was a murmur of agreement around the room. Washington walked over to the fireplace, looked at the flames for a moment, then turned and said, "Yes, it is sensible. Make the arrangements, Grayson. When they are assembled, provide them an escort of militia." Then he said to the officers: Gentlemen, return to your commands, strike camp, and prepare to march. We must start southward as soon as possible."

Wend started to leave with the others, but he heard Mercer call to him. "Captain Eckert, please remain."

He stood aside as the generals and colonels left, and only he, Mercer, Grayson, and Washington remained. Mercer said to Washington, "Sir, I suggest that the British will be in close pursuit as we make our way to Aquackanock. It may be a very near-run thing to beat them across the river. I propose that we send a small column ahead to prepare defense positions to be ready to hold off the enemy and destroy the bridge." He waved toward Wend. "I suggest that column be led by Mr. Eckert and his company and the half troop of light horse he has with him. He would be augmented by an artillery battery and a company of pioneers. They can be in position to destroy the bridge once the last of our troops pass over and, with their rifles and guns, dissuade the British advance from attempting any crossing."

Washington considered a moment, then asked Wend, "How soon will your company be here?"

"Within a few minutes," responded Wend. "I ordered them to move as fast as possible." He thought a second, then said, "And I sent my camp people ahead yesterday, along with most of our camp equipment. We can strike the remains of our bivouac and be on the way south very shortly after the company is here."

"Are you sure they won't need more rest than that?" queried Washington.

Mercer laughed. "George, they're *Valley* men."

In his turn, Washington laughed. "All right, Hugh, I understand." Then a serious look came over his face. "Captain Eckert, before you go, I have something to communicate to you. Prior to your arrival to the army, we had formed a small battalion of light troops for scouting and missions outside of normal operations. They were known as 'Knowlton's Rangers.' Regrettably, they were captured with the garrison of Fort Washington." He paused for effect. "Under the current situation, it falls to your company for those duties. You and your men come highly recommended by your governor, and Mercer tells me you have done good work in preparing for the retreat we must now undertake. As a fellow Virginian, I hope you will live up to the commission I am placing on your shoulders."

Wend looked Washington in the eye. "Both I and my men will do everything possible to meet your expectations, General."

Washington smiled at Wend. "Then, Captain Eckert, you have your orders. Godspeed, sir, and we shall see you at Aquackanock Bridge."

—~—

When Eckert arrived at the company bivouac, he found that Billy Wood and Melinda—who had not left with the other camp people—were busy loading equipment into the remaining wagon. As he talked with the Woods, the company marched into camp. Wend summoned Reese Newkirk and the three sergeants and briefed them on their mission. Soon there was a hubbub as everyone worked to pack up and stow the camp tents and cooking implements in the wagon, with Wood ready to drive.

As he stood watching, his thoughts were interrupted by a vaguely familiar voice. "Captain Eckert?"

Wend turned and saw two men standing there. One was a lithe, narrow-faced artillery captain. After a moment he realized it was the battery commander he had talked with on the day long ago when the British ships had bombarded Manhattan as they sailed north on the Hudson. The captain touched his hat with a finger and said, "Hamilton, of the New York Artillery. I've been ordered to accompany you to Aquackanock Bridge with my battery."

The other man said, "Captain Thomas Hurley, of the Pennsylvania Pioneer company. We've also been detailed to your command."

"Indeed, glad to see you both. We have a bit of work to do there and must hurry to march. When can you be ready to move?"

Hamilton said, "My men are limbering up right now. We'll be ready to leave when you are."

Hurley nodded. "We're ready to march now." He looked back in the general direction of the Hudson. "And the faster we leave, the happier I'll be for one."

Wend pointed to the Kings Way road, a few hundred yards to the east. "We'll meet you there as soon as you can manage." Then he thought of something and asked Hamilton, "How many guns do you have?"

Hamilton held up an open hand. "Five guns—six pounders."

"Well, sir," said Wend, "that ought to be sufficient for the work."

"Indeed, and I can assure you that my New Yorkers are eager for the task." And with that, the two officers turned and hurried back toward their own camps.

Very shortly the entire column was on the move: the company of foot, the artillery, the Pioneers, and the half-troop of cavalry. Wend pushed the pace, even though there was now a substantial rain, his men had spent most of the night awake, and had just finished a brisk march from their position on the Hackensack Road. Donegal kept moving along the column, "encouraging" the men as only a long-serving sergeant knew how. Wend reflected the Highlander wasn't making any friends.

Two hours after leaving the encampment, with everyone's boots heavy with mud, they came to the Passaic River and the wooden bridge spanning it. The width of the stream was perhaps 150 feet, and the bridge framing and roadway was supported by pilings of large logs wedged into the mud and stone of the river bottom. The wooden planking was wide enough to take a single wagon and, Wend judged, a column of four men abreast.

Eckert had sent Ensign Middleton and the cavalry troop ahead to scout out the lay of the land around the bridge. Now, as the column approached the bridge, Middleton rode across and joined Wend on the near side. "Sir, we can hold off the British for a long time if it comes to that." He pointed southward. "Just downstream the land around the river turns swampy. They'll ne'er cross there." He looked upstream. "And the river is quite deep in that direction. They won't get across without boats. So if we cover the bridge with artillery and firelock fire or destroy the bridge, we can hold them indefinitely."

Wend said, "Excellent, Mr. Middleton." Then he turned in his saddle and waved for the column to cross the bridge. Within a half hour, they had established their positions—Hamilton had emplaced his guns on either side of the bridge, ready to cover the approach with cannon fire. Wend had carefully positioned several squads where they could target any advancing troops.

This had no sooner been accomplished than the head of the retreating army, led by Greene and his staff, came into view. Soon they were crossing the bridge. Wend looked at the marching men and felt a sense of utter discouragement come over him. Wend and his men had not had much contact with the main army since late summer. Now what he saw was a ragtag group of men. Uniforms, where present, were ragged, often incomplete. Many men wore nothing but civilian clothes. Few had any kind of overcoat, and it seemed most soldiers were wrapped in blankets for warmth. In many regiments, there was little standardization of firelocks, with muskets, fowling pieces, and rifles often mixed in the same battalion. Among the marchers were walking wounded, and numerous carts and wagons carried sick and wounded men.

Suddenly, Wend was aware that Reese Newkirk had come up and stood beside him. "Good Lord, Wend, they're in sad shape. I wonder how long they can carry on—it's no wonder we're having massive desertions."

Wend sighed. "I fear you are right. There are many who think the end is near. You can't avoid hearing that."

There was a long silence as they watched the dreary procession, then Newkirk tapped Wend on the arm. "Look, here comes Mercer."

Wend looked along the bridge and saw the general and his staff crossing ahead of two wagons carrying wounded. Mercer, seeing them standing by the bridge, pulled up his horse and slid to the ground.

Without preamble, he pointed to the span and said, "Fairfield and his men are keeping a close watch on the enemy. The British are pushing hard with the 16th Light Dragoons and Jaegers in the lead." He pointed to the bridge. "Use the company of pioneers to tear the planking off the bridge. My preference is not to fully destroy it, or the local Jersey people will be madder at us than they already are. But it may happen that the enemy will be too close to allow for that. In that case, you must be ready to set the bridge afire. Start some fires and prepare torches in case that happens. Whatever occurs, the British must not be able to use the bridge."

Wend responded, "I understand, sir."

Mercer stood surveying the bridge for a long moment. "Once you have dealt with the bridge, you and Hamilton must march rapidly for Newark and then on to New Brunswick. That's the next place with a river crossing—a shallow ford. The enemy must be held there for a substantial time to give our column a chance to get as far ahead as possible, for it will take us a while to get boats together and cross the Delaware." He looked from Wend to Reese and back again. "I trust you understand the intent?"

"Yes, sir," replied Wend.

Mercer looked down the road southward. "I wonder where O'beirne is? His last patrol to map the location of boats along the Delaware started weeks ago. He should be back now. The information is vital to get the army across and even more essential to keeping the enemy from following us across. I wonder what could be holding him?"

Wend said, "No telling, sir. He may not be aware of the events at Fort Washington and Fort Lee. And no one is more dedicated to his duty than O'beirne. I'm sure he'll arrive in time with the information you need."

"I certainly hope so, Captain Eckert." Then Mercer went to his horse and mounted. Once in the saddle, he pointed to the bridge. "I reaffirm to you, sir, the British must not be able to use that bridge." Then he reined his horse around and was off down the road, his horse's hooves kicking up mud as it went.

In the growing dusk, with a bone-chilling wind blowing and drizzle falling, Wend warmed himself by a fire and watched as Hurley's Pioneer company, axes and pry bars in hand, worked to remove the planking of the Aquackanock Bridge. The army's rear guard had passed an hour ago, and Fairfield's half troop had been the last to cross. Now they had joined with the company and were resting their horses. The pioneers were furiously ripping off the planks and tossing them into the river. The company had started at the far end of the bridge and were working their way back to the near shore. They had just about reached mid-stream.

Donegal walked up and stood beside him, extending his hands to bake over the fire. After a few seconds he said nonchalantly, "Ah, now. You might want to take a look down the road and see who's comin' toward us."

Wend responded, "What, Mercer or some other general coming back to see what's happening?"

"Na, it's much more interesting than that. It's O'beirne and his patrol. And they got someone else with them you're not expectin' to see."

Wend turned and looked down the road and true enough, there was O'beirne, with Childers at his side. But then he saw another hunting-shirted figure mounted astride a long-legged, muscular, bay hunter. He puzzled for a moment and then recognition came: *My God! Joshua Baird!* He looked over at Donegal. "Now what the devil do you imagine he's doing here?"

"Na, my dear captain, that brain a' yours must be workin' slow today, probably because of all the worry about this bloody bridge. But there be only one reason that Peggy and Alice would have let him come up here—he's bringing that whiskey you wanted. The whiskey to buy Horner's wench away from Colleen."

Wend thought a second, then agreed. "You're right. It's the only logical reason."

Meanwhile, Shay arrived, pulled up his horse, and dismounted. He touched his cap to Wend and said, "And a lovely evening to you, my darling Captain. We're all back safe and sound from our little trip to the Delaware, and we brought you back an old friend."

"So I see, Shay. But you had better get back on that horse and find General Mercer. He's looking for the information on boats you were sent to find."

"Now, my dearest Captain, as luck would have it, we met the good general on the road makin' our way here. And I gave him a beautiful map artfully drawn up by Mr. Childers showin' all the boats for miles up and down the river." Edward had joined them. Shay grinned and put his hand on the ensign's shoulder. "I say the boy's parents can rest assured they didn't waste their money sendin' him to that William and Mary College, leastwise in the case of map drawing and writin' in a fair hand. And I am most happy to report that his honor the general was very impressed by the detail."

"Good, Shay." Wend gave him a questioning look. "But what took you so long? We were expecting you back earlier."

Shay laughed and looked over at Joshua. "Now you might want to ask Mr. Baird here, as he can give you the story in more detail than I can."

"Yes," said Wend, "what the devil is going on, Joshua? Most importantly, where is that whiskey Peggy said in her letter was on the way?"

Joshua raised a hand as if to fend him off. "Now, Wend, rein in your horses. The damned whiskey is here, but we did have a wee bit of trouble along the way."

"Joshua, trouble has always been your bloody companion. What kind of trouble did you get into this time?"

Joshua and Shay traded smiles, and then he said, "No mischief of my making.

It was a bit of thievery by some road agents." Then he went on to explain the loss and recovery of the horses.

On hearing the story, Wend raised his eyes to the heavens and then asked, "So where are the wagons and the whiskey now?"

It was O'beirne who answered. "Now, Captain, when we got back to New Brunswick, the word had just arrived about the army retreat. So we figured it would be safest to leave the wagons there, under the care of the teamsters."

Baird nodded. "That's right. We'll pick up all the whiskey when we pass through that town—all of it but a couple of kegs we gave to the militia and a certain tavern keeper for helpin' us catch them highwaymen."

Then O'beirne spoke up again. "And while ridin' back here we found that the caravan with our camp people and Mrs. Tresh are at the town of Newark, safe and sound. I told them to wait there until they got word to move on from you."

Wend said, "Good. Mercer and Washington's adjutant general are trying to decide what to do with the sick, wounded, and camp people."

O'beirne said, "But dear Captain, there's some other news you should hear. Some other things going on here in Jersey."

Wend shot the lieutenant a questioning look. "What kind of things?"

O'beirne reached underneath his hunting shirt and pulled out a piece of parchment. He handed it to Wend. Stepping close to the fire so he could make out the words, Wend could see it was a poster: A poster containing a proclamation over the name of General William Howe himself. He quickly read the words. Looking up at O'beirne, he said, "It's offering clemency for anyone who pledges loyalty to the crown, and some money to boot."

"That it is," responded Shay. "And the important fact is, many in Jersey are bloody well trippin' over themselves to accept it. After New York, there's a feelin' among the people that the cause is finished—that the war is lost. And it starts right at the top: the damned governor of the state has fled. The legislature has disbanded. And militia companies all over are goin' home, not willing to support the cause. Many people just shut themselves in their house and refuse to help the army in any way as it retreats."

Wend was digesting this news when Donegal interrupted his thoughts. "Wend, lift your eyes and look at the bridge! Those damned Pioneers are runnin' fast as their legs can carry them toward this bank of the river."

Wend looked at the men running along the bridge, then over at the far side. In the dim light he saw what he expected: The British advance guard—green coated Jaegers with a line of red uniforms behind. He took a deep breath and shouted to Donegal: "Get the torches lighted and men to run out onto the bridge to fire it! And get some riflemen to distract the light foot over there!"

Donegal didn't answer, he simply started yelling at sergeants and corporals to organize the firing of the span.

Meanwhile, Wend started walking briskly to the place where he knew Hamilton had his fire, calling out his name as he went.

But the artilleryman had already seen what was going on. He met Wend at the base of the bridge, an eager smile on his face. "I take it you want me to amuse that light foot on the other side while you torch the bridge?"

"Exactly right, Alex! Throw a few shots over there, fast as you can. It doesn't matter if you don't have firm targets. They'll move back soon as the balls start hitting the ground around them."

Hamilton, cool as ice, responded, "Well, I should expect so." Then he turned and started shouting orders to his battery.

Wend looked at the bridge and saw a string of his men running out on the planking, some carrying torches, others carrying bundles of kindling wood. Donegal had had the men gathering them from the surrounding bush during the long afternoon. In a few minutes, the first fires had been ignited in the middle of the bridge, and then Donegal and his men started working their way back to the near riverbank.

Wend looked over to where his officers were standing together with Baird. "Reese! Get the men not involved in firing the bridge ready to move. We'll be marching through the night for Newark to catch up with the army!" As he spoke, the first of Hamilton's guns spoke, the blast shattering the quiet of the evening. It was followed by the other four firing in rapid sequence, then reloading and firing again. He also saw that a squad of riflemen under Corporal Schreiber were nestled in a small clump of trees and underbrush, maintaining a hot fire in the general direction of the British. Casting a glance at the far side, he was unable to see any enemy soldiers. Clearly, the rifle and artillery fire was having the desired effect.

In a few minutes, Hamilton joined him. "Eckert, I don't see any British in sight.

Looks like they've pulled back. I'm going to stop firing. We don't have much reserve of powder."

"Indeed, Alex. And start limbering up your guns. We're getting out of here as soon as I'm certain the bridge fire is well started. You might as well get on the road now. We'll be right behind you."

Hamilton strode off, and O'beirne joined Wend. He waved toward the bridge. "Now, Captain, that's a glorious bit of arson you're creating there. Warms my Irish heart, it does. But it's sure and the local citizens are not going to be happy with you and the army if you worry about such things."

Wend leaned close to O'beirne. "Mercer was worried about that. That's why we started with just removing the planks, so it would be easy to rebuild. But he also told me that we must ensure the bridge couldn't be used by the British, and this is the only way I know how to accomplish that with their advance so close." He shrugged his shoulders resignedly. "In any case, with so many of the Jersey people ready to abandon the cause, it probably doesn't make any difference how mad they are at us."

A half hour later, with the bridge totally in flames and the Pioneer Company and Hamilton's artillery already on the road, the Frederick County Light Foot marched off toward Newark, leaving the British to figure out how they would cross the Passaic River.

"Mrs. Tresh, this is your last clean gown." Elise held up the clothing, a look of despair on her face. She waved her hand at the campsite around their two tents. It was a muddy field just south of Newark, with the tents and wagons of the Frederick County Light Foot all around them. The women and children had been in the camp for two days. The men of the company had arrived late the previous evening, having slogged down the muddy Kings Way from the Aquackanock Bridge. A chilling rain continued to fall, with the leaden sky giving little promise that it would end soon. The maid continued, "And all your shoes are coated with mud. I've tried to clean them, but to little avail." She sighed. "When shall we ever be able to dry out and clean things up and wash your clothing?"

Catherine was in a chair located under a tent fly. Before her there was a crackling fire, which unfortunately was doing little to abate the cold and nothing at all to protect her from the continuous wind. She had been living in the open and under canvas for nearly a month. She considered herself capable of enduring adverse conditions. After all, she had survived without shelter for days when escaping her first husband—that bastard Tim O'Mears. But that had been nothing like the frigid weather and frequent rain of the past weeks. She longed for the comfort of a cozy room and the well-prepared food of a proper inn.

Before Catherine could answer the maid, she spotted her husband and Wend Eckert arriving on horseback. She knew they had been visiting Washington's headquarters at the Eagle Tavern in Newark. Both men dismounted, tied their horses to a wagon, and walked toward where she sat. She called out to the colonel, "Well, Alex, what news from headquarters?"

The two men looked at each other, and it was actually Eckert who spoke up. "Mrs. Tresh, my company will be leaving here at first light tomorrow for New Brunswick. We've remained here today simply because the men and horses are exhausted after days marching through this mud."

"However," said Tresh, "you, my dear, will be headed in a different direction."

Puzzlement spread over Catherine's face. "Different direction? I don't understand."

The colonel answered, "General Mercer is assembling a caravan of vehicles going to Morristown. It's a journey of about twenty miles to the northwest. In the caravan will be men from the hospitals and women and children of the camp." He paused and smiled. "And I have arranged for you, the most beautiful of camp followers—along with Elise—to travel with the caravan. In Morristown you will be able to find some comfortable shelter. I'm told it is a very pleasant town with several inns and taverns. And once the army is safely across the Delaware River and into Winter Quarters, I shall send for you." Having said that, Tresh braced himself for Catherine to vociferously argue against the move, as she had on previous occasions.

Catherine rose and stood close to the fire, gazing into the flames, her arms crossed in front of her. The silence hung over all of them. Then she looked over at her husband and sighed deeply. Then her words surprised him. "All right, if you insist. But my dear Alex, I shall miss you the entire time we are separated." She looked around the campsite. "It will give me some time to recover from the last few weeks and clean and restore my things. But I will rejoin you at the earliest opportunity."

Surprised at her easy acquiescence, Tresh smiled at his wife. "My dear, I think you have made the wise decision. The next few days and weeks are going to be hard—and, frankly, dangerous for the army. Not like anything we have seen to date."

Wend gave a tight smile and said, "I must agree with the colonel. I'm going to counsel the women in my company to take the same action. In fact, I'm going to speak to them now, if you will excuse me." Then he waved in the direction of the Treshes' cart. "I'll have men detailed to help you get your rig loaded for the trip." He touched his hat to her and strode off.

Walking toward the rows of tents that formed the bivouac, Eckert soon encountered Donegal, who said, "Na', Wend, I got all the women together in one place. An' Lord, that wasn't easy. Word's got around 'bout the caravan to Morristown and they ain't likin' the idea, that I can tell you." Donegal led him to where all the camp women were gathered around a large fire. They were standing around, some in coats, others with blankets over their shoulders, all with some form of bonnet or cap on their heads.

Wend glanced around at the faces of the ladies and realized he had never seen a surlier collection of countenances. He took a deep breath and said, "I think you ladies know what I'm here to talk about." There were a few nods. He cleared his throat and continued, "The army is putting together a train of wagons and carts to take the sick and wounded soldiers up to a place named Morristown, which is out of danger, as much as is possible in these times. General Mercer, who is organizing it, would like as many women and children as feasible to go with it. The truth is, the upcoming days are liable to be exceptionally dangerous. You well know the British are on our heels. We'll have to move fast and may have to fight them often, perhaps every day, to get safely to the Delaware River. It's my obligation to keep you as safe as possible. So I recommend you and the children go with the caravan."

There was dead silence, and if anything, the women's faces became even more dour. Several crossed their arms in front of themselves.

Sergeant Flanagan's wife, Martha, a burly lady, and veteran of army life who everyone thought of as the 'sergeant of the women', put her hands on her hips and scowled. "I was with Henry everywhere we went with the old Virginia Regiment, and then the march along Forbes Road in '58 to take Fort Duquesne. We was guardin' the frontier in the Valley for the next five years. And then, two years ago, we was on that march into the Ohio Country under that damned Lord Dunmore with them Shawnee savages hangin' about. I ain't leavin' now just 'cause some Redcoat trash is followin' us. No, sir, Captain, neither me nor my kids is goin' to that town unless you flat out push me at the point of a bayonet."

Wend couldn't hold back a laugh. "No, Mrs. Flanagan, I have no intention of that." The other women nodded in adamant agreement. Then Annie Howell spoke up. "I fought my Ma and Pa to come along with Ben. Sure and I ain't leavin' him now."

More nods from the other women. Wend looked over at Patricia Carver, whose baby bump was very obvious. "Now, Patricia, you might want to consider it. You could have your child any day now. There will be army surgeons with the Morristown column, and they'll be setting up hospitals when they get there. That would be the safest place for you to give birth. You have to think of the child's welfare."

Patricia put her hands onto her projecting belly. "I married Jed just afore we left Frederick County, wantin' to be with him when I had his baby." She clenched her jaw in determination. "I ain't leavin' him now that it's almost time." She looked over at Martha. "Mrs. Flanagan's a midwife. I'd wager she's handled more births than any army surgeon who knows more 'bout getting' musket balls out of men or takin' off a leg than gettin' babies out." She shook her head vigorously. "No, Captain, I'm stayin' to be with Jed when it happens."

We looked around. "So you all want to stay?"

Every head nodded yes. Wend threw up his hands. "Well, ladies, I gave you the chance. Now you'll have to live with it, no matter what happens."

Martha Flannagan gave him a fierce, determined look. "You won't hear no complaints from us."

"Well, then, ladies, the whole company will march at dawn tomorrow. Make your preparations." With that, he and Donegal walked off to get the company ready.

—∞—

It was well after dark. Around Wend's tent the squad fires of the company flickered, accompanied by the background noise of a body of soldiers in camp and the voices, laughs, and shouts of women and children. Wend sat before his fire, Simon Donegal and Joshua Baird with him as the three, friends since the French War and the days of Pontiac's attacks on the Pennsylvania back country, discussed an important matter that confronted them. It was the first time they had had time for a serious talk since the action at Aquackanock Bridge.

At the moment, Baird was experiencing something of a shock. "You mean this whiskey ain't to make us some money? You're going to give it all to that Irish red-haired witch McGraw so Horner can marry his little blond wench?"

Wend responded vociferously. "No, dammit, Joshua, I have absolutely no intention of giving it *all* to Colleen. I just told her she'd get a wagon load. I didn't say *what* size. We'll put some of the whiskey in one of the company's small wagons. That will damn sure satisfy her. She's desperate for any kind of hard spirits to sell to soldiers." He looked at his two companions. "The rest of it will go to the army quartermasters—they'll pay us a good price. I've heard that they're just as desperate as Colleen for something to give the troops for their daily ration. They know that if the army can't provide a ration of whiskey or rum, we'll see desertions explode even beyond what's happening now."

Joshua took a long pull on his pipe then asked, "So just *where* is Horner? And where is Colleen and her company of scoundrels now? Where do we deliver the spirits? Jake and Elijah can't hang around for long. They got to get back to Virginia, 'cause Abbey Morgan needs them and the wagons for other work."

Donegal started laughing heartily at the question.

Joshua looked at him in perturbation, then back at Wend. "What's so damned funny? And I say again, where the devil is Colleen?"

Wend shook his head and laughed again. "That's the problem: I don't have the *slightest* idea. The last I saw her or her people was when they were crossing the Hudson from New York into Jersey at a place called Peekskill, when the British were pursuing us after White Plains. I believe she's gone to ground somewhere safe until things get sorted out with the army. She won't take any chance with her company. It represents her fortune."

Baird looked up at the night sky as if beseeching the heavens. "So what happens to all the stuff we got in those two Conestogas?"

Donegal spoke up. "When we get to Brunswick, we distribute the new shirts and coats and shoes that the ladies of Frederick County were so good as to send for the men. They need them right now."

"Yea, that's all well and good," said Baird. "But what about the damned whiskey? We got to get that out of Abby's wagons."

Wend thought a second. "We'll distribute what we can into the wagons we already have, and we'll try to pick up other wagons along the way. The army is discarding wagons, cannon, and carts every day. And you said you got some extra horses from those thieves?"

"That's right. But they ain't trained teams."

"We'll just have to make them do. And in any case, you had to give some of the whiskey to the men in New Brunswick who helped you, isn't that correct?"

"Yes, that's the damn shame."

Wend sat back in his chair and took a sip of his whiskey. "Well, one way or another, we'll find a way to transport the spirits. We'll work it out at Brunswick, and when the army is settled in Pennsylvania, I'll go talk to the quartermasters about selling it."

—m—

Shay O'beirne, had just made evening rounds of the company. He walked through the camp on his way back to the tent he and Ensign Childers shared. After yesterday's hard march and slogging around in the mud all day, his mind was focused on a stiff drink and then warm blankets. But his path led past the Treshes' tent, and he saw Catherine sitting close by the fire, arms crossed, hugging herself against the frigid night air. He reflected that even with her willowy figure bundled up in a coat and blanket, she still looked as beautiful as any woman he had ever known.

She looked up from the fire, and seeing him, called out, "Good evening, on a damned frigid night, Shay."

O'beirne stopped at the tent and put his right hand on one of the poles holding up the fly. "Indeed it is, Catherine. But lass, cold as it is, at least for tonight we aren't worried about the British."

"Indeed, Shay, there is that."

O'beirne looked around, then inquired, "Where is the good Colonel? Is he not spending the night with you?"

"He's at headquarters for one of those late night councils Washington likes to hold. He'll be back eventually, but how late I have no idea."

Shay said, "Well, I hear you are leaving us for a spell tomorrow. Off to Morristown. It happens that I was there on one of my patrols and I can report it's a *charming* village. *Small and quite rural,* but charming. And a place the British are not likely to visit anytime in the near future. I have it from Captain Eckert that once General Lee's division finally crosses the Hudson, he will probably march through there on his way to Pennsylvania." He smiled. "So it's likely to be quite safe for you until you return to the army, once we are in quarters for the Winter."

Catherine didn't reply immediately, instead she stared at him for a long minute. "Shay, we both know this isn't '*until we meet again*', this is probably *farewell*." She swept her arm in a circle, essentially taking in the world around them. "You've seen the condition of this so-called army. Men in rags. Men marching with the hides of animals wrapped around their feet instead of shoes. Men nearly starving because we lost most of our provisions at Fort Lee. Wagons, carts, artillery pieces being left behind in the mud. More men deserting every day. Alex tells me that when we left Hackensack Washington had about 5000 men. Now we're lucky if there are 3000, and that includes hundreds of wounded and sick." She scowled. "Shay, you're a professional soldier. You've fought in many conflicts. You must know this army is falling apart. The end will be weeks at the most, maybe just days. Washington must surrender or perhaps his army will simply disintegrate before him and he and his generals will be fugitives from Howe's men. Either way, the end is near."

Now it was O'beirne's turn to spend some time in contemplation. Finally, he replied. "My dear *Aiethne,* if you will *remember.* I *have* been soldiering for a long time. . ."

Catherine interrupted, "I *told you* not to call me Aiethne! She doesn't exist anymore. If you persist in doing that, it might pop out at the wrong time!"

Shay raised an eyebrow and shot her a crooked grin. "Yes, my dear. But calm yourself: It shouldn't matter if, as you say, we are unlikely to see each other again." Then he raised a finger. "But back to our conversation. It is because of my experience that I'm not so convinced as you that this army is in its 'last days.' Now, it is true we have lost a lot of soldiers to desertion, but those that remain I would say are the hardiest of the lot." He waved at the company's campsite. "Such as these men from the Shenandoah."

Catherine threw back her head and laughed. "These men? Do I need to remind you that they haven't yet been used seriously in this army? They've almost always been in the rear areas directly under Washington and haven't been in the line for any of the battles." She leaned forward and glared at him. "You know what I heard from a senior officer? The other soldiers are calling them 'Washington's Virginia Pets!"

O'beirne stiffened at the insult. "We've had our share of hard fighting—against Dunmore in Virginia." He paused to regain his train of thought. "And once Lee rejoins us—which should happen soon—Washington shall have a respectable force. I predict the General will turn and fight. Or at the very least be able to hold the core of his army together through the winter and emerge to campaign in the spring."

Catherine sat back in her chair and reflected a moment, then said, "Shay, you *dream. Dream,* do you hear me? Even my husband, who has maintained his optimism, is starting to recognize the truth. We know it's time to make plans to escape when the inevitable happens. We'll find a way to settle in a quiet place here in the colonies. The trick is to be away from the army before any surrender occurs."

After reflecting a moment, Shay said, "Catherine, you know we Irish are fey. And my instinct tells me this army isn't finished. That Washington is a stubborn man. So I'll stick to the end."

"Yes, do that! But don't say I didn't warn you when the British put a noose around your neck as a traitor!"

"A noose, my dear? Frankly, I'm more worried about the pistol of an angry husband than a British gallows." He shrugged. "In fact, like you, I plan to stay here in the colonies whatever the outcome of this rebellion. It happens I've taken rather a liking to the wenches of the land and find them quite welcoming. And you above all well know how agile on my feet I am in tight circumstances."

Catherine exploded in hearty laughter. "You're right! I've heard of some of your escapes!" She stood up, walked over to him, and put her arms around his shoulders and said, "One kiss for memory's sake!" Then she gave him a kiss directly on the lips, which he returned with fervor.

After a moment she stepped back and said, "Now get some rest, for we both face a long day tomorrow."

—ɱ—

The rain had let up by the next morning, but heavy clouds were hanging over the sky, threatening a resumption of precipitation. A cold wind continued to blow. The entire camp was up before there was any light in the sky—first to have a quick breakfast, then beginning the process of striking camp.

Alexander Tresh had returned shortly before midnight to spend the night with Catherine. Now, by the light of the morning cook fires, he supervised as Harold Moulders and Elise, assisted by two of the Frederick County men, loaded the cart.

Just after dawn the officers of the company stood together watching as the Morristown-bound caravan passed by. Wend thought it was a depressing procession, with wounded men in wagons and carts, other men, and the camp women walking. Newkirk shook his head. "They say it's only twenty miles northward to Morristown, but they're going to make slow progress of it in this muck."

Wend looked at his first lieutenant. "Reese, we're going to be slogging through the same mud all the way to the Raritan."

As they watched, the rear of the column passed by and the Tresh's cart fell in behind the last wagon, Elise handling the reins with Catherine sitting beside her on the seat. Catherine's spirited horse, prancing even in these early hours, was tied by a lead line to the rear of the cart.

Tresh waved goodbye, then he and Moulders mounted their horses and headed back to army headquarters.

O'beirne, his eyes on the departing Tresh cart with the two women onboard, looked over at Wend and said, "Last night I had a conversation with Mrs. Tresh. It was very illuminating. She said that many in the army are calling us 'Washington's Pets,' on account of that we're from Virginia and spent all our time right under Washington or Mercer and haven't been sent into the heavy fighting."

Wend thought a moment. "Well, it's not by any desire of ours. I went to Grayson and argued that we should be sent to join the forces on Long Island, way back in August. And instead he sent us to Fort Lee. You know what we've been doing since then. But I'd say that's meant more to the army than simply being a light infantry company in some battalion, particularly by setting the stage for what we're doing now. We have nothing to be ashamed of."

Edward Childers piped up. "I don't understand how anyone can say that about us. Look what we did to beat Lord Dunmore."

"Lad," responded O'beirne, "these people from New York, and Pennsylvania, and New England don't have a clue about what we did in Virginia. They haven't even heard of Dunmore."

Wend said, "Gentlemen, let's pay attention to the duties before us and if we take care to do those well, our reputation will take care of itself."

With the caravan now in the distance, Donegal, who had been standing nearby, shouted out to the men of the company, "All right you bastards! Form on the road by half companies!" With the urging of the other two sergeants, Flannagan and Wilder, the men were soon in column. The loaded company wagons were driven onto the road, with the women and children gathering behind. The only woman allowed to ride was Patricia Carver, a concession granted in light of her advanced pregnancy. She sat in the officer's wagon driven by Melinda Wood.

Wend watched and saw that the half-troop of light horse and Hamilton's artillery had also taken the roadway. Then he waved to his officers, and each went to the head of their half company. Dawn had arrived, indicated only by a gray light that barely illuminated the surrounding landscape. Wend swung up onto Sonny and, looking around from the height of the saddle, was able to see the shapes of buildings and church spires in Newark. A few lights from the town were visible.

Then, spurring the young hunter to the head of the column, Wend called out the order to march. And so they began the cold, muddy, laborious trek to the town of New Brunswick.

Chapter Fifteen

Duel at the Raritan

Wend stood together with Hamilton and Newkirk on the New Brunswick side of the Raritan River ford. It was the end of a twenty-mile march from Newark that had taken two difficult days, their progress slowed by the resurgence of rain and the deepening mud on the road. They had passed Elizabeth Town and the village of Spanktown. Now, with evening coming on, the three were shivering in the evening cold and listening to Shay O'beirne explaining what he knew about the area and the features that they would have to consider in keeping the British at bay.

The Irishman was pointing to the ford, where elements of Hamilton's artillery were still crossing. "Fortunately," he explained, "the fordable area is quite narrow, which will make it easier to defend." He pointed to high land to the north of the ford. "Those bluffs will be a good place for some of your guns, Hamilton. They will achieve longer range and then be able to fire down upon the enemy when they get closer." He turned around and faced south. "And there's another high spot over there, where others might be placed."

Hamilton said ebulliently, "Oh, indeed! I *quite* agree. We shall emplace three guns to the north and two down to the south. It will give us the ability to put the British advance in a cross-fire. We can amuse them here for quite a while."

Wend found himself amused by the enthusiastic tone in the young artilleryman's voice. The captain was only a year or two older than Edward Childers. But then a thought came to him. "Alex, how's your supply of shot and powder?"

Hamilton's face took on a more serious look. "Not that good. I'll need more if we are to put up a serious fight."

Wend said, "I'll use one of the light horsemen as a courier to Mercer with a message to get you more ammunition—if he can round it up from within the army. Unfortunately, we lost a lot at Fort Lee."

O'beirne resumed his briefing. He motioned toward a line of houses that sat close to the riverbank on either side of the road. "We could put some riflemen up there, to add their fire to that of Hamilton's guns and help discourage the British infantry if they try to rush the ford."

With irony in his voice, Wend replied, "The good people of those houses won't be particularly joyful about the prospect. They're likely to fear British reprisals after we've withdrawn from the town, not to mention the likelihood of damage during the fight. The houses could become the target for artillery."

Shay laughed. "Indeed they may. But I'm quite friendly with the local militia captain, a chap named Harwood, and I think he can apply some *cordial* persuasion to any reluctant residents."

Wend looked along the riverbank. "Tomorrow I'll put the men to digging trenches just back from the river where they'll have some protection while firing. We must be ready to hold out for some time if it becomes necessary to allow the army to withdraw safely."

O'beirne said, "There's one more thing we have to deal with. There is a farmers' wagon track parallel to this road, a couple miles south. It crosses the river on a narrow, rickety bridge 'cause the water there is too deep to ford. It won't take artillery but it will take men, horses, and light wagons. The British cavalry will surely find it and enable them to mount a flanking movement to drive us out of our positions here. It's got to be made unusable. Fastest way would be to burn it."

Wend, mindful of Mercer's reluctance to destroy the Aquackanock Bridge, thought about it for a moment. "It might be better to simply tear off the planking, but we don't have the tools." Then he had an idea. "We can send to Mercer to ensure that a Pioneer company is with the first elements of the army. I'll add that to the courier's dispatch."

"Aye," replied O'beirne, "But in the meantime, I'll go to Harwood and see if he can come up with pry bars, just in case the Pioneer don't get here in time. We could send Childers down there with a work party. He knows where the bridge is."

Wend nodded and added, "And shovels for digging the trenches. We have a few, but more would be helpful."

O'beirne replied, "I'll get on it tonight, with your permission."

"Of course," replied Wend. Then he turned to Newkirk. "Let's get the company bedded down. They've had two days of hard marching and tomorrow they'll have to get going on the trenches."

Newkirk said, "They're not going to like all the digging."

"Yes, Reese, but when the British begin their assault they'll love the trenches."

O'beirne dismounted in front of Harwood's stable just before the fading of last light. He found the militia officer graining the horses in their stalls.

Harwood looked over, saw Shay, and called out, "So you are back in Brunswick! With the army in retreat, I guess you are just passing through."

"That's a good guess, but the fact is, we're going to attempt to hold up the British at the river."

"But that will be only temporary. Everyone knows Washington is headed for Pennsylvania. One way or another, we're going to have the Redcoats and Hessians all over New Jersey."

Shay sighed. "I can't deny that."

"So, let me guess: You're here because you want something."

"Very astute, lad. I'm looking for shovels and pry bars."

"I understand the shovels. You are obviously planning to dig trenches for a stand at the ford. But what the devil do you want the pry bars for?"

"We want to rip the planking off the bridge down on the southern farm road. The British might try to use it to get across the river with light foot and horse to flank us and drive us away from the main ford." He waved a hand toward Harwood. "I was hoping you could get the men of your company to gather some for us."

"Tearing up that bridge isn't going to earn you any friends around here."

"Most of what we're doing isn't going to earn us any friends. But we're talking survival of the army, Harwood. If we don't get tools to remove the planks, we'll have to burn the damn bridge. It will be a lot harder to rebuild the whole thing than replace the planks."

"Shay, the people around here are just thinking about survival. They're terrified about what's going to happen when the British and Germans get here, as they inevitably will. And by the way, I don't *have* a company anymore. Most of them tell me they'll refuse to turn out if called. They are already worried about being reported to the British by loyalists when the crown forces arrive."

O'beirne sighed. "So you can't assist us?"

"I didn't say *that*. I'll do what I can, but I won't get much help—maybe two or three of the lads who aren't afraid of their shadows. Come back tomorrow morning, and I may have something for you."

Shay put his hand on the militia captain's shoulder. "Lad, I'll be grateful for whatever you can do."

With that, O'beirne mounted his horse and rode up the alleyway that led to the main street and then headed for the Jolly Times. A few minutes later, he walked into the crowded and smoky common room. Several of the men looked up at him, including a couple who had ridden with them on the horse chase. They immediately looked back down at their tables, avoiding his eyes. Shay looked around for Joy but, although several maids were working, didn't see the girl. The proprietor, Watkins, was at the bar, so he went up to the counter.

"Hello, George. I distinctly feel a chill in the air at the sight of an army officer."

Watkins stared for a moment, then said, "Ain't no secret the army's taken a lickin' and is in retreat, fast as they can. There's lots of worry about what the British will do when they get here."

"Aye, so I gather," responded Shay.

"When will that happen? When do you think they will arrive?"

"Not for a few days. Our army will start passing through tomorrow, and the plan is to hold off Howe's force at the river—a rearguard action to give our army some time to get well ahead of them."

Watkins' eyes opened wide. "Good God! Fighting here? There'll be destruction to the town."

"Almost certainly, George. But it's war."

Watkins, agitation showing on his countenance, gestured toward the men in the common room. "For God's sake, O'beirne, everyone's sayin' the war is over. It's just a matter of time until Washington surrenders or his army just scatters. Just days until Washington is wearin' Howe's shackles. Why the hell do you have to fight here?"

"George, calm yourself down. You know what I've been doin' the last few weeks, at least in a general way. So you know Washington's going to attempt to get the army over to Pennsylvania and collect all the boats so the British can't follow, then rebuild the army." He smiled. "There's a few tricks left in the old man yet."

Watkins scowled. "So you say." He pointed to the men in the room. "You'll never get any of them to believe it. And even if the army is safe across the Delaware, it won't do us any good here in Jersey."

"Well, George, we'll just have to see how things work out." He looked around. "In the meantime, I have some business with Joy. Where is she?"

Watkins took a deep breath and spoke more calmly. "Yes, yes, I know you're a bit taken with her. You've certainly kept enough time with the lass. Right now she's out back gettin' wood for the cook fire. That's where you'll find her."

O'beirne hurried to the back door and walked out into the yard. He immediately saw Joy by the stack of wood, loading a hand cart. It was near dark, but even so he marveled at her beauty—her golden hair and willowy figure—which had kept him interested beyond the simple effect of her agility under the covers.

"Hello, Joy," he said in a quiet tone. The girl froze in position, then slowly turned. He was gratified to see her face light up in a genuine smile. She dropped the wood she had in her hands and quickly strode toward him. The girl stopped in front of him momentarily, then reached up and wrapped her arms around his neck and gave him a long embrace.

"Oh, I knew you'd come back. I've been worried since you rode off the last time. I thought perhaps there would be a battle and I'd never see you again."

Shay ran his hand through her hair and said, "Now, lass, there will be a fight—right here at Brunswick. But not for a couple of days, so we'll make some time for ourselves before it starts."

She looked up into his eyes. "When?"

"Tonight—later. I have to go back to my company and get the men settled for the night, but I'm sure my captain will let me come back. Keep a room saved for us. Can you do that?"

"Of course. My very own—it's small, but it will serve."

"Then I'll be back just when you are getting finished."

She went back to the cart and picked it up by the handles. "I'll be waiting." Then she headed for the door to the cook room.

—∞—

Leaving Newkirk to get the company bedded down, Eckert, Donegal, and Baird had ridden southward through the town to where the teamsters were encamped with the Conestogas. They were accompanied by Billy Wood, driving one of the company wagons. When they arrived, Wend swung down from his horse and greeted the two waggoners.

Jake Cather ignored the friendly greeting and was as cranky as usual, not bandying any words. "Look, Eckert, damn it to Hell, we been sittin' here for days. We got to get these wagons unloaded and head back to Battletown. Abby's sure enough got a need for these wagons for other loads by now. She only let them go on account it was for you and the company."

Wend walked over and looked into one of the wagons and saw whiskey casks crowded onto the bed, with coats, hunting shirts, and blankets packed on top. He turned to the wagoner. "Is the other wagon loaded the same?"

Jake replied, "Damn right, Eckert."

"All right, Jake. Let's all work together to get the clothing and blankets loaded in Billy's wagon to go up to the company tonight. The men need that stuff right now. Every day seems to be colder and wetter than the one before."

"Yeah, that's fine. But what about the whiskey?"

"We're rounding up some other small wagons to carry it. We'll have them soon."

"Damn it, Wend, maybe I ought to just unload it right here into this damn mud. We need to get back to Virginia. It was a long trip, and then we had them thieves stole the horses, and it ate up the better part of a week to get them back. And Abbey is tight for money. She needs paying contracts."

"Yes, Jake, I understand. But I'll remind you that if you hadn't gotten help from O'beirne and the local militia, you'd never have gotten the animals back. You'd be stuck here and trying to figure out how to get back to Frederick County. And where would you get two Conestoga teams around here?"

The two waggoners just stared at Wend, unable to answer.

"And," Wend continued, "if you *could* find teams, how in the Hell would you pay for them? Think on that and *cool* your damned fire."

There was total silence. Wend ended it by saying, "Now let's get to work and get Billy's wagon loaded. The men need these coats."

—ʍ—

Clive Harfeld, aka *Harkness*, sat at the desk within the study of his Morristown house, a glass of brandy at hand. Mrs. Hubble, the housekeeper, had a cheery fire crackling in the hearth. Outside, darkness was gathering at the end of another wet, chilling day. The spymaster was going over some reports from operatives regarding the movements of Washington's army when the sturdy woman tapped on the door and looked in. "Sir, there's a man here to see you. A Mr. Northcutt."

Harfeld was a bit shocked. "Northcutt, you say?"

"Indeed, sir. That's the name he gave."

"Well, show him in! Immediately!"

In a few moments, the door opened again, and the housekeeper did indeed usher in none other than Barrett Penfold Northcutt. He was attired in a civilian overcoat and hat, both of which were soaked.

Harfeld said, "For God's sake, get out of those wet things and have something to warm your innards."

"I was hoping that was precisely what you would say." Northcutt handed his hat to Mrs. Hubble and then shed his overcoat, which she also took. Clive saw that the colonel was in a brown suit. Mrs. Hubble took the outer wear and then left, shutting the door behind her.

"My God, Barrett, riding about in enemy territory. What's toward?"

"I'm here to get a firsthand feel for the state of things here on the ground on behalf of Lord Cornwallis, who is leading the pursuit of the rebels. I wanted to get your impression of what's going on with the Rebel army. I trust you've got watchers out?"

"Naturally, Barrett." Harfeld tapped the papers on his desk. "I have fresh reports right here." He walked over and poured his friend some brandy. "Wish I could offer you rum or whiskey, but I've flat run out."

"I quite understand, old man." Northcutt took a deep sip of the libation. "Ah, that does satisfy on a cold night like this."

"Well, since you ask, I can sum up the condition of the rebels in a sentence: In full retreat, shedding men and equipment as they go." He smiled. "Desertion is endemic, and Washington's got less than 3000 men with him."

Northcutt laughed. "That's actually two sentences. But you made yourself clear. In fact, I've seen some of that myself on the ride up here. I should tell you, Cornwallis and Howe are quite confident that the rebels are finished. They've eased up a little on the pace of pursuit, thinking Washington's column may simply disintegrate and things can quickly be wrapped up."

Harfeld walked over to the sideboard, poured himself more brandy, then turned to Northcutt. "Barrett, do you really believe it's going to be that simple?"

Northcutt considered that for a moment, then said, "No, Clive. We both live here—we understand Americans. And I personally know Washington from my Virginia days. Met him several times in Williamsburg. I've had conversations with him." He paused and looked directly into Harfeld's eyes. "I believe Washington has too much riding on this insurrection, too much invested, and understands the likely consequences for himself to meekly surrender. And he's a forceful person who can inspire men. I believe he'll get at least one more battle out of that ragged army of his. And there's this—Charles Lee has several thousand men who have just crossed the Hudson. If Washington can unite with him, they'll have a useful force."

"Barrett, I have the same feeling as you. This is most definitely not over yet."

"Yes, to some degree Cornwallis and Howe are engaging in wishful thinking. But the whole bloody staff is doing the same thing—there's an air of jubilation in all quarters. That's one reason I've taken to the road to see things for myself. I want to take back evidence of what the Americans are still capable of doing and what they plan if we can get some hard information."

"Yes, I dare say: Inject a little reality to our British brethren." Then he thought of something. "We're about to have visitors here in Morristown. I've got a report that the army is sending wounded, sick, and camp followers here for refuge. The army is shedding impedimenta which could hinder their movements."

"Indeed, Clive, I can attest to that. I rode by that sorry caravan on my way here, just outside of town. They should be here now. I daresay the town is about to become very crowded."

"Quite right, Barrett." Then Clive added, "You must stay here; we'll talk later tonight and tomorrow. In the meanwhile, Mrs. Hubble should have supper ready."

"I should love nothing more than to accept your hospitality."

The meal was a nice one, with beef brought in from Harfeld's plantation outside town, accompanied by roast vegetables and bread baked that very day by Mrs. Hubble. It was accompanied by a fine wine Harfeld opened just for the occasion, with a pudding for sweets afterward. With the housekeeper hovering around, they talked of things beside the war over the food and wine, but afterward they retreated to the study where they could talk in private about serious matters.

It was just a half hour later that the housekeeper interrupted them, a puzzled look on her face. "Excuse me, Mr. Harfeld, but there's someone here to see you: A lady. Actually, a lady and her servant."

"This late? I presume she gave you a name?"

"Indeed, sir. It's a certain Mrs. Tresh. She says you know her."

"Absolutely! Please show her into the parlor, and I shall be there momentarily."

Mrs. Hubble departed and Harfeld quickly turned to Northcutt, a wry smile on his face. "Barrett, fortune has chosen to smile on us. This is the lady I've told you about—the wife of that Swiss Colonel serving on Washington's staff. She has given me information in the past without knowing my loyalties. With careful tact, we may be able to draw a wealth of information from her."

"Damned right, Clive. I presume she must have come in with the caravan."

"The same thought struck me. But let me talk to her and get the facts of the matter." He waved to the sideboard. "Help yourself to more brandy." Then he quickly left on his way to the parlor.

Harfeld entered the room and found Catherine seated in a chair and another woman standing by the fireplace. He realized the second woman was her maid, whom he had seen once before in the New York tea shop. Then he looked back at Catherine and was shocked. He realized that the only apt word to describe her was *bedraggled.*

He walked up to her, took her hand, and bowed slightly. "My dear Catherine, what has happened? What has brought you to Morristown on such a miserable night?"

She took a deep breath, and Harfeld thought he saw the glimmer of a tear in her eye. "Oh, Clive, Alex sent me here with a convoy of wounded and camp followers. Between this horrible weather and the loss of provisions and men, things are not good with the army. He believed I would be safer and more comfortable here in Morristown. But we found the taverns and inns are all filled with other refugees fleeing the British. There is no suitable place for a lady to stay." She hesitated, bit her lip, then with beseeching eyes, said, "So I remembered that you lived here, and we have come to throw ourselves on your hospitality."

Marvelous! thought Harfeld. He smiled benignly. "My dear, of *course* you must stay here! I have a room that will be perfect for you, and Mrs. Hubble can accommodate your maid in the servant's quarters. You must consider this your home until the situation in the war becomes clearer."

The expression on Catherine's face quickly went from desolation to gratitude. "Clive, you *can't* understand how much I appreciate this. I feel so cold and, and . . . and may I say, just plain soiled from living in camp for so long."

Clive put on his most benign smile. "Catherine, I can understand just what you are feeling." He put a finger to his chin. "And it strikes me that you have been without decent food for a long time. We have just finished our repast, but I know Mrs. Hubble still has some nice roasted beef and vegetables that she can put on the table. Would you be amenable to that?"

Catherine instantly stiffened in her chair. "Amenable? I should be exhilarated at some fresh food! It's been so long on army rations."

Harfeld turned to the housekeeper, who had been standing in the door. "Please put together something for Mrs. Tresh."

"Of course, sir."

"And Mrs. Hubble, will you please stop by the study and ask Mr. Northcutt to join us?"

Catherine raised her eyebrows. "You have another guest?"

"Indeed, my dear. Another gentleman from this colony whose acquaintance I think you will be very pleased to make."

Northcutt arrived momentarily, and Harfeld saw Catherine scan him with appraising eyes. He said, "Mrs. Tresh, this gentleman is Barrett Penfold Northcutt."

Barrett approached Catherine, bowed, took her hand, and brushed it with his lips. "A pleasure to meet you, Ma'am."

"And my distinct pleasure, sir," Catherine responded.

Harfeld said, "Barrett is staying with me while conducting business. It may interest you, Catherine, that he owns considerable land and other property in this area and is looking for buyers so that he may realize some financial liquidity."

Catherine's eyes opened wide. "Land that you desire to sell?"

Barrett exchanged glances with Harfeld and then smiled. "Indeed, Ma'am. I have held a good deal of property in this part of the country for a long time and believe this may be the time to sell some of it."

Clive beamed at Catherine. "Now my dear, I told you that there was land available around Morristown. And perhaps while you and Barrett are here, we could at least have some preliminary discussions." He spread his hands wide. "But that can wait until tomorrow. Tonight, let's get you a good meal and a long night's rest to fortify you after your ordeal."

"That sounds wonderful, Clive."

General Hugh Mercer sat behind a tiny field desk in a room of the White Hall Tavern on the main street in New Brunswick, which was serving as the army headquarters. On his desk was a stack of reports he was reviewing. At the moment, Wend Eckert stood before him, explaining the defense measures which had been taken at the river.

"General, Hamilton's artillery is in place, largely hidden by brush built up around each gun emplacement. My men have finished a line of trenches, and we've selected locations for riflemen in the buildings along the river. We're as ready as we can be for the arrival of the British column."

Mercer nodded. "It sounds like you've done what is possible." He looked up from papers on the desk and said, "Virtually all of the army has passed over the river. Only Fairfield's troop remains north of it, watching for the approach of the enemy. It won't be long until Cornwallis' division arrives."

"Yes, sir. I'm getting frequent reports from Fairfield." Wend changed the subject. "One other thing: I sent Ensign Childers and two squads down to a small bridge on a farmer's road about two miles south of our position at the ford. He's got pry bars and axes and has orders to remove the planking from the bridge. He went out this morning and will be back any time. I have held off taking that step, but went ahead now that the cavalry has reported the British are approaching."

"That's all good. The army will bivouac here tonight and start the march toward the next town to the south, Princeton, in the morning. Washington is planning to stay here for a couple of days, where we can get Fairfield's reports."

Wend ventured to ask a question. "Sir, our column is greatly diminished in size. What is the situation with General Lee's force? I know that he was summoned to join the main army. When is he due to arrive?"

Mercer didn't answer immediately. Instead, he stared into the distance, his jaw tight. Finally, he responded, "Eckert, you have just asked the question that is on Washington's mind constantly." He stood up and looked into the hearth where a small fire burned. "In fact, the real question is not *when*, but *if* he will arrive—arrive in time to help us."

Wend was startled by Mercer's words. "Sir, I don't understand."

The general clasped his hands behind his back. "The fact is, we are not sure General Lee has indeed crossed the Hudson. He has sent Washington a letter arguing that he should remain separate, on our flank, in order to distract the enemy, and gave us no hard statement of his location." He turned his head to look directly at Wend. "His plan would be a good tactical consideration if we were certain that we could maintain our strength. But as it is, I must tell you that our force here is down to less than 2,600 effectives, and more men are taking their leave every day. Beyond that, with the expiration of enlistments in a few weeks, it is likely we shall be down to no more than a few hundred men. Our only hope to remain an effective force is to join the two divisions."

Wend was shocked. "I don't understand why Lee won't comply with the order, sir. He must understand our situation."

"*Of course* he understands our bloody situation!" Mercer took a deep breath to control his emotion, then spoke in a low voice: "As a fellow Virginian, I will confide this to you: The man is conspiring to replace Washington in command. We have information from friends in Congress that Lee has been writing letters critical of Washington to various congressmen and explaining how he would conduct the war if in command. And not only to the politicians—he has been corresponding with some of the senior officers throughout the army pushing the same idea, soliciting their support. He's plainly calling into question Washington's competence and judgment." He took a deep breath. "In my opinion, Lee is waiting for this column to disintegrate so that he will have the largest, most effective force in the field and then demand the generalship of the army."

Wend was shocked. "I had no idea, sir. What can Washington do to counteract him?"

"George has not been passive. He has sent his own correspondence to Congress, particularly to our delegation, explaining what he considers the best way forward. And he has urgently asked for a division of General Gates' northern army, two brigades at least, to be ordered to join us at forced march. They could be here by late December if the orders are given promptly. That would sustain our size until newly recruited regiments could arrive."

"Well, General, that is at least hopeful news. Two brigades will surely help."

"Hold your enthusiasm, Eckert. It's not certain. I will tell you that Gates is also a competitor for command of the army—an *eager* competitor. He, like Lee, had considerable experience in the British Army. And he has vocal supporters in Congress who would like to see him in command." He gave Wend a meaningful stare. "So it's possible he may find a way to delay sending those troops if he thinks it would hurt Washington and help his cause."

There was a long pause. Then Wend said, "Sir, it appears all we can do is make sure this column makes it safely across the Delaware and then see how the chips fall."

"Sadly, Eckert, that is the precise situation." Mercer moved over and looked at his map pinned to a wall. "That is what we must concentrate on. I'm told the Governor of Pennsylvania has his naval galleys hard at work rounding up the boats, both for our crossing and to deny them to the British, and we have put Glover's Massachusetts battalion of Marblehead fishermen at the head of the column, so they may provide the same invaluable services they have in the past." He turned back to Wend. "Your part, along with Hamilton, is to delay the British here at Brunswick."

Wend raised his hand. "We're as prepared as possible, sir. Hamilton's guns will be essential."

"Indeed, Eckert." Then a thought hit Mercer. "Did Hamilton get that powder and shot we collected from the column?"

"Yes, sir. He's quite happy with his supply now."

"Then it's up to the two of you." He thought a while, then a cloud came over his face. "Wend, I've just spoken plainly to you out of frustration at the situation. I'll trust you to keep all the comments I made about Lee and Gates close to your chest. We don't need the men losing any more confidence in our leadership than has already occurred."

"Of course, you have my assurance, General."

—∾—

Joy lay in O'beirne's arms in the bed of her room at the Jolly Times. Both were exhausted after frantic lovemaking. She reached up and put her arms around his neck and shoulders. "I'm so glad you could make it here tonight."

A serious look came over Shay's face. "Yes, the first lieutenant was gracious to grant me permission. But, my dear Joy, I fear this may be our last night together, at least for a good while. The British have resumed their march toward New Brunswick. I don't know precisely when they'll arrive, but it will be soon. We've got a cavalry patrol out watching them."

"Then there will be a fight at the river. You'll be part of it."

"Indeed. We're to hold the British a while to let the army get farther ahead."

Joy put her head next to his. "But it will not be long until they're here. The British and their German mercenaries."

"It's a certainty, my dear."

"Shay, I'm afraid. Everyone's talking about how soldiers treat townspeople after a battle. They run wild, taking food, taking valuables, stealing animals." She looked up at him, the fear obvious in her eyes. "And they force their way with women."

"I shouldn't think something like that would happen here. It's not like you are foreigners to the British. That kind of marauding usually happens when a foreign army occupies part of another country. And the British want to persuade the people to give their loyalty back to the crown. I suspect they'll keep the soldiers reined-in tightly. They're even offering pledges for people to sign renouncing their support of the rebels and renewing their allegiance to the King. It wouldn't do to have the men running amok if they expect people to do that."

"Still, Shay, I'm afraid." She bit her lip and looked him in the eye, then said beseechingly, "You'll be leaving after the battle. *Take me with* you. I could become a camp woman, at least for a time."

He looked at her with startled eyes. "You come along?"

"Yes, yes, Shay! I could be so helpful in camp. I can cook and I'm strong. I could be good help."

O'beirne hesitated almost a minute, ordering his thoughts. "Joy, nothing would please me more. But I can't do it. The women with the company are all married to soldiers. We can't just take someone along—the women get a ration based on their marriage." He sat up and put his arms around her. "You'll be safe here. The men of the town will protect you. Just stay here in the tavern, out of sight as much as you can from the troops marching through. And the way things are going, it's not likely to be safe with our army. In fact, many of the women have already been sent away."

Disappointment spread over Joy's face. Shay knew he had to give her something to look forward to. "And I'll be back as soon as possible. Either Washington's army will rally, or the war will end. In either case, I vow I'll be back."

Tears rolled down the girl's face, then she hugged him tightly. "Oh, Shay, it started out with you giving me money. But you must know, soon enough, I began to crave our nights together." She looked toward heaven. "God knows how an Ulster Scot girl fell in love with an Irishman, of all things. But it happened, and now I want to be with you all the time."

Shay put his hand under her chin and lifted it so their eyes were locked. "My dearest, I told you I will be back, no matter what happens. Shay O'beirne is a *survivor.* And I do have what they call the *Luck of the Irish.* After all, I'm fortunate enough to be here with you tonight. So you must take care of yourself and wait for me." He pulled her close and kissed her. Then he said, "Now, I must get dressed and get back to the company, or Lieutenant Newkirk will be after me with a sharp stick."

Joy laughed. "Not immediately. One more time tonight, if I'm not to see you for who knows how long." She gave him a knowing look. "It will be quick. I know how to make you come *fast.* And then you can go back to your company." As she spoke, one of her hands slipped down to caress his manhood, and he felt a surge of excitement run through his body.

Shay laid back on the bed, a huge look of pleasure on his face. "Well, then, lass, if that's the way it's to be, work your magic!"

"Captain Eckert!" It was the voice of Corporal Schreiber. "Captain, that Lieutenant Fairfield and his men are comin' in! They're fording the river now."

Wend had been talking with Hamilton, seated together before a campfire for warmth. The two captains turned to watch the horse troop splash across the ford. Hamilton remarked, "The British must be close. That's Fairfield's whole troop."

"I fear you are right. He'd have left men to observe if they were some distance away."

Hamilton pulled a watch out of his pocket. Looking down at it in the bright morning light, he observed, "I make it just before 11:00."

"Well, sir," replied Wend, "this happens to be the first day of December. I expect it will be a day we shall always remember."

Fairfield urged his mount up onto the river bank, then rode over to where the two men now stood. Looking down from the saddle, he smiled broadly. "Well, my dear sirs, to quote a famous phrase, 'The British Are Coming.'"

Wend said, "Very cute, Fairfield. What force and how far away?"

"A troop of light horse—of the 16th Light Dragoons. They'll be here in a few minutes. We had a very brief clash with them. A few shots fired, and we retired at the gallop. Behind them is an advance guard of light foot—both British and Jaegers. And they are followed by a mixed column of British line troops and Hessian Grenadiers."

Wend responded, "You'd better ride down to the White Hall Tavern and report all this to the staff. I suspect Washington will want to question you himself." He motioned to the horsemen. "Have your ensign move the troop to shelter and dismount, as a reserve."

Having seen Fairfield making his report, the company officers and Donegal joined the two captains. Newkirk said, "What's toward, sir?"

Wend responded, "The enemy is just behind Fairfield's troop. Get the men into the trenches." He looked at O'beirne. "And get your riflemen up in the buildings." He raised a finger. "Now listen carefully, all of you: Keep your men on a short leash—no firing until the order is given. We don't want to give away our positions before the enemy begins their assault. And in any case, we must husband our shot and powder."

He turned to Donegal. "Get the women and children together and have them pack up. Have Baird take charge and assign two other men. As soon as they're ready, get them moving south through the town to pick up the whiskey wagons. Then they are to head south on the road as fast as can be managed. We'll catch up with them after the fight."

Donegal didn't immediately respond. After a moment he said, "Na, my dear Captain, that I'll do, but I'm thinkin' that we ought to have Martha Flanagan and one other woman stay with the company. There may be men who will need tendin' to after the fight begins."

"All right, Sergeant. A good thought. Make it happen."

The officers hurried off to get men into position while Eckert and Hamilton moved to a clump of bushes near the river's edge where they could observe the far bank from cover. Soon there was a rush of men hurrying to their positions in the trenches and the riverside buildings. Wend could see Hamilton's gun crews forming up at each of their cannon.

It wasn't a long wait. No sooner were the men in position than two red-coated horsemen appeared on the road at the North side of the river. The two sat their horses, observing the ford and the town. One pointed to a six-pounder, barely visible over the bushes.

Hamilton said, "Well, Wend, now they know we have artillery in place."

"Yes, Alex, but they don't know how many. That gun was the least well-hidden of the lot."

At that moment, one of the cavalrymen shouted out loudly and waved down the road, as if summoning someone. Shortly thereafter, the full troop trotted into view, then pulled up at the river bank. An officer scanned the southern bank with a telescopic glass. Reese Newkirk, who had joined them, said, "We could do some major damage to that troop with a volley of rifle and musket fire."

Wend responded, "Yes, Reese, but I don't want them to know our strength. Let's keep them guessing until their foot troops attempt to cross." He added, "Fire at the dragoons only if they try to ford the river, which I think is unlikely."

In a few more minutes, the troop pulled back about a hundred yards and dismounted, except for one horseman, who kicked his horse into a gallop and headed back from whence the troop had come. Hamilton said, "Obviously a courier to the head of their column."

"Undoubtedly, sir," remarked Wend. Then he commented, "I should say that the festivities will begin in earnest within the next hour."

—⁂—

Wend watched as Joshua Baird, mounted on his tall hunter, led the small caravan of wagons carrying most of the company's camp equipment and the group of camp women and children southward down the main street of New Brunswick. Two men of the company, their muskets slung over their shoulders, escorted the group.

It was just under an hour since the troop of 16th Light Dragoons had arrived at the Raritan ford. Now all the Frederick County men were at their stations in the trenches or at windows in the upper floor of town buildings. Hamilton's artillerymen were at their guns, and the youthful captain was inspecting the readiness of each gun and crew.

Donegal, watching from the bush beside the riverbank, quietly called out. "Wend, pay attention now. Sure and I see some of those green-coated Jaegers comin' up the road."

Wend quickly joined the Highlander. The Jaegers were indeed advancing. As he watched, they deployed into the bush, taking position in the wooded areas along the northern side of the road. Behind them came companies of red-coated light foot, who in open skirmishing formation presently deployed to the south of the road.

Then the silence of the afternoon was broken by the sound of fife and drums in the distance. Simon looked over at Wend. "That'll be the line battalions of their advance guard. They'll be the ones who make the assault across the ford."

"Yes, I've no doubt that's their intent. But we've got to break them up before they start to cross."

"Well, na, Wend. I'm thinkin' in the main that will be Hamilton's job."

Wend nodded. "Yep, at least at the start. We'll back him up with our firelocks." He looked over to see Hamilton approaching.

Without preamble, the artilleryman said, "I propose to open fire when the foot column approaches the ford. At least two of my guns can send balls right down the road. Each shot will cause multiple casualties, make them break ranks to seek cover, and take time to plan a further advance."

"Alex, you can open the dance whenever you think proper. And when the Redcoats start to break, we'll keep them hunkered down with rifle fire and musketry."

Hamilton just grinned, then ran back to his guns.

Donegal stared at the departing artillery captain. "Eager lad, isn't he?" Then he pointed to the positions of the soldiers across the river. "I'll wager they're going to try to pick off the gunners once they start firing. We'll have to try to distract them."

Wend looked back at the buildings where the riflemen were hiding. "They'll be the best for that work—they're high enough to get a good view of where the Jaegers and light foot are hiding and can fire down on them." He tapped his friend on the shoulder. "Quick: Find O'beirne and tell him to put his men to work as soon as Hamilton starts firing."

As Donegal departed, Newkirk, who was supervising the men in the trenches, came up. By this time, the drums of the British column were getting louder, and Wend was able to discern that the fifers were playing *The British Grenadiers.* Newkirk came over and said, "They'll be in sight any moment now. What are your orders?"

"Keep the men down until Hamilton starts firing and the column starts to scatter. Then have your men fire at will to take as heavy a toll as possible. But have them be careful to stay under cover: Undoubtedly the Jaeger riflemen, firing from cover, will attempt to pick off our men. O'beirne's men will try to keep them pinned down."

Wend watched the road, waiting for the first sight of the column. As he watched, Donegal returned. "O'beirne knows what to do and is lookin' forward to it with glee in his eyes."

Wend was about to answer when the redcoats came around a clump of trees, marching in column of fours. In the middle of the battalion, Wend could see a color guard with the Union Flag and a regimental standard. An officer rode a prancing horse at the head of the column. Catching sight of the river, he raised his hand, and the battalion halted. Other officers on foot came running to join him. They gathered around in discussion, obviously making plans for the assault.

Donegal unslung the musket from his shoulder. “Well, lad, the time is nigh. We’ll soon have the smell of powder in our nostrils.”

At that moment, the cluster of British officers broke up, returning to their companies. And almost immediately, a body of troops—Wend estimated a company—broke ranks and began advancing in loose formation for the ford. Just as they reached the water, the silence was broken by the loud bang of one of Hamilton’s guns, followed almost immediately by a second. The effect was dramatic. Several men fell. One dropped into the water, clearly dead or dying, and floated downstream. Several other soldiers of the advanced company were hit, blood flying. Wend looked at the rest of the column and saw that the balls had continued down the road, putting holes in the ranks of the formation. As he watched, officers yelled and the men started to take cover.

Wend shouted out to Newkirk, “Fire at will!”

The lieutenant and the men of the trenches had obviously been eagerly waiting, and a volley of shots rang out. Wend looked back at the British column and saw men drop to their knees or simply fall over. Many others ran, looking for cover in the trees and bush along the road. More shots rang out, this time from O’beirne’s riflemen. Wend saw the mounted officer’s horse buckle and go to the ground. The officer himself was thrown off and tried to crawl to cover. Then he suddenly collapsed to the ground and lay still, obviously hit by a rifle ball.

Now there was general firing from all the guns of the artillery battery, and the shot kicked up dirt in the road. Wend saw men who had flopped to the ground after the first cannon fire flung up in the air by the balls. He thought, *If they had survived the first cannon fire, the second round had finished them.* There was a period of silence as Hamilton’s men reloaded, and then firing began again. Now all Hamilton’s guns were firing rapidly, concentrating their aim on the woods and bush on either side of the road, firing blind with the intent of hitting men hiding there.

After several long minutes, the artillery captain signaled cease-fire to all his gun crews. He called over to Wend, “I’m holding fire until I have some visible targets. In any case, it’s a chance for the guns to cool off.”

Donegal tapped Wend on the shoulder. “Na, I got to tell you, we got an audience.”

“Audience? What the devil do you mean?”

“I mean a brace of generals. Includin’ the big man himself.”

Wend's head spun around and saw several officers sitting their horses in the street about 100 yards away. He soon recognized Washington and Mercer. As he watched, Mercer spurred his horse forward. Wend got up from his crouching position and hurried to speak with the general.

"General, take care. There are rifle marksmen in the bush on the far bank."

Mercer nodded and swung down from his horse. Wend joined him by the animal.

The general waved to Hamilton, who came running to join them. When the artillery captain arrived, Mercer said, "You gentlemen have done well so far." He waved back at where the staff sat their horses. "The staff and all other remaining parts of the army are leaving posthaste and intend to march southward to Princeton, twelve miles hence. It is important for you to make every effort to hold the British until dark to give us time to be clear." He looked at the two with questioning eyes. "Do you consider that possible?"

A devilish look came over Hamilton's face. "Not only feasible, but doing so will be a pleasure."

Wend stared at Mercer. "We'll hold even if it means close fighting with bayonets and hatchets here at the river bank."

"Good. Now Wend, when you leave tonight, leave Fairfield and a detachment of his light horse to watch what the enemy does."

"Aye, sir. I was planning on that."

"Good. Then we shall not dally further. I hope to see both of you in the encampment at Princeton." Mercer shook hands with both of them. "Here's to your success and personal good fortune." Then he quickly mounted and rode back to the staff. Wend saw Washington and him exchange a few words, and then the staff turned and rode off southward.

Wend looked at Hamilton. "Alex, I assume the British will shortly bring up more troops and plan to rush the ford." He looked across the river and up the hill. "And I should be very surprised if they didn't place some artillery up on that ridge."

Hamilton stared at the height on the north side of the Raritan. "I've no fear of that. My lads will be ready to duel it out with them."

"Then, Alex, let us make ready for what may come."

—m—

The second assault came in mid-afternoon. Wend had expected to see an artillery battery taking position at the crest of the hill which rose above the northern side of the Raritan, but instead a strong column of Redcoats came into sight. It immediately broke ranks, and in loose formation, headed for the river at the rush, bayonets fixed, not taking time to fire. As they charged, the British and Hessian light troops in hiding near the banks took up a rapid fire which appeared to have the aim of suppressing Hamilton's artillerymen and Wend's soldiers in their trenches.

It was to no avail. The New York artillery, now firing grapeshot, opened a withering fire that cut through the regulars, opening gaps in their ranks. But with officers waving their swords in encouragement, they sturdily advanced at the run, their first company plunging into the flowing river. That slowed their advance as they waded through the stream. Hamilton's guns began firing at will, each gun shooting as soon as they had reloaded from the last round. The Frederick County men, in the trenches and the buildings, fired as rapidly as they could reload after each shot.

The Redcoats made it to mid-stream before they faltered in the face of the combined artillery, rifle, and musket fire. Many bodies floated downstream. The men remaining on their feet hesitated a moment, the officers still screaming at them to advance. Then, first by individuals, then en masse, they turned and fled out of the river and into the shelter of the trees and bush on the far side, more falling as they retreated amidst the storm of lead chasing them.

Wend shouted the cease fire to both the artillery and the light foot. A silence quickly descended over the ford. It lasted a few seconds but was then broken by an uproar of spontaneous, triumphant cheering from both the New Yorkers and Virginians. It went on for nearly a minute.

When silence returned, Donegal came up and said, "Na, that was a right brisk action. And the lads are proud of what they done. But we took some fire from the Light Bobs on the far banks. We got wounded—five of them that need lookin' after. Sure, I need to get them back to where Martha Flannagan and Melinda Wood are waiting."

"Of course, get them out of the trenches right away."

"And there be somethin' else. It be Private Jed Holwin, in Corporal Sanders' squad. The lad took a ball in the head. He had just taken a shot at a Redcoat and was watching to see if he got a hit instead of ducking back down into the trench to reload like he should have. One of those Jaeger riflemen got him. It's sure he never felt anything. One moment he was lookin' at an enemy, the next he was standin' a'fore the Lord, trying to explain why he should stay in Heaven instead of bein' sent down to Hell." Simon grimaced. "I'll get his body out of the trenches. We'll put it on one of the horses, so we can bury it somewhere down the road when we got time for grave digging."

Wend took a deep breath. Holwin was the first death in the company since they had marched away from Frederick County. He thought, *The first, but undoubtedly only the first of many.* Then he simply nodded to Donegal.

The afternoon wore on with little more action on the British side of the river. The battalions that had attempted the forced crossing at the ford remained off the road, under cover. Meanwhile, Hamilton's men quickly swabbed out their guns and ensured adequate ammunition was available at each position. Wend took time to walk back to where the five wounded men were being taken care of by the women. He asked Martha Flannagan their condition.

The heavyset woman motioned to four of the men. "They're taken care of, at least for now." Then she pointed to the fifth man. "But Caldwell, there, he got a more serious wound. Right up on his right leg, just below the hip. He's needin' a surgeon's care right quick, or it's sure he'll lose that leg. Can we get a doctor here in town?"

Wend thought a moment. "I'll send out Ensign Childers to find one. But we've got to take Caldwell with us, else he'll end up a prisoner. And he's not likely to fare well if that happens." He looked over at the officer's wagon, which had been left behind to carry the remaining camp cooking gear. "We'll make room for him there. We'll be in Princeton tomorrow and will get him to an army surgeon."

Wend went back to the company position and sent Childers out on his mission of mercy. Meanwhile, there was still no activity over on the British lines, and looking up at the sky, he realized there was less than two hours until evening dusk set in. He wondered what the chances were that the day would finish without further conflict.

The answer came in less than a half hour. Reese Newkirk called out to him, "Wend, look up on the ridge on the other side of the river."

Wend looked and saw it: A battery of horse-drawn British guns had appeared in the road and was deploying to a clear area on the south side of the track and would afford a good field of fire. Within a few minutes they were being unhitched from their limbers, and gunners were manhandling them into position. Wend quickly strode over to where Hamilton stood with his lieutenant. "Alex, I assume you see what's happening on the ridge?"

Hamilton's eyes were glued to the crest of the hill, and he wasn't smiling now. "Indeed, sir. I see. Six pounders, by the look of them. It appears things are about to get more serious. Clearly they realized they can't take the ford until they've neutralized my guns."

Wend said, "Can your six pounders elevate to take them on?"

Hamilton nodded. "Yes, we've got enough height on this bank, and they'll be well in range. But clearly we're going to have a bit of a duel, whenever they're ready to begin."

Wend responded, "If we can hold them off until dark, we'll have done our duty. But it could be hot times until then. When do you think they'll be ready to begin their bombardment?"

Now a smile broke out on the young captain's face. "It matters not. We're not waiting for them to open the cotillion. I can make it hot for them and slow down their preparations." He looked over at Wend. "That is, if you have no objections to my opening fire first."

"Alex, do what you will."

Hamilton shouted orders to his men and soon every gun was manned. The young captain himself went along and personally aimed each piece. Then on signal, all were fired within seconds of each other. Wend looked up at the ridge and saw eruptions of dirt and underbrush in front of, behind, and in one case next to the British guns. The artillerymen scurried for cover.

Wend looked over and saw the New Yorkers frantically working to reload. Hamilton ran to the first ready gun, made adjustments to its aim, and fired it himself.

Reese Newkirk had come over and was standing beside Wend. Suddenly he exclaimed, "Jesus! He's hit one of their guns!"

Wend looked up on the hill and was shocked to see that a gun in the center of the enemy battery had been knocked off its carriage, the carriage itself flipped over with one wheel separated from the axle and lying on the ground. Dirt and debris were still flying, and several men lay on the ground. He turned to Newkirk and said, "Damned if Hamilton doesn't know his business!"

"Seems so, sir!"

More of Hamilton's guns were firing, the balls kicking up dust around the enemy positions. Newkirk remarked, "It's undeniable that he's got their range!"

Wend nodded, but then pointed to the ridge. "Despite Hamilton's efforts, they're getting ready to fire. Now it's our turn to take some punishment."

Within a minute, two of the enemy guns opened fire. Wend heard a shriek as one of the balls flew over their head and harmlessly hit the ground in a grove of trees just off the road fifty yards behind them. But there was also a loud crashing sound almost simultaneously, and Wend turned to see a ball had hit one of the houses behind the river, smashing part of its facade.

Newkirk said, "They're overshooting." He gritted his teeth. "But they'll adjust their aim, and I wager they'll be closer to target with the next shots."

Just then, several of Hamilton's guns fired in rapid sequence, the shot landing in front of and behind the British battery. But the enemy gunners stuck to their business and returned fire. Newkirk had been right: Several balls landed right behind the New York guns. Another hit just behind the company trenches, in fact no more than a few feet from where Eckert and Newkirk stood.

The lieutenant said, with excitement in his voice, "Sir, I suggest we take to the trench ourselves!"

Wend didn't answer; he simply walked to the trench in front of where they had been standing and dropped down into it. Newkirk joined him, as did O'beirne, who had just arrived. The Irishman said, "Well, bless Mother Mary, we got the riflemen out of those buildings just in time!"

Wend looked up into the sky. He saw heavy cloud cover and realized darkness would come early. "Gentlemen, barring something I don't expect, this will be over within the half-hour. The cannonade, however effective, will not drive us out of our positions. They'll need an infantry assault to do that, and I've seen no effort to stage another one."

O'beirne looked at the other side of the river and nodded. "I say they plan to regroup overnight. They'll bring up reinforcements, probably a battalion of grenadiers, and make a foot attack after dawn."

Wend replied, "That's my thinking also." He smiled, "And they'll be successful, because we will be gone."

At that moment, there was an eruption of cannon fire from the British battery. Everyone in the trench dropped to ensure maximum protection, and instantly there was the shriek of balls passing over them. Suddenly, there was the sound of an explosion close by.

O'beirne rose to look out of the trench. "Damnation!" he exclaimed. "That one got one of Hamilton's guns! It's blown to hell, and that explosion was the gun's supply of powder going up!"

Wend jumped up and saw that the barrel of the nearest gun had been knocked off the carriage, and the carriage itself was torn asunder, the fragments spread all over. Several men of the crew lay still on the ground, obviously dead, while others were clutching wounds.

Then Wend saw Hamilton, who was standing at one of the other guns. His face was the picture of pure rage, his hands balled into fists. But he remained like that for only a few seconds. Then he rapidly moved to the nearest gun, sighted on the British battery, ordered the crew to make adjustments, then seized the slow match from a gunner standing nearby. Sighting carefully again, a smile came over his face, and he touched the match to the gun. The piece jumped back as it fired. Wend quickly turned to see the fall of the shot and was exulted to see a direct hit on one of the enemy guns. A cheer went up from all of the men, both artillerymen and light foot.

Wend was surprised to see a flurry of activity on the ridge. Horses were being brought in and hooked up to the artillery pieces. As he was staring, he heard Shay exclaim, "Damn, they're moving the guns back over the crest of the ridge where Hamilton can't hit them."

"Indeed, Shay," replied Wend. "They've lost two of their six guns. Since they're just moving them back, not away down the road, I believe they are indeed waiting for tomorrow for their next attack."

Wend jumped up out of the trench and walked to where Hamilton stood, hands on hips, watching the British activity. "Alex, I think it's over. You've convinced them to pack it in for now." He looked at the darkening sky. "Dusk is upon us, and my expectation is that the British are done for the day."

Without taking his eyes off the ridge, Hamilton nodded. He stood thinking for a long moment, then he looked at Wend. "It's time for us to make plans to get out of here."

"Yes, I intend to leave under cover of darkness, with bright campfires set, tended by Fairfield's troop, to confuse the British about whether we are here."

Hamilton replied, "There's a problem with that: We'll make a significant amount of noise limbering up and loading ammunition. It will carry through the silent night air, and they'll understand we're pulling out."

Wend grinned. "That had occurred to me, Alex. I have a plan: a plan that will generate noise to cover your activity and convince the British we are remaining in our positions." He started to walk off but said over his shoulder, "And I'll organize that now."

Wend walked back to the trenches and called his officers together, including Fairfield and Ensign Middleton. When they had all arrived, he said, "Gentlemen, we're pulling out of here just before midnight. But we need to convince the enemy we are remaining overnight." He looked at O'beirne. "And you, Shay, must play an important role."

A diabolical expression came over the Irishman's face. "Ah, my darling captain, do you want me to organize a small raid on our compatriots across the river, as a distraction to convince them we remain ready to fight?"

"I admire your spirit, sir, but I plan nothing so dramatic or dangerous." Wend broke into a broad smile. "Now, since we've been together these months, I'm well aware that you have a magnificent Irish singing voice and are familiar with a great many songs and ballads."

Puzzlement came over Shay's face, as well as the others. "Now, my Captain, that's true enough, but I vow you leave me a *wee bit* bewildered."

Newkirk asked, "What do you have in mind, Captain?"

"Well, gentlemen, hitching up the guns to their teams and getting them out of here will cause a distinct amount of noise, no matter how cautious Hamilton and his men are. So we will build up our campfires, and Shay will organize the men to sing loudly as if we are having a merry old time here and fully intend to stay. And Mr. Childers, you will arrange for a robust ration of whiskey to the men to encourage their taking loud voice."

Understanding spread among the officers. Shay laughed and said, "And so the fires and singing will cover the noise of the departure of the guns."

"Precisely, Shay. And once the guns are on the road, we shall withdraw by squads." He turned to Fairfield. "Geoffrey, the light horse will remain behind to stoke the fires during the night and make enough noise to convince the enemy we are still in camp. And then, of course, tomorrow you will act as rearguard to keep watch on the enemy advance."

Then Wend looked up at the sky and saw that dusk was upon them. He said, "Now that nightfall approaches, let's get the fires stoked up and feed the men the best meal we can, for we have a long night march ahead of us and they will need all the energy they can muster."

When dusk turned to darkness, bright cooking fires were flaming along the lines of the Frederick County Light Foot and the New York Artillery Company. Presently, the loud singing of happy, lusty voices could be heard all along the southern banks of the Raritan. Meanwhile, with the utmost quiet that could be achieved, Hamilton's men withdrew their remaining four guns and started down the road through New Brunswick toward the town of Princeton. After the artillery were on their way, the singing tapered off as if the men were bedding down for the night. Moving quietly, squad by squad, the company followed the artillery southward through the town. As they went down the main street in route step, a few people, standing along the street in silent groups, watched them go. Here and there the soldiers could see faces looking out of windows.

As they passed the Jolly Times Tavern, Wend was surprised to see the front door flung open and a lithe, blond-haired young girl emerge. Dashing up to Shay O'beirne, mounted on his horse, the lass took his hand and they exchanged a few words. Then the Irishman spurred his horse forward and the girl turned and returned to the tavern.

Wend maneuvered Sonny until he was close by O'beirne. "Well, Shay, it seems you've made some attachment during your time in the town. A very young attachment."

"Aye, my darling Captain. You well know I'm not a man for dallying long with any particular lass, but I must admit this one has managed to get under my skin."

Wend grinned. "You know my feelings about tavern maids. I found one who, as you say, got under my skin and could not be left behind. Could it be you are emulating your captain?"

For once O'beirne's face took on a serious look. "I shall have to measure my feelings as time goes on. But I'll not deny I have given the lass my promise to visit her again when things are settled, one way or another."

Wend grinned at his lieutenant. Meanwhile, he thought of a moment long ago on a dark night at the crest of North Mountain in Pennsylvania when he had first realized he loved Peggy. They had been driving a wagon carrying her sister—severely wounded in a mill explosion—to a doctor in Carlisle. Then a wheel spoke had cracked during a sharp turn. They had had to work together to make emergency repairs, lacing a rope around the spoke to hold it together. Peggy McCarty had labored shoulder to shoulder with Wend, working as hard as any man. When the spoke had finally been repaired enough to continue, they had spontaneously embraced in emotion, and he knew that sooner or later they would be wed.

Wend turned his mind back to the present and simply said to O'beirne, "Shay, sometimes with females, matters of emotion overtake us at the most unexpected moments." With that, he spurred his horse and returned to the head of the column, steeling himself for a long, cold night's march.

Chapter Sixteen

Travail at The Delaware

The carriage, pulled by a team of matched bay horses, followed the wagon track westward from Morristown, passing over rolling, wooded hills, and well-tended plantations. It was, for a change, a clear, sunny day, although the morning air was quite crisp. Catherine Tresh, in her warm cape and covered up to her shoulder by a thick traveling rug, sat in the cushioned rear seat of the carriage next to Clive Harfeld. Across from them in the forward, rear-facing seat lounged Barrett Northcutt. It was the second day after her arrival at Harfeld's place. She had spent the previous day recovering from the travails of traveling with the army, enjoying her host's food and drink while Elise cleaned and pressed her wardrobe.

Seeing the day dawn without heavy cloud cover or threat of rain, Clive had suggested that the three of them take a drive so Catherine could see the land in the rural area beyond the town. She had enthusiastically agreed and now found herself enthralled by the beauty of the countryside. She looked between her two escorts. "Gentlemen, this is such lovely country! Just the kind of which I have always dreamed. And it must be quite fertile, for these farms are so obviously prosperous!"

"Indeed, Catherine," responded Harfeld. "I'm happy to say each acre produces an excellent volume of high quality grain. And the grazing pastures provide excellent grass for the cattle." He waved at a field they were passing. "Of course, things are now quite dormant, but I can assure you that you will get good, profitable crops of grain for sale and milling. A farm in this area can provide a handsome income."

Catherine sighed. "That is just what we are looking for. But I wonder if we will ever be able to manage the price of such a plantation."

"Well," replied Harfeld, "Land is the business of both myself and Barrett. We are the men to help you find the best property to fit your purse."

"I've never felt better about our prospects. I was hesitant about coming up to Morristown, but I now realize how fortunate it was. And of course, I will always be indebted to you for your hospitality."

They rode on for some distance and then a substantial mansion at the end of a long drive came into view. It was surrounded by stables, farm sheds, open fields, pastures and groves of trees. "My, what a beautiful place," remarked Catherine. And such a lovely setting." She pointed to a sign at drive which proclaimed, *Barrister's Rest*. "My, what an intriguing name."

The two men exchanged smiles, then Clive said, "I will accept your compliment, for both the manor and the name, Catherine."

Barrett laughed, "That's Clive's plantation, Mrs. Tresh. And I can assure you it is quite spacious and well-appointed inside."

Harfeld said, "That's our destination, Catherine. I thought we might take luncheon there before journeying back to the house in town."

"What a lovely idea, Clive! I shall so enjoy it."

The carriage driver turned the vehicle into the drive and in a few minutes they were entering the manor house. Once in the hall, an African butler took their outer clothing, and Catherine and Barrett were seated in the parlor while Clive went to see about arrangements for the meal.

He was back in a few minutes. "Well, our arrival was a bit of a surprise, but I think the staff will be able to put together an acceptable repast." Harfeld walked over to a cabinet near the hearth. "While we wait, should we have a bit of brandy to finish off the last of the chill from the ride?"

After a tasteful and convivial lunch they retreated to Harfeld's cozy study. One of the servants had lit a fire and the room was bright and warm. Barrett helped Catherine into a wingback chair and took a seat in another. Clive provided more libation. Then, when all had a drink in hand, Harfeld looked at Catherine. "My dear, I think you've gotten a good impression of the type of land available in this area and understand how suitable it is for the estate which you have in mind."

Catherine smiled. "I think that goes without saying. But I fear prices for such provident land may be beyond our resources. Realistically, I imagine we shall have to look further toward the west for something that we might afford."

Harfeld and Northcutt exchanged glances. Then Clive said, "Catherine, what would you say if we could present you with an arrangement that would put you in possession of substantial acreage—say 250 acres—in this vicinity at extremely favorable price? At a price which would be well within your resources."

Catherine stiffened in her chair and her face took on a sharp look. "Obviously, I should be extremely interested. But I'm at a loss at why you should make such an offer." She looked between the two men, who were gazing at her with clear interest in their eyes. "Why would that be to your benefit?"

Harfeld took a sip of his brandy. Then he rose and took a pair of cigars out of a box on his desk, handed one to Northcutt, then went to the fireplace and lit his tobacco with a taper and did the same for Barrett.

Catherine sat staring at both of them, a puzzled look on her face.

Finally, Northcutt said, "My dear Catherine, I believe it's time for us to be completely honest with you about our situation and yours."

Harfeld nodded. "Quite right, Barrett." Then still standing before the hearth, he said, "Catherine, let me fully introduce you to Barrett. His full title is *Colonel* Northcutt and his regiment is the King's Loyal Virginia Legion."

Catherine's face tightened as she looked at Northcutt and her hands gripped the arms of the chair. Then she said in a quiet tone, "I would be a fool not to understand that is a Loyalist regiment."

"Quite correct," replied Clive. Colonel Northcutt is seconded from his regiment to the staff of General Howe himself."

Catherine's head snapped back to Harfeld. "And clearly that makes you also a loyalist." She raised her eyebrows. "And in fact I should presume you are actually a spy. It fits with you traveling around the countryside so frequently." Then she had a further thought. "You've been pumping me for information about Washington's army."

Harfeld spread his hands. "I must plead guilty, Catherine. And I apologize for the months of deception."

"And obviously," she continued, "You want me to do something for you—in exchange for a land deal. You want me to betray the cause my husband has taken up."

Harfeld made a tight smile. "Catherine, in our conversations, it has become quite clear that you understand full well that this so-called Patriot Revolution is in its last weeks, perhaps last days. Washington's army is in dire straits."

She raised her hands in supplication. "Indeed that's true. But if that's the case, why do you need me to do something for the British? I don't understand."

Harfeld went over to the desk and sat down. "That's a very perceptive question, Catherine. So let me explain." He took a pull on his cigar and said, "Frankly, Howe and his senior generals are of the opinion that the war is over. They think they can simply let the Patriot army to its own devices and it will soon disperse." He turned to Northcutt. "Do you agree with me on their belief?"

"Completely, Clive. Catherine, I've been party to discussions by the generals of the army. They were pressing the Americans hard. But in view of the condition of the Rebel army and the support they are losing in New Jersey, Howe has directed that Cornwallis, who is leading the pursuit, to ease up, rest his troops and take time to let his supply trains catch up." He paused, then said, "But Clive and I, and frankly some other officers, are not sure that is correct. We know the Americans and we know Washington. We believe they are likely to turn and make at least one more serious fight. Or find some other way to continue the struggle, such as withdrawing to a safe local and recruiting a new army." He paused to let that sink in. "In any case, that could be costly to the British cause and perhaps cause the war to go on longer than necessary."

Then Catherine surprised them. She raised her finger and said, "I will concede you that point, gentlemen. My husband is of the same opinion; that Washington may persist in the fight and actually try to find a way to strike back at Howe."

"Ah, Catherine, you have already helped us by confirming that sentiment of ours."

"But Clive, that brings us back to my original question. What do you want of me? I assume you want me to become some sort of spy."

Barrett said, "We want to expedite your return to the army. As the wife of a senior officer, you will have access to whatever Washington is planning. If we could get advance warning of his intentions, the army could be prepared and take action to prevent his success. It could shorten or precipitously end the war."

Clive added, "And there is a personal factor in this: If we supply vital information to Howe, information which hastens the Rebel capitulation and saves the crown time and fortune, there certainly will be some valuable rewards for our efforts. To wit, property and land confiscated from the traitors. Both we and you, my dear, could benefit."

Catherine sat staring into the fire for a long time. The silence in the room hung heavily over all of them. Then she turned back to the two waiting men. "Gentleman, I did not come to the status of a middling woman by the gift of birth. Before I attained that status by marrying Alexander, I had to live by my own efforts." She raised her eyebrows and looked each of them in the eye. "So you can understand that I have had to make certain compromises along the way." She took a deep breath. "Which means that I know how and when to do what is necessary to improve my situation, however distasteful some might consider my actions. So now suffice it to say I see your proposition as my best course forward."

A smile spread over Harfeld's face. "So you'll cooperate with us?"

"Wholeheartedly from this moment forward." She raised a finger. "So, when I'm back with the army, how would I get word to you?"

Clive said, "We have many watchers and agents, traveling men in our web. Usually peddlers or of some other like trade. We will give you a set of secret words by which they will identify themselves. And a code with which to write secret messages."

"You obviously are well organized."

Northcutt laughed and said, "We've been at this for months now. We have a highly effective system. And now, my dear Mrs. Tresh, you are part of it. A very welcome part of it."

Catherine's face took on a serious expression. Then she leaned forward and said, "However, gentlemen, there is one more question which must be resolved."

Northcutt frowned. "And what might that be, my dear lady?"

"I need some assurance beside your word about my reward for helping the crown. I need something written, pledging that I will in fact receive the land you gentlemen have so enthusiastically promised me. Let's be frank: The end of a war can be quite messy. And promises can be forgotten or ignored in the ensuing confusion. Surely my cooperation is worth a formal land contract?"

Harfeld grinned broadly. "You are, indeed, Catherine, a woman of the world. Before you leave I will draw up what you require and you shall have the signed original."

"Excellent, Clive."

Harfeld held up a finger. "But, in return, I will also have you sign a copy of General Howe's proclamation of loyalty to the crown, which people all over New Jersey and New York are signing. That will be my guarantee that you have truly joined our cause."

Catherine made a crooked smile. "When I have that contract in hand, I will have no objection whatsoever."

Northcutt picked up the Brandy decanter and refilled all three of their cups. "Let us toast our newly minted partnership and it's successful outcome."

—∞—

Wend walked into the large building in Princeton which normally housed the College of New Jersey. It was devoid of students and professors, who had all fled in the face of the expected arrival of the British, and it had become the staff headquarters when Washington's army entered the town. He immediately encountered an aide seated at a table in the hall, who looked up and said, "General Mercer is expecting you, Captain." He pointed down the hall. "Second door on the right."

Wend tapped on the door and then tentatively opened it. Mercer, seated at a desk, looked up and waved him in. "Well, you didn't waste any time getting here, Eckert."

"We had just arrived and the company was going into camp when I got your message. I came as soon as I got the word, sir."

"Yes, before we say anything else, I wanted to tell you that Washington is quite satisfied with your stand at the Raritan. He believes no one could have done more."

"Well, the real work was done by Hamilton's guns. He severely discouraged the British and forced their battery to withdraw."

"Yes, that lad does have a way with artillery." Then without any further preliminaries, Mercer said, "Did you get Fairfield's message from the courier who just came in?"

"Indeed, sir. He said he had ridden right from you to me. I must say, rather startling news. Cornwallis has occupied New Brunswick but seems to have, at least for the present, suspended the pursuit."

"Yes. Washington and Grayson and I put our heads together trying to figure out why they've stopped. It seems most likely that they are waiting for their supply train to catch up and re-provision their column. And perhaps regroup their force and send out parties to secure control of the populace in the area of Jersey that they have occupied."

"I wonder," replied Wend, "How long they'll stay there."

"We have no idea; we'll just have to depend on Fairfield to keep us advised." He paused a moment, then said, "In any case, it gives us the opportunity for most of the army to stay here for a couple of days to rest and recover. Then we'll proceed to the Delaware."

"My men have been marching hard and could certainly use some time in bivouac."

Mercer laughed. "I'm sure they could. But I'm going to disappoint you on that point. While the rest of the column rests, you are to get down to the Delaware posthaste."

Wend looked up at the ceiling and sighed. "I should have guessed."

Mercer smiled but didn't comment. Instead he continued, "We're sending you, Hamilton, and Glover's battalion down to the ferries around Trenton to prepare for the crossing." He motioned Wend to join him at a table where a map had been laid out. He moved his hand along the Delaware. "That lieutenant of yours, O'beirne, personally knows where all the boats are. You and Glover are to work together to move them to the crossing points as soon as possible. Then we'll march the army down and get across." He hesitated a moment. "You need to work fast, because Cornwallis could take up the pursuit at any time and we would have to get the army down there at forced march if that happens."

"Right, sir. I understand."

"Now, Eckert, we expect the main column of troops to cross right at Trenton. So Glover will concentrate most of his seamen there along with the appropriate number of boats. And Hamilton is to emplace his guns at the edge of the town so he can take the British under fire if they are in close pursuit by the time we're crossing."

Wend nodded his understanding.

Mercer put his finger on a point upstream of Trenton. "That's Coryell's Ferry, four miles north of the town. To expedite the speed of crossing, we'll send our supply train, with all the wagons and carts, to cross there. You and a detachment of Glover's men will collect enough boats and particularly flatbed rafts able to transport the vehicles across without delay."

"Aye, sir. That should be straightforward."

"Precisely, Eckert." Then he looked up at Wend. "I know your men are tired, and as you said, could use some time in camp. But I must insist you leave at first light tomorrow."

"We'll be ready." Then a thought hit Wend. "Sir, if I may be so bold, have we heard any more from Lee's column? Are they due to soon join us?"

Wend saw the general's face tighten. "You may. And the answer is that Lee has crossed into Jersey, but remains in the north, doing nothing but sending us written arguments about why he should stay there." He looked at Wend with real anger in his eyes. "We are in dire straits with regard to the size of our column, barely above two thousand, and the man refuses to reinforce us. Washington has just dispatched a message with the sternest language I have seen yet summoning Lee to join with us. If he does not march immediately upon receipt of that letter, there will have to be a reckoning. A reckoning Washington would not like to face, but that he may not be able to avoid." He reflected for a second. "But Eckert, that's not your worry. Your job is to get down to Trenton and prepare for us to cross the river. So I'll not delay you any longer."

"Yes, sir. We'll be ready to march at dawn."

The long column marched southwestward along the King's Way under a driving rain. Wend and Reese Newkirk rode side by side at the head of the column, followed by Donegal on foot. Behind them was an extensive cavalcade: In the lead the musket half-company led by Ensign Childers and Sergeant Flannagan. Next were Hamilton and his New York Artillery, now reduced to four guns, the horses working hard to pull the heavy weapons through the ruts and deepening mud. After them was a cluster of all the women and children from both companies. Then came the wagons—one driven by Billy Wood carrying the officer's baggage, messing gear, and provisions. Other wagons carried the company's tents and camp equipment. Behind them were the wagons transporting the precious whiskey, Bringing up the rear were the riflemen of the other half company, with O'beirne and Sergeant Wilder at their head.

They were climbing a rise when a lone horseman, on a tall hunter, appeared at the crest. He was dressed in a hunting shirt and leggings and carried a rifle slung over his shoulder. A wide brimmed floppy hat protected his narrow, stubbly bearded face from the rain. Suddenly he waved rapidly to get the attention of the column and pointed down the far side of the hill, then waved again in a manner summoning watchers to join him.

Wend turned to Newkirk and remarked, "Joshua is having a grand time playing scout just like the old days of the French War. And he's loving getting away from the women of Eckert Ridge for so long a time."

Reese smiled. "Aye, he does seem to be enjoying being with the army." He pointed toward Baird. "Looks like he's *really* excited about something further down the road."

"Yes, it seems so. I'd better ride up and see what it's all about. You take the column, Reese."

Wend touched his heels to Sonny and the young stallion responded immediately. In a minute he had joined his old friend at the ridgetop. "All right, Joshua, what's got you so worked up?"

A grin spread across Baird's face. "Sure and I'll tell what's up. Damned if we ain't got the answer right here in front of us to something we been puzzling over mightily."

"Joshua, for God's sake, stop talking in riddles. What are you trying to say?"

Baird pointed down the far side of the hill. Wend looked and saw in the distance a group of wagons stopped on the road. Then he looked harder. "Damn! It's Colleen!"

"Aye, the very same and she's in a peck of trouble. Two of her wagons are off the road and layin' on their side."

Wend pulled out his glass, snapped it open, and put it to his eye. After looking for a few moments, he lowered it and said, "*Trouble* is right. The road has been cut into a hillside and apparently these rains made it so muddy one side gave way under the weight. The two wagon rolled down and over. The bows have been broken or stripped away, the canvas tops are off the Conestogas, and the contents strewn all about."

"Yep, Wend, it's a big problem for them. But it's also trouble for us. Our wagons got to get past that spot. We're gonna have to fix it or cut a way around it."

"Damn, it, you're right. And it's going to be even more of a problem for Hamilton's heavy cannons." He shut the glass and said, "Let's ride down there and figure out what has to be done."

The two rode toward the wreck at the gallop. As they got close, Wend saw that two of Colleen's smaller wagons, the ones that carried the women, had made it past the muddy point. Stopped on the road before the cave-in were the other two Conestogas and Horner's cart. Wend saw the women of the company working as they pulled out any cargo remaining in the two wagons in order to lighten them. To his surprise, other than Horner, who was down by the fallen wagons with the women, he saw no other men. He thought, *That's curious: Colleen has at least four waggoners and a couple of other men in her company.*

Then, as they reached the site of the wreck and passed the two wagons still on the road, he caught sight of Colleen. Wearing a heavy coat, she was standing by one of the overturned wagons, directing her girls as they collected the spilled items. As he pulled up his horse, she looked up and saw him sitting there.

Her face lit up. "Wend! Wend!!! I don't know how you happen to be here, but you are a sight for sore eyes." Then a inquisitive look came over her face. "But where is your company?"

Wend looked back up the road to the ridge-line, where the head of the column was now visible, and pointed. "Here they come. They'll be here in a few moments."

"That's wonderful! We'll need the help of some strong men to get these wagons back upright."

Wend waved his hand over the whole area. "Where are all your men? I know you have several with your company."

She looked at the heavens, then replied, "When the damned wagons went down the hill, all the hitch pins broke and one of the teams got spooked and ran off. The men are out trying to find them."

Wend had a thought and asked, "We haven't seen you since Peekskill. Where have you been? And where are you going?"

"After we crossed the Hudson, we went north for a while to be safe from the British and camped out until we found out where the army was headed. Then we got word it was going to cross the Delaware down near Trenton. So we went westward through Morristown and Basking Ridge and then south to find a ferry. I'm planning to be waiting and ready for business when the soldiers arrive on the other side." She looked back at the overturned wagons. "But we need to get these wagons back on the road if we are to get to the river." She beseechingly looked up at him. "That's why I need your help."

Suddenly Joshua spoke up. "Hell, Colleen, it's gonna take more than just righting those wagons. One of them has a broken wheel. It's off the hub and some spokes is broken clean through."

"We got a couple of spares. But we need to get it upright and on a jack before we can fix it."

At that moment, an idea came over Wend and it was all he could do not to laugh out loud. He looked up to see the company had arrived and Newkirk had halted them.

Colleen looked over at the soldiers, relief spreading over her face. "I've never been so happy to see soldiers. For God's sake, Wend, give the order for them to come down and get the wagons back on their wheels. It won't take long. And I can see that you've got several teams. We can use them to tow the wagons back up onto the road."

Wend grinned at Colleen. "Well, I'll be glad to help. But of course, there will be a price for doing it."

Colleen glared up at him. "A price? What the Devil do you mean?"

"I'm just playing by your rules, Colleen. How many times have I heard you say *everything* has its price."

She balled her fists and put them on her hips. "All right, I'll play your game. What is your damned price?"

"Emily Crider. Before we do anything, she gathers up her clothes and other belonging and joins Horner in his cart—permanently. She's released from her servitude to you."

Astonishment, followed by outrage burst out all over Colleen's face, which turned bright red. She screamed, "Damn you to Hell, Wend Eckert! We had a deal. A *firm* deal. A wagonload of whiskey for the girl. And I'll damn well make you stick to that!"

Keeping his voice very calm and smooth, Wend smiled and replied, "Now my dear Colleen, conditions have changed. That whiskey deal is off. You have immediate need of services only I and my men can provide." He waved his hand taking in the wrecked wagons. "Unless you have some other way of getting them fixed and on the road." He turned and pointed to the collapsed roadway. "And you also need us to fix that road enough for the rest of your wagons to get through." He shrugged. "Frankly, my dear Colleen, I don't think you have any choice. We're under orders to get to the river ferries posthaste. I'll be delaying on my own authority if I do linger and help you. So, if you decide you don't want our assistance, we'll be on our way and none of my men will raise a hand to help."

Colleen bared her teeth. "You contemptible *Bastard!!!*"

"Now Colleen, you can fume and curse all you want, but the fact is if you want me to help you out of this fix, you must give up the girl right now."

All the women had gathered together a short distance from their mistress. Emily stood in front, her face aglow with hopeful anticipation. Horner had come up to stand by Wend, his face also excited.

Wend pushed the issue. "Well, Colleen, what's it going to be?"

She stood there staring at him for a long time, hot fury in her eyes. Then she closed her eyelids and sighed deeply and the stiffness went out of her body. Without looking at the young girl she called, "Emily, get your things. You are no longer part of the Red Vixen Sutler Company. And if I never lay eyes on you again it will be too soon."

Emily let out a great sob of joy. She ran to Horner and, throwing her arms around him, the two held a long embrace. After allowing them a few moments, Wend said, "There's time enough for that later, Horner. Hurry and help her get her stuff."

Wend watched as the two young people hurried off to collect Emily's things. Colleen was still standing, hands on hips, chin thrust out. At that moment Newkirk rode up with Hamilton at his side. He said, "We came to see what needs to be done. He looked over at the road. "Looks like the rain water flowed down the side of the hill onto the road and turned the dirt into slush."

Wend nodded. "Exactly right. I want you to put half the company at work cutting through the underbrush beside the firm side of the road, so we can get the wagons over on solid ground." He motioned down to the overturned wagons. "Send the rest of the company down to right those Conestogas. And see if we've got someone who can jack up a wagon and put a new wheel in place."

Newkirk looked at the wreckage. "We'll get them back up. And I believe Holt has been a wagoner in the past. I'll get him on that wheel."

Just then Wend heard Hamilton's voice. "Why, Mrs. McGraw! Good to see you again. I wish it were under better conditions."

Wend turned to see Colleen look up at the artillery captain and a smile come over her face. "And it's my pleasure, also. Are you traveling with Captain Eckert?"

"Yes, ma'am. We're headed for Trenton."

"Alexander, it's been since May since we met the last time. But we can talk after we get my wagons back up on the road." And with that Colleen walked back toward the wagons, shouting for the girls to get back to work.

Wend, a bit surprised, looked at Hamilton. "Alex, how do you happen to know Mrs. McGraw?"

"Oh, yes, we met at Fraunces Tavern in Manhattan last Spring. She was having supper there with Lieutenant Fairfield. I was with a couple of other officers and we barged into their private dining room." He laughed, "We all wanted to meet the notorious Mrs. McGraw. I must say, we were all taken with how handsome she was, not to mention her jolly personality."

Wend tried not to show his surprise. "Geoffrey Fairfield *knows* Colleen?"

Hamilton grinned. "I should say so, sir. They are known to dine together often." Then a furtive look came over his face and he leaned closer to Wend and said in a softer voice, "Confidentially, there is a rumor going around on Washington's staff that they were seen leaving the Britannic Crown Inn together *very early* one morning."

"Indeed, sir. How *interesting*." Wend smiled to himself and thought, *So, Geoffrey and Colleen are an item. He never would have guessed, but thinking it over, he could see the affinity which might develop between the two.* Then it immediately occurred to him that it might well be a useful bit of information in the future.

Then he turned his mind back to the business at hand.. "Alex, we're going to need several horse teams to get those Conestogas back up on the road. And they must be powerful, well trained teams. Your limber horses fill the bill. I would ask that you allow them to be used for the purpose." He waved at the road and all the wagons backed up because of the cave in. "And we must clear all of this if we are to proceed."

"Of course, sir. They'll be at your service." Hamilton waved back toward his guns and men. "I'll get right to it. We'll be prepared by the time you have the wagons ready to be moved."

Wend looked over at Baird, who still sat his horse next to him. "Joshua, it's already late in the afternoon. It's going to be coming onto nightfall by the time we get this all done. I suggest you scout ahead and find a nearby meadow or field big enough to take our column plus Colleen's company for the night."

"That would be my pleasure!" He sighed in relief. "For a moment, I worried you were going to ask *me* to go down there and help gather up all that women's stuff." He grinned again, pulled Beau around and was off at the trot down the wagon track.

Wend sat in front of his fire, reflecting on the long day and how tired he felt. Baird had found a suitable bivouac, consisting of a meadow with scattered trees, only a mile beyond where the wreck had been. It had taken until dusk to fix the wagons and get them back up onto the road. About halfway through the process, Colleen's men had returned with the six horse team that had stampeded. Working with axes and shovels, Wend's and Hamilton's men had cut a widened road through the bush so that all the wagons and guns could pass. Now all were sharing the same encampment.

Wend's eyelids were heavy when he unexpectedly saw Colleen McGraw walking toward him. He thought, *Damn, I can't handle any more of her anger, at least at this moment.* So he felt some trepidation when she walked right up to his fire. She stood there for a moment looking at him.

Wend, taking the initiative, said, "Has that Irish anger of yours cooled down yet?"

She made a thin smile. "It's only *half* Irish. My father was Irish but mother was Ulster." She sighed. "And yes, I've had time to cool down. I admit you got the best of it and that I would have done the same thing. In any case, I'm here on a practical matter."

Wend warily cocked his head. "What might that be?"

She pointed to another chair. "May I sit down?"

Wend rose and helped her into the seat. "All right, Colleen; what's on your mind?"

"*Whiskey*. The matter of a wagonload. I still need it—once the army gets into camp across the river, the men are going to want it and will be willing to spend whatever money they have on it."

"They don't have much, most men probably have none. Pay for the whole army is in arrears."

Colleen put her head back and laughed. "You'd be surprised how much money suddenly appears when it's a matter of liquor or sex. Certainly in the purses of the officers. I assure you there will be a market for it."

"So you want to buy the amount we talked about?"

"That's right. You've got at least three of those farm wagons full of kegs. I walked by them myself. I want one of them."

"I was planning to sell all them to the army quartermaster. They need spirits for the daily ration."

"Wend, for God's sake, all you'll get is a written promise from him. And the way things are going, you 'll likely never see real payment." She raised an eyebrow and smiled. "I've got hard coin. It shouldn't be a difficult choice."

Colleen reached into a pocket of her coat and pulled out a bag and handed it to Wend. "That's what I'll pay for one of those wagons. Hard money and you know damn well you won't get a better offer."

Wend opened the bag and dumped the coins into his hand. He quickly counted it then looked at Colleen. "All right, it's a deal. You can take your wagon when we leave tomorrow."

"No, as part of the deal, I want you to continue to have it driven as part of your company until it's across the Delaware. That way it will be an official army wagon. Whoever is controlling the crossing may not be hospitable to me. I fear I may have to search for another place to cross and I don't want the extra encumbrance."

Wend nodded. "I understand. It's a deal—all the whiskey will cross with my company. You can take custody on the far side whatever happens."

"Thank you, Wend." Then she gave him a coy look. "I wouldn't be surprised if you had some of your whiskey close at hand."

"Are you asking for a drink?"

"It would be nice. Sharing a bit of libation to celebrate that we are at peace again. And of course, even someone who's just half Irish is still fond of the spirits."

Wend got her a cup of whiskey and one for himself. They had just taken their first sip when Wend thought he heard the faint sound a horse's hooves pounding at the gallop. He stiffened, then leaned forward in his chair, cupping a hand to his ears. "Someone is pushing a horse really hard, coming down the road from the North."

Wend stood up and strode over to where he had a view of the wagon track. He didn't have long to wait. Momentarily a horseman came into sight, a shadowy figure in the night. Having seen the camp, the rider pulled up, then turned his horse into the bivouac area. Realizing it must be a dispatch rider, Wend waved vigorously and called out "Over here!"

The horsemen came toward him and it was clear that he wore the uniform of a dragoon. Wend looked at Colleen. "That's one of the Palmetto Light Horse. Then he recognized the man; it was Trumpeter Bloom.

Bloom pulled up before Wend and flung down from his heavily breathing animal. "Sir, I have a message from General Mercer!" He handed a leather dispatch case to Wend.

Meanwhile, Reese Newkirk, having seen the courier, had joined them. "What's toward, sir?"

Wend looked at Bloom. "Do you know what's in here?"

"Not exactly, sir. But I do know what it's about: the British are heading this way. They stayed a few days in Brunswick, not advancing at all. But now there's a flying column on the way. Jaegers, dragoons, and Highlanders. Coming fast, from what I heard."

Wend had opened the case and was reading the dispatch. "Bloom's right. Mercer says a British detachment is on a forced march toward the Delaware, probably aiming to try to impede the crossing. He says our army has left Princeton and is marching as fast as possible for Trenton and the supply train, under a Quartermaster Colonel Longwood, is headed for Coryell's Ferry as fast as they're able." Wend read further. "He says we're to get there as soon as possible and make sure enough boats are ready to ferry the train across." He looked over at Newkirk. "I wonder where Glover's men are? They left Princeton after we did."

Bloom interjected, "I can answer that, sir. They are encamped about an hour up the road. I stopped to give the news to Glover. He said they'd break camp before dawn and head for Trenton and send a detachment to Coryell's."

Wend turned to Newkirk. "Get the word out. We'll also leave before dawn. Ensure the men get to sleep *now.* Tomorrow will be a hard day." He looked up at

Bloom. Same for you, Trumpeter. I'll be sending you back to Mercer in the morning with a dispatch telling him when I expect to get to the ferry."

Newkirk and Bloom hurried off and Wend turned to Colleen, who had heard everything. He asked, "What are your plans?"

Colleen drained her cup and stood up. "Same as yours. I intend to stick with you like a fly on sugar. My wagons will be ready to roll when you leave."

Without another word she strode off rapidly toward her company's campsite.

—∞—

The Frederick County Light Foot, accompanied by The Red Vixen Sutler Company, arrived at Coryell's Ferry in mid-afternoon. Hamilton's New York Artillery Company had left them at the fork in the road which led to Trenton. The ferry landing on the Jersey side was nearly rural—just a couple of houses and a farmstead in the distance. Wend could see that there was a more substantial village on the Pennsylvania side. The ferry itself was not large, able to carry one Conestoga sized wagon and its team at once.

Wend had been told that a company of Glover's Marblehead Regiment would arrive to assist with crossing the supply wagons. So Wend was surprised when a larger force, at least two companies, arrived at dusk. Even more surprising was that Colonel Glover himself was riding with the column.

Glover was a lean bodied man, who was dressed in civilian coat and jacket in lieu of an officer's uniform. He dismounted and walked over to where Wend was warming his hands over a newly built fire. "I take it you are Eckert. Never met you, but Mercer gave me a description."

"Indeed I am, sir." Wend shook hands with the Massachusetts colonel. "I know you by your reputation and the work your men have done."

"Yes, and clearly we're about to become sailors again. Now, I understand you have an officer here who knows where all the boats are along the river."

"That would be Lieutenant O'beirne. Actually, my Ensign, named Childers, also has been involved in locating the boats."

"That's good, because we've got to get cracking on rounding them up and getting them to Trenton and here. I've brought two companies here to Coryell's Ferry. One, under Captain Elias Richards, will stay here to build rafts and control the boats for the crossing at this point. The other will get the boats and move them to here and Trenton to transport the troops across." He looked out at the river, then remarked, "I expected to have more time, but as I assume you are aware, the British are coming fast."

Wend said, "Indeed, sir." Then he summoned his officers and introduced O'beirne and Childers. Glover asked Shay, "Where is the biggest concentration of boats? Boats large enough for our work."

Shay motioned northward. "You want what they call *Durham Boats*. They're made for hauling ingots from a couple of iron works up the river from the next ferry, McConkey's. There are many of them there. A road runs right along the river which will take us there."

Glover thought a moment, then said, "We don't have any time to waste. Do you know that road well enough to get us there by night march?"

The Irishman grinned broadly. "Both Childers and I have ridden it many times. I'll get you there in daylight or dark of night, rain or shine, my good Colonel."

"Then we'll get started right away." He turned to Richards. "You and your company stay here and start construction of the rafts. We'll need several to get all the conveyances over before the British arrive. We'll drop some boats off here tomorrow."

Having gotten mounted, O'beirne and Childers led Glover and one company northward. Meanwhile, Richards and his company got busy. Wend asked him where he would get the materials for the rafts. The Marblehead captain pointed to a grove of trees just south of the road that lead up to the ferry landing. "There's our rafts, we just have to cut them down." He looked at Wend. "I assume, coming from the backcountry of Virginia, you have men who are handy with an ax?" He pointed to a wagon which had accompanied them. "There are axes in there, along with rope and spikes to hold the logs together. With two companies of men, we should be able to fell enough trees for three rafts capable of accommodating large wagons."

Wend looked at the grove and said, "We have our own axes, and I can assure you that you'll get all the help you need from us."

Richards pointed to an area next to the landing. "We'll assemble them over there, on the bank, where it will be easy to get them into the river."

"Well, you're the sailor, Elias, so we'll take direction from you."

Richards grinned. "Actually, I'm a shipwright. I build fishing boats for a living, which is appropriate for the work ahead of us. But then, of course, I've also done a fair share of time at sea."

Wend looked at the sky. The sun was setting, it's waning light reflected in the waters of the Delaware. "It's too late to get started on those trees tonight, but I propose we begin at first light tomorrow."

"Indeed, sir." responded Richards. "But I'll go over and mark the most suitable trees while there's still light, and tonight we'll get our tools ready to save time in the morning."

—∞—

The construction of rafts was well underway by mid-morning on the day after their arrival at Coryell's. Crews of men from both companies were busy chopping down trees and trimming off the branches. Another crew, with a team of horses, worked to drag the logs to the river bank.

Meanwhile, Colleen had started getting her company ferried across the river. By noon, two of the big Conestogas had been transported to the Pennsylvania side and the waggoners were hitching up the team to the third, so as to be ready when the ferry returned.

Then things changed drastically.

Wend and Richards were standing together at the riverbank. They were discussing the need for men to shovel the grade of the embankment in order to facilitate launch of the rafts and later to serve as a ramp for wagons to be driven onboard. Then one of the Marblehead seaman standing nearby pointed to the ridge-line to the east and said, "Captain, we got company. Wagons coming down the road."

Wend looked to see a long train of wagons—Conestogas, smaller wagons, and carts—rolling down the hill toward the ferry. At the head of the column rode two mounted officers. As he watched, the officers spurred their mounts and headed to where he and Richards stood. Soon they were close enough to see one was a colonel and the other a captain.

The two pulled up a few feet away and Wend walked over. The colonel was a man who looked to be in his forties and seemed to be a dandy. He was dressed in a finely tailored uniform with considerable gold braid and wore a powdered wig under his cocked hat. Looking down at Wend he announced, "I am Colonel Hiram Longwood; Deputy Quartermaster of the army. To whom am I addressing myself?"

"I'm Captain Wend Eckert of the Frederick County Light Foot Company and this is Captain Elias Richards of the Marblehead Regiment."

"Ah, yes, *Eckert*. You are the man I was told would be here." He looked around, displeasure clearly registering in his eyes. "Now, Captain, I was told you would have boats and barges ready to transport my wagons and men." He glared down at Wend. "But I see nothing."

"Colonel, we got here last evening, as did Colonel Glover and his men. That should have been in plenty of time because we didn't expect you until tomorrow at the earliest. You must be aware that we have just learned that the British have taken up the pursuit again." Wend waved upriver. "In any case, Glover is off getting the boats. They should be here shortly." He motioned toward Richards and his men. "These men are building rafts, which obviously will take some time." He turned and pointed to the ferry, which was just arriving from the far bank. "As you can see, at present, the only way across the river is the ferry, which can handle one Conestoga and its six horse team at a time or two small wagons. You can start ferrying yours over, but obviously it will be a slow process."

Longwood stood up in his stirrups and looked around. Displeasure spread across his face. "Indeed, sir, we shall get started *immediately*." He pointed toward Colleen's wagon that was now hitched and waiting for the ferry. "Whose wagons are those?"

"Those are Mrs. McGraw's—she runs a sutler company."

Longwood narrowed his eyes and said dismissively, "Captain, I'm *well aware* of Mrs. McGraw and the—ahem—*services* she provides." He turned to his aide. "Captain Harlow, stop that wagon from boarding the ferry. Only official wagons will be transported until our entire train is across the river. We have precious little in provisions and supplies for the army after the disaster at Fort Lee and I'm taking no chance on losing anything to the hands of the enemy. Mrs. McGraw will have to wait. One of our wagons will straightaway board the ferry when it arrives." He looked over at Richards. "And you, sir. May I ask precisely when do you expect to have your rafts ready for service?"

Wend saw a flash of irritation sweep across Richard's face at the tone of

Longwood's voice. But he answered respectfully, "As you can see, we are just getting started. But we should have one or two ready by late afternoon. We plan on a total of three, which will allow a steady shuttle when complete."

"Well, sir, my order is for you to expedite construction to your best ability. Spare no effort or time."

Richards responded, "Colonel, I should have done that in any case."

The aide, Harlow, having stopped Colleen's Conestoga, rode past, waving to the first of the supply wagons to drive up to the landing. Then he came back and Longwood said to him, "Sir, find a suitable site for my tent. We shall obviously be spending the night here at the river."

Meanwhile, Richards spoke up. "Colonel, here comes Glover and the boats."

Wend turned around to look at the river and saw a flotilla of large boats being rowed down the river. Many of them were towing another boat. He said, "Well, Colonel, there's enough boats for both here and Trenton."

One of the leading boats headed for the embankment just beside the landing. It touched the shore and Glover himself jumped out. He climbed the bank and briskly walked to where they stood. Without ceremony or any enthusiasm in his voice, he said, "Hello, Longwood. I see you have arrived." He pointed to the boats and said to Richards, "We're going to drop some of the boats for you and take the rest down to Trenton, to use in ferrying the main column."

Wend said, "If I may ask, Colonel Glover, where are O'beirne and Childers?"

"While we were requisitioning these boats from the iron works, two row-galleys from the Pennsylvania navy came up river. O'beirne is showing them where other boats are along the shore so that they can be towed over to the western side and beached or destroyed to keep them out of the British hands. Your officers should return on horseback tonight or on the morrow."

Then a thought came to Wend. He turned to Longwood. "Sir, do you know where the main army troop column is?"

"Indeed, Captain. They were right behind us and took the road to Trenton. I should imagine they will be there this afternoon."

Wend asked, "If the column is nearing Trenton, is there some rearguard to hold the British in check? Or at least warn us of their approach?"

Longwood waved his hand dismissively. "Of *course,* sir. There's a battalion supported by militia. And of course, the Palmetto Light Horse is watching the enemy's advance. He looked at Glover and Richards. "The fact is, you gentlemen need to concentrate on speeding our crossing."

Glover said, "With the troops soon arriving at Trenton, I must get downriver to organize the crossing." He nodded to Longwood and then Wend, and headed back to his boat.

Wend looked back at the landing fifty yards away, where the first army wagon was boarding the ferry. He caught sight of Colleen, hands on hips, watching as the wagon rolled aboard, her own Conestoga now sidelined. Even at that distance Wend could see the anger on her face and was happy that, at least this time, it wasn't directed at him.

Chapter Seventeen

The Rearguard

It was near noon on the day after the supply train had arrived. Wend stood on the river embankment watching the Marblehead men as they carried out the laborious process of transporting the army's supply wagons over the Delaware. Each raft, with a wagon aboard, was towed across by a Durham boat, the oarsmen laboring hard to pull the awkward, low-riding log vessel against the current. Seamen aboard the rafts provided some modicum of steering with a long oar they called a *sweep*. Each raft was escorted on the upstream side by a second boat, using a line attached to the raft to help it stay perpendicular against the current.

The men of the two companies had labored overnight to finish the rafts. That effort had allowed ferrying of the wagons and carts to begin just after dawn. At first, things had gone slowly, but the pace had increased as the sailors perfected their procedures for handling the barges. Now, at any given time, one barge was loading, a second was on its way to the far bank, and a third was unloading or on its way back. Richards had also commandeered the ferry and placed a number of his own men onboard, so it worked faster than under the owner's crew. All the remaining vehicles were now organized into two lines, one for the raft shuttle, the other, smaller line for the ferry.

The Frederick County Light Foot's vehicles were at the end of the line for the ferry, Longwood having given them a priority lower than his own supply wagons. Colleen, angry and frustrated, sat beside a fire, waiting for the military vehicles to be ferried across.

Wend walked over and joined her. "Mrs. McGraw, I must say you look highly perplexed."

"Who the Devil wouldn't be?" She waved toward the far embankment. "Two of my Conestogas are on the far side, and the rest are stranded here. I have no idea when—or if—I'll get across. Or maybe I should just take that road along the river and head north. I understand there's another ferry a few miles north of here."

"It's no good, Colleen. That ferry's been shut down by the Pennsylvania Navy. It's at the west bank and won't run again any time soon. And the same for other ferries farther northward."

"What if I just go north to a safe campsite? At least I'll make sure I don't lose anything."

Wend shook his head. "That's possible, but you may spend weeks there. No telling when the ferries will start again."

She gritted her teeth. "Damn, damn, damn! If only that bastard Longwood had arrived a couple of hours later, I'd be across the river with all my wagons and people."

"Well," responded Wend, "it shouldn't be more than a few hours now, and I'll do everything I can to get you over rapidly once they're finished with the supply wagons. I'm sure Richards will help you."

Just then Colleen looked eastward and stood staring for a long moment. Then she pointed up the road. "Look, there's one of Fairfield's men, riding like the Devil is chasing him!"

Wend spun around to see the dragoon gallop up to Longwood's tent, where the colonel was sitting in a chair before a crackling fire, talking with his aide seated beside him. Wend watched as the dragoon threw down, then spoke something to the colonel. Instantly both men sprang to their feet. Longwood started pacing back and forth, and the aide ran toward the riverbank where Richards was standing.

Wend commented to Colleen, "Something's going on. Something that has agitated Longwood."

Colleen said, "It can't be anything good. And in case you haven't noticed, Captain Harlow is now coming over here at the run. We're going to find out what it's all about momentarily."

Harlow arrived, breathing heavily. "The Colonel wants to see you posthaste. There's a problem."

Wend said, "So what is it, Harlow?"

The aide looked at Wend and then glanced at Colleen, as if trying to decide how much to say. "It's the rearguard. They've been attacked and broken. We have to decide what to do. Now, please come with me to see the Colonel."

By the time they had arrived, Richards was also present. Longwood stood, hands on hips, his eyes riveted on the eastern ridge as if he was expecting British troops to appear momentarily. Then he faced the Marblehead captain. "Richards, how long do you estimate it will take to get all these wagons across?"

Richards scanned the lines of remaining vehicles. "Well, sir, including all Eckert's wagons and Mrs. McGraw's, three to four hours, if nothing happens to delay us."

"Forget McGraw's vehicles. It's the army wagons which are urgent."

He looked at Richards and Eckert, anxiety visible in his eyes. "Now, gentlemen, here's the situation as reported by the courier: the British column attacked our rearguard early in the morning. Jaegers and cavalry first, which our foot and militia rebuffed. But then the Highlanders mounted an assault and the militia panicked and ran off. The Continental battalion fired two volleys, but then, when the firing didn't slow the Highlanders, the men, without orders, started to fall back. Soon discipline failed and they started to run. It seems their enlistment is up next week, and nobody wanted to face bayonets so close to going home. So most of the men broke ranks and melted into the woods. The British cavalry and Highlanders pursued, and a goodly number were captured. Fairfield says all that is left between us and the enemy is his troop and a handful of the infantry. There's no way they can stop a British advance; the enemy could be here in two hours if they push it. However, when the courier left the hill where Fairfield was observing, the British had halted to rest and reform, organize the prisoners, and deal with their wounded."

Longwood turned to Richards. "Sir, you must do everything in your power to expedite the passage of our wagons. You *must* find some way to speed things up."

Richards looked over at the riverbank. "The truth is, we're moving as fast as we can." He shrugged. "We'll keep at it. But you might want to pick your most important wagons to get priority, so if the enemy approaches, we'll leave behind only the lowest priority."

A look of anger appeared on the colonel's face. "The priority is *all* of the wagons and I will accept nothing less." He turned to Wend. "Captain Eckert, we must buy more time. Here are your orders: Muster your company and march out to form a new defense line. You must endeavor to hold the enemy back to enable us to complete the crossing. You will join Mr. Fairfield at his position and delay the British at all costs."

Wend felt a lash of anger. "You want a hundred men to hold an isolated position against at least a full battalion of Highlanders? They're the hardest hitting troops in the British Army! And what will become of us even if we succeed? How will we—or at least our remnants assuming we can disengage without being captured—cross the river considering we will have cavalry and Jaegers on our heels?"

Longwood stared at Wend with a stone face. "Mr. Eckert, there is no alternative. We will wait as long as possible for you. But I will not sacrifice a single one of these wagons."

Wend stiffened at the colonel's words and his temper took over. He lashed out, "No, not a wagon, but you will sacrifice my company—the finest light foot in the army—and Fairfield's cavalry, which have been Washington's eyes since the beginning of this campaign." He pointed to the far side of the river. "I say, with the army as weak as it is, the preservation of a hundred twenty well-trained and disciplined light foot and cavalry is far more important than some quantity of supplies. Replacement provisions can be obtained in Pennsylvania, but not trained men."

A sneer came over Longwood's face. "Ah, yes, Mr. Eckert. Of course your men are irreplaceable—Washington's *Pets,* as they're called throughout the army. *Virginia* men supposedly so valuable they've received the cushiest assignments and have never been committed to real battle."

Wend shot back, "Most men would say the fight at New Brunswick was real battle."

A knowing look came over Longwood's face. "And I would say a battle performed mostly by Hamilton's guns."

Wend fought to control the rage which nearly overwhelmed him. He took a deep breath and then said, "Colonel, I would suggest another plan that might save both wagons and men. Instead of marching out a couple of miles to meet the enemy, we form a line on that ridge." He pointed to the heights to the east. "And wait until Fairfield falls back there ahead of the enemy advance. If the British see a line of troops, they'll have to pause to let their Jaegers feel out our strength and organize for an attack. It may buy just as much time as your proposal, and it would give time to get Fairfield's men and horses on the rafts to cross." Wend stared at Longwood. "And while the British were deciding what to do, we could disengage and have at least a chance of getting across if Richards could have his men waiting with boats."

Richards interjected, "Eckert's idea has a good chance of working, Colonel. Boarding men is far faster than loading horses and wagons. They could jump in the boats and we'd be away before the British could close in."

Longwood's face turned vividly red. "Now listen, I will not stand for this insubordinate behavior! Eckert, get your company formed and march to join Fairfield! Posthaste, do you understand?" Then he turned to Richards. "And you get back to the business of ferrying those wagons as fast as you can manage." He took a deep breath and glared at Wend. "You have your orders, sir! Now start moving."

Without saying another word, Wend headed for his company area where the officers and sergeants, seeing that something was happening, had gathered.

Newkirk waved toward Longwood's tent. "What's toward, sir? Everyone seemed agitated over there."

Wend quickly summarized the situation. "So, gentlemen, we're to attempt to stop the British column. Form the half companies with the men in light order for battle. No packs, only necessary accouterments." He turned to Donegal. "Get me Billy Wood and Horner and Baird. They'll stay here and organize the women and the camp to get everything across the river. Richards has promised me he'll do everything they can to get everything over."

Newkirk asked, "And what about us? Are we to be sacrificed?"

"I won't lie to you. Our chances aren't good, but Richards told me he will have his men ready with boats waiting for us until the last moment. He'll stay until he sees the British coming over the ridge." Wend looked at each of them in turn. "If he sees that, he'll know we aren't coming back."

They all departed to make preparations, and soon Billy, Horner, and Baird arrived. Wend explained the situation and said, "You and the women and Sergeant Flannagan's sons have got to get everything over the river."

Joshua held up a hand. "Whoa, Wend. I'm goin' with the company. Nobody's saying Joshua Baird shirked a fight. Besides, you can use another rifle."

Wend was about to argue, but then realized it would be futile. He paused and looked the two of them in the eye and said, "Now listen: If the worst happens to the company, I'm charging you with getting all the women and children back to Winchester."

The two men nodded. Then Wend reached into the pocket of his overcoat and pulled out the purse Colleen had given him for the whiskey. He handed it to Horner. "I'm also charging you with seeing that this gets to Peggy. She'll need it to see Eckert Ridge through the winter and pay Mrs. Morgan for the use of her wagons."

Billy said, "I'll get your horse ready for you, Mr. Wend."

Wend shook his head. "No, Billy. No horses for this fight. Get them over the river." Then Wend reached out and patted first Horner and then Billy on the arm. "Now get started. It must be done quickly, for we don't know how soon the enemy might be here."

The two men went off. Wend looked around and saw Colleen standing near her wagons, arms crossed, concern written all over her face. He walked over to join her.

"I heard! I heard what's happening! And what that bastard Longwood is doing to you. It's villainous, that's what it is! You haven't a chance back there!" She looked over at his camp. "All he's thinking about is not losing his damned wagons."

Wend said, "That's as it may be. But here's what you've got to do: Get everything ready to move. I talked to Richards before he went to his boats. He'll do everything he can to help you. But if he can't get you across, you'll have to go north like you talked about, real fast. It would be your only chance to stay out of British hands."

Colleen nodded her understanding. Then she sighed. "He's sacrificing you, heartlessly sacrificing you just so he can brag that he got everything over the river."

Wend smiled. "Be of good heart, Colleen. We aren't lost yet. And I have a few ideas which might help us." He pointed to the ridgeline. "Just keep your eyes on that crest to see us returning."

He started to leave, but she pulled him back and looked into his eyes for a prolonged moment. She put her hand to her lips and then tenderly touched it to his cheek. "God go with you, Wend Eckert." Then she quickly turned and strode back to her camp. There Edna joined her, and the two stood watching as Wend hurried to his own tent, got his sword and pistols. By the time he had done so, Donegal had formed the company. In a few moments, they formed into a column of threes and were marching along the road up the grade to the ridgeline. In five minutes, they were out of sight over the crest.

Edna turned to Colleen. "Well, I fear that's the last you will see of that company and Wend Eckert. I'll make sure we are ready to move, be it to those barges or up the River Road."

Colleen stood with her eyes closed for a long few seconds. Then she sighed and said very quietly, "Yes, yes, Edna. You just do that."

—∞—

Fairfield's dismounted troop was sheltering in the bush on the top of a low, tree-covered ridge, the horses secured behind the hill. With them were a cluster of about fifteen foot soldiers, clearly the remnants of the Continental battalion who had chosen to stay around when their comrades fled.

Wend stopped the company below the crest and went ahead to find Geoffrey seated on a log with his two sergeants and ensign. Fairfield had a lighted cigar in his hand, and the sergeants were puffing on pipes.

Fairfield exhaled a stream of smoke and then said without preamble, "We saw your column coming when you came over the last hill. What the hell are you doing here?"

Wend looked around. "Fairfield, we need to talk. In private."

Quinn laughed and commented to McCrae, "This can't be good news." The others laughed.

Fairfield rose to his feet and led the way about thirty feet distant. "All right, so what is this all about?"

"I'll tell you in a minute. First, what are the British up to?"

"They've been resting and recovering after destroying the Continentals." He pointed along the road to another hill a few hundred yards eastward. "They're just over the crest—there's smoke from campfires. I figure they were having tea or some such thing. But we've seen signs they are about to start advancing again." He pointed to the tree line on the far ridge. "There are Jaegers moving around in the bush. They could advance in a skirmish line at any time."

Wend took it in, then said, "All right. Here's the word: We—your troop and my company—have been ordered to make a stand. We're to delay the advance of the British column as long as possible so the last of the army's supply wagons can get across the Delaware. Colonel Longwood, the Deputy Quartermaster of the army, says we need to hold them as long as possible."

"With no more than 120 men? That's insane! There are two battalions of Highlanders over there. They'll cut us to mincemeat with their bayonets and broadswords and enjoy every minute of it!"

Wend smiled in irony. "Fairfield, for once you and I are in complete agreement."

"So what the hell are you doing here? Why didn't you just tell that ass Longwood to go to hell? To tell the truth, I would have shot the bloody fool, burned the wagons, and gotten all the troops across the river."

"A pleasant thought, Fairfield, but not practical."

"Well, fighting a thousand Highlanders is not practical."

"I have no thought of engaging the Highlanders. While marching up here, I've worked out a plan which has a chance—small but possible chance—of delaying the British column without us having to fight the Highlanders."

Fairfield threw up his hands. "And what is this grand plan of yours? I can hardly wait."

"Simply put, we make their advance—the light dragoons and Jaegers—think they are facing at least a battalion. If we can do that, they'll have to delay while they report to the column commander and he organizes for a full assault." Wend shrugged. "It will buy time, and we'll pull out before the Highlanders are ready to attack. Then we'll march rapidly back to the river, where Captain Richards of the Marblehead Regiment is waiting to transport us."

The lieutenant's face screwed up in skepticism. "So how precisely do you propose to achieve that happy outcome?"

"We're going to spread my company out along the ridge in what we call field squads of about ten men each. They'll be separated by gaps of maybe thirty or fifty feet, and hidden as much as possible in the trees and bush. My men have been trained to fight that way—far enough apart to extend the line, but close enough to support each other with their fire."

"But the cavalry and Jaegers will close in to feel you out. Sooner or later they'll discover it's not really a full battle line."

"We're not going to let them get close enough to do that. That's where your troop comes in."

"And just what does that mean?"

"It means that, moving under cover, you are going to get over into the bushes of that little hillock over there," he pointed toward a small, tree-covered hill, "We will slow the Jaegers with rifle and musket fire. Meanwhile, you'll be ready to make a surprise charge into the Jaegers on their right flank as they advance on our line. Once you attack, we'll also rise up out of our positions and charge down the hill at them. Their reaction will be to fall back upon the main column." Wend pointed toward the enemy position. "And then they'll have to take some time to make plans. That's when we surreptitiously pull out and head for the river. It will take a while for them to discover we've gone."

Fairfield looked perplexed. "Keeping the horses hidden as we move to that position will be difficult."

Wend shook his head. "No, it won't. You'll be going on foot, and your charge will be dismounted."

"What? What? Eckert, you have *really* gone crazy."

"It may be crazy, but it's the only plan I can think of which might get you back to that rich widow in Charleston and her rice plantation on the Ashley River."

"But on foot? For God's sake!"

"You are called *dragoons* for a reason, because you are supposed to be able to fight on horseback or on foot. You've got carbines and pistols." Then Wend pulled the real surprise. "In any case, we're going to send the horses back to the river before anything else happens."

"You're out of your damned mind, Eckert. Why would we do that?"

"Because it will take time to get them onto the barges and across the river. If we don't send them ahead, it may take too long to do that if the British are close behind. You might survive the fight but lose your mounts. And, Geoffrey, if we don't get out of here, at least the army will have the use of trained cavalry horses, which are desperately needed."

Fairfield said in a sarcastic tone, "I'm impressed with your thoughtfulness for the well-being of the army. Maybe they'll give your widow a medal in memory of your heroic actions."

Wend ignored his biting tone. "Regardless of how you feel, detail some men to lead the animals back to the river landing and get them started immediately." Wend turned to go. "I've got to go brief my officers and sergeants. I suggest you do the same."

"Yes, and when Quinn hears about this cockeyed plan, he's liable to come after you with his bloody saber."

Wend responded in a dry voice, "Fairfield, are you saying you can't control your men?"

Without waiting to see how Fairfield would react, Wend went back to his officers and sergeants. Then he led them to a place where they could look eastward to where the skirmish would take place while still shielded by the bush. Newkirk pointed to the tree line on the ridge to the east. "I make out Jaegers in the bush over there."

Wend nodded. "You're right. And Fairfield says there are also a troop of the 16th Light Dragoons and two battalions of Highlanders."

O'beirne interjected, "Highlanders? They'll bloody well run right over us."

"They would," replied Wend, "if they got a chance. But we're not going to let them. Now all of you be quiet and listen." Then he told them of the plan he had explained to Fairfield.

O'beirne remarked, "It's a classic hold and flank attack plan." He shrugged. "It just might work."

Donegal said, "Na, it's Bushy Run all over. It worked then against the savages, even when I 'na thought it had a chance."

Wend said, "It's a little of both. But in any case, it's all we've got. Donegal, go form the field squads and personally place them in the most advantageous positions, both in good cover and at what you judge as the most favorable distance between each other."

Joshua said, "I can't believe we're going to have to trust in that Fairfield and his pack of scoundrels. They'll just as likely to run away as charge."

Wend responded, "You're right, Joshua. So I'm sending along a little bit of insurance." He turned to Newkirk. "Send one of our field squads along to strengthen the flanking force. Pick the one with your best corporal in charge."

Newkirk grinned. "That would be Schreiber and his squad. He's as big as either Quinn or that other sergeant, McCrae."

Then Wend had an idea. "And Joshua, you go along too. I'll tell Fairfield you're going because you can pick out a path through the woods that will give them the least chance of being discovered. Between you and Schreiber being there, it ought to keep them to their business."

A half hour later, all the dispositions had been made. The cavalry horses were on their way back to the river; the line of squads had been formed; and Fairfield's troop, augmented by Baird and Schreiber's squad, had departed for their position on the flank. Wend, Newkirk, and Donegal lay under cover and looked eastward over the field, which was spotted with trees and patches of bush.

Suddenly, Donegal said, "I hear cavalry."

Wend looked up the road and soon saw a troop of light dragoons come into sight over the crest of the eastern hill. They were trotting in a column of twos, but once they arrived in the meadow, a trumpet sounded and they smoothly deployed into a single rank with wide intervals. An officer, pennant bearer, and trumpeter were out front. Wend looked over at Donegal. "Wait until they are in easy musket range, then give the order to fire. Have some of the riflemen ensure the officer goes down."

Donegal nodded and moved off. Wend watched the troop come on at the trot, spreading out more as they advanced. Newkirk said, "They're not sure where we are or at what strength. They're feeling us out."

"They'll know pretty soon."

At that moment, Wend heard Donegal shout the order to fire. It was followed by a ragged volley from the squads, with the sharp, high-pitched crack of rifles and the deeper sound of the muskets plainly evident.

Newkirk said, "They got that officer and the man with the pennant. The trumpeter turned and fled."

Wend replied, "As has the rest of the troop. Look at them go—they're heading for cover." He sighed, "Well, the ball has now formally begun."

Donegal came back, crouching as he moved to stay under cover. "Well, the lads did their job. That was a good volley."

Newkirk nodded. "Indeed it was." Then he stopped to stare. "I see some mounted officers at the top of the hill. Looks like Highland officers, from their clothing."

Wend pulled out his glass and opened it. He studied the officers for a while. Then he handed it to Donegal. "Tell me what you see, Simon."

Donegal looked through the glass. Then he lowered it and looked at Wend. "They're wearing coats with blue facings, and their plaid is the dark sett."

Wend said, "That's what I thought. The regiment we least wanted to see."

Newkirk said in a puzzled voice, "What does that mean?"

It was Donegal who responded. "That means it's the 42nd Foot. The Royal Highland Regiment. The Black Watch itself."

Wend looked at his first lieutenant. "Even more, it means Donegal and I are facing men we marched and fought with in Pontiac's War. We always worried it could happen. Now it has."

Donegal said, "Aye, that's the truth. But if your plan works right, praise the Lord we won't have to be shootin' at them today."

Wend looked at his friend and answered, "All we can hope is that the Jaegers advance as expected in skirmish formation and that Fairfield does his job."

An hour after the Frederick County Light Foot had marched off to meet the British column, Colleen stood on the riverbank, watching the progress of the ferrying operation. Then suddenly, she heard the sound of gunfire—distant, but clearly gunfire. One burst of firing, then it was silent again. She realized it was Wend and his men beginning the engagement with the British.

As she listened for more firing, she noticed that some soldiers were striking Colonel Longwood's tent, and his aide was leading their horses toward the ferry. Longwood himself walked over to where Richards stood. Colleen moved closer so she could hear the conversation.

Richards saluted and said, "Good afternoon, Colonel." He pointed toward the east. "It sounds like Eckert is engaged."

Longwood returned the salute and said, "Indeed, sir, it appears that is the case." He paused, and both men listened, but there was still no more gunfire. Then he turned back to Richards and said, "I just wanted to say you have done marvelous work here. It is clear that we have dodged the bullet, as it were, that the last of our wagons will be over soon, well ahead of the British arrival." He looked around. "That being the case, I have decided that it is time for me to cross the Delaware, to get the wagon caravan organized to rejoin the army. And of course, for me to personally report our success here to Washington. He will be very happy."

"I'm sure, sir."

"Indeed. And once you have transported the last of the wagons, you and your men can retire across the river yourself."

Richards stared at Longwood for a long few seconds, then said, "What about Mrs. McGraw's wagons?"

Longwood glanced at Colleen, then back at Richards. "I'll leave that to your discretion, Captain. If you feel that time permits, you may do so."

"And Colonel, what about Eckert and Fairfield and their men?"

Longwood stared into the distance for a moment, then said, "I fear it is most likely they will be lost." He shrugged. "Regrettable, but such things happen in war. And as with Mrs. McGraw's company, I leave that to your discretion. But heed me on this: You are not to put your company in danger waiting for them. You and your men are too valuable to the army." He looked over at the ferry. "Ah, yes, I see that my horse and baggage have been loaded. I must be off. Good fortune to you, sir."

Colleen watched as the colonel and his aide boarded the ferry, and the sailors immediately shoved off and began pulling for the far side. Then she walked over to Richards. "You *are* going to get us to the other side, aren't you?"

The captain stared at her for a moment, an inscrutable look on his countenance. Then a wry grin broke over his face. "Mrs. McGraw, one thing I know for sure: If I left you and your company here to fall into British hands, I'd never be able to show my face around the army again. Of course we're going to get you over!"

"Bless you, Mr. Richards. I assure you the Red Vixen Company will always have a place in its heart for you and your men."

Then suddenly there was the sound of many galloping horses. Both of them spun around to look up the road to the east. Richards exclaimed, "My God, cavalry! It must be British light dragoons!"

Colleen looked hard, then put her hand on Richard's arm. "Look again, Captain! Most of the saddles are empty. And see the uniforms of the riders? It's Fairfield's horses being led by a few men!"

"You're right, Mrs. McGraw." He shook his head. "I don't understand."

Then Colleen had it. "They've been sent back! Sent back to be transported across the river."

In a few moments, they arrived, and the men, with some difficulty, got the horses stopped. The animals, excited by the galloping, were snorting and pawing the ground. One of the dragoons threw down and strode over to Richards. He saluted and said, “Are you Captain Richards, sir?”

“Indeed I am.”

“Corporal Dowd, sir, of the Palmetto Light Horse. Captain Eckert sent us back. He said you are to get the horses across the river. They’ll all be a’comin’ back soon, but they might have the British right on their tails, if you take my meanin’, sir. And we don’t want to lose the horses.”

“Right, Corporal, I understand. We’ll load them right away.”

Colleen grinned. “I knew it! Leave it to Wend Eckert to think of something like that. His mind is always two steps ahead.”

Richards looked over at Colleen. “Mrs. McGraw, if I may be somewhat forward, it’s well known in the army that you are close friends with Lieutenant Fairfield. But it sounds like you also have some personal familiarity with Captain Eckert.”

Colleen smiled. “Mr. Richards, long before I ever met Fairfield, when I was a nineteen-year-old tavern girl, Wend Eckert and I were friends.” She gave him a meaningful look. “The *closest* of friends.”

Richards’ eyebrows shot up in surprise, and he was about to say something more when there was a burst of gunfire in the distance, followed by the sound of steady, continuous firing by many men.

Colleen looked over at the captain. “Well, that means the real fight has now well and truly begun.”

Staring into the distance with concern in his eyes, Richards simply nodded.

Part IV

Washington's Guides

Chapter Eighteen

Respite in Pennsylvania

General Hugh Mercer walked through the camp of the Continental Army, or more precisely, the portion of the army directly under the Commander in Chief, General George Washington. The crossing of the Delaware at Trenton had just been completed, and the troops and the other people of the army, weary after many days of retreat through cold, wet November and December weather, sat around campfires in a field on a hillside just west of the river. They were a bedraggled-looking lot, with a full uniform being a rarity. Many were dressed in ragged, filthy civilian clothing with a blanket over their shoulders for warmth. Mercer had no good muster, but the total of men in the camp could not be over 2400 men, with many not fit for active service. Now, with dusk coming on, the men, women, and children were cooking their meager rations for the evening meal. Mercer looked up to the crest of the hill, where a solitary tent had been erected. It was Washington's headquarters, and that was where the general was headed.

In a few minutes, Mercer walked past the headquarters sentry and pushed through the tent flap. The inside was crowded to capacity as Washington presided over a council of senior officers and aides. Colonel Grayson, the Adjutant General, was reading a report on the strength of various brigades. He finished up by saying, "The total number of men fit for duty is just over 1700, sir." Washington looked over and held up his hand to interrupt Grayson. He asked, "Hugh, what did you see in Trenton?"

Mercer responded, "I went down to the ferry landing and looked over the town with my glass. I can vouch that the British have arrived. There was at least a troop of dragoons and some light foot in the main street." He looked around the room and remarked, "We got the last of our men and artillery over the river just in time."

Grayson looked up from his reports. "But we haven't heard from Longwood at Coryell's Ferry. I worry what has happened to them."

Just at that moment, there was the sound of someone clearing his throat at the tent flap. Then a confident voice said, "Well, I am here now, and I can give you the happy assurance that all of our provisions and military supplies have been transported safely across the river. The wagons are on their way here now."

Mercer saw that Longwood, standing at the entrance, had a broad smile on his face and looked quite satisfied with himself.

Washington turned to the quartermaster. "That is indeed very good news, Colonel Longwood." Then a thoughtful look came over his face. "And when will Captain Eckert's company and the Palmetto Light Horse arrive? They were also to cross at Coryell's. We need their services to help find a proper, secure place for my headquarters and a favorable location to bivouac our troops."

Longwood's self-satisfied smile evaporated, and a look of anxiety came over his countenance. He cleared his throat again, then, not daring to look into Washington's eyes, said in a very soft voice, "Sir, I fear they are unlikely to be coming at all."

Washington stiffened, as did others in the room. It became deadly silent. Then he said in a severe voice, "Colonel, what *precisely* do you mean that they are *unlikely* to be coming?"

"Sir, with numerous wagons still on the Jersey side of the river, we were about to be attacked by a pursuing British column. The rearguard battalion had deserted in the face of an attack by Scottish Highlanders. I had no choice—no choice, sir—but to send Eckert and Fairfield to attempt to hold them off while I got my wagons over the river."

Mercer looked at Washington's face. He knew the many mannerisms of his old friend and saw that, under a face with tightened muscles, George was seething. He prayed the commander in chief would be able to contain himself, for although it was rare, he had seen Washington lose control and break out into a terrible fit of rage.

But it was one of the aides who spoke up. "My God, those two companies are our best-equipped and disciplined units! The very eyes of the army. With them lost, what shall we do?"

Washington, still controlling himself, said in a very stern voice, "Colonel Longwood, I wish that you had burned some of your wagons and saved those men, for we have so few with us who have their skills."

Longwood's face turned beet red, but he said nothing.

Washington added, "Sir, you said it is unlikely that those units survived. Did you not wait to see the outcome?"

Longwood, now visibly disturbed, bit his lip, then said, "I thought it my duty to cross over to the Pennsylvania side and organize my supply train."

Mercer thought, *Oh, shit! Now the old man is going to let loose and give Longwood a piece of his mind.*

But at that moment, there was the noise of a galloping horse approaching, followed by excited voices outside the tent. Then a young aide burst into the tent and said, "General Washington, there's a courier here from Congress!" He stood aside, and a dispatch rider entered.

The rider looked around until he saw Washington. Then he went to him and handed him a tubular dispatch case. "Sir, I've been instructed to pass this directly to you."

Washington took the case, extracted the rolled paper, and opened it up. All eyes were on him as he read the words. Then he looked up and around at all the gathered officers. "It's from the presiding officer of Congress, Mr. John Hancock. It says that the entire assembly has fled Philadelphia and is seeking safety in Baltimore." He read some more. "It also says that their last act before departing was to delegate all decision-making regarding the army and campaign to me."

Colonel Joseph Reed, one of Washington's longest-serving and most trusted aides, looked around at the other officers. He nervously wetted his lips and, with a tremor in his voice, said to Washington, "General, the loss of Eckert and Fairfield aggravates our already desperate situation. The adjutant general just said we have only 1,700 effective troops available here, and we all know that the majority of those are due to go home at the end of this month—less than three weeks from now. Over the retreat, we have lost much of our artillery and other equipment. The men are in rags."

Mercer intervened. "What are you trying to say, Reed? Speak directly."

The colonel took a deep breath, wetted his lips, and said, "Regrettably, I must suggest that perhaps this is the time to think about discussions with the British on some sort of terms—on a negotiated settlement, at least for this part of the army. It is well known that General Howe is empowered as a peace commissioner and would desire nothing more than to end this war with some sort of reconciliation. In Jersey and New York, he is offering clemency to anyone who signs a declaration of loyalty to the King. And if we went to him while we still have some military viability, I submit his terms would be more generous than if we were to be virtually destroyed on the battlefield or our army had disintegrated through desertion. I would also point out that if the British were able to get across the river in the next few days, we would be hard-pressed to put up any real resistance."

There was dead silence throughout the tent. Mercer looked around the gathering and thought he saw at least some other officers with sympathetic looks in their eyes. He looked back to Washington, who he could see was organizing his thoughts.

But it was Nathaniel Greene who first broke the heavy silence. "Colonel Reed, I fear you are too pessimistic. Although our strength here has been greatly reduced, we know that Charles Lee's division has crossed into Jersey and can be here soon. Moreover, we know that a strong column from General Gates' northern army is marching to reinforce us posthaste, and new regiments from Pennsylvania, Virginia, and Maryland are promised to join us within weeks."

Someone cleared his throat, and Mercer realized it was their Swiss volunteer, Colonel Tresh. Tresh said, "Gentlemen, I do not normally venture to speak in matters of this kind, but it appears that the next fortnight will represent great danger to your cause. When, and only if, these reinforcements arrive, the cause of the colonies may become viable again. But in the meantime, I say that Reed is speaking a degree of reality. If the British were to cut off Lee in his march across Jersey, or find enough water transport to strike us on this side of the river, it could mean the destruction of this force. I fear that if Washington's main command were to be destroyed, the rest of the divisions may not have the spirit to carry on, and the rebellion will collapse."

Washington stiffened. He looked around the gathering, defiance on his face. Then he spoke in a grim but determined tone. "Gentlemen, hear this clearly: As long as this army—and particularly this part of the Continental Army—exists, our cause lives. This army *is* the Revolution! There will be *no more* talk of surrender or terms of any kind." He held up a finger for emphasis. "Understand this: Even if all fails and there remain only a few men with the colors, I will retreat to the Valley of Virginia, plant my flag on the Blue Ridge, rally to me the Ulster-Scots of that region, and make my last stand for liberty amongst a people who will never submit to British tyranny whilst there is a man left to draw a trigger."

There was, if possible, an even deeper silence. Most eyes were on their defiant commander, but Reed looked down at the ground. Tresh stared straight ahead. Mercer was trying to think of proper words to reduce the tenseness of the situation and get back to making plans for the army to move to a secure bivouac, but then he heard something which took his mind off that. It was the sound, thin and barely perceptible, of a single fifer playing a march, and the faint accompaniment of a drummer tapping out a cadence.

Every head turned to listen, not sure of what they were actually hearing or what it meant. The fife and drum were steadily getting louder. It was Washington himself who asked the question on everyone's lips. "What unit is that marching toward us? Pray, someone find out."

"I'll look, sir." It was Gibbs of the Guard who spoke and immediately opened the flap of the tent and strode out into the bivouac area. He was back in less than a minute. "General Washington, you may want to come out and see this."

The Commanding General hurried to join the captain, followed by all the others in the tent. Gibbs pointed down the long hill toward the river. "There, sir. Coming along the river road from the North. A horse and rider have just emerged from behind that clump of trees. At this distance, I can't quite be certain of the rider, but I know for sure that's Eckert's tall hunter—one of the best pieces of horseflesh in the army."

Washington stared for a moment. The young, spirited horse pranced to the music as its rider—undoubtedly Eckert—reined him back into control. As the general watched, the leading ranks of the company also emerged, led by a sergeant wearing a Highland bonnet, accompanied by a young fifer and drummer. The group was followed by ranks of men wearing distinctive black hats with the rear brim turned up. A thin smile crossed the general's face, and he looked around until he met Longwood's eyes. "Colonel, it appears that your report of the destruction of the Frederick County Light Foot was somewhat inaccurate."

Longwood stuttered, "Well, I was not present . . ."

Washington cut him off. "A *good point,* Colonel. Your report might have been accurate if you had remained with your command to see the outcome of your orders."

Longwood stiffened, and his face flushed at the rebuke.

As the company, marching in column of threes, made the turn onto the road which led up the hill from the ferry, Washington asked the assembled officers, "What is that sprightly tune the fifer is playing? I vow I've never heard it before."

It was Tresh who answered. "It's a British marching song, sir. I've often heard it played by their battalions in Europe. The name is 'The Girl I Left Behind Me.'"

Washington grinned. "Well, we shall have to have all our fifers learn it."

Meanwhile, Gibbs said, "I wonder how it is that so many of Eckert's men have overcoats," he paused and said, "although they are not uniform but of many different styles and colors."

Mercer, standing beside Washington, replied, "At least they have them, as opposed to most of our other men." He thought a second, then said, "Perhaps they were sent by the people of Frederick County."

Now the column was much closer, and signs of the recent battle were becoming visible. Mercer saw wound dressings on some of the men, and a few soldiers were struggling to keep the marching pace.

Then he saw that behind the main formation of the company were more seriously wounded men walking, some of them being supported by the women of the company. And then, to his surprise, Mercer saw none other than Mrs. McGraw helping support a young soldier.

Gibbs saw her at the same time. "Why, that's Colleen McGraw! The Red Vixen herself!" He looked harder and exclaimed, "And all of her girls are helping those men."

Mercer said, "Indeed it would seem so." He looked further down the hill and saw the Red Vixen wagons as well as the wagons of the Frederick County company. He noted that one of the company's open wagons was carrying men too hurt to walk, being attended by a burly, middle-aged woman. Then he looked further down the hill and saw Fairfield's troop coming at the walk behind the wagons. He looked over at Washington. "It appears Eckert has managed to preserve both his company and the South Carolina troop."

Washington looked over at his friend and said, "Indeed, Hugh. At this grim moment, Mistress Fortune has chosen to grant us a small favor."

Eckert, seeing the Commanding General and knot of officers around him, ordered the company to form before them in two ranks. The wounded men, women, and children and wagons halted where they were on the road. Fairfield's troop rode up and formed behind the foot troops.

When all were in place, Wend ordered the company to present arms and salute Washington.

Washington returned the salute and then said, "Captain Eckert, we are glad to see you. Please report your condition."

"Aye, sir. Frederick County Light Foot, all present and correct. In the late action as rearguard, we had four killed, thirteen seriously wounded, and one missing. But were able to withdraw in good order after throwing the enemy back in confusion."

At that moment, Private Thompson, standing in the forward rank just in front of Washington, groaned and then collapsed to the ground. Immediately Colleen and one of her girls came running and helped the private to his feet. Colleen looked over at Washington and shot him a coquettish smile, and then the two women, each with one of Thompson's arms over their shoulders, escorted him back to a wagon.

Washington's eyes followed as they went, and Wend swore he could see a faint smile on the commanding general's lips.

Then Washington turned back, now all business, and said, "Captain Eckert, take your column to a bivouac at the crest of the hill and be ready to move at dawn to locate a proper site for our camp and headquarters."

Wend responded, "Aye, sir," and then ordered the column to continue its march.

As they departed, Mercer leaned over and whispered to Washington, "I'll be damned if it doesn't seem that some sort of alliance has been formed between Mrs. McGraw and Captain Eckert."

Washington looked after the departing company, then answered, "I had never seen Mrs. McGraw so closely before. She is as attractive as the junior officers have remarked on in the mess. And despite her rather unsavory reputation, I concede it is comforting to see her helping Eckert's men in their time of need."

Mercer laughed and said in a wry tone, "George, *unsavory* is in the eye of the beholder. I can tell you that the young officers would not use that word in reference to Mrs. McGraw or her girls."

A twinkle appeared in Washington's eyes. He put a hand to his chin and replied, "Ah, yes, Hugh, I can quite understand their point of view."

In the evening dusk, Captain Ernst Ludwig Wolff, commander of the Fourth Company of the Hesse-Cassel Jaeger Corps, pulled up his horse at the gate to the yard of the substantial farmhouse sited just north of Trenton. Earlier in the day, it had been requisitioned as the headquarters of General Lord Charles Cornwallis, and now the windows were brightly lit. Wolff could see officers standing around, drinks in hand, in both the hall and what appeared to be the parlor of the building. Loud conversation and laughter wafted out to his ears. He swung down from his mount, and a soldier came to take the reins.

Entering the hall, he saw that officers from not only Cornwallis' own staff but also senior officers from the various regiments which had participated in the pursuit of the rebel army had gathered. Obviously, something of a celebratory party was in progress—stewards were carrying trays of drinks, and plates of finger food were on tables. In fact, the hall, parlor, and dining room were full of men in high spirits.

Wolff, never one to reject a cup of libation, picked up a drink from a tray offered by a steward and had just taken his first sip when he heard his name called out. He looked around and realized the source of the greeting was none other than Lord Charles himself.

The general had extended an open palm in his direction and said loudly so that the entire company could hear, "Ah ha! And here is our valiant Captain Wolff of the Jaegers, whose company has been so effective in leading our pursuit. Sir, I am told you had quite a *spirited* skirmish with a rebel battalion near Coryell's Ferry this very afternoon."

The room became silent, and Wolff sensed all heads turning toward him. He took a quick sip from his cup and said, "Indeed, although I would not characterize it thus, sir. A spirited engagement would have been one where we met and overcame our opponent after a brisk fight. It began that way but did not end in a favorable outcome." He looked around the room. "It started with normal skirmishing as we moved forward to feel out the enemy, who was hidden in the forest on a low hill. We had just begun when the rebels fired several volleys, hitting some of our men and forcing us to stop and take cover. Then they charged with much more spirit and determination than I have experienced so far in this campaign. They came at us screaming like demons with bayonets and war hatchets and with no hesitancy about using them. We were forced to stop and close ranks to receive them."

Cornwallis interrupted, "They forced the issue with cold steel? I say, that is *most* unusual for the colonists."

Wolff responded, "They came on with great enthusiasm, your Lordship, a situation which I found quite shocking. But that was only the initial part of the action. Just as we engaged them on our front, we were assaulted on our right flank by dismounted dragoons." He looked around the room. "In just a few instants, we lost six men killed and numerous wounded, by far the most casualties we have taken in the campaign. And to add insult to injury, one of the dragoon sergeants, an ugly looking man with a scar on his face and a missing ear, knocked down one of our trumpeters with the flat of his saber and captured a hunting horn." He shook his head. "In the face of all that, I was forced to precipitously withdraw to the support of the 42nd in my rear, leaving dead and injured men on the field."

The general reflected a second, then said, "My dear Wolff, of course you did the proper thing. As I have told you before, we must preserve your Jaegers, for they are our most cherished and accomplished light foot." He took a sip of his libation and then added, "And in any case, we are informed by Colonel Stirling that you were confronted by overwhelming force—at least a battalion of rebel infantry."

Wolff reflected a moment, then said, "That is the estimate which I gave the colonel, but must now admit I was seriously mistaken. Information has come to me that, in fact, we faced only a single company of light foot and a small troop of dragoons."

Colonel Thomas Stirling, who was standing near one of the tables with Charles McDonald beside him, said, "My dear Ernst, how can you be so sure? I saw the engagement, and I concurred with you that, given the heavy fire you received from a very wide front, it could have been no less than a battalion."

Wolff responded, "It happens we took a prisoner, sir—a cheeky young private who was quite prideful and ready to tell us about his company. It seems there were no more than 100 light foot, all from the Shenandoah Valley. The cavalry were a troop of twenty men from Carolina."

"It appears that this company—known as the Frederick County Light Foot—has a very imaginative commander. He has developed a technique to spread his men out in squads at wide intervals with the explicit idea of confusing an enemy about their strength. The young lad was quite excited to tell us that, and also that they have trained rigorously and with great discipline in skirmishing before they joined the army." Wolff looked around the room with a wry smile on his face. "I regret to concede this, but today they were a match for us, General."

Cornwallis looked down at the cup in his hand, thinking for a moment. "I wonder who this back-country captain is who knows so much about the tactics of skirmish warfare that he can challenge your Jaegers, the finest light infantry in Europe?"

"Actually, sir, we know his name, and it is at least one positive aspect of the entire situation: He is, in fact, a German gunsmith of Jaeger stock from my own province of Hesse-Cassel."

Cornwallis threw back his head and laughed. "So we have a battle of the Jaegers! A bit droll, I must say." There were laughs around the room. Then the General added, "Do we have the gentleman's name?"

"Indeed, sir. The young private says it is *Wendelmar Eckert*."

Suddenly a voice said, "In fact, his friends call him simply *Wend*. Wend Eckert." Everyone looked around and saw that it was Stirling who had spoken.

Cornwallis looked bemused. "Are you saying you know this fellow, Thomas?"

"Quite well, sir. Or at least I did. He scouted for me during Pontiac's War in '63, fourteen years ago, when he was a youth. He was the smartest colonial I ever worked with. Previously, he had scouted for Bouquet on his march to relieve Fort Pitt. I would postulate that he learned much of his skill at warfare during that campaign. There is hardly a better teacher than Henry Bouquet." Stirling turned to McDonald standing beside him. "And, as it happens, Charles owes his life to Eckert."

McDonald nodded. "Indeed, Lord Charles. At the Battle of Bushy Run, he killed a Shawnee warrior who was standing above me with hatchet raised to strike. He put a pistol ball into him from thirty yards away."

In an astonished tone, Cornwallis exclaimed, "Major McDonald, I can hardly credit that! A pistol shot at ninety feet?"

"I vow it is true, sir. The man is an extraordinary marksman with rifle or pistol. The day after the battle, he put a rifle ball into the head of a warrior who was harassing our column—a shot to the head at 200 yards, sir." McDonald looked around the room. "And I will confide that Eckert has in his possession my gorget from the 77th Highlanders as a gift for saving my life."

In a thoughtful tone, Cornwallis said, "An extraordinary story, sir." Then he looked back to Wolff. "Well, Captain, it would indeed seem true that you encountered a most worthy opponent on the field today."

Wolff set his chin and looked directly at the General. "I most sincerely agree, sir. And mark my words: If fortune grants me the opportunity to meet this Eckert in battle again, I will return the favor of today's action manyfold. My men and I desire nothing more than to meet the Frederick County Light Foot on even terms and show them who are the better men."

Cornwallis smiled. "Well spoken, Captain Wolff! You have a most commendable record in our service, and I have no doubt you will prevail if given the opportunity." He looked around the room. "But I fear you may *never* have the chance. We have received word through our spies that the division of rebels across the river under Washington has less than 2000 effectives and is diminishing every day through desertion and expiration of enlistments. General Lee, whose force is to the north of us, has somewhat more, but he is facing the same problems."

Then Cornwallis, in a loud voice, addressed the entire room. "Gentlemen, I have an announcement: Today I received a dispatch from General Howe. Based on the reports of conditions in the rebel army and the extreme weather we are encountering, he has decided to end this year's campaign immediately. Most of the British troops will withdraw to winter quarters in eastern Jersey and New York. A line of outposts along the Delaware, mostly manned by our German allies, will be established to keep watch on the rebel army, such as it is. General Howe is of the opinion that by the time spring arrives, there may be no such thing as a rebel army."

There was a buzz of comment around the room.

Cornwallis paused, looking around to observe the effects of his words. Then he made a further announcement. "Gentlemen, as many of you know, my beloved wife is afflicted with some serious infirmities. General Howe has graciously granted me leave to return to England to wait upon her. So I will be completing a few matters over the next few days, turn over command to General Grant, and then I shall ride to New York to take ship for England. If my services are needed for a renewed campaign, I will return in the spring. But as I said, all indications are that it will be unnecessary. So at this time I would like to commend you all for your service to me and to the Crown and wish you good fortune."

There was a round of applause from the officers, and then they returned to their conversations. Wolff made his way to where the two senior officers of the Black Watch stood. "Colonel Stirling, I wanted to thank you for the kindness your regimental hospital is showing to my wounded men. I hear they are receiving excellent care."

Stirling replied, "Our honor, sir. I vow they fought valiantly and deserve the best care available, which I am proud to say is the case with the hospital of the Black Watch."

Wolff answered, "There is one favor I would ask: I would like to ride back with you to your camp this evening so as to visit with my men in the hospital."

Stirling waved his hand. "Ernst, that would be our pleasure. We shall be leaving shortly and would enjoy your company on the ride."

The camp of the Black Watch was along a stream a short distance from the site of the afternoon's skirmish. Although the regiment had not had any serious wounded, the hospital had been pressed into service to treat the numerous cavalry and Jaeger casualties. They had been working for hours, and darkness had descended, so now they labored by the light of campfires and candle lanterns.

Mary Fraser had been busy assisting Surgeon Potts, administering to the wounded from the German Jaeger company. While a few had wounds from gunfire, several had more grievous bayonet and hatchet wounds. These were harder to deal with and required urgent attention.

There were also numerous injured from the troop of the 16th Light Dragoons, virtually all suffering from firearm wounds inflicted by the rebels' devastating first volley that had killed many, including the lieutenant troop commander. Kathryn

O'Hara led several nurses, providing comfort to these men until Potts had time to look at them.

Potts and Mary were attempting to close up and sew a Jaeger's bayonet wound when Susan, one of the nurses working on the dragoon wounded, came to the tent, a look of distress on her face. "Doctor, they just brought in a man who's in very bad shape. He was lying on the field, not moving, and it was thought he was dead, but then he suddenly started groaning, and two men carried him in. I think someone needs to look at him right away if he's to survive."

Potts looked up from his work, stared into the distance, considering for a moment, then looked over at Mary. "Miss Fraser, go take a look at him and let me know your opinion. If he's really in need, we'll get to him next."

Mary said, "Right away, Mr. Potts." She followed Susan to a tent down the row of hospital tents.

As they got to the tent, Susan said over her shoulder, "I should have mentioned it's an officer. A young cornet."

Mary immediately felt a sense of panic. She thought, *My God, a cornet of the 16th! What if it's Nevin Haldane?* She stopped where she was, fearing to enter the tent.

Susan looked back. "What's the matter, Mary? You look like you have seen a ghost. Please hurry!"

Mary took a deep breath and followed her into the tent. There were several men lying on blankets.

In a quiet voice, Susan said, "Here he is."

And then Mary's worst fears were realized. The young man's face was layered with dirt and caked blood, but even so, she could make out the features of Nevin. His eyes were closed, but he was breathing in a labored manner. Steeling herself, she knelt down beside him and then said to Susan, "He's been hit in the chest, and he's got a grazing wound to the side of the head. Help me get his clothing off so we can see the extent of the chest wound."

Together they were able to get his coat and then his shirt off. His torso was encrusted with dried blood, and more was oozing out of the wound. "Susan, get water and washcloths so we can clean it."

Even before cleaning, Mary could see the seriousness of the injury. Nevin's only hope was quick removal of the ball, but she realized it was near the heart and extraction would be extremely difficult—and it was entirely possible he would not survive the shock of the operation.

Suddenly, Nevin's eyes opened a slit and fixed on Mary's face. Then he opened them wide. "Mary! Mary! It is you! I thought I saw you a today when we rode by the wagons of the 42nd on our way to the skirmish. Or rather, I saw part of your face and the auburn hair of the exact shade I remembered." He stopped and caught his breath. "But I couldn't be sure it was really you." Then he slowly, laboriously reached out and took her hand, the grasp so tight it was painful. He struggled to get words out. "I wanted to tell you that I didn't believe what they were saying about you, that you had intentionally killed Uncle Gerald out of spite, out of a lovers' argument. I knew you would never betray Aunt Elspeth by having an affair with her husband. I knew Gerald must have tried to have his way with you and you were defending yourself." He gasped again. "Mary, believe me, you have nothing to worry about from me."

Mary took a deep breath, feeling a surge of relief. Then she said, "I believe you, Nevin. But that's not important now. Please, *please* stop talking. Save all your strength. We'll have the surgeon here immediately and get that bullet out."

He was able to smile slightly, then said sadly, "We never did get to have that ride out onto the moors you promised me." Then Nevin closed his eyes but held on to Mary with all his strength.

Susan came in with the water and washcloths. Mary said, "Here, I'll do that. You go to Potts and tell him this officer needs his attention as soon as he can manage. I'll stay here to clean him and get him ready for surgery."

Susan hurried over to the tent where Potts was working. As it turned out, he had just finished with the young Jaeger's bayonet wound. Susan told him about the cavalry officer's situation. Potts stood up. "All right, let's go take a look."

They had just arrived at the tent when a young dragoon officer rode into camp at the trot and pulled up his horse in front of them. Following him was a canvas-covered wagon. The officer swung down from his saddle and, seeing Potts, walked up to him and said in a rather haughty tone, "Sir, may I *presume* you are the surgeon of the 42nd?"

Potts looked the young man over and said, "You may. And what is your business, sir?"

"I am Cornet Banastre Tarleton of the 16th Light Dragoons."

The surgeon said dryly, "Yes, I couldn't have missed the uniform of Burgoyne's Beauties."

Ignoring the doctor's tone, the dragoon officer waved back toward the wagon. "I'm here to pick up the body of Lieutenant Witherspoon and also transport Cornet Haldane, who I understand has been wounded, back to the regiment."

Potts waved to the tent. "I'm just about to take a look at young Haldane. He's taken a bullet in the chest. I would say he must stay here until we've extracted it and *he has* some time to regain his strength."

Tarleton raised his chin and looked along his nose deprecatingly at Potts. "Sir, I will inform you that we of the 16th make it a practice of taking care of the members of our mess ourselves. I can assure you we have a most competent surgeon, and our camp is not far distant."

Potts, his ire up, responded tersely, "Cornet, you don't seem to understand. The man is *desperately* wounded and *lay* on the battlefield for hours before he was found barely alive. I don't believe he would survive transport in your wagon."

Tarleton's face took on an obstinate look. "Now see here, Surgeon Potts . . ."

At that moment, Mary emerged from the tent. Potts said, "Cornet, this is Miss Fraser, our Matron of the Hospital. She has been tending to Haldane." He turned to her. "Mary, tell Mr. Tarleton that moving him now would be fatal."

Mary looked at Tarleton for a long moment. She noticed he was staring at her as if he could see her body under her garments. Mary ignored the man's brazen look and turned to the surgeon. "No, Mr. Potts, I think it's absolutely appropriate for the cornet to take Mr. Haldane, and the sooner the better. The wagon trip will cause him no discomfort."

Potts' head snapped around, confusion in his eyes. "Mary! What are you saying?"

In a weary tone, Mary replied, "It's quite all right, sir. Cornet Haldane expired just a few minutes ago, and I'm sure his comrades of the 16th would like to pay him their last respects."

Stirling, McDonald, and Wolff rode into the 42nd camp with the moon fully up and stars shining in the cold December night. The colonel turned to his companions and said, "I'm going up to headquarters to see McDougal about the evening reports. Charles, would you be so good as to show Captain Wolff to the hospital and have Potts give him a report on his men?"

"Certainly, sir," responded McDonald. Then he waved to the Jaeger captain and said, "Come with me, Ernst, we'll ride down to the hospital."

In a few minutes they arrived at the two rows of tents which constituted the regimental hospital and dismounted. A tall, thin, angular-faced nurse wearing a stained white apron was standing before a fire where a large pot of boiling water hung on a tripod. She was stirring dressings in the process of being cleaned. McDonald said, "Mrs. O'Hara, could you find Surgeon Potts? Captain Wolff would like information on his wounded Jaegers."

Kathryn looked at the two men and, without stopping her stirring, said, "You'll na' find the good doctor here. He's been workin' on the wounded all day, and he just went up to the mess to get somethin' to eat." She looked at them with a mischievous smile and continued, "I shouldn't be surprised if he dunna' fall asleep over his plate, the man's so exhausted." She put the ladle down and said, "Why don't I get you the Matron? She can tell you as much as the Surgeon about how they are doing."

"Indeed, I agree," the major responded. Kathryn dried her hands on the apron and hurried off to find Mary.

In only a few minutes Kathryn was back, and Ernst could see she was followed by another nurse. As they approached, he realized the second nurse was a striking woman, perhaps in her late 20s, of medium height, lithe figure, and a pretty, if not outright beautiful face crowned with shiny, dark auburn hair. Even more stunning were her green eyes, which exuded warmth and intelligence. Wolff felt himself catching his breath at her attractiveness.

McDonald said, "Ernst, this is Miss Mary Fraser, our Matron of the Hospital. She is considered equivalent in rank to an ensign, manages all the nurses, and is the surgeon's chief assistant."

Wolff said, "Ah, yes. I understand. And it is a pleasure to meet you, Miss Fraser."

Mary acknowledged the introduction and said, "Captain Wolff, I understand you are here to look after your wounded." She motioned to the tents. "Why don't we take a walk through the hospital, and you can see for yourself how they are doing?"

"Please lead, Miss Fraser."

Mary took him through the tents, and Wolff spent a little time with each man. When they finished and were outside the last tent, Mary said, "As you can tell, many of the men had wounds from hatchets or bayonets. Bayonet wounds are the hardest to sew up because of their triangular shape; they destroy so much of the skin. They also go deep into the body, which can lead to very serious damage. In some cases, they never fully heal."

"Indeed, ma'am, I quite understand. I trust Doctor Potts and you have done your best."

McDonald, who had been waiting, joined the conversation. While they were talking, Wolff heard the sound of a flute and a violin begin to play. He turned around and saw several musicians standing in the center of the camp, with the Highlanders gathering around and taking seats on the ground.

Mary said, "I see the men are taking the opportunity for some entertainment. We haven't had much chance lately because of all the marching we've been doing in pursuit of the colonists, but I hear that is over now, and it appears the men are celebrating."

As they talked, Wolff noticed a tall, burly piper coming toward them. The piper touched his hat to Wolff and McDonald, then said, "Mary, my love, the men want you to dance for them. It's been a long time since they've seen you."

Mary smiled faintly. "Tavish, this has been a sad day. Men have died. I don't have the spirit for a dance tonight, but I will sing, if the men will be happy with that."

"Now Mary, dear, they'll be pleased with whatever you want to do."

McDonald said, "Yes, Mary, do sing. You know how they love to hear you, and it's fitting with the end of the campaign upon us."

Mary took off her apron and tossed it into camp chair, then walked with Tavish to where the other musicians were tuning their instruments before a large fire. Cheers and loud clapping erupted from the assembled men and camp women. She spoke for a few seconds with the musicians, then turned to face the crowd. She said, "We're a long way from home on this cold December night, so I'll sing a song about returning to Scotland."

The instrumentalists began playing a slow introduction, and then Mary began, "You take the high road, and I'll take the low, and I'll be in Scotland afore ye..."

Wolff was astonished at the sweet, true sound of her voice. He looked at the men, who listened with rapt attention and longing in their eyes. He turned to McDonald and whispered, "My God, such a beautiful voice. Where did she learn to sing like that?"

Charles McDonald laughed. "It's not just singing. She has many accomplishments; the lass is a first-rate nurse and a governess of children for wealthy landowners." He looked over at Wolff and said, "I am very proud of her and consider her my goddaughter, although we are not truly related."

"My dear Charles, how can that be?"

"More than twenty years ago, at the start of the French War, I recruited her father to the old 77th Highlanders from a tiny village in Scotland. And Mary and her mother came along. She was a mere child holding onto her mother's skirt. Her father soon became a sergeant and was killed in a futile battle before Fort Duquesne at the Forks of the Ohio in 1763. Her mother immediately remarried to keep her rations, but later in the campaign against the Spanish, both she and her new husband died at Havana of yellow fever. Thenceforth, Mary was raised by the regimental chaplains, first in the 77th, then the 42nd. She came to the Black Watch with me because she had no natural relatives in Scotland. So she is a true daughter of the regiment."

"There are many like that in all armies, but she speaks and acts like a middling woman, not a camp follower."

"That is of her own doing. From her youth, she had ambition. She became a dedicated student, learning to read and consuming every book she could get her hands on. Many a night I've seen her sitting by a fire, leaning over a volume on her lap. She pestered the chaplains for more information and, as a young woman, she became the best, most knowledgeable nurse in the battalion."

"That is most commendable."

"Indeed, Captain. And you will be astonished to learn that she was present at the Battle of Bushy Run and, in fact, was gravely wounded by a Shawnee rifle ball. It was thought she would die."

Wolff's eyebrows shot up, and he stared speechless at the singing girl.

McDonald continued. "She survived by a miracle, and when the regiment went home a few years later, Stirling and I were able to get her a position as governess to a fine Highland family, where she served for seven years."

Puzzled, Wolff asked, "Why is she here now?"

"When this rebellion broke out, she volunteered to return to the regiment, which of course would normally be impossible unless she were married to a soldier. But Stirling and I appealed to the Proprietary Colonel, General Lord John Murray, who, learning of her background and realizing she was as much a part of the regiment as any soldier, agreed to appoint her to the position of Matron of the Hospital."

Wolff thought a moment. "Charles, it puzzles me why such a talented and beautiful woman is not married to a husband of substance."

"She could be betrothed in an instant if she were interested. I tell you, all the subalterns of the regiment are infatuated with her. We have numerous young officers who will inherit estates and titles. Were Mary to agree to marry one of them, she could soon be Lady Mary."

"And why does she resist such a happy outcome?"

McDonald looked over at Wolff. "Because, since her youth, she has been infatuated—nay, deeply in love—with a colonial. A youth who was the gravely wounded sole survivor of a massacre on Forbes Road by a band of Mingo Indians in 1758. The company Mary was with found him lying on the road nearly dead. She and her mother nursed him and he had her heart from the beginning."

"And why were they not married? That would have been a natural outcome."

"A twist of fate intervened, Ernst. The lad acted as a scout for Bouquet on the Bushy Run campaign, but he went on a mission deep into the Ohio Country, and when he returned, the regiment had left Fort Pitt, and he was mistakenly told that she had died of her wounds from Bushy Run. He ended up marrying another woman."

Wolff said, "My God, a tragic outcome. And so Mary has carried the torch for him since then, to the exclusion of others?"

"Unfortunately, true. I have endeavored to match her with some of the best young men of Scotland, but she resists all my efforts."

Wolff shook his head. "Who is this man to whom she maintains such loyalty, even though he lives with another woman?"

McDonald looked over at the German with a droll look in his eyes. "He is a man of German heritage, just like you. In fact, a Jaeger. His name is *Wend Eckert.*"

Ernst exclaimed in shock, "My God!"

"Yes, my dear fellow, the very same man you have just this day pledged to destroy in battle. Can we not agree life is full of strange ironies?"

Wolff stood frozen, staring at the singing woman who had the rapt attention of scores of men.

McDonald put his hand on Wolff's shoulder. "I will leave you puzzling over that strange story of fate and life. I must make my evening rounds." And with that, he strode off along the line of tents toward the regimental headquarters.

Wolff stood riveted, listening as Mary finished her song and then sang another. Then she bowed to her audience and, having thanked the musicians, walked back toward the hospital. When she was near him, Ernst touched his hat to her and said, "Miss Fraser, may I have a word?"

She smiled and said, "Of course, Captain. What is on your mind?"

"While you sang, Major McDonald told me of your background and how you came to be the matron."

Mary laughed. "I have known the major since I was a child at my mother's skirts. He has looked after me since I was orphaned in 1763, and he fancies himself my protector."

"Yes, Miss Fraser, so I gathered. But he told me much about your life," he paused and looked into her eyes, "including why such a lovely and accomplished lady as yourself remains unmarried."

A guarded expression came over Mary's face. "And you believe that is because... ?"

"For the reason that you are enamored of a certain colonial man you met as a child."

A touch of irritation flashed in Mary's eyes, and her face flushed. She cocked her head and responded, "Much as I esteem him, sometimes Charles says too much."

"I can understand you feeling that way about personal matters. However, I thought you might want to know something that might be of great interest to you."

Mary Fraser put her hands on her hips and said, "And pray tell, what might that be, Captain?"

"Just this: The man who led the troops which confronted us today, whose men inflicted the wounds you have been treating, is someone you know."

Wariness showing in her eyes, Mary said slowly, "I was in America for seven years. I know many colonials. Who might you be speaking of?"

"A man named Wend Eckert, of Jaeger heritage like myself, currently Captain of the Frederick County Light Foot, from the Shenandoah Valley in the colony of Virginia." He watched as that sank in and saw her body stiffen. Then he pointed westward and said, "I can tell you he is encamped tonight just a few miles away, on the other side of the Delaware."

Mary's eyes opened wide, and he was gratified to see her head slowly turn in the direction of the river. She stared for a moment, and to Wolff, her eyes seemed full of longing and her mouth slightly open. Then she turned back to him. Now he could see suspicion and a touch of anger in her eyes. "Why do you choose to tell me this?"

"I am always interested in learning about the men who I come up against, and from what McDonald tells me, you are the person who can provide me much information *on* this Captain Eckert."

Mary's eyes drilled into him for a long minute. Then she spoke in a quiet but determined tone, "If Charles McDonald told you about the relationship between Wend Eckert and me, then it should be clear—*very clear*—to you that I would not say a word that would help you." She abruptly said, "Now I must go check on the well-being of your men. Good night to you, sir." She turned and strode off rapidly toward the hospital area.

Wolff grinned to himself. *So McDonald's story had been accurate.* Clearly the woman, after the long passage of time, was still infatuated with Eckert. Now he must figure out a way to make use of that in his quest to destroy the man who had killed his soldiers and sullied the reputation of him and his company.

Chapter Nineteen

Secret Movements

Shay O'beirne, sitting his horse, watched as Sergeant Flannigan put three field squads of the company through their paces in a piece of pastureland. It was just east of the army encampment in Upper Makefield Township, an area several miles west of the Delaware in which farms and large estates were intermingled. They were not far from Washington's headquarters, which was in the substantial brick house of one of those estates.

Flannagan had had the squads at rigorous skirmish drill for a busy hour. Shay was considering whether he might suggest that the sergeant give the men a rest when he spied something which pushed thoughts of drill and exercise out of his mind. Looking up the wagon track that ran alongside the field, he saw approaching in the distance an elegantly dressed woman on horseback followed by a horse cart. As they got closer, he was pleasantly surprised to realize it was none other than Catherine Tresh on the horse and her maid, Elise Moulders, driving the cart.

Spurring his horse, he trotted eastward to meet the new arrivals. Catherine gave him a smile and a wave and pulled up her horse. Shay stopped his animal alongside hers and doffed his hat in greeting. "Catherine, my dear, I vow it's a pleasure to see you again. But you were thought to be in Morristown. How in the devil have you gotten across the river and found us at this rural spot? And in any case, what moved you to leave the comfort of that town to return to a rather barren army camp?"

“Shay, you know I feel a good wife should be with her husband. I left the army only because of the terrible weather we were having and because every piece of clothing I had was fouled by mud. I was able to resolve that situation in Morristown, and so now I have made my way back.”

“Yes, but how in the world did you get across the Delaware?”

“There are some ferries to the west of Morristown which the militia have allowed to run again. There are no British in the area—they normally stay further to the south, except for a rare cavalry patrol. The ferryman told me he retreats to the western riverbank when there’s any word of a patrol in the area. And after all, life and commerce must go on.” She smiled. “So it was no trouble getting over the river.” She looked around at the camp with curious eyes. “I don’t suppose you would happen to know where my husband would be?”

Shay turned in the saddle and pointed to the brick house, about a quarter mile distant. “That’s the Keith house, which is Washington’s headquarters. All the staff officers are living in tents nearby. I’m sure one of Washington’s aides can help you locate the colonel.”

“Of course! Thank you, Shay.” Catherine turned and called back to the cart. “Come along, Elise. We’ll find Colonel Tresh and move into our new quarters.” She grinned at the Irishman and then urged her horse onward toward the Keith Manor, followed by the cart.

In a few minutes she pulled up her horse in front of the house Shay had pointed to. Catherine prepared to dismount, and a young private came to take her reins. An aide, a captain whom she recognized but whose name she didn’t remember, arrived to hand her down.

“Good afternoon, Mrs. Tresh. This is quite a surprise.”

Catherine nodded. “I love surprising people, Captain. I’m told my husband might be inside. Is that correct?”

“Indeed, ma’am, he’s in a meeting with General Washington and other senior officers. It will be my pleasure to escort you.”

The young officer took her arm and led her into the hall. “Ma’am, if you excuse me, I’ll go into the meeting room and let the Colonel know you are here.”

Catherine had to wait only a brief minute, and then Alex burst out of the room, a great smile on his face. “My dear, I had no expectation of seeing you so soon! But it is my great pleasure that you are here!”

"Oh, dear Alex, I couldn't wait until you sent for me. I do hope you are not upset?"

"Of course not! Let me get my hat, and I will take you to my quarters."

Meanwhile, General Mercer had also come out into the hall. He said, "Please be patient with me, Mrs. Tresh, but since you have just come from Morristown, I have some questions for you."

"Why, General Mercer, I shall be most pleased to help you in any way possible, but I cannot fathom what news I would have that would benefit you."

"It is just this, Mrs. Tresh: We are vitally interested in the location of General Lee and his division, which should be moving westward on roads leading through Morristown. Did you see or hear anything about the progress of the general?"

Catherine gave Mercer her broadest smile. "Well, I'm most glad to say I *can* help you in this matter. The fact is, General Lee's troops marched through Morristown while we were there and encamped a small distance to the west of the village. They were still lingering there when we left two days ago."

A look of concern came over the general's face. "You say they were remaining in bivouac at that point? You saw no preparations to continue their march?"

"Yes, General. They seemed to be in no hurry to move."

Mercer stared into the distance for a while, then smiled thinly at Catherine and said, "Mrs. Tresh, you have been very helpful." Then he turned and quickly strode back into the room.

Alexander gave Catherine his arm and escorted her out of the house. He looked over at his wife and said, "I'm afraid you will be back to living under canvas for a time, my dear."

"Well, I have had the respite of living for the last few days in a snug, well-warmed house. So I am fortified to withstand the rigor of it, at least for a while."

Tresh took the reins of her horse in one hand and her arm with the other. "It is but a short distance, we can walk it, Catherine." He signaled for Elsie to follow them with the cart.

As they walked, Catherine asked, "Alex, General Mercer seemed very concerned about the location of General Lee and his men. If I may, what was that about?"

Tresh considered his words for a minute, then said, "Well, if you will remember, I told you that I expected Washington to make some sort of desperate move against the British—a final chance to save this rebellion."

"Yes, I certainly remember. Is Mercer's query somehow connected to that?"

"Not *somehow*, but *crucially*, my dear. Unless Lee's force is merged with the few troops which remain with Washington, there is no chance of an effective attack."

"So they are anxiously waiting upon Lee's arrival." She reflected a moment. "If Lee is so important, why is he delaying his march?"

"That is precisely the point, Catherine. He is playing games with Washington. There is a belief that he is waiting for Washington's force to disintegrate, leaving him in a position to claim supremacy in command."

Catherine thought about that, then said, "Alex, if I may ask, what is this strike that Washington is planning?"

Tresh replied, "There are a series of outposts along the river which the British have set up to watch the rebels here, mostly manned by large detachments of Germans. Washington is proposing to cross the Delaware back into Jersey and attempt to destroy one of them. It would be a great encouragement to the rebel spirit and might bring in more recruits. In other words, it has the potential of keeping the Patriot cause alive."

"Indeed, Alex. It would be a bold move. Do you know which of these posts will be attacked?"

"No, that has not yet been determined. Militia in Jersey are being requested to scout out the posts to see which would be the most advantageous to attack." At that moment he stopped and motioned to a pair of tents. "Well, my dearest, behold your newest home."

Catherine said, "Elsie and I shall do our best to make it comfortable."

Tresh replied, "I know you will, dear. Now I must return to the meeting, but I shall be back to keep you company as soon as possible."

Catherine stood watching her husband walk off to the manor house. She thought, *I have just arrived and already have obtained news that Harfeld and Northcutt will find useful.* She had been told that one of their spies would contact her shortly and was delighted to be able to immediately demonstrate to them how much information she would be able to provide.

Wend entered the Keith House and went to the reception desk in the hall. He announced himself to the young captain sitting there. "I'm here at the bequest of General Mercer."

"Ah, yes, Captain Eckert. The General said to send you right in." He pointed to a door at the far end of the hall.

Wend tapped on the door, and immediately Mercer's voice summoned him to enter. "Morning, sir. I came as soon as I got the word."

Mercer nodded and motioned for him to sit down in front of the desk. Then, as Wend took the seat, he reached down to a paper on his desk and said, "Here's your commission as major in the Continental Army."

Shocked, Wend quickly scanned the paper, then looked up at Mercer. "Sir, the commander of an independent company is normally a captain. Why am I being promoted? Does this have something to do with the fight at Coryell's Ferry?"

"Washington thinks you deserve the rank, but there's more to it than your commendable action in that skirmish. It's being done at this moment because Washington has an important job for you to do, and ranking as a major will carry more weight in the performance of the task."

Wend stared at Mercer for a second, then said, "Sir, with all due respect, you are talking in riddles. What in the devil's name is this all about?"

"In short, Eckert, it's about General Lee. I've spoken to you before about his intransigence, about his disregard for Washington's guidance to him."

"Yes, I certainly remember that."

"I'm sure you have heard rumors around camp about the possibility of the army making a surprise strike against the British."

"They are quite rampant."

"Simply put, Eckert, the rumors are true. The staff is working on plans to strike one of the outposts that Howe has set up along the Delaware. We're still working out which one and the details of how to do it, and it *has* to be done soon. We need Glover's men to get us across the river, but his regiment is due to be mustered out in January. Moreover, it can only be done if Lee's division can be consolidated under Washington's command. We simply don't have enough effective men otherwise, and we don't know when the brigades from Gates' army will arrive. So if anything serious is to be done, Lee's men must be here as soon as possible." He stood up and crossed his arms. "But Lee has consistently and aggressively refused ever stronger requests from Washington to unite with us. George has been extremely deferential to Lee, given his experience and seniority. However, yesterday something happened which changed everything."

"Sir? What was that?"

"Washington saw a letter from Lee on the reception officer's desk. Mistakenly believing it was to him, he opened it, only to find that it was a letter to Colonel Joseph Reed."

"Lee was writing directly to Reed? But why?"

"Because Lee has been corresponding with Reed, apparently since the battles around New York, expressing his disdain for Washington's leadership, and Reed has been at least somewhat sympathetic in that opinion. As Washington read, it became apparent that Lee is gathering a cabal of allies to wrest command of the army from him."

"But it is known throughout the army that Reed is one of Washington's longest serving and closest aides."

"That, Eckert, is *precisely* the problem. Lee has evidently been working to convert many officers' loyalty from the commanding general to him."

Mercer paused to gather his thoughts. Wend spoke up, "You wouldn't be telling me this if I wasn't to be involved in some move against Lee."

"Very good, Eckert. Washington plans to send Lee a direct, preemptive order to immediately cross the Delaware and bring his division at forced march to join us here, and you are the fellow who will deliver it. Let me be frank: At this moment, Washington doesn't know who in the army he can trust. So he feels if he can trust anyone, it is those of us from Virginia. We three are at this moment all who are aware of the complete situation."

Wend grinned. "I don't suppose there would be any use for me to decline the order? I don't envy being in the middle of a fight between generals."

"No jesting, Eckert." Mercer rose from his desk. "This discussion has all been preliminary. Washington is going to personally instruct you on the details. Come with me to meet with him."

Feeling very wary about the impending interview, Wend followed Mercer across the hall and into Washington's office.

The Commanding General was seated at a desk, studying papers. He looked up when the two of them entered. He smiled knowingly at Wend. "Ah, good morning, *Major* Eckert."

"I appreciate your confidence in me, General, for whatever it is you are about to order me to do."

A wry smile crossed Washington's lips. "Well, as usual, you are quite to the point, Eckert." He looked down at his desk, moved the papers he had been studying aside, reached down into a drawer, and pulled out three envelopes. He spread them out in a precise line across his desk, then looked up at Wend. "As I'm sure General Mercer explained, it is imperative that Lee's division march immediately to join us here. Your mission will be to ride to Lee's camp and make sure that happens." He waved his hand over the envelopes. "These are lettered 'A', 'B', and 'C'. Envelope A contains an order from me to General Lee directing him to begin his march to join us within the hour of its receipt. Once having read it, he is to tell you that he will comply. You are to remain in his camp until the march begins. If he does not comply in every detail, you will give him Envelope B. It is an order relieving him of his command and placing him under your arrest." Washington looked up at Wend. "Do you quite understand what I have said?"

Wend felt a lump in his stomach, but he responded, "Quite, sir."

Washington continued, "Envelope C is the order to Lee's deputy, General Sullivan, to assume command of the division and immediately commence marching to this camp. You will, of course, deliver that to him only in the case Lee has been relieved."

"I understand," Wend said. Then he asked, "What is the latest information about the location of Lee's division?"

It was Mercer who answered. "Mrs. Tresh came into camp yesterday. She says Lee's men were encamped just west of Morristown when she left that town, and it appeared to her there was no plan to depart. We are also aware that the local militia is allowing a ferry on the Delaware to the west of that vicinity to operate for regular travel. That is where you should proceed to cross."

Washington said, "Now, Major, you will need a strong escort to ride with you, not only for protection, but to assist you in guarding Lee if he is placed under custody. I would suggest a squad of the Palmetto Light Horse, but I will leave the precise composition up to you." He looked down at his desk and said, "And I think you will agree it is urgent that you depart as soon as you can make ready."

"I shall ride this afternoon, sir."

Washington nodded. "That will not be too soon." Then he gathered up the three envelopes and handed them to Wend. "Major Eckert, I wish you godspeed in your journey. I have no doubt you will carry out your mission to the advantage of this army and our cause."

"Lord Cornwallis, I appreciate your taking the time to see me on such short notice and at such a busy moment for you." Northcutt looked around the room; present were Cornwallis, General Grant, and Colonel Souders, Cornwallis' adjutant general. Cornwallis was at his desk, packing some personal papers into a leather valise as he prepared for his impending trip to New York and on to England. The massively rotund Grant, his girth barely covered by his uniform coat and his thighs looking as if they were about to burst out of his breeches, sat, drink in hand, in a chair beside the desk while Souders stood near one wall, having just entered with Barrett.

Cornwallis responded, "Actually, Colonel, I'm rather glad you appeared at this moment, because it gives me a chance to acquaint Grant here with your function for the army. General Grant is taking over as my relief and will be coordinating the watch on our estranged and misguided friends across the Delaware."

Northcutt looked over at Grant and said, "I'm, of course, quite acquainted with your illustrious career, sir, both in the army and as a member of Parliament, and it will be my honor to serve your needs."

Cornwallis turned to Grant. "James, Northcutt provides us with an invaluable service. He organizes our relations with the loyal colonists, but more importantly, and speaking frankly, he is our chief spy. He's built up a commendable network to keep us informed on the activities of the rebels."

Northcutt took the opportunity to speak up. "Sir, that is precisely my reason for meeting with you today. I have some urgent information which has just come into my possession—information about Washington's plans for future action."

A disdainful expression came over Grant's face. "I should think Washington's future plans would mostly encompass simply trying to preserve his own freedom when the impending collapse of the rebel army becomes reality."

Barrett took a deep breath and was marshalling his words for a reply when Cornwallis spoke up. "James, Colonel Northcutt does not agree with the generally held opinion within our army that the rebel resistance is all but over. He, alone in his conviction, believes that they have at least one more shot in their cartridge box, as I might put it."

Northcutt felt a flash of frustration and anger at the tone in Cornwallis' voice, but contained himself and said, "It's not just my opinion, gentlemen. I have direct evidence that the rebels are planning an attack."

Grant leaned forward. "Do you jest, sir? It is consensus that Washington has no more than 2000 starving, skimpily clothed, ill-disciplined soldiers in his camp. My God, the rebels need all their energy simply to survive in this frigid weather. What could he possibly achieve against our force?"

Souders spoke up. "Barrett, what is this evidence that you have about the rebel intentions? And how did you obtain it?"

Northcutt cleared his throat. "Gentlemen, my spymaster, who goes by the nom de guerre of *Harkness*, after diligent effort, has developed a source at the highest level in Washington's camp. To wit, the wife of a senior staff officer, who is providing us with direct information about their plans."

Barrett was pleased to see that got their attention. Cornwallis stopped gathering his papers and turned to stare, Grant stiffened in his chair, and Souders raised his eyebrows.

It was Cornwallis who spoke. "Pray, please give us a detailed explanation."

"Harkness has been cultivating the friendship of this lady, who is the wife of a Swiss professional officer who joined the colonial cause last spring. He first met the lady in New York and has kept in contact with her since then. She has realized the futility of the rebel situation and has become an informant to ensure the future of both she and her husband after the collapse of Washington's army." Northcutt looked at each of the officers, who now stared at him with rapt attention. "The lady transmits information to us through a traveling peddler who is part of our web."

Cornwallis asked, "And precisely what news has she provided at this time?"

Northcutt responded, "Washington is gathering reinforcements. He expects to receive a reinforcement of over a thousand men from Gates' army in northern New York. And Lee's force, which has lingered on our northern flank and is now encamped west of Morristown, will be brought across the Delaware to consolidate with the men directly under Washington. That will establish a field force of upwards of six thousand men. The intent is that they will cross the Delaware and attack one of the outposts we have established on the eastern side of the river."

Paterson asked, "And at what outpost and on what date will this ostensibly occur?"

Barrett replied, "That has not yet been determined by Washington. They have their own spies and are studying which place to attack."

General Grant scowled and said, "Northcutt, let's be *honest*. The fact is you can't give us any details of this supposed plan, of which I must say I am highly skeptical. How can we prepare for such an attack unless there is firm information? It would be foolish to warn our subordinate commanders about something so nebulous. And, in any case, they already know to be on watch for activity by the rebels. That's why they are positioned along the river."

But Cornwallis had a serious look on his face and put a hand to his chin. "Still, James, I have found that, when dealing with Washington, caution is the watchword. There is ample reason why my staff and I call him the 'Old Fox'. He sometimes does the most unexpected." He walked over to a table with a map spread out upon it and bent over, studying the area. He beckoned to Grant. "Sir, join me here."

With some effort, Grant pushed himself up and out of the chair and then walked over to the table. Cornwallis had his finger on Morristown. "Lee is somewhere to the west of here, and as long as he stays there, his presence could endanger our northern flank. But in actuality, he has made no move upon us. If what Northcutt says is true, he should be making haste toward the river at a point where boats can ferry his men, guns, and supply train across."

With little interest in his voice, Grant said, "Yes, Charles, that's logical."

"Well, it will be up to you, James, but I would say it might be prudent to send a strong cavalry patrol up there to observe Lee's movements, or lack thereof. Will he stay in place, or march to join Washington as Northcutt expects? That will tell us a lot about the validity of this information." He looked over at Grant. "Harcourt's 16th Light Dragoons are currently quartered nearby at Pennington. I would suggest giving him the order to send a squadron-sized patrol up north. The information they gain might be comforting, one way or another."

Grant stared at the map for a few seconds, then remarked, "Yes, Charles, I quite agree." He smirked and added, "And in any case, it wouldn't do to let Burgoyne's Beauties become too comfortable in their quarters, would it now?"

—m—

Donegal, riding beside Wend, commented, "Na, sure, and we damn well oughta' to be pretty near Lee's camp."

Wend nodded in agreement. After departing the army camp, they had ridden north for two days and then camped near the river at a town named Tinicum. The ferry had taken them across early the next morning, and they had ridden all day through hill and low mountain country, alternating forest and farmland. They camped overnight and got away at dawn the next day. Riding behind him and Donegal were Sergeant Quinn, Trumpeter Bloom, a squad of eight dragoons, and four mounted riflemen of Wend's own company, led by Corporal Schreiber. Wend had decided on bringing a robust number of men in case they ran into a British patrol. In reply to Donegal's comment, he said, "That's why I sent Joshua ahead to scout. He can smell out an army camp miles away. If we're close, he'll find them."

That was soon the case. They rode on for a few more minutes when their friend came into sight at the top of a hill, sitting his hunter as he waited for their approach. Wend and Donegal trotted on ahead of the column to meet with Baird.

The scout waved eastward. "They be 'bout two miles ahead, in a little valley just west of Morristown."

Wend asked, "Did they look like they were getting ready to move?"

"Nary a sign of that, Wend. I talked with some men on picket duty. They been there for days and ain't heard a word about getting ready to march."

Wend swore under his breath. He had been hoping to avoid a confrontation with Lee. Now it looked like it was definitely in the offing.

Donegal remarked, "I take it you ain't lookin' forward to your meeting with his Highness the General."

Joshua grinned and said, "I wouldn't be surprised if when old man Lee finds out why you be here, he don't sic that whole pack of dogs of his on you and have 'em chase you all the way back to the river."

Wend stared into the distance. "Thanks, my old friends, you're really making me feel good about my prospects."

Donegal said, "Hey, now with you bein' a lordly major, this should be all in a day's work for you."

Wend said loudly, "Damn you both to Hell. That's enough." He looked back to see the column was about to join them. "Well, let's hurry to the camp and get it over with."

He waved his arm for the whole group to proceed at a trot.

They rode into camp and soon found the cluster of tents which formed the headquarters. As they rode through, officers and men stared at them, realizing they were outsiders. Wend dismounted in front of a tent flying a general's standard. An aide, muffled up in an overcoat and scarf, sat at a desk near a fire.

Wend introduced himself and said, "Sir, I am here with dispatches for General Lee from the Commander in Chief. Please take me to him."

The aide, a young captain, looked up at Wend with a bored expression on his face. Then he slowly got to his feet and stepped closer to the fire. He made a crooked grin and said, "I'm afraid that's not possible."

Wend asked, "And why not?"

"The General is not in camp." He stood there staring at Wend, not deigning to provide any more information.

Wend hesitated a moment, not sure how to proceed. Then he made a decision. "Then I trust General Sullivan is here?"

"He is indeed. Do you desire to see him?"

"That should be obvious—this very minute."

"All right, Major. Follow me." The aide led him to a nearby tent and announced him. "General, there's another courier here from General Washington. This one brought a troop of light horse with him."

Wend strode impatiently past the aide into the tent. Sullivan was sitting at a writing table reading something. He was a man of middle height, stocky build, and black hair. The general looked up at Wend and said, "And you are, if I may ask?"

Wend told him his rank and name. "I'm here directly from General Washington with important dispatches."

"Yes, we've been getting a lot of aides visiting us from Washington. I'm sure your dispatches are just as important as the others." He held out his hand. "Give it to me. I assure you General Lee will see it upon his return, whenever that may be."

"I have orders to present it to Lee personally. It is for his eyes only. I'll ask you to relate where he might be."

Sullivan looked up at Wend, hostility visible in his eyes. "If you are so bloody eager to see him, I'll be glad to inform you." He got up and went to a table where a map was laid out and motioned for Wend to join him. "Well, Major Eckert, General Lee has retired to an inn called *The Widow White's Tavern* in this village—Basking Ridge—to take his leisure for a couple of nights. It's about seven miles away if you are determined to see him immediately."

Wend looked at Sullivan. "I am quite determined." Wend hesitated, then said, "At this moment I am not able to tell you precisely what is in the dispatch for the general, but I should advise you to prepare your division to march."

"Well, Major Eckert, indeed that sounds very serious. But you know General Lee has his own ideas about the movement of this division, and he is a very stubborn man."

"So is General Washington. I suggest you consider that and remember who is the commander of all our forces and ultimately directs their movement."

Sullivan stared at Wend. Wend returned the look and thought, *Undoubtedly he now realizes I have direct orders for Lee to act, not just another polite request.*

The general put his hands on his hips, bit his lip, and looked down at the map. Then he turned to Wend. "I shall begin making preparations for the division to move in the morning, assuming Lee concurs."

"Excellent, sir. I would say that by the time I return, you can count on being able to see your duty clear."

—ꟾ—

Wend and the escort arrived at Basking Ridge in the late afternoon after a brisk ride of over an hour. It was a tiny village astride an intersection of two wagon tracks. There was a store just off the intersection, and, as luck would have it, a couple of farmers stood talking beside a hitching rail. A wagon with a sleepy-eyed horse was parked before the store, and a saddled horse was tied to the hitching rail. Wend rode over. "Good afternoon, gentlemen. I am Major Eckert of the Continental Army, and I'm looking for a place called the Widow White's Tavern."

One of the men, a stout fellow dressed in rough clothing, said, "This sure is a busy place today. It happens another troop of cavalry just came through." He looked over at his friend and winked, then turned back to Wend. "Except they was British. Dragoons dressed in pretty red coats." He pointed down the road and said, "They rode right through like they knew where they were going, and that was in the direction of the Widow's place. It ain't but a matter of a quarter mile down the road." He bit his lip. "Can't have been fifteen minutes."

He had no sooner spoken than the sound of a single gunshot was heard. Wend realized it was in the direction of the tavern. Everyone turned and looked toward the sound, but nothing was to be seen.

The man said, "I'm bettin' that was at the Widow's place, sure enough."

Wend replied, "Undoubtedly." Then he pulled Sonny around and rode over to where the column sat their horses. He explained what had transpired with the men at the store.

Quinn's face twisted into a wry smile. "I'd say the British got to Lee afore we did." He looked at Wend. "Well, Major, what you gonna' do about this?"

"We are—very carefully—going to scout out the situation, Sergeant." Wend thought hard for a moment. Then he said, "Joshua, Donegal, Quinn, the four of us and trumpeter Bloom are going to go up and see what's happening at the tavern." He turned to Schreiber. "Corporal, there is plenty of forestland along the road. Find a place to hide the men and horses but stay ready to ride. Come fast to join us if you hear Bloom's trumpet."

Wend waved to the other four, and they rode off in the direction of the tavern. When they had gone a couple of hundred yards, he waved for them to dismount. "Bloom, take the horses into that grove of trees and wait there for our return."

The four of them left the road and moved as stealthily as possible through the wood and bush toward the tavern. In just a few minutes they had it in sight, and Wend found a hiding place where they could observe what was going on. And that proved to be quite a bit. The building was ringed by dragoons. A man in a blue Continental uniform lay still near the front door of the tavern. Nine horses were tied up nearby.

Baird pointed toward the dead man. "Well, that's what that shot was all about. He must have been the sentinel."

Wend nodded. Then suddenly the tavern door opened, and a man Wend recognized as Lee came out along with two aides. Right behind them, pistol in hand, was a British officer and a dragoon.

Joshua whispered, "I know that dragoon officer! His name is Tarleton. He's the one O'beirne sneaked up and got the drop on when our horses teams were stolen."

Wend said, "Well, he's turned the tables today. He's captured the second senior general of the army."

Quinn said, "Besides that cornet, I see only eight dragoons. We got double the men. Let me steal back and bring them up. We can take the whole lot of them and free Lee."

Wend's immediate instinct was to agree with Quinn. But then another thought—actually a myriad of thoughts—ran through his mind. He recalled why he had been sent on this mission and the urgency of Lee's division joining Washington. He struggled mentally for a few long seconds. Finally, he made his choice.

Quinn pushed him again. "Eckert, shall I bring up the rest of the troop?"

Wend took a deep breath. "No, we'll just observe. There's too much chance of Lee getting hurt if we attack." He felt all of them staring at him, not believing his decision.

Quinn looked at him with fire in his eye. "For God's sake, Eckert, what the hell is keeping you from giving the order? There's a general about to be taken away and you're doing nothing!"

Wend just stared at the sergeant. The issue was too complicated to explain in a few words. Then in an instant, the necessity of explaining evaporated.

Suddenly Quinn's head snapped around, and he looked down the road. He put his hand to his one good ear. "Damn, I hear horses coming at the gallop! Lots of them!"

The noise of pounding hooves got louder, coming fast. Then suddenly over thirty horsemen, all in the uniform of the 16th, came up the road and pulled up in the yard in front of the tavern.

Quinn said, "It's a bloody full squadron of dragoons!"

Wend saw an officer at the head of the column raise his arm into the air and order the halt. "Cornet Tarleton, what is toward?"

The officer holding the pistol said, "Colonel Harcourt, that loyalist who told us the general was here was right! I have the honor of presenting Major General Charles Lee of the so-called Continental Army. He has surrendered to me and my men."

Harcourt stared at Lee for a moment. Then said, "Damn fine work, Tarleton! General Grant sent us up here to find out what Lee was up to, but he'll be absolutely delighted to have a little talk with the general himself."

Lee spoke up. "I presume, Colonel, that I and my aides shall be treated with all the courtesies of war."

"You will be treated to all the courtesies that a former officer of the British Army who rises in rebellion against his King is entitled to. But ultimately General Howe will decide what to do with you." Harcourt looked around. "Mr. Tarleton, I assume the general and his aides have horses out in the tavern stable. Get them mounted posthaste. I intend to leave here immediately and get back to Grant's headquarters as expeditiously as possible." He pointed at the prisoner. "When the rebels find out we have Lee, they'll likely mount some sort of pursuit."

Within a few minutes, the cavalry and their prisoners rode off to the south. Wend and the others came out of their hiding place. Turning to Quinn, Wend said, "Send Bloom back to have the patrol join us here at the tavern. I'll be inside, finding out precisely what happened."

Wend sat at a writing table in the room Lee had occupied, writing a dispatch to Washington. He had related the capture of Lee and was finishing with the report that Sullivan and his men would be marching immediately to the ferry at Tinicum. He was just finishing when Donegal came into the room. He carried a tankard of ale in his hand and sat down on the other side of the table.

"Wend, you ought to know that Quinn is down in the common room tellin' all who would listen what a coward you are for not tryin' to rescue Lee. I'd na be surprised if Joshua didn't take a swing at him any time now."

"Yes, Donegal, and if we had attempted to save Lee, we'd be prisoners of that Colonel Harcourt right now, who would have arrived just in time to scoop us up."

"Sure and that's true, but you could na have known he was commin."

Wend sighed. "And how do you feel about it, Simon?"

"I've been knowin' you since you was a lad in '63—thirteen years now. And I know you ain't afeared of man or beast. But I'm sure and puzzled by you being so hesitant to try to free Lee."

Wend put the quill down and looked into the eyes of his old friend. "Simon, hear me out: There's much more at play here than I can tell you now. It's about the army, congress, and the games generals play amongst themselves." He pointed in the direction of the tavern yard. "I had to make a quick decision out there. I may have made the wrong one, but it's done now and for us at least, it happened to keep us out of harm's way. And someday I'll be able to tell you all the details. But for now, I just need you to be a good soldier and friend and help me get General Sullivan and his division back to the army where they are needed."

"Of course you got that. Weren't never any question. I just wanted you to know what Quinn is sayin'."

"Thank you, old friend. And now, before people start throwing punches, tell Quinn to get Bloom and come up here to see me."

The two of them arrived shortly. Wend could smell ale on the sergeant's breath.

Quinn looked at Wend with a surly scowl. "You wanted to see us, Eckert?"

Wend frowned at Quinn. "Let me remind you it's *Major Eckert,* Sergeant."

Quinn raised his eyes to heaven, then looked back at Wend. "Yes, Major."

"Good." Wend pointed to the paper on the table. "Now I need to send Bloom back to army headquarters with a dispatch to Washington. It tells him what happened to Lee and that the division is on the way."

"Right, sir. Bloom's the man to do it."

"He's got to get there as fast as possible, so Washington can make plans. Make sure he's got a strong horse up to being pushed for two hard days. And get food for Bloom to carry so he won't have to find it along the way." Wend folded and sealed the dispatch and handed it to the trumpeter. "You've got an important job, Bloom. And you need to ride right away."

"Right, sir. I'll get it done."

The two men left and Wend stood up, grabbed his hat and descended the stairs to the common room. Most of the troop were sitting around, cups in hand. Wend said, "You all had better settle up with the tavern, we're riding out to Sullivan's camp immediately."

Wend started to leave, but the proprietress left the counter and barred his way. "Now see here, Major. There's a reckoning to be made."

"Mrs. White, I just told the men to pay for their ale."

"It ain't their spirits I'm worried about, but that damned general spent two days here, eatin' and drinkin' and sleepin' in my best room, and I ain't been paid a penny for all of that. Who's goin to pay me?"

Wend sighed. "Mrs. White, I would pay you from my own pocket, if I had the money. But all I can say is that you must go to the army for your recompense. I suggest you correspond with the quartermaster general or see him personally."

"The Devil you say! All that means is I'll never get my money!"

"I am truly sorry, Ma'am." Wend touched his hat to her and then waved at all the men. "All right, get mounted. We're riding immediately."

Alexander Tresh, the collar of his heavy overcoat turned up to shield his neck from the frigid wind, trudged through the late night over the frozen ground from Washington's headquarters to his tent. He was surprised to see his wife, heavily bundled up in coat and scarf, sitting before the fire.

"My dear Catherine, why are you sitting out here? I should have imagined you would long ago have been in your cot under the covers."

She responded, "Because it's far warmer in front of the fire. I vow I'd freeze in the tent." Then she asked, "Why are you so late coming home? You've been at headquarters all day and into the night."

"Well, Catherine, I can tell you this has been a momentous day."

She sat up and put her gloved hands nearer the flames. "What's happening, Alex?"

"A courier came in from Major Eckert today with startling and important news." He explained the mission Wend had been sent on. Then he said, "The news, my dear, is that General Lee has been captured by the British."

"My God, Alex! This is a disaster. He's got the most brains of any of the rebel officers. We've seen how Washington has bumbled through this campaign."

"Now, my dear, be charitable. Washington is a very smart man, but he doesn't have the military experience of Lee. But he certainly does have the presence and patience for an army commander. The men loyally follow him."

Catherine sighed. "If you insist, Alex." She looked up at him. "But what took so long at headquarters?"

"The other part of the courier's news is that Lee's division, now under Sullivan, has left its encampment near Morristown and is marching to join us here. Some of Glover's men have been dispatched with boats to ferry them across the Delaware." He stopped and looked at her meaningfully. "And that, in turn, means that Washington has made the final decision to attack the enemy."

"You mean one of the outposts along the river?"

"Precisely, my dear. That is what took so long. Washington, Greene, Mercer, and of course Glover were bent over maps making the necessary plans. I was privileged to be a part of the discussion." Tresh sat down in a chair beside his wife. "You know, my dear, you are quite correct: It is much better beside the fire."

Catherine ignored her husband's comment. Instead, she bit her lip, then looked over at him. "Alex, did they go so far as to decide which outpost to hit and the day of attack?"

Tresh hesitated a moment, staring into the fire. Then he said, "It is most confidential, my dear, but I will keep nothing from you. The place is Trenton, where there is a garrison of 1500 Germans under a certain Colonel Rall, and the date is the 25th. The army will be transported across the river by Glover and his men at a ferry directly east of here and will attack Trenton at dawn."

"Washington's going to attack on *Christmas*?"

"Yes, Catherine. You must admit that it will certainly be the last thing the Germans will expect."

Catherine sat staring into the fire. Then she asked, "Alex, would you be so good as to get me some of the whiskey? It will help ward off the chill."

As her husband complied, Catherine sat thinking very hard, thoughts and ideas spinning in her head like debris in a whirlwind. By the time he had returned with her libation, she had made up her mind. She said, "Alex, the plan seems like a very dangerous move for the army. To cross the river in the dark of night, march miles south, and stage an attack without being discovered seems almost impossible. And merely crossing the Delaware is highly dangerous. There were ice flows when we crossed earlier this month, and clearly things can have only gotten worse with this cold weather. And if the attack fails—I mean, you have told me yourself the German Grenadiers are some of the best soldiers in Europe—it could be the end of Washington's army."

"Sadly, you are quite correct, Catherine. It will be extremely dangerous. At every step of the movement there is the *great chance*, some would say the *likelihood*, of disaster. Washington is taking an extraordinary roll of the dice. I think no rational gambler would take the bet on a positive outcome."

Catherine did not respond. Instead, she put down her cup and stood up. She walked to the other side of the fire and paced back and forth several times, her arms crossed in front of her chest. Then she came around to the near side of the fire, stood behind her husband's chair, leaned over, and put her arms around him. Then she whispered into his ear. "Alex, I must tell you something."

"What, my dear? You do look very disturbed."

She straightened up and spoke normally. "It's about the time I spent at Clive Harfeld's house in Morristown. I'm afraid something happened there that I must tell you about."

Tresh's head spun about, a look of great anxiety in his eyes. "What are you trying to tell me?"

Catherine laughed. "No, Alex. I wasn't in bed with Clive. My darling, I'll always be true to you."

"Forgive me for doubting you, my dear, but what is it that is so serious?"

"Well, Alex, you know that Harfeld is a lawyer and deals in land sales." She paused and then said, "But he confessed to me that he is much more than that."

Puzzled, Tresh asked, "And what is that?"

"Alex, he is General Howe's chief spy in this area. He runs a web of watchers and couriers to keep the British Army informed of the rebels' movements and plans." She felt her husband's body stiffen as if he had just received a shock. "And he made me an offer which it was impossible to refuse."

Tresh turned his head, and their eyes were just a few inches apart. "And what was that offer?"

"Just a minute, Alex." She hurried into the tent, then quickly returned. There was a paper in her hand. "Obviously, he wanted information on Washington's plans, and in return, he and another officer, a Colonel Northcutt, promised me—or rather us, Alex—a substantial estate at a price we can afford."

Tresh took a deep breath. "Of course, you refused."

"No, Alex, I *accepted*. I have already provided them with information since my return. That peddler who visited a few days ago acts as a courier to Harfeld and Northcutt." She handed him the paper. "This is a contract."

Tresh quickly scanned the paper. "My God, Catherine! How could you do such a thing!"

"It is for us! To secure the life we have desired, to obtain the life for which we traveled to America. For God's sake, the rebel cause is hanging by a thread. Its collapse is imminent. You just admitted that Washington's gambit to attack Trenton is a last desperate gasp, and if it fails, as is likely, the war is over. We must think of ourselves now. If we get detailed word to the British warning of the attack, we will secure their gratitude and indebtedness to us."

"Catherine! I have pledged my support to the Americans. It would be dishonorable to betray them!"

"The Patriot cause is doomed! Doomed, don't you understand? The bloody rebels haven't paid you a farthing or given you a command. And it is no longer the time to think about honor; it is the time to secure both our *safety* and our future. For God's sake, you must accept what everyone knows in their heart: It is over! Soon Washington and his collaborators will be fleeing for their lives, probably to end up on the gibbet or before a firing squad. Think of how the King treated the Highland rebels after the Battle of Culloden."

Tresh turned and looked into her eyes, and she felt the stiffness leave his body. "Catherine, I must admit there is much truth to what you say. I have maintained my support for Washington, hoping for some reversal in fortune, but there is no sign it will happen."

"Alex, please think of *my* safety. I don't want to be forced to go on the run like some desperate criminal fleeing the sheriff."

Tresh sat staring into the fire for what seemed an eternity, Catherine holding him tight in her arms. She whispered, "Alex, think of this: You are not as young as you once were. Soon enough you will have to stop soldiering, much as you enjoy it. This is your path to a comfortable retirement."

Finally, Tresh said in a weary voice, "What is it you would have us do?"

"There is no time to wait for the peddler to come back. I will go myself to warn this Colonel Rall in Trenton and he can get the word to the British commander. They will spring a trap for Washington when he advances on the town."

"Catherine, how will you get there? How will you get across the river?"

"The peddler told me about a loyalist man who has a boat hidden near Trenton. He said I should contact this man in an emergency—I have a secret word to identify myself—and he will row me across. I'll leave tomorrow on horseback and be in Trenton by dawn the next day. You will stay here and perform your duties as if nothing has changed."

"But how will I explain your absence, Catherine?"

"Just say I couldn't stand the cold. I went to a village nearby to board in a house for a few days' respite. No one will suspect anything is amiss." She kissed him on the cheek. "And soon this war will be over—Harfeld and Northcutt will ensure your safety, and we will be reunited."

She kissed him again. "It's a good plan, Alex. It *will* work. And in a few weeks we shall be looking over our new land in Jersey and beginning a new life."

Alexander Tresh sighed and then slowly nodded. "Yes, Catherine, you are right. It is indeed time to think of ourselves."

Reese Newkirk stood before the officer's fire in his dress blue officer's uniform with O'beirne and Childers looking on. He asked, "I say, does everything look proper?"

It was Shay, leaning back in a camp chair before the fire, who answered, "Oh, my esteemed First Lieutenant, you are quite ready for a parade, not to mention sitting on a court martial." He was referring to the fact that Reese had been appointed to the board of a court martial due to convene within the half hour at headquarters.

Childers, sitting beside O'beirne, agreed. "You do look very good, Reese. By the way, what did the poor fellow do to merit a court?"

"I'm not quite sure, something about misappropriation of supplies or some such." He pulled out his pocket watch. "And I must be off if I'm to be on time." He made a final adjustment of his sword belt, nodded to the others, and strode off toward the mansion.

Shay pulled his overcoat tighter, looked up at the overcast sky and said to Childers, "It's been so damned long since I've seen the sun I likely won't recognize it when we actually have a clear day." He pointed to the wood pile and said, "Be a good lad and toss a few more splits into the fire."

Edward stood up and started feeding the fire. Then he looked over at Shay. "I was talking with Mrs. Flannagan. She says Patricia Carver is going to have her baby any time now."

"Aye, it'll be a blessed event, but it's a great shame the child will never know its father."

A serious look came over Childers' face. "Well, Jed is listed as missing, and nobody saw him shot or go down in the rearguard action. There's a chance he was captured. Maybe he'll be traded or come back after the war."

"Sure, and there's a small chance Private Carver will return someday, but I have little hope, lad."

Just then, Melinda Wood, who had been working at the cook fire nearby, came over and said, "The Treshes' servants—the Moulders—are here wantin' to talk to you, Lieutenant O'beirne."

Shay looked up to see the two of them standing near the cook fire. He noticed that they seemed to have anxious expressions on their faces. "Well, tell them to come over, Melinda."

They approached and stood close to each other, arm in arm. O'beirne asked, "What is it you wish to speak to me about?"

Harold Moulders looked over at Childers and said, "With respect, Lieutenant, could we talk privately?"

Shay was puzzled at what was bothering the couple. Edward took the cue, saying diplomatically, "Actually, it's nigh on time for me to make rounds of the company camp." He donned his hat, rose, and touching it to Elise, strode off at a brisk pace.

O'beirne said brightly, "Now there's a lad who knows his manners." Then he turned back to the Moulders. "But what is it that you wish to talk with me about? I must say, you both look very serious."

Harold Moulders took a deep breath and said, "In fact, sir, it is a grave matter we have come to speak to you about. It concerns Mrs. Tresh."

"Now, Moulders, why would you want to discuss something about Mrs. Tresh with me?" Shay thought, *For God's sake, did Catherine let something slip about our relationship before she met Tresh?*

"It's just this, sir. We thought, she is Irish, as are you, and we have seen you talking to her many times. So we thought we could confide in you and ask your counsel about a matter we have discovered." He looked over at his wife. "Or I properly should say, Elise has discovered."

O'beirne raised an eyebrow. "And what is it you believe you have discovered?"

Elise responded, "Mr. O'beirne, last night I was bringing some clean clothes back to Mrs. Tresh's tent, and I overheard them talking—talking about betraying the army."

O'beirne stiffened and half-rose from his seat. "What? You can't be serious."

Moulders said, "Ja, she is, sir. Elise, now you tell him precisely what you heard."

"Well, a lot of the time they were whispering, but I was just beside the tent, and I heard much of it. Sir, when we was in Morristown, we stayed at a certain Mr. Harfeld's place, and Catherine told the colonel that this man was an important spy for the British. And he convinced her to get information for him. She said he promised to get them land, a plantation, if you will, if she would cooperate. And Mr. O'beirne, that is what Catherine wants more than anything else; I know that from bein' with her for a year now." She stopped to organize her thoughts. "Well, the colonel had told her that the army was going to attack Trenton at Christmas, so she's goin' to go to Trenton to warn them."

"When is she planning to leave?"

"That's it, Mr. O'beirne. She rode out on her horse just a little while ago. She said to me that she was lookin' for a place to hire a room to stay warm, but I heard them say last night that would be her excuse for leavin'. So it's sure she's on her way to warn the British."

Shay thought hard. He wanted to disbelieve what he was being told, but he knew Catherine craved wealth and land more than anything else. It had the ring of truth. Then another thought struck him. "Why didn't the colonel go with her?"

It was Moulders who answered, "They planned for him to stay, so no one would suspect what was happening. If both of them disappeared, the army staff would know something was amiss."

O'beirne realized it all made sense. He thought for a moment, then asked, "How the devil is Catherine going to get across the river? The ferry at Trenton is not running, and there's a picket stationed there."

Elise responded, "I heard her say there's a man loyal to the British who's hiding a boat near to Trenton. He's prepared to take her across."

O'beirne jumped up. *Damn,* he thought, *it all was feasible. And Catherine was daring enough to do it—or at least attempt it.* He asked, "How long ago did she leave? As exact as you can remember."

Harold said, "It was no longer than an hour ago."

Shay paced back and forth for a few moments. Then something occurred to him. He stopped and stared at Moulders. "Why are you telling me this? You are betraying your master and mistress. You have been in long service to Colonel Tresh."

It was Elise who spoke first. "I think you have it *wrong,* Mr. O'beirne. They are *betraying* us. What will become of us? Who knows what will happen if the army is defeated or collapses?"

Molders added, "We talked this over last night. We have been loyal to the colonel and Catherine, but it is time for us to look out for ourselves. We want to stay in America and work in our own interest, maybe find a small farm where we can support ourselves."

O'beirne made up his mind. "All right, the both of you. Go back to your quarters and stay there. Don't tell anyone else what is going on and act normally with the colonel. He must not suspect that you have told anyone what they are doing. Do you understand?"

They nodded in unison. Then Harold asked, "What are you going to do, Lieutenant?"

O'beirne said, "I'm going to immediately ride after Catherine. We can't let her get to Trenton, or even somehow get word across the river. I must cut her off." He picked up his hat and told them, "You have done the right thing. I'll make sure that the army knows about your loyalty. Now I must ride."

He went into his tent to get his pistols and sword. When he went back out, Childers had returned. He said, "If I may ask, what was that all about with the Moulders?"

O'beirne put his arm on Childers'. "Edward, Catherine Tresh is betraying Washington's plans to the British. I'm riding to stop her."

Childers said, "My God!"

Then Shay had a thought. "And I might need assistance. You are coming along to help catch her. I'll explain things as we ride."

Childers' face broke into a look of shock. "Shouldn't we get some of Fairfield's dragoons to come with us?"

Shay pulled the ensign close and said in a low voice, "No, Edward. This is *officers' business.* Don't say a word about what we are about to anyone when you get your horse and saddle up. Do you understand?"

"Yes, sir."

"Let's go then. We have a hard ride, and I fear there is some very dirty work ahead of us."

Chapter Twenty

River of Ice

It was coming on nightfall as Wend Eckert, weary from a long, hard ride, his clothing soaked by freezing rain that had persisted along the way, dismounted in front of army headquarters. The rest of his detachment had headed straight for their bivouac area after arriving back at the encampment. He went up the steps and into the house's hall, where a captain sat at the desk, and asked to see General Mercer.

Mercer heard his voice and hurried out of his office. "Eckert! We've been waiting for your return. Washington wants to see you immediately." He waved for Eckert to join him as he went to Washington's door and knocked. Then he swung it open and announced, "Sir, Eckert is here."

Wend followed Mercer into the office. Washington was leaning over his desk with a paper in hand. He dropped it and sat back in his chair as Wend entered. Then he said, "Welcome, Major. I am, of course, quite eager for your report, particularly the details of Lee's capture."

Wend stood in front of the desk while Mercer leaned against a wall, arms crossed in front of his chest. Wend said, "First, sir, before I get to Lee, you should know that when I left Tinicum Ferry yesterday, most of Sullivan's division had crossed. Only some artillery and supply wagons remained to be ferried. I expect they'll be here sometime on the morrow."

Washington nodded in satisfaction. "They can't arrive too soon. Now, sir, your account of how Lee came to be captured."

Wend explained how Lee had gone to the isolated tavern miles from his division headquarters.

Mercer interrupted. "Damn, what could the man have been thinking?"

Washington said, "Hugh, that is the prime question and one to which we may never have the answer." Then he motioned for Wend to continue.

Wend explained how, after meeting with Sullivan, they had made their way to Basking Ridge only to find the tavern surrounded by British dragoons and Lee in their custody.

Mercer asked, "And you made no attempt to rescue Lee?"

This was the question Wend had feared. He took a breath and said, "I considered it, sir, but was afraid the general might be injured or killed if an exchange of fire ensued. In addition, I feared that if we failed and sustained heavy casualties, no one would be left to inform Sullivan about the situation." He looked at Washington and Mercer in turn, then continued, "And in any case, a full squadron of dragoons arrived almost immediately. So, even if we had prevailed at first, we then would have been captured."

Washington didn't say anything immediately. He stared at Wend for a few seconds, then rose from his chair, walked slowly over to the fire and gazed into it for a moment, his hands clasped behind his back, lost in thought. Then he turned, a strange look in his eyes, and said, "Yes, yes, Major. I believe you did the right thing. It is unfortunate that Lee is lost, but your action was quite correct, and indeed you have provided valuable service."

Relieved, Wend said, "Thank you, sir."

Washington gave a slight smile and continued, "Now, Major Eckert, things are progressing quite rapidly here. Decisions have been made. We shall be in action in just a few days. Return to your command and ensure it is ready in all respects, for you will have an important role in what ensues."

"Yes, sir." Then Wend followed Mercer out.

"Come with me to my office, Eckert." Mercer shut the door after Wend. He sat down at his desk, filled his pipe, lit it, and took a good draw. Then he looked skeptically at Wend. "Eckert, I'll say straight out I don't believe what you said in there. I mean the part about Lee's capture. Not for a minute!"

Wend started to reply, but Mercer cut him off. "Frankly, I think you made a decision to let the British take Lee without any interference."

Wend didn't know precisely how to answer. He said simply, "Sir, the circumstances were as I explained."

Mercer pointed the stem of his pipe at Wend. "Here's the truth: You let them take Lee because it meant a certain end to his insubordination. He'd have no more opportunity to prevent his division from rejoining the army or foment discontent about Washington's command. You took it upon yourself to end the problem that way."

Wend took a deep breath. "Sir..."

"Don't say anything more. The truth is, I damn well believe you made the right decision." Mercer grinned. "And I can tell you with certitude that George believes the same thing. He'll never say it out loud, but when he was standing by the fire and you were explaining, there was a glint in his eyes. I've known him a long time, and I tell you he was glad that Lee was decisively out of the picture. If you had ended up relieving Lee by use of that letter, he would have gone to Congress and personally made his case against Washington. Now that won't happen as long as he's the guest of General Howe."

Mercer waved Wend to a chair in front of the desk. "Now that's an end to it. Sit down, Eckert, and I'll brief you on what's about to happen."

Wend took his seat. "I assume you mean the attack on one of Howe's outposts."

"Indeed. Confidentially, it's going to happen on Christmas."

"My God, that's just a few days away."

"Precisely. And the place we're going to strike is Trenton. Colonel Rall's brigade."

Wend responded, "It was Rall's Grenadiers that led the charge at Fort Lee. They were the ones who bayoneted many of our men, even as they were trying to surrender."

"Yes, that's quite true. But while attacking Rall will constitute a welcome bit of vengeance, that's not the reason we're hitting his brigade. Trenton is the closest enemy outpost and has a convergence of roads which will facilitate our approach." He hesitated a moment and said, "And that's where you and Fairfield come in. You'll be the first across the river and will scout the roads and help scoop up anybody who could give away our approach."

"Certainly I welcome the opportunity."

Mercer said, "Washington thinks your men are the best troops for the mission." He reached down to his desk and picked up a folded paper. "This is a rough map of Trenton and the roads around it. It's been put together by local Jersey militia. Take that back to your bivouac and study it well."

Wend took the map and stood up. "If that's all for now, I'll get back to my tent." He smiled. "I admit I need some rest."

"I'm sure, and you well deserve it. But I have one more thing before you go." He handed him a small pamphlet.

Wend looked at the little booklet. It was just a few pages, and the title read, *The American Crisis.*

Mercer said, "Do you know the name 'Thomas Paine?'"

Wend searched his mind. "It sounds familiar, but I can't place it. Sorry, sir."

"Paine is the man who wrote '*Common Sense.*' Does that mean anything to you?"

"Yes, General. I remember reading that. It was a rationale for defying the King, published in newspapers all over the colonies at the beginning of the war. Very forceful arguments."

"Damn right. It helped to light the flames of our cause. Well, for your information, Paine has been along on this campaign, serving as a volunteer aide to General Greene. That essay you have in your hand is meant to stir up enthusiasm among our troops and the citizenry in this dark moment."

"Given our situation and the condition of our soldiers, that's going to take a bit of doing."

"Well, it's strongly and emotionally written. If anything can pump up morale, that will do it. Washington wants it read to all the men throughout the army. Have your officers read it to the men of your and Fairfield's units."

Wend scanned the opening phrase. It began, 'These are the times that try men's souls . . .' He looked up at Mercer. "Compelling and true words. Well, it can't hurt." Then in a weary tone, he said, "I'll be on my way, sir."

Mercer smiled. "You do look weary, sir. Rest well, Wend Eckert."

Shay O'beirne and Edward Childers galloped over the crest of the low hill just west of the Delaware across from Trenton and pulled up their horses. The lights of the town shone brightly across the river.

Childers pointed down the road. "Shay, look, there's a fire with men around it."

"Aye, Lad, that'll be the militia picket watching the river and Trenton. Let's ride up and have a word with them."

They rode to the fire, which was about a hundred fifty yards from the river. As they approached, the circle of men seated around the flames turned to look at their visitors. The two officers dismounted and walked to the fire. All the men were heavily bundled against the cold and held cups in their hands.

Shay said, "I'm Lieutenant O'beirne of the Frederick County Light Foot. Who's In charge here?"

A man in his late thirties, in a heavy overcoat, raised his hand but made no effort to rise from his seat on a log. "I'm Newly. Sergeant Newly of the county militia. What's your business, sir?" Then he pointed at their horses. "The way them animals is lathered up, it must be damned urgent."

Shay ignored his words and said, "We're looking for someone and have some questions to ask of you."

One of the other men spoke up in a jocular tone, "You may have questions, I ain't sure we got any answers."

The rest of the group laughed. O'beirne thought, *They're pretty jolly because they've undoubtedly got liquor in those cups.* Ignoring their mirth, Shay asked, "Have you seen a woman come past? Riding a tall, spirited bay horse?"

Newly said, "Aye, that we did. 'Weren't but maybe fifteen minutes ago. Fine lookin', well dressed, middling woman, I'd say. Damned strange to see a woman like that out in this weather, what with all the cold and snow fallin'. But she stopped and asked if we knew where a fellow named Webber lived. We couldn't answer, since ain't none of us from this town." He waved down toward the ferry landing. "She headed for the river. Perhaps she stopped at the tavern there, right at the ferry."

O'beirne looked down toward the river, then thanked the sergeant. He motioned to Childers. "Come on Edward, let's go check the tavern."

They mounted and headed for the river. Childers remarked, "Look at the lights in the tavern windows. They're very inviting. Perhaps she's there, warming up and making inquiries."

"I damn well hope we could be so lucky. We'll go take a look."

They pulled up their horses at the landing. The ferry itself sat forlorn at its moorings, having been idle since the army had crossed in early December.

Shay also saw something else. "Damn, Edward, look at the river!"

Childers stared a moment and exclaimed, "My God, it's solidly packed with ice. There are big, solid flows, all jammed together."

"Yes, and no boat is going to be able to navigate through that mess."

Then O'beirne looked over at the tavern and saw something else. "See there, Edward! It's Catherine's horse! Tied at the rail."

"God, yes, Shay! Maybe we are going to be lucky after all."

They both dismounted and tied the horses next to Catherine's. Then they rushed to the front door and pushed through it. O'beirne quickly scanned the common room, only to see it was empty save for two men by the fire, ale in hand, and the proprietor at the bar.

"She's not here," said Childers, disappointment in his voice.

Shay said nothing but walked up to the counter. The proprietor said, "What's your choice, sir?"

"Information: I'm looking for a young woman. Pretty, with black hair and in heavy overcoat." He pointed over his shoulder. "Her horse is out there. She might have inquired about a local man—someone named Webber."

"Yeah, she was just here. And she asked about Charley, all right. I was a bit surprised and figured she must be tryin' to get across the river. Everyone knows Webber has a boat hidden. He takes people across the river at night, for a bit of hard money." The man grinned. "You army people got the ferry shut down and took all the boats what could be found, but Charley was smart enough to hide his. He figured there was goin' to need to be some commerce over the river."

"So did you send her to this Charley Webber?"

"Yeah, I told her where he lives, his place is right along the riverbank just to the north. But she ain't getting across any time soon. You saw the ice in the river. No boat gonna' get through that."

Shay said, "Yes, we saw. But why is it so jammed with ice here? Upriver there are plenty of flows and chunks of floating ice, but it's not solid."

"It happens every year right at this point. The river narrows and there's a sharp bend just below the town. The frozen chunks choke together and form sort of a dam of ice."

"All right, so did the woman take a room here? Is she upstairs?"

"Naw, she just stormed out of here. Real upset she was. I figure she went somewhere else. Maybe to look up Charley even though it won't do her no good."

Shay leaned over the counter and grabbed the proprietor. "I think you're lying. Her horse is still outside. Where is she?"

"Why the devil would I lie? I tell you she just walked out of the tavern and I ain't seen her since. She was only here for a few minutes."

Suddenly Childers, who was standing near a window, called out, "Shay, we need to go outside. There's something you want to see." He turned and went through the door nearly at the run.

Shay thought, *What the Hell?* But he followed Childers outside.

The ensign was standing at the riverbank beside the ferry, staring hard across the ice toward the lights of Trenton. He turned to O'beirne. "I thought I saw something moving out there! Like a person, Shay!"

"The Devil you say!"

Edward was pointing. "There! Look! Just past that upended ice flow. It*is* someone moving and I swear it looks like a woman!" He turned to his companion. "My God, Shay, she wouldn't try to cross on foot, would she?"

O'beirne felt a dread feeling in his stomach. He said, very softly, "If there's any woman who would dare it, it's Catherine Tresh." He scanned the ice, hoping against hope Childers' eyes were playing him false, that it was some sort of illusion. But then he saw a figure emerge from behind a high, broken and slanted slab of ice nearly six feet high. His heart skipped a beat and he knew it was Catherine. Instantly his stomach knotted up. "Good God, Lad, you're right. It's her!"

"What are we going to do, Shay?"

"There's only one thing for it, Lad, I'm going out there to catch her."

"I'll not let you go alone. Two of us will have a better chance of stopping her."

Shay walked down the bank to the edge of the ice. He pulled out one of his pistols and checked the priming.

Childers asked, "You're not going to shoot her, are you?"

"We'll try to grab her alive. But I'll shoot if I must. She can't be allowed to get to Trenton." He took a deep breath and said, "All right, Edward, are you ready?"

Childers nodded. "Let's go."

It was hard going. Much of the ice was covered with a layer of snow, which helped with their footing. But in places the wind had driven it bare and they slid and slipped on the slick surface. Each of them fell a couple of times. They had to dodge around huge chunks of ice. But there was even more of a hazard—in places the ice wasn't stable, the flow not packed tightly against others, so that it would tip when you put your weight on it. One such almost got Shay. But he sensed the movement of it, and was able to jump back before his leg went into the cold water. He found a section of ice more solidly wedged against another and was able to pass by it and keep going.

They tried to move fast, for she had a good lead on them. And after a few minutes, Shay saw Catherine about thirty yards ahead. She was making slower progress than they were—moving bent over to keep her balance. And he saw that her smaller-sized boots meant she wasn't as steady as they were.

Shay screamed out, "Catherine! Catherine! It's Shay! I know what you are about! Come back—you'll never make it!"

Catherine dodged behind a high piece of ice. Then he heard her voice shouting in the night. "I'll make it, Shay. You of all people should know I've faced dangers worse than this. And if you had any sense, you'd join me. The rebels are done."

"Aiethne, Aiethne—no one knows you are an informer. I swear I've told nobody. Only the Moulders know, and they won't talk if you return. Come back now, and there will be no consequences. I vow I'll say nothing."

"You're a fool, Shay. The die is cast. And I'm finally going to get what I've been praying for all my life." Then there was a high-pitched laugh.

O'beirne shouted in desperation, "Aiethne, for God's sake, listen to me. Come back; it's too dangerous."

But his words were answered only by silence. O'beirne looked at Edward, who was staring at him with a puzzled expression. He called, "Come on, Childers. I think she's moving again. We must catch her."

They struggled on for another few minutes until O'beirne realized they were near the center of the river. The lights of Trenton and those of the tavern on the west bank looked equally distant. He was worried that he had not caught sight of Catherine since their exchange of words.

Childers called out, "I think we've lost her. She could be hiding behind one of the piles of ice! We'll never see her in this darkness. And out here in the middle, there are a lot more soft spots."

Shay responded, "We've got to keep going. She'll be taking as straight a line toward the lights of the town as she can. We'll move as fast as possible, try to get ahead of her, and cut her off when she reaches the riverbank."

"Shay, this is crazy. I tell you, she's gotten away."

"Edward, just keep moving!" Shay pushed on through the dark, Childers paralleling his movement about twenty feet to the north of him. And then, as luck would have it, there was a break in the cloud cover, and moonlight bathed the river.

Just a few moments later, the quiet was broken by a piercing shriek of panic, followed by another. O'beirne called out, "Lad, she's in trouble. And she's not far away." Then he shouted, "Aiethne! Keep calling! We'll come to you."

"I'm here! Here! Help me! I'm in the water. Oh, God, help me."

"For God's sake, keep calling out, Aiethne! It's the only way we'll find you."

"Here! Here! There's a high piece of ice flow by me!"

Childers pointed and shouted, "I see her! She's not fifty feet away! She's fallen through!"

Then O'beirne saw her and, throwing caution to the wind, ran toward her, slipping and sliding, once falling to his hands and knees. When he was within ten feet of her, he saw what had happened: In her hurry, she had stepped into a soft spot, then slipped feet first into the frigid water. Now she was bent over, her arms spread out on the ice, the weight of her torso laying on a solid piece while her legs were in the water.

Shay stopped where he was, wary about the firmness of the ice between him and Catherine. Breathing heavily, Edward joined him.

She screamed again, "For God's sake, hurry!"

Childers said, "We need to grab her arms and pull her out." He took a step toward her.

O'beirne grabbed his arm and held him back. "Lad, look at the ice in front of you."

Childers did so and exclaimed, "Damn! It's all cracked."

"That's right, Lad. It's thin and cracked. It won't hold our weight, leastways if we're standing up."

Catherine sobbed, panic in her voice, "Oh, Shay, I can't feel my legs anymore."

O'beirne dropped to his knees, then flattened out on the ice. "Lad, I'm going to try to crawl out toward her. It might support me if I'm spread out. Hold onto my ankles so you can pull me back if I start to sink."

O'beirne inched forward toward her position. Finally, he was within three feet of her. He stretched out his right arm so that his gloved hand was near hers. "Now, Lass, you must move an arm toward me and stretch out so you can hold my hand."

She was shivering violently, her hand and arm shaking. Slowly, with great effort, she moved it toward Shay and after what seemed like an eternity, touched her hand to his. Quickly he clasped it. "Now, I'm going to try to pull you out. But you've got to help by pushing on the ice with your other hand."

"I can hardly feel it. And the water is moving—it's pulling hard on my coat and skirts."

Shay called to Childers, "I can't move her, I can't get any grip on the ice. You've got to pull on my legs, Lad! I'll push with my free hand."

Edward did so, and was able, inch by inch, to move Shay backward. Catherine pressed down on the ice with her free hand and finally her body started to come upward, out of the water, and on to the ice.

O'beirne said, "Aiethne, we've got you. By God, we'll have you out of the water in just a moment."

And then to his horror, the ice under her torso cracked and she sank back into the water. Her hand slipped out of his and the current sucked her away. The weight of her overcoat and skirts pulled her down deeper into the water. In a moment only her head was above water and she uttered one final blood curdling shriek.

O'beirne screamed her name, "Aiethne, Aiethne!"

And then her head disappeared and she was gone under the thick ice.

Shay felt rising panic, fearing that he would sink also, but Childers, acting quickly, dragged him back to more solid ice. He looked up at the young man, about to thank him, but saw that he was staring at the water where Catherine had disappeared, his face contorted in utter horror and tears streaming down his cheeks. Childers said, "She was so close, so close to being safe. And then, then . . ." He stared silently at the place where Catherine Tresh had disappeared.

O'beirne was able to get to his feet. He put his arm around Edward's shoulders and said in a soothing voice, "Lad, it's done. We did what we could. And in the end, the sad truth is that she doomed herself." He turned and looked back to judge the distance to the tavern. "Now I'm damned wet and freezing. I need to get to a warm place. I've no desire to join Catherine in Hell. Leastwise, not for a few more years. Let's make our way to the tavern and the heat of its hearth."

O'beirne and Childers entered the common room of the ferry tavern. Everything was the same as when they had left, with the two men near the fire and the proprietor working at the bar.

O'beirne was shivering violently, and he immediately stripped off his soaked overcoat and uniform coat. He walked toward the hearth and pulled out a chair from the men's table, put it directly in front of the fire, and draped the clothing over it. The two men stared at him. Shay, returning their stare, said after a moment, "I'm sure you gentlemen won't mind if I dry the damned things. They just been in the river."

Then he walked over to the counter. "Sir, what might your name be?"

"Presley, Thomas Presley."

"Well, Thomas, I need some whiskey. Whiskey or rum, whichever you might have."

Presley responded, "Sir, I haven't had any of either for weeks. You'll have to do with a little brandy."

O'beirne glared at him. "Brandy will do for starts, but I'll wager you've got a private stock of whiskey or rum that you've husbanded for your best patrons. I'll pay you well. Get it for me!"

"I tell you I don't have any such." The proprietor placed a small glass on the counter and poured some brandy into it.

Shay downed it in one gulp. Then he walked around to the rear of the bar, pushing Presley out of the way, and began searching through cabinets.

The proprietor glared at O'beirne and exclaimed, "Who the hell do you think you are? You can't do this! Get away from my spirits." He took a step toward the lieutenant, reaching out as if to grab him.

Childers, who had also taken off his overcoat, was standing near the bar. He leaned across the counter and put a restraining hand on the proprietor's shoulder. "Sir, with all respect, I shouldn't interfere with him, if you value your well-being. I might point out that he's an Irishman, he's mad, and he's got a gun in his belt."

The proprietor looked at Edward with a touch of fear in his eyes and stopped moving toward O'beirne. At that moment, Shay shouted out, "Here's the bloody stuff! I damned well knew he had some stashed somewhere!" He had pulled the cork from a large jug and was smelling the contents. "Whiskey! Raw smelling, not like Eckert's, but it will do well enough!" He reached to a shelf and grabbed two cups, handing them to Childers. "Here, take these to a table." Then he put a hand into a pocket, pulled out some coins, and threw them onto the counter. "Here, there's your tariff! And more than enough." Then, carrying the jug, he roughly pushed past the owner, who shrank out of the way, and joined Edward at the table.

O'beirne poured a full cup of the whiskey, downed it immediately, then poured a cup for Childers and another for himself. The two men sat quietly drinking the liquor.

Childers glanced around and saw that the men at the hearth were staring at them, as was Presley. He remarked to O'beirne, "I'm afraid they don't know how to take us."

His companion scowled. "Let them damn well think what they may. We've had a rough night's work."

"Indeed, Shay, that we have. The Devil knows we participated in a tragedy out there on the river. But I will confide that there's much I don't understand about this night's events and about Catherine. And for that matter, about you."

"Lad, don't spend too much time pondering what happened. Sometimes there are no good answers for what people end up doing."

"It's not so much what Catherine did which puzzles me. It's about what was between *you and her*. Many times out there on the ice you called her *Aiethne*, not Catherine. I'd be a fool not to realize that you knew her well, that you were familiar before she was married to Tresh, and that Catherine is not her real name. Now Shay, we have ridden together today and shared the hellish events out on the river. Perhaps you would honor me by explaining the mystery?"

O'beirne gazed into the distance for long seconds. Then he turned to look at Childers, a great sadness in his eyes, and Edward thought for a moment he was going to explain his past with Catherine. But instead he said, simply, "Perhaps, lad, when some time has passed and the pain has faded and I'm sufficiently in my cups to talk about it, mayhap then I'll tell you the tale. But for now let's just say it was a long time ago and in another land." He shrugged, "And in any case, now the wench is dead." He closed his eyes and was silent for a while.

Momentarily, Childers spoke up. "That's not original. That's a paraphrase of a line in a Christopher Marlowe play. But it is appropriate."

The Irishman slowly opened his eyes and looked at the ensign. "Lad, I've said it before, and probably will again, your father didn't waste his money by sending you to that William and Mary school."

They sat silent for a while, then Shay looked over at the hearth. "We'll let the coats dry some more and finish this whiskey. Then, lad, we've got a hard ride back to the camp."

Chapter Twenty-One

New Orders

George Washington, sitting at his desk, read through the report as Mercer and Grayson stood watching. He looked up, sadness in his eyes. "All I can say is, Mrs. Tresh died a terrible death."

Mercer said, "There's no denying that, sir. But, regrettable as that might be, the important thing is that she was stopped before she could get to the British with her information about the attack."

"Yes, Hugh, you are quite right. The fact is we owe Lieutenant O'beirne and Ensign Childers a debt of gratitude."

Grayson spoke up. "No doubt of that, sir. But the next question is: What shall we do with Colonel Tresh? Should I prepare the order for a court martial?"

Mercer said, "Normally that would be in order. But this is a damned bad time to have to go through all of that, not to mention the probability of an execution. And the truth is, Tresh is more a victim of his wife's actions than an active participant in a conspiracy—it seems clear that he took no actual part in transmission of information. And there's another factor: Gossip will spread through the army about why Tresh is being tried. It may spur a lack of confidence among the officer corps. His experience and judgment are certainly respected throughout the army. If they perceive that this all happened because he had lost faith in our cause, disenchantment could spread. God knows there's already enough of that going around. Above all, it will all be a distraction at a time when we need to focus on organizing the attack on Trenton. We need the full support among the officers and men if the movement is to be a success. That was the whole purpose of getting Paine's pamphlet published."

Washington got up and paced the room. "Hugh, I think you are right. With the number of officers who would be sitting on a court martial, word would undoubtedly become public that we have had a spy and that might lead to the British getting some rumor of the impending action." He put a hand to his chin. "My sense is, it might be better to deal with this in a quieter way."

Grayson asked, "What do you have in mind, sir?"

Washington held up a finger. "Let's remember that Congress approved of Tresh joining the army and sent him to us. I have it in mind to write a report to the military committee explaining what happened and send Tresh under guard to them for disposition of his case. They can prosecute him if they desire, or they could just put him on a ship back to Europe."

Mercer smiled. "Knowing those politicians, the latter most likely will be their choice. In any case, he and his escort won't be in Baltimore until after Christmas. By that time our attack will be finished, the outcome will be settled one way or the other. And there'll be no chance in the near term for word of his wife's perfidy to leak out."

Washington said, "That is my thinking." Then he asked, "Where is Tresh now?"

Grayson said, "He's confined to his quarters. I tasked Eckert to post guards from his company."

"All right," replied Washington. "Order Captain Gibbs to provide a mounted escort from my Guard to take him to Baltimore. And they're to leave as soon as possible. Today would not be too soon, but without fail I want Tresh out of here by dawn tomorrow." Then Washington thought of something else. "What about his servants—the Moulders—who informed us of this situation? We are as much indebted to them as to O'beirne and Childers. What will become of them?"

Mercer said, "Leave that to me, sir. I had a discussion with Eckert. He has an idea about a way to send them to a place where they'll have the opportunity to prosper."

The commanding general went back to his desk and seated himself. "Excellent, gentlemen. I will leave the details to you and consider the matter resolved."

Grayson departed but Mercer lingered. Washington looked up at his friend. "You want to talk about something?"

"Indeed, sir. I wanted to ask what we're going to do with Eckert and his company. Virginia regiments are due to arrive soon. Should he and his men be put under one of them as their light company? That would be normal."

Washington sat at his desk thinking. "Frankly, it has been very useful having a scouting and skirmishing unit under my personal command. And there's no question that Eckert and his men have performed excellent service."

"My sentiment exactly, sir. We've used them as a successor to Knowlton and his men. I think we should keep it that way, but build on it and permanently align them with the Palmetto Light Horse." He hesitated a moment, then said, "And there's something else, George: A new troop of cavalry, from Maryland, arrived in camp today. Frankly, they don't have much experience—their duty was mostly ceremonial, such as escorting the former royal governor. But they could be quite useful given the proper leadership and training."

Washington looked up, a gleam in his eye. "Are you suggesting what I think you are?"

"George, let me put together the idea on paper and I will speak to you about the details very soon."

"I shall be waiting expectantly, Hugh."

There was a gray sky at dawn as Eckert walked with Gibbs of the Life Guard toward Tresh's tent. Along with them were a lieutenant and four dragoons from the guard, leading horses, including one for Tresh. Wend could see the colonel, fully dressed and in a heavy overcoat, hands clasped behind his back, standing in front of the fire. Two men from the Frederick County Light Foot stood near him, with muskets in hand.

Tresh looked up and saw their approach. He said, with irony in his voice, "Ah, Captain Gibbs, I see you have brought my guard of honor." He reached down to a camp chair and picked up a pair of saddlebags. "I was told I could take only what could fit into these."

Gibbs said, "That's correct, sir." The captain reached for the bags and handed them to the lieutenant. "Colonel, this is Lieutenant Boughten. He and his men will escort you to Baltimore." Boughten touched his hat to Tresh, then went over and laced the saddlebags to the colonel's horse.

There was a heavy silence as Boughten worked. Wend broke it to say, "Colonel, I came along to say farewell. We've marched together and shared the same campfire. I respect your experience in the art of war and deeply regret this turn of events. I wish things had played out otherwise."

Tresh's lips formed into an ironic smile. "Well, sir, I thank you for your kind words. I spent last night reflecting on the events of the last few days. The only consolation I can take is that I am not the first man who has been led into folly by a beautiful woman, and that I shan't be the last."

Wend nodded agreement. "I'll not disagree with you on that, sir."

"In any case, I loved Catherine so much that I could never have exposed her."

The expression on Tresh's face turned serious. "It will comfort me to believe that you understand I myself did *not* take any action to betray the trust the army and General Washington put in me. My fault was not having the fortitude to expose the actions of my wife." He shrugged. "However, I will admit that is, in itself, enough of a sin for me to face a reckoning by the authorities in Congress." He stood staring into the distance. "But in all seriousness, I vow that I would have preferred to be tried by a board of officers and face a soldier's punishment."

Wend said, "I can understand that." Wend reached into a pocket of his overcoat and pulled out a flask. "Here is some libation to warm you through your journey."

Tresh took the flask and put it in his own pocket. "If that is some of your own very fine whiskey, it will indeed be a comfort. You have my thanks, sir." Then a serious look came over his face. "One further question: What is to become of the Moulders? Regardless of what has occurred, they gave me years of faithful service, and I would not see them hurt by the events of the last few days."

Wend replied, "Have no worry about that. We have made plans for them to go to a place where they can prosper."

"Ah, Eckert, that is as comforting as the whiskey in my pocket."

Boughten said, "Colonel, if you are ready, let us mount and be off."

The escort mounted. Gibbs called out to his lieutenant. "God be with you and your men, Boughten. And come back as soon as you can!" Then he touched his hat to Tresh. "And Godspeed to you, sir. I hope Congress is in a mood for leniency."

Alexander Tresh swung up into his saddle, then swept his hat off in salute to Eckert and Gibbs. "Gentlemen, it's been a pleasure to serve with you, and I wish you fortune in the events of the coming days."

With that, Boughten signaled for them to ride, and the group left at the trot. The two officers watched as they headed through the camp and then turned onto the road that would take them south.

As they were watching, Donegal joined them. "Begin' your pardon, sirs! I got some news for you."

Wend looked at the sergeant. "And what might that be, Simon?"

"Ah, now, it's good news, you can surely say. Patty Carver has had her baby. Mrs. Flanagan just got it out of her. Bit of bother, it bein' her first one. But Martha knows her business."

The two officers smiled. Wend asked, "And what variety of baby did she have?"

"Sure and it's a bonnie little soldier. Got a strong voice too, I was just there to see him."

Gibbs waved in the direction of the departed Tresh and his escort, then looked over at Wend. "Well, the army just lost one and gained one."

Wend raised his eyebrows and sighed. "True enough. But here's the sad part: His father, Private Jed Carver, has been missing since the skirmish we had with the Jaegers east of Coryell's Ferry."

—ꟺ—

Wend and Joshua walked to the former Tresh campsite. Baird was leading his horse, which was saddled and loaded with his bedroll and saddlebags. Andrew Horner, Billy Wood, and the Moulders were standing by Tresh's cart.

Horner said, "Mr. Eckert, they're all loaded and ready to go. And Catherine's horse is tied to the rear."

Harold came to attention and touched his hat to Wend. "Captain Eckert, are you sure that we are allowed to take all these things? The possessions of the Treshes? And Catherine's horse?"

Wend put his hand on Moulder's shoulder. "I can assure you it is perfectly fine. Neither of the Treshes will have any further use for these things. General Washington himself has blessed it, and you will need them to get started in your new life."

Wend looked over at Baird. "Harold and Elise, this is my friend Joshua Baird. He knows Pennsylvania like the back of his hand. He's going to guide you to a place called Sherman Mill, which is in a fertile valley north of the town of Carlisle. His sister and her husband, a minister, live there and will shelter you while you take some time to decide your future. You may want to stay in Sherman Valley, or you may decide you want to travel somewhere else. If you decide to farm, there is plenty of good land around there, but there's even more land available further west."

Harold nodded. "Ja, ja, my Captain. I grew up on a farm in Germany before I went to the army as a youth. I think that is what we will do." He put his arm around his wife's waist. "We are excited that we will soon have our own place for the first time, but I will have to relearn much about farming, particularly how it is done here. It has been so many years."

Joshua said, "Reverend Carnahan and my sister Patricia are the very people to get you used to the way things work here in America. And Paul knows his way around Pennsylvania 'bout as good as I do. We'll talk about all that while we be on the road."

Wend looked at the sky. "It's coming on noon. Time for you to start if you are going to put a goodly amount of miles behind you today."

Elise said, "We thank you so much, Mr. Eckert, for all you have done for us, but I am a little frightened—this is a strange land, and everything is new to us."

Wend grinned. "Elise, this is America. It's a new land to everyone who is here. You are as much an American as anyone else, and don't forget that." He took her hand and said, "Let me help you up to your seat."

Once she was in her seat, Harold Moulders shook Wend's hand and then took his place on the cart and picked up the reins. Meanwhile, Joshua had mounted up. Wend walked over to him and said, "You got that bag of coins for Peggy safe with you?"

Joshua patted one of the saddlebags. "Right here."

"Well, have a safe journey to Sherman Mill and then down to Winchester. I'll trust you to give my love to Peggy."

"Shit, Wend, she don't need me to tell her that." Baird turned to the cart and waved to Harold. "Get that horse started! Let's make use of the light we still got!"

The two men from Eckert Ridge stood watching as Joshua led the cart and its occupants westward through the camp. In a few minutes, the little caravan disappeared around the trees at a turn of the road.

Horner looked over at Wend. "Well, sir, another good German family to make their home in America."

Wend laughed. "Yes, Andrew. Harold Moulders is not like us two Germans, who ended up marrying Ulster women instead of good German girls."

"Well, sir, I do have to say that at *night* I very much appreciate being married to an Ulster girl."

Wend grinned and put his hand on Horner's shoulder. "Yes, there is *definitely* that, Andrew. But I caution you to do all you can to avoid an argument with an Ulster wife."

A dour expression came over Horner's face. "I have already learned that, sir."

—ꟿ—

Night had fallen as the officers of the Frederick County Light Foot sat in camp chairs by their fire. The evening meal was finished, and Melinda was busy cleaning up the dishes from the table. Each man had a cup of whiskey in his hands, and conversation was desultory, the officers lost in their own thoughts.

Then Wend heard the voice of Donegal. "Na' Captain, I have someone you will love to see." He looked up to see the sergeant walk out of the darkness, a broad smile on his face. Surprisingly, Patricia Carver was standing beside him, holding her newborn in her arms. And then Wend saw something that made him jump up from his seat: Also standing with Donegal was Private Jedediah Carver.

He was dirty and unshaven, but he also had a wide grin on his face. Patricia, her eyes filled with tears of joy, said, "Captain, God has brought Jed back to me and his son! It's a miracle."

Wend said, "Indeed it is, Patricia! For God's sake, Carver, what happened to you? You weren't with us when we withdrew from the skirmish."

Carver touched the side of his head. "Truth is, sir, I took a hard knock from a Jaeger's rifle butt, and I passed out. Then, after you all was gone, they saw I was alive and took me to their camp."

All the other officers had gathered around to hear the story. Puzzled, Wend asked, "But how is it you are here? How did you escape?"

"Well sir, it's a bit of a story. They took me to see their captain. And he asked me all sorts of questions about who we were and particularly about you. He was pretty startled when I told him you came from a Jaeger family back in Germany."

O'beirne laughed, "Indeed, I expect he was. He was fighting a man from his own principality."

"But," said Wend, "that doesn't explain how you got here."

"Sir, the fact is, they let me go. That captain, his name is Ernst Wolff, and he sent me back with a message just for you. He made me memorize it."

Wend nodded. "All right, let's hear it."

Carver stiffened and, reciting like a child in class, said, "From Captain Wolff of the Fourth Company of the Hesse-Cassel Field Jaeger Corps to Captain Eckert of the Frederick County Light Foot Company: You have surprised us on the field once, but we accept the challenge and are eager to meet again. I vow that next time it is you who will be running in defeat. You will learn to your regret the skill of the Hessian Jaegers."

Newkirk laughed out loud. "Well, it seems this Captain Wolff has laid down a marker. But I think it will be he who relearns the lesson we taught him the other day."

Wend looked around at his officers. "Gentlemen, Reese is right. We'll pick up that marker and throw it back in this Captain Wolff's face!" Then he thought of something else. "And when we meet the Jaegers, we'll taunt them with their own hunting horn that Quinn took from them!"

O'beirne interject, "Indeed we will; trumpeter Bloom has been practicing the chase call on that horn!"

There were grins all around. Then Wend asked Carver, "You say they released you, but how did you get across the river and find your way here?"

"I ran into some Jersey militia. They knew a man with a boat, and he rowed me across. Then it weren't hard to find out where the army camp was."

"Well, Private, we're glad you are back. Now you and Patricia get to your campfire, have something to eat, and spend some time holding your son."

Donegal ushered the family back into the camp, and as they left, Fairfield, who had been down at his troop's bivouac, joined the other officers. The cavalryman sat down next to Eckert. "I just heard something interesting while talking with Sergeant McCrae down by the picket line."

"And that would be?"

"A new cavalry troop has joined the army. They rode in today and camped on the western edge of the camp. McCrae said he walked down to take a look and found out they're from Maryland."

"Well, that will likely take some of the load off of your men."

"Perhaps." Fairfield then held up a copy of Paine's pamphlet. "Well, I just sat watching as Ensign Middleton read this whole bloody thing to my troop." He looked over at Wend. "A damned waste of time if you ask me."

Ensign Childers spoke up. "I read it to my men. They listened carefully and were quite impressed. Paine's ideas are quite compelling. They asked if they could keep our copy for a while because some of the men wanted to read it again."

Wend replied to Fairfield, "Well, Geoffrey, despite your thoughts, Washington thinks it will have a positive effect on the men—to motivate them for the upcoming movement against Trenton."

Fairfield stared at Wend, disdain in his eyes. "They can be as motivated as you please, but it's not going to make this damned insane plan any more successful. The whole bloody idea is a fantasy." He held up the pamphlet. "And this is supposed to make it all better!" He tossed it into the fire. "The fact is this Trenton idea is likely going to be the destruction of the army. And if it's not, it will be wrecked and the end will be only a matter of time."

"Well, if you feel so strongly about it, you have my permission to seek an audience with Washington to give him the benefit of your wisdom."

"Don't be such an ass, Eckert. But I'll tell you that even Quinn thinks this is a stupid idea. And you know he loves a good fight."

Suddenly a familiar voice spoke out of the darkness beyond the fire's light. "Mr. Fairfield, if you are so discouraged, I'll take you to see the commanding general myself. We can go tonight." All heads turned to see General Hugh Mercer step into the firelight.

Fairfield jumped to his feet. "Sir," he sputtered, "My apologies! I vow I was tired after a long day and just releasing some anxiety in what I thought was a private moment."

Mercer said dryly, "Yes, I'm sure you thought no senior officer could hear. You are quite right that it is risky. But I must remind you that our only chance of success is if every officer wholeheartedly supports Washington's plan. I hope, with your doubts now off your chest, we can expect that from you, Mr. Fairfield."

Geoffrey took a deep breath. "I pledge that support with every bone in my body, sir. The Palmetto Light Horse will do its part come what may."

"I feel very reassured, sir." Mercer grinned broadly. "Well, back to matters at hand, gentlemen," said Mercer, motioning to all present. "I have someone here you'll all want to meet." He beckoned a figure who had been barely visible in the background darkness. "Join me, sir."

A tall, blond-haired, well-coiffed officer with a thin, high-cheekboned face, dressed in an expertly tailored uniform consisting of a short, light blue shell jacket, white breeches, and highly polished black boots stepped forward. He held a blue and white dragoon helmet in his hand. Mercer said, "Gentlemen, permit me to introduce Captain Warren Bradley of Maryland's Anne Arundel Light Horse. He and his men have just joined the army." He turned to Wend. "Captain Bradley tells me you two are acquainted."

Wend grinned at the newcomer. "Yes, we worked together on a rather interesting piece of business for Virginia and Maryland last year. We had to stop some of Lord Dunmore's men who were trying to raise the Ohio tribes against our border." He held his hand out to Bradley. "Good to see you again, Warren."

"And I you, Wend." The two shook hands.

"Excellent, because you will be working together again on a long-term basis." Mercer looked around at the assembled officers and said, "Gentlemen, permit me to read a section of tomorrow's general orders for the army." He took out a folded paper from his pocket, opened it, and moved to where the fire would illuminate it. He said, "This is the first article of the orders and I quote: 'It is the Commanding General's pleasure to constitute a new formation of the army, to be under his direct orders. The name of the organization shall be *The Legion of Continental Guides*. It shall be composed of the Frederick County Light Foot Company, the 1st Troop of the Palmetto Light Horse, and the Anne Arundel Light Horse Troop. The commandant of the Legion will be Major Wendelmar Eckert of Virginia. This legion of light horse and foot will serve as the army's main reconnaissance formation, performing scouting service and assisting the army in the establishment of contact with the enemy before battle. In addition, the legion will perform such other special duties as the commanding general may from time to time order.'"

Mercer stood up and looked at Wend. "Congratulations on your new command, Major Eckert."

Wend nodded. "This is a signal honor, sir."

With a twinkle in his eye, Mercer said, "Confidentially, gentlemen, I can say that General Washington is most pleased to be able to have a scouting unit formed by companies that all hail from south of Mr. Mason's and Mr. Dixon's line of demarcation." He looked around and winked with a grin on his face. "But seriously, I wouldn't go bragging about that to the rest of the army. We don't want to be seen promoting what our northern friends might call *favoritism*."

There was a round of hearty laughter. When it had subsided, Mercer said, "There's more news—a round of promotions. Since Eckert will command the entire legion, Mr. Newkirk will be promoted to Captain of the Frederick County Light Foot. Lieutenant O'beirne will be promoted to first lieutenant. Ensign Childers will be promoted to second lieutenant of the company." The general grinned. "And not to ignore South Carolina, our skeptical friend Mr. Fairfield will be promoted to captain. The paperwork for all this will be ready tomorrow. You all richly merit promotion, and you have my congratulations."

Wend looked around at the officers. "Sir, I can assure you that every officer and man of the Legion of Continental Guides will strive every day to live up to the confidence that General Washington has shown in us."

Mercer nodded. "I have no doubt, Major." Then he cleared his throat and said, "Now, it happens that the army quartermaster has informed me that he has recently purchased a quantity of whiskey from none other than you, Major—whiskey distilled on your very own farm and which he says is of exceptional quality and quite memorable taste." He smiled broadly. "Might I assume that some of that same libation might be available at hand for a toast?"

Wend laughed. "Of course, sir." He called out, "Mrs. Wood! Bring the whiskey and cups for the General and Captain Bradley!"

Melinda called out from the other side of the tent. "Yes, sir. Mr. Eckert, sir! I be right there!" Momentarily, she hustled out, jug in one hand and cups in the other.

Wend said, "Fill the cups for General Mercer and Captain Bradley, then all the others."

When she had finished, Mercer held up his cup. "To the Legion of Continental Guides! May it lead the army with excellence and courage as its watchwords, and may its history be one of glory in the service of our cause! Gentlemen, I give you the Guides!"

There was a round of "The Guides!" and every man drained his cup.

Mercer looked around. "One further word. In a few days, as we have discussed, the army will march on a daring expedition with the fate of our endeavor in the balance. The Guides will lead the main force into battle. Tomorrow, I will meet with Major Eckert and provide his detailed orders for the movement. So, in the coming days, steel yourselves, study what you must do, and ensure your men and equipment are ready for the most difficult yet important days of their lives. And I know when all is finished we shall be proud of your contribution to the victory which we must win if our infant nation is to survive."

There was a profound silence as everyone thought on Mercer's words. Wend was surprised when it was Geoffrey Fairfield who broke the silence. He said, "General, I can assure you that the Palmetto—" he hesitated—and then resumed, "that the *Guides* will be ready and proud to be in the van of the army when the time comes. You will be able to count on our full dedication and utmost effort to ensure success!"

Mercer raised an eyebrow, and a rather crooked smile crossed his face. "Thank you for that, Mr. Fairfield. In my heart, I was sure that the doubts you expressed earlier in the evening were but a transitory emotion. And now I can go back to General Washington and tell him that he has the full confidence and enthusiastic support of all of The Guides! And so, gentlemen, I bid you a good night."

Without further words, Mercer strode off toward headquarters, all eyes on him as he disappeared into the darkness.

It was Warren Bradley who spoke first. "Well, it seems we Marylanders have arrived just in time for action. And there is no one we would rather ride into battle with than the men of Virginia and Carolina."

Shay O'beirne exclaimed, "Well said, my darling Captain." He strode over to the table where Melinda had left the jug. He picked it up and said, "Now, tomorrow, lads, as the general has said, we must put our snotty noses to the grindstone and get ourselves and our lads ready for the fight. But I say tonight we celebrate in honor of our new regiment and make good work of finishing off this jug." He proceeded to make the round of officers and fill their cups.

Wend looked over at Bradley and laughed. "As you can tell, this fellow is our own resident Irishman, a rogue who is equally good at holding his liquor, squeezing a tavern maid, and swapping lies. And even more important, a real devil when the fight is on."

Bradley downed some of his whiskey, winked, and said, "My dear Wend, I may be a planter of the Maryland Tidewater and not one of you stalwart Shenandoah border men, but I was able to figure that out all on my own."

Wend laughed. "Bradley, I can confidently predict we're going to get along famously."

The End of
Retreat From New York

Author's Historical Notes

The battles around New York and the long retreat across New Jersey constitute a complex challenge for the novelist. Initially, my intent was that the story should focus exclusively on the retreat. The idea was to show the travails of Washington and his army in escaping from the British and surviving to fight another day. But then it became evident that for context, some attention would have to be paid to the events of the actual campaign and the defeat in the Continental Army's first large-scale open-field confrontation with a European Army. It was complicated by the fact that the New York campaign extended over many months with significant intervals of inaction. This, in turn, led to the requirement for more research and increased the length of the narrative, all of which added to the time required for completion, so that this book's publication is two years since the previous in the series. For all the readers who have been enthusiastically asking when the next volume would be available, I can only say I hope that when reading *Retreat From New York* you decide that the story was worth the wait.

A related consideration was whether or not to include the Battle of Trenton in this narrative. After deliberation, I decided that it would detract from the main focus of the novel, which is the efforts of Washington and his leadership team to preserve the army after the defeat in New York. I also found it more logical to cover Washington's Winter campaign of December 1776 – January 1777, including the Christmas attack on Trenton, the Battle of Assunpink Creek (Second Battle of Trenton), the Battle of Princeton and the march to winter quarters at Morristown as a single progression. Readers of the Rebellion Road Series can expect to see that story in the next novel.

As is my custom in Forbes Road/Rebellion Road Series novels, the following notes are intended to provide some background information on certain individuals, relationships, and events mentioned in the narrative and to point out the most egregious departures from actual history in weaving the fictional story.

Washington's Generalship. New York was Washington's first experience commanding a large force in an open field campaign, and it's clear that he made some mistakes. Examples: not withdrawing the troops from Fort Washington before they were trapped by the British, leaving his flanks open to British attacks on Long Island and Brooklyn Heights, and splitting his force into fragments after the Battle of White Plains. Washington's rivals, General Charles Lee and General Horatio Gates, were indeed correct in some of their criticisms. But Washington learned rapidly and came out of the campaign a more competent commander. He also had something neither Lee nor Gates had, and that is a command presence which instilled great trust and loyalty in his officers and men. It was during this campaign that Washington gained the important understanding that the preservation of the army was actually the central requirement of his generalship, for as long as the army existed, the Patriot cause was alive. Incidentally, the statement Washington makes in Chapter 18 that if all else failed, he would retreat to the Blue Ridge, plant his standard, and rally the Ulster people about him to fight to the end, although sometimes quoted in articles and books, was probably never expressed so succinctly by him. In fact, there are several versions of the statement. But whether he actually said it or not, it is a good way to exemplify his defiance and determination, and I couldn't resist putting the words in his mouth.

It's also important to realize that Washington, in commanding the Continental Army, was necessarily engaged in the politics of managing a political and military coalition. He was dealing with thirteen entities that at the time considered themselves independent. Thus, like Eisenhower in World War II, who had to be tactful and even-handed in his treatment of the Allies, Washington had to act in a way that satisfied the sensitivities of each state. He was always worried about showing favoritism toward the southern states and especially Virginia. For example, this often affected the selection of generals; they had to be apportioned fairly among the states. This led to some very good tacticians not being appointed as early as their achievements merited. A prime example was the delay in promotion of Daniel

Morgan to brigadier general for so long that in 1778 he actually left the army in frustration. Finally, in 1780 he was recalled to the colors, promoted to general, and then orchestrated the tactical masterpiece of Cowpens.

The Persona and Plotting of General Charles Lee. Although academic historians tend to hedge their words about Lee, it's pretty clear that in late 1776 he was angling to replace Washington as commanding general of the Continental Army. He was corresponding with members of Congress and some of Washington's closest aides in order to establish alliances with people who would back him at the proper moment. He also knew that once his division rejoined the main force, he would no longer be in direct command of a troop unit. Hence his refusal to bring his men to join Washington despite increasingly urgent appeals from the army commander.

The account of Lee's capture at Basking Ridge in the narrative is part history, part fiction. A squadron of the 16th Light Dragoons was in fact sent to the area on a reconnaissance, and Tarleton was leading an advance patrol when a loyalist resident of Basking Ridge told him about Lee's presence at Widow White's Tavern. He then rode there and attacked Lee's guard detail. Some were killed, and the rest ran off. Lee was taken into custody, and shortly thereafter the rest of the squadron, under Lieutenant Colonel Harcourt, the regimental commandant, arrived. The exploit earned Tarleton fame and promotion from cornet to captain and started him on his meteoric rise to lieutenant colonel and command of the British Legion at the age of twenty-six. Upon learning of Lee's capture, General Sullivan immediately marched to join his division to Washington's force in Pennsylvania. Wend's fictional role in the events was, of course, woven around the historical action.

It was also true that Lee's appearance and personality largely precluded meaningful relationships with women. Hence his frequent use of prostitutes to satisfy his carnal needs, as fictionally portrayed by the hiring of Emily Crider from Colleen McGraw's bevy of girls. It's not clear why he left his command to stay in a Basking Ridge tavern miles away from his troops. Some accounts attribute it to the desire for sexual relations with one of the women at the tavern, while others simply say he was looking for comfortable lodgings. There is a story that after Lee was exchanged out of captivity and returned to the army at Valley Forge in 1778, Washington extended him the courtesy of a bedroom next to his own in the headquarters house. Lee promptly arranged to bed the prostitute wife of a sergeant. George and Martha, trying to sleep, were forced to listen to the exuberant sounds of Lee's sexual activity throughout the night.

For more details on Lee's capture, see: Christian M. McBurney, *Kidnapping The Enemy: The Special Operations to Capture Generals Charles Lee & Richard Prescott* (Westholme Publishing LLC, 2014)

Mercer's Role. As in the narrative, historians credit General Hugh Mercer with suggesting to Washington the idea of retreating across New Jersey and sheltering in Pennsylvania behind the natural barrier of the Delaware River. And as a long-standing friend of Washington, he was indeed a key, influential advisor in the early days of the war. However, I've amplified his role a bit in order to highlight the problems associated with the retreat and provide a fictional channel between Wend and army command. The patrols of the kind undertaken by O'beirne and Childers to make preparations for the withdrawal and crossing into Pennsylvania are also fictional. However, some preparations were indeed made, such as identifying the locations of boats and ferries, largely by militia and the Pennsylvania row galleys, which were actually on the river.

For further background: Michael Cecere, *Second To No Man But The Commander In Chief* (Heritage Books, Inc, 2015)

Wend Eckert's Encounters With John Paul Jones. Although Wend's interactions with Jones onboard the *Lady Felicity* and at the City Tavern in the first chapter are of course pure fiction, they *could* have happened since the *Providence* indeed escorted a convoy of six colliers to Philadelphia during that general time frame. My purpose was to use Jones to introduce the reader to the essential role that seapower would play in the New York campaign.

The Hesse-Cassel Jaeger Corps. The Hessian Jaegers are perhaps the most well-known element of the German mercenaries that augmented the British during the Revolution. They were highly effective opponents to the American rifle companies and certainly had an influence on the formation and tactics of later light forces in the Napoleonic wars. The British rifle regiments used the Baker rifle, which was quite similar to the pattern of the Jaeger Rifles, as opposed to the American long rifle. And the most well-known of the Jaeger officers was Captain Johann Ewald, largely because of his widely published diary of daily activities during the war. Historians have found it particularly useful in adding color and first-person illustrations to their works. Ewald of course inspired the character Captain Ernst Ludwig Wolff. Whereas Ewald commanded the third company of the Jaegers, Wolff commands a fictional fourth company. I decided to use a fictional character and company in the role of opposing Wend so that their presence could be arranged wherever convenient for the fictional narrative.

The fictional conversation between Cornwallis and Wolff regarding conserving the lives of Jaegers is based on an actual statement by the general to Ewald that he considered the Jaegers worth ten of the Americans in the skirmishing role.

For further information on the Jaegers see: Johann Ewald (Auth), Joseph P. Tustin (Editor),*Diary of the American War,* (Yale University Press, 1979). A concise account of the overall Hessian military role in the Revolution is: Brady J Crytzer, *Hessians: Mercenaries, Rebels, and the War For British America* (Westholme Publishing, 2015).

The Stand at New Brunswick. Hamilton first distinguished himself by the performance of his battery at White Plains. Then his rearguard action at the New Brunswick river crossing was highly effective, delaying the British long enough to allow the escape of Washington and the Continental Army. His actions at White Plains and New Brunswick brought him to the attention of army leadership. Later, the effectiveness of his battery at Trenton added to his reputation and eventually resulted in his promotion and assignment as aide-de-camp on Washington's staff and later chief of staff. While historical descriptions of the action at New Brunswick mainly focus on Hamilton and his artillery's role, they also mention that he was supported by army riflemen. So it was logical to have Wend and his light foot work with Hamilton at the Raritan and at other engagements during the retreat. For Hamilton's role in the war, see: Phillip Thomas Tucker, PhD, *Alexander Hamilton's Revolution: His Vital Role as Washington's Chief of Staff* (Skyhorse Publishing, 2017).

The Spying Game. There was considerable spy/informer activity during the run-up to the attack on Trenton. There was at least one British spy in the Continental army camp with some level of access to Washington's plans. There is no certainty of his or her identity. In any case, the individual was able to provide warning of the attack, but it was dismissed by the British as impossible. It is also true that Washington had at least one spy, a shopkeeper in Trenton, who was reporting enemy strength, quartering arrangements, and tactical dispositions. So the fictional role of Catherine Tresh as portrayed in the story is clearly consistent with the events and environment that existed.

River Ice at Trenton. The jam-up of ice in the Delaware at Trenton, which ultimately was the scene of Catherine's demise, reflects the actual situation that occurred during that extremely cold winter. While upriver, although there were floating chunks of ice, they impeded but did not stop Washington's part of the army from crossing to attack Trenton. But the full plan envisioned a three-pronged attack: (1)The main force under Washington successfully crossed at McConkey's Ferry and made the actual attack at Trenton. (2) A force under General Cadwalader was to cross below Trenton and attack the small garrison at Bordentown, to cut off any reinforcement, and (3) A force of 700 militia under General Ewing was ordered to cross at the ferry crossing right at the town. He was to secure an important bridge at Assunpink Creek on the south side of Trenton to prevent retreating Hessians from getting away. This third force couldn't cross precisely because the river was jammed up with ice flows as described in the manuscript.

Acknowledgments

I'm grateful to many individuals and organizations for their assistance in producing this fifth volume of the Rebellion Road Series. Pamela Patrick White extended permission for the use of her painting, *Bitter Winter at Jockey Hollow*, for use on the front cover and for promotional purposes. Then there are the "beta" readers for this manuscript, including Dick Batiste, Spencer Dejarnet, Tripp Butler, and my son Mike Shade, who provided valuable feedback. This is the fifth book for which *Elite Authors* publishing organization provided design work for the cover and interior, as well as digitally formatted the finished product for upload to the online booksellers. Their production values and technical competence are uniformly excellent. Finally, as always, I owe thanks to all the readers who have followed Wend, his friends, and antagonists through all the books of the Forbes Road/Rebellion Road Series and contacted us through the Rebellion Road Facebook page and other media to express their appreciation for the stories and advance their ideas for the future of the characters and story line.

Robert J. Shade
Sunshine Hill Farm
Madison County, Virginia
January 2026

www.ingramcontent.com/pod-product-compliance
Lightning Source LLC
LaVergne TN
LVHW020647110826
845149LV00012B/1937

* 9 7 9 8 9 9 4 6 5 8 2 0 8 *